P9-CEP-320

The
Half-Made
World

TOR BOOKS BY FELIX GILMAN

The Half-Made World

The Half-Made World

Felix Gilman

A TOM DOHERTY ASSOCIATES BOOK

NEW YORK

THE HALF-MADE WORLD

Copyright © 2010 by Felix Gilman

A Tor Book
Published by Tom Doherty Associates, LLC
175 Fifth Avenue
New York, NY 10010

www.tor-forge.com

Tor® is a registered trademark of Tom Doherty Associates, LLC.

ISBN 978-0-7653-2552-5

First Edition: October 2010

Printed in the United States of America

0 9 8 7 6 5 4 3 2 1

ACKNOWLEDGMENTS

The excerpts from the treatise the precocious ten-year-old Liv reads in chapter 20 are drawn partly verbatim from Hans Gross's 1911 *Criminal Psychology*.

Huge thanks are due to my editor, Eric Raab, for invaluable comments and support, and to my agent, Howard Morhaim, without whose efforts this wouldn't be here, and to Sarah, for all the usual reasons.

THE
HALF-MADE
WORLD

H⊙⠃ The General Died

~ 1878 ~

The General lay flat on his back, arms outflung, watching the stars.

A rock pressed into the base of his spine. He'd hit his head and turned his ankle when he fell, but the rock was the worst of his pain. Other sensations were leaving him, but the rock, obstinately, persisted; yet he was powerless to move. He was powerless to will himself to move. Between his will and his body, there was the *noise*.

A dark cloud passed before the stars, and their light was shadowed, then returned, cold as ever. He watched the night sky over the mountains burn and wheel, hiss and dance, shudder and fall.

The General was losing his mind.

There were no trees—no pines. He lay in a bare hollow, a high flat stony clearing. The General and his last most loyal twenty-two men had been caught in their desperate flight between the Line behind them and the cliff's edge before them.

If the General could only have mustered the will to turn his head, he would have seen the mountain's peak. It was dark, and forked like a gesture of benediction. It had been his destination, before this—this unfortunate interruption. It would have been better, he thought, to have died watching the mountain than the stars, which were meaningless.

In the end, no shots had been fired. No words exchanged or warnings given. The Linesmen's awful weapon had simply come whistling out of the night sky, fallen like a stone at Lieutenant Deerfield's feet, and poor young Deerfield had gone pale, eyes wide, turning to the General for last words; then the *noise* had begun, the mad awful *noise*, and Deerfield's wide eyes had filled with fear and blood, and he'd toppled one way and the General had toppled the other, and now they both lay where they fell.

The weapon had quickly burned through its fuel and gone silent, but the terrible noise still echoed in the General's mind. The noise split his mind in two, then in four, then into scattered pieces. The echoes ground him to finer and finer dust. The process was frightening and painful.

※　※　※

The General was a man of extraordinary character. He'd built the Red Valley Republic out of nothing—hadn't he? He'd preserved it against all enemies and all odds, he'd taken the mere words of politicians and philosophers and he'd *beaten* the world into their mold. As the noise crashed rhythmlessly back and forth across his mind, he held tightly to his pride—which maybe slowed the process of disintegration but could not stop it.

For twenty years the Republic had flourished, and it had been the finest moment in the history of the West; indeed, the finest of all possible moments, for the Republic had been constructed in accordance with the best possible theories of political virtue. Gun and Line and their endless war had been banished—the Republic had been an island of peace and sanity. It was gone now, ten years gone, undermined by the spies and blackmailers of Gun, crushed by the wheels of the Line, never to return. But it had lasted long enough to raise a generation of young men and women in its mold, and it was for those young persons that the General wished he could somehow utter, and have recorded, some noble and inspiring last words; but all that now came to his shattered mind were fragments of old fairy tales, curse words, obscenities, babble. He thought he might be weeping. He couldn't tell.

※　※　※

He was vaguely aware of the Linesmen going through the bodies around him. He could see them out of the corner of his eye. Squat little men in their grays and blacks stepping dismissively over the bodies of heroes! They stopped sometimes and knelt down to use their dull-bladed boot-knives to silence murmuring throats. They went like busy doctors from patient to patient. The General's men lay helplessly. A bad way to end. A bad way for it all to end.

Would the Linesmen notice the General, still breathing? Maybe, maybe not. There was nothing he could do to stop it.

One more section of the architecture of his mind crumbled to dust, and for a moment he entirely forgot who he was, and he became preoccupied with his memories. He'd been a leader of some kind? He'd had some great final duty, which had brought him up into these damned cold ugly mountains; he forgot what it was. For some reason, he remembered instead a fairy tale his nursemaid had told him, many, many years ago back in green Glen Lily, in Ulver County: a tale regarding a prince who set out from his father's red castle bearing nothing but a sword and, and, an owl, in search of the princess, who . . . no, bearing a *message* for the princess, who . . . the princess was a prisoner, chained in a tower, ebony-skinned, beautiful black hair to her waist, bare-naked . . .

A Linesman stepped over him—black boots momentarily blocked out the stars. The Linesman's black trousers were worn and smeared gray with dust. The Linesman shouted something, something the General couldn't understand, and moved on, not looking down.

The General clutched at the scattering dust of himself and recalled that this was not the first time he'd lain outside at night, under the stars, among the dead, bleeding and dying. Indeed, a night like this had been the making of him, once. As a young soldier he had been wounded in the shoulder by a lucky shot at the battle of A . . . at the battle of . . . at the field of gorse and briars, by the stone bridge. He had been left for dead in the first retreat and spent the night among the dead, too weak to walk, strong enough only to hold his jacket to his shoulder and pray for the slow bleed to stop, and to watch the cold stars. He'd been very young then. There he had learned to dedicate his soul and his strength to a bright distant purpose, to lay his course by a remote star. He had learned to be *heroic* and not to fear death. So he'd told too many generations of fresh young recruits.

The recruits hadn't been so fresh or so young, or so many, in re-cent years—not since the horrors of Black Cap Valley. Not since all was lost. Not since the Line drove them into the hills and the woods and the back alleys like bandits, not since the army of the Republic, reduced to a desperate fierce remnant of its former glory, became a matter of secret meetings and disguises and dead-drops and mid-night explosions and code words and signals. He remembered! No—he remembered only the codes, not why they were sent. Matters of great weight and significance hidden in the lines of humble everyday domestic correspondence—*The children are growing tall and strong* meant *The weapons are ready to be retrieved*—he struggled and grasped at codes and symbols. . . .

He remembered they sent messages encoded, among other things, in fairy tales, in letters that purported to be addressed to much-loved children safe at home. He remembered writing, *Once upon a time, the Prince of Birds looked down from the Mountain over his kingdom and was unhappy*. It meant something secret; it conveyed maybe good news, more likely bad, because all the news had been bad for ten years; he couldn't remember what.

He tried to recall the names of some of his men—many of whom, perhaps all of whom, lay scattered on the mountainside around him, their own minds ruined and crumbling like his own. No names came to him. What came to him instead were the faces of three Presi-dents, three of his masters: Bellow, big-bearded, who was once only Mayor of Morgan, who drafted the Charter; Iredell, little wiry bril-liant man, who was the first to sign it at Red Valley; stout but sim-pleminded Killbuck, who in retrospect was perhaps a sign of the Republic's rapid decline.

But his memory of Bellow's bearded face was perhaps confused with an illustrated king from the storybook his nursemaid read to him.

The noise kept sounding in his head, and he forgot Bellow for-ever. The noise ricocheted madly back and forth against the cham-ber of his skull like a bullet. The *meaninglessness* of the noise was its worst quality. He forgot his battle standards. He recalled, then forgot again, the stables at Glen Lily, where he first learned to ride and read and hold a sword. The stables were long since ground under by the Line. He recalled with sudden sickness that he had a daughter of his own, whom he had not seen for years, for all these years of hard campaigning, of hiding in the hills, of raiding and harrowing the Line. He wrote letters; she always waited for him to come home. Now he never would.

He'd sent her a last letter, from the foot of the mountains, just days ago: there was something very important in it, but he couldn't recall what. Something about these mountains and these stones on which his mind now bled. He recalled that he signed and sealed it with a reckless wild abandon. He said things it was dangerous to say. He had set years of discretion and secrecy aside. He remembered thinking, *Secrecy is behind us now. If we win through, the earth will shake.* He forgot why.

He remembered, terribly vividly, the stink of Black Cap Valley, after the battle, its mud and vile flowers black and glistening, slick with red blood. One of his sons had died there. He forgot where the other one had died.

※　※　※

A Linesman stepped back over him, knocking his head sideways, so that he could no longer see the stars. He saw instead the shuffling legs of the Linesmen and the body of Lieutenant Deerfield. Deerfield! A good man. He wore trappers' furs, not his old red uniform, because the days of splendid red uniforms were long gone. He was pale and dead.

Behind Deerfield, the General saw the body of Kan-Kuk, the stone-caster, the Hill-man, *his* Hill-man. His ally among the First Folk. There were a great many secrets about Kan-Kuk in his last letter. The General had forgotten them all.

Kan-Kuk's naked bone-white body jerked and flopped like a landed fish. Kan-Kuk's long skinny arms flailed like stripped branches in a storm. Kan-Kuk tore at his wild mane and ripped away greasy black fistfuls. That struck the General as strange; the General was fairly sure that he himself was still, very still. Perhaps the mind-bombs affected different species of person in different ways. Or perhaps the General himself, without knowing it, was also thrashing and flailing and screaming. Everything was very numb; he couldn't be sure.

The General wondered if Kan-Kuk would rise again. It was said of the Folk, and perhaps it was only a fairy tale, like the story of the princess and the prince and the mountain . . . It was said of the Folk that when they died, and were buried, they rose again, in due season, immortal, like a song or a dream—or like the masters of Gun and Line. If Kan-Kuk were to be buried, and to rise again from the red earth, would his mind recover, or was Kan-Kuk ruined now, too? His fine, strange mad mind, now ruined.

It was at Kan-Kuk's request that the General had gone on this last mad mission. Those were the terms of their deal. People had said for years that the General was mad to keep a Hill-man around like that, and maybe they were right. Now the General remembered what Kan-Kuk promised: that his people had a secret. A Song, Kan-Kuk had called it, though the General had thought: *a weapon*. A weapon to bring peace. An alliance between resolution and atonement for peace and goodwill, that oldest dream. The General would have tended his garden in his old age, grown roses perhaps. Kan-Kuk's people had been ready to share it at last, to forgive, again, at last. There was a cave, there was a cave in the red navel of the world, there was drumming, there was the City of the First Folk, for they, too, were fallen from greatness. Down in the dark, fallen. There were, so Kan-Kuk whispered, to have been tests of courage and virtue and . . .

※ ※ ※

Now a song sounded in the General's head, but it was a terrible one, not peaceful, not a cure for anything, but a gathering torrent of mad noise. Kan-Kuk! The General remembered Kan-Kuk and then forgot again, forever. Kan-Kuk and Deerfield. The names of Putnam and Holmes occurred to him as well. The echo in his mind grew and thundered rhythmically over and over like horses' hooves. The names of Halley and Orange surfaced from the sinking ruin of his mind, and he remembered that Orange was once from the Twenty-third Regiment of the Third Army of the Republic, before the Third Army was lost at Black Cap. The echo of horses; it was tearing him apart, but for a moment it made him think of *escape*—he imagined that the horses were thundering an escape, thundering new hope.

He could escape one more time; he could regroup. Regroup what? He forgot. The black boots of a Linesman stopped in front of him. The echo was not rhythmic—the horses that galloped across his mind were limping, falling, screaming. What shattered the soul, what set the brain's delicate architecture bleeding and crumbling, was that horrid senseless arrhythmia. The General recalled and forgot the names of Holmes and Mason and Darke. A Linesman bent down and gripped Kan-Kuk's beard and forced back the hinge of his long white neck and silenced him with a boot-knife. (Would he rise again?) The rhythm of the Linesmen's noisemaker was *not* horses, of course, nothing so natural; it was the sound of Engines. The Linesmen, being already mad, were inured to it, but to the General it sounded out madness, worse than death. He recalled that the battle standard of his first regiment, which he made the standard of this desperate rump of the Republic, after Black Cap, bore two eagles. The eagle was a noble bird. He recalled a story regarding a prince who set out from his father's castle of red rock into the mountains with nothing to accompany him but an eagle, no course to follow but the course the eagle's black wings marked across the blue sky. He couldn't recall why, and it frustrated him. *Begin again: Once upon a time and it was the last time I went into the mountains to find . . .*

✳ ✳ ✳

"That one."

"Where?"

"There."

"Right. I see him."

Private (Third Class) Porter, soldier of the Line in the First Army of the Gloriana Engine, stood over the body and poked it with his foot. An elderly fellow, weather-beaten, dark-skinned but with a startlingly silver-white beard. His eyes, which stared blankly up into Porter's own, were a deep vibrant green, which Porter disliked. The pupils had collapsed almost to pinpricks. That often happened with the mind-bombs. The old man didn't respond to a poke in the ribs or when Porter nudged his head from side to side with the blood-slick sole of his boot.

Still breathing, just about, but the mind was gone. Porter's back ached after the long chase through the mountains, and he couldn't be bothered to bend down to finish the old man off.

"Already dead," Porter lied.

Private (First Class) Copper looked around him. The hollow was strewn with bodies. "Good. That's all of them, then. All gone. Might as well do that savage, too, shut him up. Soap."

Private (Second Class) Soap drew his knife, yanked the jerking, shrieking Hillfolk fellow up by his mane, and took care of business.

Porter gave the old man another poke with his boot. "Who do you think they were?"

Copper shrugged. "No one important. Who cares? They're dead now."

"Wonder what they were doing up here."

"Trespassing," Copper said. "Where they didn't belong."

"Odd-looking bunch, though."

"Shut up," Copper said. "Not our place to ask questions."

"Yes, sir. Sorry, sir."

"Been a long night," Copper said. "I want to get back to bed. Leave these idiots for the crows."

BOOK ONE

OUT TO THE EDGE OF THINGS

CHAPTER 1

The Departure

~ 1889 ~

One fine spring afternoon, when the roses in the gardens of the Koenigswald Academy were in bloom, and the lawns were emerald green, and the river was sapphire blue, and the experimental greenhouses burst with weird life, the professors of the Faculty of Psychological Sciences met in the Faculty's ancient August Hall, in a handsomely appointed upstairs library, where they stood in a little group drinking sherry and saying their good-byes to their colleague Dr. Lysvet Alverhuysen—*Liv* to her friends—who was, against all reasonable advice, determined to go west.

✳   ✳   ✳

"You'll fall behind, Dr. Alverhyusen." Dr. Seidel shook his head sorrowfully. "Your work will suffer. There are no faculties of learning in the West, none at all. None worth the name, anyway. Can they even read? You won't have access to any of the journals."

"Yes," Liv said. "I believe they can read."

"Seidel overstates his argument," Dr. Naumann said. "Seidel is known for overstating his arguments. Eh, Seidel? But not *always* wrong. You *will* lose touch with science. You will *rip* yourself from the bosom of the scientific community."

He laughed to show what he thought of the scientific community. Handsome and dark of complexion, Dr. Naumann was the youngest of the Faculty's professors and liked to think of himself as something of a radical. He was engaged in a study of the abnormal or misdirected sexual drive, which he regarded as fundamental to all human activity and belief.

Liv smiled politely. "I hope you'll write to me, gentlemen. There are mail coaches across the mountains, and the Line will carry mail across the West."

"Hah!" Dr. Naumann rolled his eyes. "I've seen the maps. You're going to the edge of the world, Dr. Alverhuysen. Might as well hope to send mail to the moon, or the bottom of the sea. Are there mail coaches to the moon?"

"They're at war out there," Dr. Seidel said. "It's very dangerous." He twisted his glass nervously in his hands.

"Yes," Liv agreed. "So I've heard."

"There are wild men in the hills, who are from what I hear only very debatably human. I saw a sketch of one once, and I don't mind admitting it gave me nightmares. All hair and knuckles, it was, white as death, and painted in the most awful way."

"I won't be going into the hills, Doctor."

"The so-called civilized folk are only marginally better. Quite mad. I don't make that diagnosis lightly. Four centuries of war is hardly the only evidence of it. Consider the principal factions in that war, which are from what I hear not so much political entities as religious enthusiasms, not so much religion as forms of shared mania. . . . Cathexis, that is, a psychotic transference of responsibility from themselves to *objects* that—"

"Yes," she said. "Perhaps you should publish on the subject."

If she listened to another moment of Dr. Seidel's shrill voice, she was in danger of having her resolve shaken.

"Will you excuse me, Doctors?" She darted quickly away, neatly interposing Dr. Mistler between herself and Seidel.

It was stuffy and dusty in the library; she moved closer to the windows, where there was a breeze and the faint green smell of the gardens, and where Liv's dear friend Agatha from the Faculty of Mathematics was making conversation with Dr. Dahlstrom from the Faculty of Metaphysics, who was terribly dull. As she approached, Agatha waved over Dahlstrom's shoulder and her eyes said, *Help!* Liv hurried over, sidestepping Dr. Ley, but she was intercepted by Dr. Ekstein, the head of her own Faculty, who was like a looming stone castle topped with a wild beard, and who took both her hands in his powerful ink-stained hands and said: "Dr. Alverhuysen—may I abandon formality—*Liv*—will you be safe? Will you be safe out there? Your poor late husband, rest his soul, would never forgive me if I allowed . . ."

Dr. Ekstein was a little sherry-drunk and his eyes were moist. His life's work had been a system of psychology that divided the mind into contending forces of thesis and antithesis, from the struggle of which a peaceful synthesis was derived, the process beginning again and again incessantly. Liv considered the theory mechanical and unrealistic.

"I have made my decision, Doctor," she reminded him. "I shall be quite safe. The House Dolorous is in neutral territory, far from the fighting."

"Poor Bernhardt," Dr. Ekstein said. "He would *haunt* me if anything were to happen to you—not, of course, that I would expect that it would, but if anything *were* to happen—"

Dr. Naumann insinuated himself. "Hauntings? Here? Sounds like you'll miss all the *real* excitement, Dr. Alverhuysen."

Ekstein frowned down on Naumann, who kept talking: "On the other hand, you won't be bored—oh my no. No place out there is neutral for long. No matter how remote your new employer may be, soon enough *you-know-what* will come knocking."

"I'm afraid I *don't* know, Dr. Naumann. I understand things are very turbulent out there. Excuse me, I must—"

"Turbulent! A good word. If you cut into the living brain of a murderer or sex criminal, you might say what you saw was *turbulent*. I mean the forces of the Line."

"Oh." She tried to look discreetly around Dr. Ekstein's mass for sight of Agatha. "Well, isn't that for the best? Isn't the Line on the side of science and order?"

Dr. Naumann raised an eyebrow, which Liv found irritating. "Is that right? Consider Logtown, which they burned to the ground because it harbored Agents of the Gun; consider the conquest of Mason, where . . ." He rattled off a long list of battles and massacres.

Dr. Alverhuysen looked at him in surprise. "You know a lot about the subject."

He shrugged. "I take an interest in their affairs. A professional interest, you might say."

"I'm afraid I don't follow their politics closely, Dr. Naumann."

"You will. You will." He leaned in close and whispered to her, "*They'll* follow *you*, Liv."

She whispered back, "Perhaps you should travel that way yourself, Philip."

"Absolutely under no circumstances whatsoever." He straightened again and consulted his watch. "I shall be late for my afternoon Session!" He left his glass on a bookshelf and exited by the south stairs.

"Unhealthy," Ekstein said. "Unhealthy interests." He glanced down at Liv. "Unhealthy."

"Excuse me, Dr. Ekstein."

She stepped around him, exchanged a polite *good luck, good luck to you, too,* with a gray-haired woman whose name she forgot, passed through a cool breeze and shaft of dusty afternoon sunlight that entered through the oriel window, heard and for nearly the last time was delighted by the sound of the peacocks crying out on the lawns, and deftly linked arms with Agatha and rescued her from Professor Dahlstrom's droning. Unfortunately, Agatha turned out to be a little too drunk and a little too maudlin, and did not share any of Liv's nervous excitement. She blinked back tears and held Liv's hand very tightly and damply and said, "Liv—oh, Liv. You must promise you'll come back."

Liv waved a hand vaguely. "Oh, I'm sure I will, Agatha."

"You must come back *soon.*"

In fact, she hadn't given a moment's thought to when she might return, and the demand rather annoyed her. She said, "I shall write, of course."

To Liv's relief then, Dr. Ekstein tapped on a glass for silence, and quickly got it, because everyone was by now quite keen to return to their interrupted afternoon's work. He gave a short speech, which did not once mention where Liv was going or why, and rather made it sound as if she were retiring due to advanced senility, which was the Faculty's usual procedure. Finally he presented her with a gift from the Faculty: a golden pocket watch, heavy and overly ornate, etched with sentimental scenes of Koenigswald's mountains and pine forests and gardens and narrow high-peaked houses. The occasion was complete, and the guests dispersed by various doors and into the stacks of the library.

❋　❋　❋

The Academy stood on a bend in the river a few miles north of the little town of Lodenstein, which was one of the prettiest and wealthiest towns of Koenigswald, which was itself one of the oldest and wealthiest and most stable and peaceful nations of the old and wealthy and stable and peaceful nations of the old East.

Six months ago, a letter had arrived at the Academy from out of the farthest West. It was battered and worn, and stained with red dust, sweat, and oil. It had been addressed to *The Academy— Koenigswald—Of the Seven.* Koenigswald's efficient postal service had directed it to Lodenstein without too much difficulty. "Of the Seven" was a strange affectation, initially confusing, until Dr. Naumann remembered that four hundred years ago, Koenigswald had— in an uncharacteristic fit of adventurism—been one of the Council of Seven Nations that had jointly sent the first expeditions West, over the World's End Mountains, into what was then un-made territory. Perhaps that fact still meant something to the westerners; Koenigswald had largely forgotten it.

Strictly speaking, the letter was addressed not to Liv, but to a *Mr. Dr. Bernhardt Alverhuysen,* which was the name of her late husband, who was recently deceased; but her husband had been a Doctor of Natural History, and the letter sought the assistance of a Doctor of Abnormal Psychology, a title that more accurately described Liv herself. Therefore, Liv opened it.

Dear Dr. Alverhuysen,

I hope this letter finds you well. No doubt you are surprised to receive it. There is little commerce these days between the new world and the old. We do not know each other, and though I have heard great things of your Academy, I am not familiar with your work; my own House is in a very remote part of the world, and it is hard to keep up with the latest science; and therefore I write to you.

I am the Director of the House Dolorous. The House was founded by my late father, and now it has fallen into my care. We can be found on the very farthest western edge of the world, nestled in the rocky bosom of the Flint Hills, northwest of a town called Greenbank, of which you no doubt have not heard. West of us, the world is still not yet Made, and on clear days, the views from our highest windows over Uncreation are unsettled and quite extraordinary.

Are you an adventurous man, Dr. Alverhuysen?

We are a hospital for those who have been wounded in our world's Great War. We take those who have been wounded in body, and we take those who have been wounded in mind. We do not discriminate. We are in neutral territory, and we ourselves are neutral. The Line does not reach out to the Flint Hills, and the agents of its wicked Adversary are not welcome among us. We take all who suffer, and we try to give them peace.

We have able field doctors and sawbones in residence, and we know how to treat burns and bullet wounds and lungs torn by poison gas. But the mind is something of a mystery to us. We are ignorant of the latest science. There are mad people in our care, and there is so little we can do for them.

Will you help us, Dr. Alverhuysen? Will you bring the benefit of your learning to our House? I understand that it is a long journey, rarely undertaken; but if you are not moved by the plight of our patients, then consider that we have all manner of mad folk here, wounded in ways that you will not find in the peaceful North—not least those who have been maddened by the terrible mind-shattering noise-bombs of the Line—and that your own studies may prosper in a House that provides such ample subject matter. If that does not move you, consider that our House is generously endowed. My father owned silver mines. I enclose a promissory note that will cover your travel by coach and by riverboat and by Engine of the Line; I enclose a map, and letters of

*introduction to all necessary guides and coachmen on this side of
the World; and finally I enclose my very best wishes,*

> *Yours in Brotherhood,*
> *Director Howell, Jr., the House Dolorous.*

She had shown the letter to her colleagues. They treated it as a
joke. Out of little more than a spirit of perversity, she wrote back
requesting further information. All winter she busied herself with
teaching, with her studies, with the care of her own subjects. She received no reply; she didn't expect to. On the first day of spring,
rather to her own surprise, she wrote again, to announce that she
had made her decision and that she would be traveling West at the
first opportunity.

※　※　※

Now she couldn't sleep. The golden watch ticked noisily at her bedside and she couldn't sleep, and her head was full of thoughts of distance and speed. She'd never seen one of the Engines of the Line and
could not picture what they looked like; but last year she had seen,
in one of the galleries in town, an exhibition of paintings of the
West's immense vistas, its wide-open plains like skies or seas. Perhaps
it was two years ago—Bernhardt had been alive. The paintings
had been huge, wall-to-wall, mountains and rivers and tremendous
skies, some blue and unclouded and others tempestuous. Forests
and valleys. The *panorama*: that was what they painted in the West.
Geography run wild and mad. There'd been several with bloody
battles going on at the bottom of the frame: *Fall of the Red Republic,* or something like that, was especially horrible, with its storm
clouds of doom clenched in the sky like sick hearts seizing, thousands of tiny men struggling in a black valley, battle standards
falling in the mud. They always seemed to be fighting about *something,* out in the West. There'd been half a dozen depicting nature
bisected by the Line; high arched rail bridges taming the mountains
or railroads shaving the forests away; the black paint blots that
were the Engines seeming to *move,* to drag the eye across the canvas. There were even a few visions of the very farthest West, where

the world was still entirely uncreated and full of wild lights and lightning storms and land that surged like sea and strange beautiful demonic forms being born in the murk. . . . Liv remembered how Agatha had shuddered and held herself tight. She remembered, too, how Bernhardt had held her in his heavy tweed-clad arm, and droned about Faculty politics, and so she had not quite lost herself in the paintings' wild depths.

Now those scenes rushed through her mind, blurred with speed and distance. The House was a world away. She could not picture traveling by Line, but she imagined herself leaving town by coach, and the wheels clattering into sudden unstoppable motion, and the horses rearing, and the coach lurching so that all her settled life spilled out behind her in a cascade of papers and old clothes and . . .

It was not an unpleasant sensation, she decided; it was as much exhilaration as terror. Nevertheless she needed to sleep, and so she took two serpent-green drops of her nerve tonic in a glass of water. As always, it numbed her very pleasantly.

❋ ❋ ❋

Liv settled her affairs. Her rooms were the property of the Faculty—she ensured that they would be made available to poor students during her absence. She consulted a lawyer regarding her investments. She dined almost nightly with Agatha and her family. She canceled her subscriptions to the scholarly periodicals. The golden watch presented an unexpected problem, because of course her clothes had no pockets suitable for such a heavy ugly thing, nor was she sufficiently unsentimental to leave it behind; eventually she decided to have a chain made and wear it around her neck, where it beat against her heart.

She visited her subjects and made arrangements for their future. The Andresen girl she transferred into Dr. Ekstein's care; the girl's pale and fainting neurasthenic despair might, she hoped, respond well to Ekstein's gruff cheerfulness. The Fussel boy she bequeathed to Dr. Naumann, who might find his frequent sexual rages interesting. With a satisfying stroke of her pen, she split the von Meer twins—who suffered from cobwebbed and romantic nightmares— sending one girl to Dr. Ekstein and the other to Dr. Lenkman. An excellent idea, as they only encouraged each other's hysteria. She wondered why she hadn't done it years ago! The Countess Romsdal had nothing at all wrong with her, in Liv's opinion, other than being too rich and too idle and too self-obsessed; so she thought Dr. Seidel might as well humor her. She gave Wilhelm and the near-catatonic Olanden boy to Dr. Bergman. She sent sweet little Bernarda, who was scared of candles and shadows and windows and her husband, to a rest cure in the mountains. As for Maggfrid . . .

Maggfrid came crashing into her office, late in the afternoon. He never understood to knock. The shock made her spill ink on her writing desk. He was in tears. "Doctor—you're leaving?"

She put down her pen and sighed. "Maggfrid, I told you I was leaving last week. And the week before that."

"They told me you were leaving."

"*I* told you I was leaving. Don't you remember?"

He stood there dumbly for a moment, then hurried over and began to mop at her desk with his sleeve. She put her hand on his arm to stop him.

He was nearly a giant. His huge hands were scarred from a multitude of small accidents—he didn't have the sense to look after himself properly. Someone who didn't know him might have found him terrifying—in fact, he was gentle and as loyal as a dog. Maggfrid was her first subject and, in a manner of speaking, her oldest friend.

Maggfrid's condition was congenital. His own blood had betrayed him. Sterile, he was the last of a line of imbeciles. Liv had found him sweeping the stone floors of the Institute in Tuborrhen, where she herself had spent some years in a high white-walled room, in a fragile state, after the death of her mother. He'd been kind to her then. Later, when she was stronger, he'd been happy to be her test subject; he was always simple and eager to please. He would answer questions for hours with his brow furrowed with effort. He bore even the more intrusive physical examinations without complaint. There were three ugly scars across his bald head, and a burn from a faulty electroplate, but he didn't mind. She couldn't heal him—she had quickly realized he was beyond mending—but he'd provided subject matter for a number of successful monographs, and in return she'd found him work sweeping the floors of August Hall.

"Doctor—"

"You'll be fine, Maggfrid. You hardly need me anymore."

He began mopping up the ink again. "Maggfrid, no . . ."

She couldn't stop him. She watched him work. He scrubbed with intense determination. It occurred to her that she could get up, walk away, lock the office behind her, and he might remain standing there, implacably scrubbing in the darkness. It was a sad thought.

Besides, she might need a bodyguard; she would need someone to carry her bags. It was even possible that fresh air, adventure, new scenery would do him good. It was certainly what *she* needed.

She put a hand on his arm again. "Maggfrid: Have you ever wanted to travel?"

It took nearly a minute for his big pale face to break into a grin; and then he lifted her from behind her desk and spun her like a child, until the room was a blur and she laughed and told him to let her down.

✳   ✳   ✳

She spent her very last day at the Faculty on the banks of the river. She sat next to Agatha on an outstretched blanket. They fed the swans and discussed the shapes of clouds. Their conversation was a little forced, and Liv wasn't at all sorry when it drifted away, and for a while they sat in silence.

"You'll have to a buy a gun," Agatha said quite suddenly.

Liv turned to her, rather shocked, to see that Agatha was smiling mischievously.

"You'll have to buy a gun, and learn to ride a horse."

Liv smiled. "I shall come back quite battle-scarred."

"With terrible stories."

"I shall never speak of them."

"Except when drunk, when you'll tell us all stories of the time you fought off a dozen wild Hillfolk bandits."

"Two dozen! Why not?"

"No student will ever dare defy you again."

"I shall walk with a limp, like an old soldier."

"You will—" Agatha fell silent.

She reached into her bag and took out a small red pocket-sized pamphlet, which she handed solemnly to Liv.

According to its cover, it was *A Child's History of the West*, and it had been published in somewhere called Morgan Town, in the year 1856.

Its pages were yellow and crumbling—hardly surprising, given that it was several years older than Liv herself. Its frontispiece was a black-and-white etching of a severe-looking gentleman in military uniform, with dark features, a neat white beard, a nose that could chop wood, and eyes that were somehow at once fierce and sad. He was apparently General Orlan Enver, First Soldier of the Red Valley Republic and the author of the *Child's History*. Liv had never heard of him.

"I'm afraid it's the only book I could find that says anything about where you're going at all," Agatha said.

"This is from the library."

Agatha shrugged. "Steal it."

"Agatha!"

"Really, Liv, it's hardly the time for you to worry about that sort of thing. Take it! It may be useful. Anyway, we can't send you off with nothing but that horribly ugly watch."

Agatha stood. "Be safe," she said.

"I will."

Agatha turned quickly and walked off.

※　※　※

Grunting, Maggfrid heaved up Liv's heavy cases onto the back of the coach. The horses snorted in the cold morning air and stamped the gravel of August Hall's yard. The Faculty was still sleeping—— apart from the coach and the horses and a few curious peacocks, the grounds were empty. Liv and Agatha embraced as the coachman stood by, smoking. Liv hardly noticed herself boarding the vehicle— she'd taken four drops of her nerve tonic to ensure that fear would not sway her resolve, and she was therefore somewhat distant and numb.

The coachman cracked the whip and the horses were away. The

die was cast. Liv's heart pounded. Balanced on her lap were the *Child's History of the West,* the ugly golden watch, and a copy of the most recent edition of the *Royal Maessenburg Journal of Psychology.* She found all three of them rather comforting. Maggfrid sat beside her with a frozen smile on his face. Gravel crunched, the lindens went rushing past, the Faculty's tall iron gates loomed like a mountain. Agatha gathered up her skirts and ran a little way after the coach, and Liv waved and in doing so managed to drop her copy of the *Journal,* which fluttered away behind her down the path. The coachman offered to stop, but she told him keep going, keep going!

CHAPTER 2

A GENTLEMAN OF LEISURE

Riverboat, due south from Humboldt, through night and red rushes, through neutral territories. Long-legged herons stalked the banks. The riverboat came as a roaring invader into their silent muddy world: its vast dark weight and the golden light and swirling thumping piano music pouring from its windows sent the birds panicking into flight like shots had been fired. . . .

But it was only a gambling boat, a private enterprise chartered out of the Baronies of the Delta, three decks of music and drinking and whores and con men and business travelers and suckers. It carried no cannon. Its great paddle wheel clattered and splashed. (The Folk who turned it were discreetly locked away below.) It was painted scarlet and blue, rimmed with brass, flying a variety of flags; it was quite pretty in the torchlight. A young man in pinstripes vomited over the side while his girlfriend picked his pocket. Six blond and prosperous farmers staggered out of the bar arm in arm, singing a song about fighting. The floor of the bar was bright with spilt whiskey and broken glass, and the pitch and yaw of the boat sent a constant whirl of men and women around and around in drunken circles about the roulette wheel and the dice tables and the knots of men clutching tightly to their cards and their little heaps of coins and worn, sweaty banknotes.

Everyone was talking much too loudly about sex, about business, about crime, about war—and about plans for when the War was over, which always got a laugh. A man with a quick mind and sharp hearing could have picked up valuable intelligence—and Creedmoor had a passably quick mind and the ears of a fox. But he was retired, and happily so, and so he shut his ears and let the babble wash over him. He liked to be among people; he liked the noises and smells of crowds. This wasn't peace. There was no peace and there never would be. But it was close enough.

He sat in a half-dark corner playing cards with strangers. His back was to the wall, just in case.

The table was playing the Old Game, with the suits they used in the towns of the Delta—rifles, shovels, wolves, and bones. A game of bluff and cunning: Creedmoor excelled at it. There was a rich-looking man in a green necktie and glasses, a less rich-looking man in a brown suit with a bald head, and a stupid-looking young man called Buffo who'd joined the boat that morning from a one-street town called Lezard, with bloodstains on his boots and a burlap sack full of clinking gold coins. No questions asked. Buffo balanced a black-haired green-eyed girl on his lap, who seemed to like it when Creedmoor smiled at her. Everyone was substantially less rich than they'd been at the start of the evening, except for Creedmoor and the girl, who appeared to be a neutral party.

Creedmoor had joined the boat two days ago in a town called Humboldt, where some old enemies had spotted him. He'd been sitting on a painted bench on Humboldt's waterfront, watching the young women go by in their blue and green summer dresses, when his peace had been shattered by the sound of Engines and the smell of smoke. Even before he saw it, he sensed the black staff car coming down the dirt road behind him. *Linesmen.* He jumped up, walked quickly but calmly down the pier, and bought a ticket for the first boat out. In the old days, he might have stayed and fought, but he was tired of fighting. Anyway, he was only passing through Humboldt on a detour to avoid the Shrike Hills, which, when he'd last been that way thirty years ago, were full of drowsy little villages. Now, to his great annoyance, the hills were being flattened and built over by the

Line—farms replaced by factories, forests stripped, hills mined and quarried to feed the insatiable holy hunger of the Engines.

He was happy enough on the boat. He hadn't been traveling anywhere in particular anyway. It was six years since he'd last heard the Call. It was impossible to avoid his masters or escape them, but he did his best to make himself appear both idle and useless to them—a burnt-out case. It appeared to be working well enough. He regarded himself, provisionally, as a free man.

More money changed hands. The rich-looking gentleman in the necktie gave a sad laugh and tossed his last crumpled bills in the air. Creedmoor deftly snatched them.

"You're a devil, sir."

"Not tonight," Creedmoor said, and smiled.

Creedmoor's hair was a little thin, brown turning gray; his face was red and lined and rough. He looked like he came from Lundroy peasant stock, which he did. If you saw him smile, you might think he was still a young man; if you saw him sometimes when he thought he was alone, he might look a hundred years old. The three men who sat across the table from him behind rapidly diminishing piles of money had seen a simple old man. Now, Creedmoor judged, at least two of them were considering drawing a weapon on him. He hoped they wouldn't be so foolish.

Creedmoor's hoard of bills and coins grew, big and glittering and beautiful. The rich-looking gentleman staggered drunkenly off, cursing in disgust. The black-haired green-eyed girl moved herself from Buffo's lap to Creedmoor's.

Buffo sneered in disgust and spat on the floor.

"I'll ask you not to do that," Creedmoor said. "Lowers the tone."

Buffo's bloodshot eyes narrowed and his leg started to twitch. He appeared not to have slept in days. He stared at his cards and muttered *old fool* and *whore*, the latter presumably addressed to the girl. He repeated it: *whore, whore, whore.* The girl laughed, high and cheerful. Creedmoor liked her. She had an unfortunate black wen on her lip but was otherwise lovely, and Creedmoor put his arm around her and was happy.

❋ ❋ ❋

When he woke the next morning in his cabin, his head hurt so dreadfully that for a moment he thought his old masters were Calling to him. That was how they announced their presence: with pain, and noise, and the smell of blood and fire. He began to plead and make excuses. He was answered with silence, and it quickly became clear that he was experiencing nothing more extraordinary than a hangover.

The boat lurched. The girl was squeezed into his bunk, and her arm with its fine dark hairs was draped across his own scarred chest. Her green eyes looked at him curiously. He hoped he hadn't spoken out loud.

❋ ❋ ❋

He passed the day in a deck chair with a romantic novel. He pulled his hat down over his eyes and warmed in the sun like an elderly alligator. The river shone white behind and blue ahead, and the broad plains were baked brown and encircled in the distance by dark pines and blue mountains. A few farms, no towns. No Line—not yet. The plains were a hazy emptiness, uninhabited land, a vast and vague beauty, not yet shaped or Made by anyone's dreams or nightmares.

He ate no lunch. Sometimes he forgot.

A shadow fell over him and woke him. It was the girl, blocking the orange haze of the afternoon sun. She looked pale and nervous, and Creedmoor quite forgot what he'd liked about her. He also forgot her name.

"John," she said, "I've been thinking. . . ."

John was his real name. He didn't recall giving it to her, though admittedly he'd been drinking lately. He sure didn't see how it was any business of hers to be using it. His face set into a scowl.

"This boat stops in Aral," she said. "And from there it's not too far north to Keaton, or even Jasper. And there's work on the stage there, and everyone says I'm pretty enough. And I know you got money. And I know you're smart, smarter than any of these boys here, and I don't know what you do for money, but I know it ain't regular, and what I mean is if you wanted to travel together . . ."

"I'm not going to Keaton. Or Jasper."

"Wherever, then. I'm sick of working this boat, John. I want to see the world."

"The world's a bloody awful place," he said. "This boat is as good as it gets." And he pulled his hat down again, so he wouldn't have to see the hurt look in her eyes.

Once she'd stormed off, he went back to his novel. He saw a happy ending coming, but he didn't believe in it.

He dozed in his deck chair. He woke again in the evening, disturbed by the distant whine of ornithopters. Every one of his old muscles tensed, and a sour taste of fear rose into his mouth. He lifted his hat just enough to examine the red evening sky; otherwise, he was still. After a few moments he saw them, miles off, six black specks moving in formation high over the plains. Advance scouts for the Line. They bled smoke—they scored black lines across the sky. The whine became a drone then a clattering whir of iron wings as they passed overhead, and Creedmoor quietly pulled his hat down over his face. The drone faded again and he untensed.

He ate alone in his room, worrying boiled meat from the bone with his teeth.

❋   ❋   ❋

Buffo put on a kind of show in the bar that night. The young man had slicked back his hair and pressed his suit and cleaned the blood from his boots, and looked quite handsome. He leaned on the bar and shouted over the noise of the boat. The black-haired girl was back with him. He was throwing money around and telling stories of how he'd won it—as he drank and swayed, his story shifted, so that first he'd been a famous gambler, and then he'd made his fortune running rifles to the besieged towns of Elmo Flats past the blockades of the Line, and then he'd robbed a bank in Jasper City, and then he'd invented a wonderful new headache cure but been cheated out of the patent by a cunning little Northerner.

If Creedmoor was any judge, every word of it was a lie, but Buffo's audience only grew throughout the evening. Creedmoor drank alone. Sometimes Buffo caught Creedmoor's skeptical eye and scowled, and Creedmoor smiled, and Buffo bared his teeth and lost the thread of his latest story. The girl seemed angry with Creedmoor, too. And those 'thopters had quite soured Creedmoor's mood.

※ ※ ※

Buffo began a new story.

"... and that was where ... that summer ... after the, you know, after I was saying how I robbed that bank in Keaton, I mean Jasper, and ... can I trust you all? Come closer, can I trust you to keep a secret? I fucking well ought to be able to, all the drinks I bought you ... that was where I got *this*."

The boy fumbled drunkenly in his jacket. He pulled out a small and cheaply made revolver, snagged it on his tie, and dropped it on the floor. He recovered it and then slammed it down on the table.

He said, "Yeah." People drew nervously away from him.

"That *is* what you think it is," he said, loosening his tie.

"Let me tell you. Let me tell you. They don't recruit just anyone. Only the bravest and wildest are chosen by the Gun to be its Agents. They'd had their eye on me for months, I reckon—maybe since I did that bank in, in Shropmark, maybe since I broke out of the jail in White Plains, maybe since the shooting in ... but that's another story. Don't touch that weapon. Don't none of you even fucking *look* at it. There's a demon in that weapon. A god in it. In *me*. That was—I was in a bar in, in that town, just by myself, just quiet, because you see what you people don't know is that when you rob a bank, see, you have to stay quiet, you can't go spending your money, you have to be even more quiet and innocent than if you were actually innocent, if you're smart. And so a man came to me in the dark, and he was dressed all in black and he had a black hat and he had red eyes, and they say that's how you can tell, because they're not like ordinary men anymore. *We're* not like ordinary men anymore. He sat down beside me and he said, 'I've got a proposition for you.' What would you say, what would you say if they asked you? I mean, they *wouldn't* ask any of you—they take only dangerous men. They take only wicked men. They take only the worst of the worst and the best of the worst. Robbers and murderers and anarchists. I've been—I've known all of them, Abban the Lion, Blood-and-Thunder Boch, Dandy Fanshawe, Black Casca,

Red Molly—I've had her—all the legends. All the stories. What would you say, if they asked? All that power. You'd live forever, or at least you'd never be forgotten after you're gone. But the War . . . I mean the Line covers half the World. And it's always growing. And it has Engines, and 'thopters, and bombs, and a million fucking men. And all Gun has is—is us. Heroes. Is it worth it? They can't win. They can't win. The Line's going to get them all in the end. That's—that's what I'm doing here, see, I have a mission. A mission for the Gun, against the Line. I'm part of it. The Great War. I'd say it's worth it. I'd say. I'd say yes if they—"

Buffo's eyes were darting all around the bar. His audience was uncertain, drawing slowly away from him. The black-haired girl had busied herself elsewhere. He didn't seem to notice.

"*Fuck* yes, it's worth it." He banged his weapon again on the table. He stood suddenly, swaying, and tore open his shirt to bare a wiry chest. "You can't kill me. They made me strong. I'm not like you anymore. Shoot me. Shoot me or stab me if you dare."

No one took him up on his offer. He didn't say anything else. After a while, he wandered out into the night, snatching up his money but leaving the cheap revolver forgotten on the table. Creedmoor followed.

※　※　※

Creedmoor waited until Buffo had finished pissing over the side before he spoke.

"That's a dangerous story to be telling."

The young man turned and stumbled against the rail. His face was in darkness, but shafts of light from the windows crisscrossed his hands and body. The riverboat's great paddle wheel turned and turned in the darkness behind him, and the night sky above was full of ink-black clouds.

"We're a long way from any Stations of the Line out here," Creedmoor said, taking a step closer. "And you'd know if any of the Line's men were aboard, because they stink, and they're stunted and pale, and you can always spot 'em. They grow all packed in together in their big cities, and the smell of oil and coal smoke never leaves 'em. And anyway they never go anywhere without their machines, and their vehicles, and their Engines. But even so. Even so. Rumors fly faster than birds and faster even than Engines."

With the assistance of the rail, Buffo stood straight. "I'm not scared of Linesmen."

Creedmoor paused and shook his head. "The Agents of the Gun, now, I hear you can't tell them apart from ordinary men. Or even women. Except that every one of them carries the weapon that houses the demon that rides them and barks at them and makes them strong. Yes? But how would you know—because who doesn't carry a weapon these days, and aren't all weapons a little monstrous in their way? Fortunately the Gun's Agents are few and far between, because you're right—the Gun takes only the worst and wickedest. But if there were Agents aboard, they might not like your stories."

Buffo shrugged.

"And these are neutral territories we're passing through now, and these people are businessmen and farmers going to market, and they may be playing at being wicked people for a night while they're away from their wives, but they do not love Agents of the Gun. The Great War will come to them eventually, they cannot stay neutral forever—Line is too greedy and Gun too ruthless—but for now they are neutral and happy that way. They may slit your throat in the night."

"I don't care what they think." Buffo waved dismissively, and nearly fell over.

"They don't care for bank robbers either, come to that. Not after the story's over. How did you come by that money, really? Who did you kill for it? I'm curious."

Buffo spat at Creedmoor's feet.

"Fair enough." Creedmoor spoke quieter as he came closer to where Buffo swayed. "And if there were a man aboard who'd retired from the Great War, he might not want you telling stories either. You might bring down unwanted attention. You might disturb his peace. You might bring back bad memories; you might with your lies tarnish glorious memories. A man like that might politely ask you to shut up, and get off at the next town, while you still have your money and your neck. What do you say?"

Buffo shoved Creedmoor's shoulder and said, "Leave me alone, old man." So Creedmoor, sighing, slapped Buffo's hand aside and lifted him struggling by the collar of his shirt, and reached down into those depths of his spirit where that savage inhuman strength lay, and hurled Buffo over the edge, out into the night, arcing high into the air and far past the white water rushing over the boat's wheel. The boy's arms and legs pinwheeled in the air and coins rained from his pockets. He splashed down forty feet behind the boat in a slow dark bend of the river.

Creedmoor looked around; no one seemed to have noticed the brief struggle or heard the distant splash. Buffo's tiny figure trod water, waving his arms and shouting, but the music drowned out his voice and the boat left him behind.

Creedmoor noticed that the boy had dropped a fistful of notes on the deck. His back ached a little as he stooped to gather them up.

The green-eyed girl waited on Creedmoor's table that night. She kept looking around anxiously, as if wondering where her stupid young man had gone. Creedmoor tipped her well.

✳ ✳ ✳

He woke at noon, lurching bolt upright in his bed. Pain stabbed at his head, and he staggered to the window, where a red-hot sun burned and the smell of the river was stagnant and made him sick. The pain—the smell of blood and cordite in his nostrils—there was no mistake this time. He'd forgotten—he'd forgotten how it hurt, when they Called. For six years, he'd been idle and alone in his soul. He'd locked away those memories; his wounds had healed. Now he felt his master kicking down the doors and Calling for him. The world moved very slowly around him—outside the window, the paddle wheel turned as slowly as the long centuries of the Great War—and a fly crawled with infinite patience across his knuckles. He'd gone to sleep in his clothes, and his collar was suddenly choking him. The weapon—the Gun—the temple of metal and wood and deadly powder that housed his master's spirit—sat on the floor by the bed and throbbed with darkness. All the room seemed to bend and sway around it. Creedmoor couldn't face looking at it yet.

The voice sounded in his head, like metal scraping, like powder sparking, like steel chambers falling heavily into place.

—Creedmoor. You are needed again.

CHAPTER 3

The Black File

It was the morning of the first day of the third month of the year 1889—or 296 in the reckoning of the Line—and Sub-Invigilator (Third) Lowry sat in a small ill-lit office, filling out forms. The tall moonfaced clock that loomed behind Lowry's shoulder had just informed him, through a series of insistent whistles and clacks that still to this day induced anxiety, though Lowry was now thirty-two years old and had been a soldier for twenty-two years, that the time was 14:00. He had not slept in two days. The bags under his eyes were like big black zeros, and the stubble on his jaw was a palpable disgrace. Every hour on the hour, he took one of the dark gray antisleep tablets, which were not to be confused with the light gray appetite-suppressant tablets, or the chalky libido-suppressants, or the black intellect-sharpeners. He had work to complete.

His office had one small square window, too high to allow any view that might distract him; nothing was visible through it except slate-gray clouds. That view never changed. In the haze of industry that surrounded Angelus Station, it was always gray. For all Lowry knew, the sky beyond those smog-clouds might be blue or white or any other horrible thing, but down here it was gray.

His office echoed with the sound of machinery outside, his typing inside. Angelus Station was preparing for the return, refueling, and rearming of its Engine, which occurred every thirteen days and was always a vast undertaking. No delays were tolerated. Every machine and process of the Station was being pushed to capacity. Lowry pecked away at the keys, slowly, one-fingered, taking infinite agonies over the composition of his reports, on which his career might depend.

Not only was his office small, but a tangle of pipes and cables poked through its walls at roughly head height, carrying important fuels and heating and cooling fluids from one part of the Station to another, clanging and steaming and occasionally dripping warm acrid water onto the back of Lowry's neck. A person not familiar with the operations of the Line might infer, from Lowry's surroundings, that he was low-ranking; that would be wrong. In fact, Lowry occupied a position somewhere in the middle range of the upper reaches of the hierarchy of Angelus Station's several hundred thousand personnel, military and civilian, a hierarchy that was almost as complex and convoluted as the Station's plumbing. However, the Line believed in keeping its servants humble, the more so the more responsibility that was entrusted to them. The Angelus Engine's Sub-Invigilators (Second) and (First) had even smaller offices than Lowry's. The Invigilator had no office, as far as Lowry knew, and possibly did not exist except in the form of a signature on certain official documents. The higher ranks and civilian administrators were a mystery to Lowry, one it was not his business to investigate.

Three identical black-and-gray uniforms hung from the pipes behind Lowry's back. They made him feel like unfriendly eyes were spying on him, which he put down to sleep deprivation—he wasn't imaginative, normally.

His office had one single decoration: a copy of the commendation that had been issued to his unit of the Angelus Engine's Second Army for its part in the capture and execution of the Agents Liam "the Wolf of the South" Sinclair and Goodwife Sal. It was sixteen years old.

On a shelf over his desk he had a copy of the Black File. It was his most treasured possession. It occupied twelve thick black volumes, and every one of its pages contained top-secret intelligence on the Line's great enemies, the Agents of the Gun. It was not widely circulated. Lowry had undergone a six-month review process before being permitted to read the thing, and another two-year review to be permitted to possess a copy.

He had made a special study of the subject of the Agents, and believed himself to be something of an expert. His hatred of them was unusual even by the standards of officers of the Line. No particular reason why. They just disgusted him, was all. He was a simple man.

The Wolf of the South and Goodwife Sal were both in the Black File, under DECEASED. Since their bodies had been burned, it was, Lowry supposed, their final resting place. Six years ago, Lowry had been an adviser to an operation that had killed Blood-and-Ashes Morley, at the cost of only forty-six Linesmen, which had earned Lowry himself a footnote in the Black File. Now he was engaged in filing his report on the recent death of Strychnine Ann Auburn. It was an exquisitely tricky business. If all went well, it would earn him a second footnote in the File; however, the slightest trace of vanity or ambition could earn him demotion, disgrace. The Line did not tolerate vanity or ambition in its servants.

SUMMARY

The first joint operation between the forces of the Angelus Engine and the forces of the Dryden Engine since the Razing of Logtown in Year 267 can be judged to have met with total success. Command structures were successfully integrated to ensure effective hierarchy and full obedience while leaving adequate operational independence to ensure prompt and effective action. Casualties were inconsequential. The Dryden Engine's forces assaulted the enemy's position and rightly claim a significant portion of the credit for the execution. ~~However, intelligence provided by Sub-Invigilator (Third) Lowry of the Army of the Angelus Engine proved essential to the success of the operation~~

However, it is important to note that intelligence operations contributed significantly to the success of the operation. The efficient interchange of information is critical to the Forward Progress of the Line, and though personal ambition is irrelevant to that Progress, a full record must be made. ~~Sub-Invigilator (Third) Lowry of the Army of the Angelus Engine designed the intelligence-gathering operations which~~

~~Sub-Invigilator (Third) Lowry of the Army of the Angelus Engine~~
~~participated in the intelligence-gathering operations which~~

The Angelus Engine permitted its personnel to oversee the intelligence-gathering operations that led to the tracking of the Agent, Ann Auburn, aka Strychnine Ann, aka Strychnine Auburn, see H.22.7, R.251.13, to the town of Corbey, northeast of Gibson City, see L.124.21. Mathematical analysis of the patterns of her attacks located her in the vicinity of Corbey, and questioning of locals provided her precise location. Among numerous personnel whose duty it was to participate in those operations were Sub-Invigilator (Third) Lowry . . .

When he'd finally crafted his report—not to his satisfaction, exactly, but to a point where nothing further could be done to protect himself—he delivered it into the pneumatic tube at the far end of the hallway, *thrusting* it in the decisive way one might thrust a bayonet into someone's gut. Then he staggered across the littered and crowded and smog-haunted Concourse to his dormitory building. It was cold out, so it was probably night. He took a fistful of sleeping pills and was immediately unconscious.

In his dreams he saw the Agent, Ann Auburn, once again. She'd been tall, much taller than Lowry, black-skinned, shaven-headed, gold-ringed, strikingly beautiful if you liked that kind of thing, which Lowry did not. A real arrogant bitch. She'd been hiding among sympathizers in Corbey Town, in a loft over a barn like an animal, which had not diminished her arrogance, and had been striking at Line cargo transports along the river and roads. The Dryden Engine's forces had encircled the town, launched poison-gas rockets, then closed in. Lowry had watched through a telescope from a safe distance as the cornered woman fought her way out snarling and laughing through fire and blood and the billowing blind-eye-white haze of deadly gas, killing and killing until finally her wounds dragged her down, too numerous and too deep for her masters' power to heal. . . .

But in his dream he stepped *through* the 'scope's crosshairs and was down in the killing ground, walking with the same strutting immunity as the Agent herself.

Stand down, lads. Let me show you how it's done.

He seized her long thin neck and slammed her against a wall. She moaned. He yanked at her hooped gold earrings, and she cried out.

See, lads? It's simple. It's all a question of authority.

He slapped her, made her nose bleed, made her beg wordlessly.

You just have to show them who's in charge.

Lowry typically didn't dream, not unless he'd miscalculated the dosage of his various standard-issue performance-enhancing chemicals, and so he experienced it all with shocking intensity and pleasure.

❊ ❊ ❊

He woke in a guilty panic. He was alone in the room—the three other men with whom he shared his billet were awake, gone, packed. The room's narrow window opened over the Primary Concourse, and Lowry knew at once, from the sounds of the machines and crowds, that the Engine had returned. There was no shouting, no cursing, no talking at all; in the presence of the Engine, the Station's personnel worked in near-silence, in respect or terror or awe. Lowry had been born and raised in the basement levels of Angelus and was as attuned to its crowd noises and machine noises as it was possible to be.

And the thing itself waited on the Concourse below, its metal flanks steaming, cooling, emitting a low hum of *awareness* that made Lowry's legs tremble. . . .

Quick calculation: He'd slept for rather more than sixteen hours. He was due to report to the staff of the Engine some two or three hours ago.

He dressed, ran out into the corridor, and threw himself in stumbling terror down the dormitory's concrete staircase, still fumbling with his spectacles, and stepped out onto the crowded wide-open Concourse, where he was obliged, under the eyes of Authority, to walk, never to run, and to show the proper indifference to his own individual fate.

Two great busy Halls with roofs of iron girders and dirty green glass processed the Engine's passengers and crew. One Hall handled civilians and outsiders who'd purchased passage; one handled military personnel. Lowry reported to the latter. He waited, in agony, under the eye of disapproving clock faces, in a queue that zigzagged back and forth across the floor's greasy tiles in much the same way that the Line ran across the continent. He presented his papers at the counter and said, "Sub-Invigilator (Third) Lowry, reporting."

Behind the counter sat a woman with a tautly wound bun of steel-gray hair, a long sharp nose, distant eyes. She studied a roll of typed paper and said, "No."

"What?"

"No."

"I said *Lowry*, woman. I have orders to go east with the Engine to Archway. See here?" He pointed at his papers.

"See here?" The woman pointed at *her* papers, under *I* for *Invigilator (Sub) (Third)*, where his name significantly did not appear. Her finger was stub-nailed and abominably stained with black ink.

"There must be some mistake."

That was impossible, of course—the Line made no mistakes. He said, "I mean, *I* must have made some mistake," in case anyone important was listening.

She shrugged and bent down over her paperwork. Lowry saw that she kept three steel pens shoved into the back of her hair, one of which was leaking; they looked like loose wiring, or vents for internal machinery.

He pressed his face up against the grille in the glass and whispered, *"Please."*

She looked up at him with blank contempt, sighed, and waited for him to go away—which, after what felt like hours, he did.

He pushed through the crowd, which parted nervously around him. Part of his mind was trying to calculate *causes*—had he been removed from service for his tardiness? Had the Auburn Report, despite his best efforts, contained unacceptable traces of pride? Had he spoken blasphemy in his sleep? Had he contradicted, without remembering it, some superior officer, had he—? Part of his mind was trying to calculate *consequences*: Should he fear only for his career, or also for his life? Most of his mind was blank.

"Sir?"

He didn't hear it at first.

"Sir?"

The gray-haired woman was calling him. He slumped back to the counter, numbly expecting further humiliation.

"Sir." She sounded suddenly anxious, apologetic, and that made him stand up a little straighter. He leaned forward and snapped, "What?"

She handed him a short telegram. "Sir, I apologize, I . . ."

"Shut up," he said.

He read the telegram. It didn't take long, and it left him entirely confused.

"Kingstown," he said. Far to the West—indeed, the Line's westernmost point. At least two weeks away. The Angelus Engine was going east, which meant that he would have to wait for the Archway Engine to pass through, which would take him only as far as Harrow Cross, from where perhaps the Harrow Cross Engine would take him west to . . .

"My apologies, sir," the woman said. "In all the rush, sir, I forgot—"

He smiled at her, baring bleached teeth. "What's your name, woman?"

❋ ❋ ❋

The telegram said:

FOR SUB-INVIGILATOR (THIRD) LOWRY OF THE ARMY OF
THE ANGELUS ENGINE:

KINGSTOWN STATION
SETTING ASIDE ALL OTHER BUSINESS
WITHOUT DELAY

It was unsigned.

CHAPTER 4

ANCIENT HISTORY

Creedmoor left the riverboat that same night. He leapt from the boat's stern and landed knee deep in riverbank mud, among reeds and turtles and toads and snakes. He laughed and thought to himself,

—The glories of your service, once more, once again.

And his master's voice answered,

—Yes, Creedmoor. Our glories. Go north. There, over those hills, through those trees.

—We have business there? Someone you want me to kill?

—Not necessarily. We need a fire, Creedmoor. Our Lodge burns, just as it always does, and you must hear this from all of us.

—I remember. Would you care to explain the urgency?

—You have been idle too long. Go north.

The boat's lights slowly drew away down the river, leaving Creedmoor alone in the night. With a sigh he blinked, once and then again, until his eyes adjusted. A gray film settled on his vision, each detail of the world painfully clear and intense, each rustling reed knife-sharp. The night-sight: the vision of the Guns. For six years, Creedmoor had lived among crowds and lights, and he'd almost forgotten the world the way the Guns saw it.

Toads and snakes! He slogged forward through the reeds and muck, and frogs trilled and black kingfishers fled from him, calling their shrill rattling call.

—That way, Creedmoor.

The voice hurt—it buzzed, it scraped, it burned—and the Gun that housed his master throbbed like a wound at his hip—but the pain was becoming familiar again.

He clambered up the banks and over a green mound of earth, and when he turned around, the last sign of the riverboat was gone.

*   *   *

There was no refusing his masters when they Called. Creedmoor knew that very well.

When a man first entered the service of the Gun, his masters promised strength, freedom, glory—it was impossible at first to imagine ever wanting to saying no to them. For the first ten years or so, man and weapon would exist in a wild and exhilarating unity of purpose. That was how it had been for Creedmoor. He'd been lost and drifting when the Gun first took him—too old still to be a rootless boy—no honest job, no family, more creditors than friends. Every grand cause he'd taken up in his wanderings had failed him, one by one. Liberationism—the Church of the White City Virgins—the Knights of Labor—even the fucking *Smilers*. He'd been considering settling down somewhere and devoting himself to the serious study of alcoholism and despair. The Gun had raised him up and made him extraordinary. For ten years, he fought for them all across the many fronts of the Great War, he schemed and murdered and bribed and seduced and blackmailed for them, and he did it joyfully.

But the Gun's Agents were wild and unruly, and sooner or later, they all began to resent their servitude. And then their masters would give them the Goad. It always happened—sooner or later. They seemed to take a certain satisfaction in it. Sometimes it had to be done twice or three times, rarely more often.

Creedmoor had spent all afternoon in the riverboat's bar, drinking like a condemned man and flirting desperately with the waitresses. When night fell and his master said,

—Go now.

. . . he'd gone. He didn't want the Goad.

*   *   *

He marched north through the dark of a gum tree grove, through thin bone-white trunks. They put him in mind of Hillfolk. Mud sucked at his boots. The throb of bullfrogs got on his nerves. He'd taken off his necktie, and his jacket was already torn. The ground sloped up sharply and he broke through the trees and out over the marshy plains.

—That way, Creedmoor.

—What do you want from me? Just tell me.

—You must hear it from all of us. We must visit our Lodge.

—This is an important errand? I'm honored.

—All our purposes are important. And you *are* honored.

Marshland gave way to grassland. He walked alone under a stark moon, breathing deeply in the cold air and—it was ridiculous! But there was no denying it—he began to feel the old joy again. Already he felt younger and wilder than he had for years. His legs were tireless. The Gun banged rhythmically against his hip, and his master said,

—That way. Why are you smiling?

—I would rather not serve you. But if I must, I might as well try to do it gladly.

—Good, Creedmoor. We like our servants joyful.

He came to the crest of a low rise, and jumped a fence of wood and wire. Now he was on grazing land—he saw the tracks and droppings of goats. In the distance on the edge of a hill, he saw the sharp outline of a farmhouse.

—There, Creedmoor.

—A farm.

—Yes.

—Are we borrowing eggs?

No answer. He jogged briskly uphill. A worn and stony trail led him up to the farmhouse. It was a ramshackle cabin of logs and mud and corrugated iron. Its roof raised up a weathervane in the shape of a bird, probably some local Baron's crest. Its door was adorned with an upturned horseshoe. Some simple people believed that iron would keep away wild Hillfolk, on the theory that it reminded them of their brethren's chains. Creedmoor doubted its efficacy even on Hillfolk, and certainly it was wasted on him.

His master said,

—Yes. In there. This will do. They have a fire.

There *was* a fire burning inside, and smoke at the chimney. Two dogs chained to a post in the ground outside started to whine and bark. Dogs didn't like Creedmoor. They smelled the demon that rode him.

—Our kin will join us in fire. First kill the inhabitants.

With a sigh, Creedmoor knocked on the door.

❊   ❊   ❊

The cabin was cluttered with pots and pans, with pelts and hooves and animal bones, with the worn wooden paraphernalia of farmer's work. Two-tined forks and a battered old hoe. A churn? Creedmoor wasn't sure what half of it was. He hadn't done a day's honest work in his life since he was a printer's apprentice back in Lundroy.

A low fire smoldered in the corner. The cabin had one inhabitant, by the name of Josiah, a wiry old man, bent like a fishhook, with a beard like a goat's.

Creedmoor didn't kill him. Instead, though it made his master displeased—*because* it made his master displeased—Creedmoor decided to drink with him.

Josiah had some awful poisonous stuff in a wooden keg, which he sipped from a ladle, and had already been unsteady drunk when he opened the door.

"Come in," he'd said. "Come in, I got nothing left to steal. My only daughter ran off to Jasper City with a swarthy fellow to be an actress, so you won't be stealing her neither. Sit down! Have a drink."

"Don't mind if I do." Creedmoor sat. In the interests of caution, he refused Josiah's brew—there were limits, after all, to the strength the Guns could give a man—and he drank from a bottle he'd stolen from the riverboat. Noticing a battered old rifle on the wall, and some tattered flags, Creedmoor asked if the old man had been a soldier, and soon they got talking about long-forgotten wars.

—Kill him and be done with it, Creedmoor.

—I don't see the necessity.

The voice sulked and snarled and scraped in Creedmoor's head. He ignored it.

Josiah had fought for the Delta Baronies thirty years ago, in the north, in a battle in which he still to this day believed was in support of an alliance with the young Red Valley Republic—though Creedmoor happened to know that the local Baron was acting secretly in furtherance of a scheme of the Guns. Creedmoor didn't bother to set the old man straight. He made up some wild lies about his own military heroism. The old man swallowed it all up, eagerly, drinking and talking and talking . . . A lonely life out there, Creedmoor thought.

When the old man finally fell over in a dead drunk, Creedmoor carried him outside and left him with his barking dogs in the yard, and went back inside and shuttered the windows and bolted the door.

—We told you to kill him, Creedmoor.

—I didn't see the necessity. Don't worry, my bloodthirsty friend. I'm sure there's killing to come.

—A sacrifice. Blood. To bring the Lodge here.

Creedmoor sighed, and rubbed his graying temples. Then he unbolted the door, stepped outside, and shot one of the dogs. As he bolted the door once again, he said:

—That will do.

—A dog. Undignified.

—I know your preferences. Do you care enough to punish me? Time's wasting.

—Then stoke the fire.

—Good.

—We will remember this.

—Of course.

He heaped the fire with wood, and then with pelts, and then poured raw spirits onto it, and soon the cabin was dark with smoke, and red flames leapt high on the edges of Creedmoor's hazy vision, and the fire roared and burning logs snapped with gunshot noises in a mad frantic rhythm. The Song of the Guns, the echo of their terrible voices. Creedmoor's master said,

—Listen.

❋ ❋ ❋

Creedmoor's master's name was Marmion. It hardly mattered, though; they were all much the same.

How numerous were the Guns? Creedmoor wasn't sure. Some of them had several names, and some of them had no names at all, but went by the names of the particular Agents who carried them. They were immortal spirits, but their manifestation in this world was in the form of weapons of wood and metal and ivory and powder. Sometimes when their Agents died or their vessels were destroyed, they vanished from the world for decades, sulking in their Lodge; sometimes they came back at once, hungry for revenge. Some of them were carried by famous generals or warriors; others favored spies and blackmailers and murderers, and might never be known to history at all. Creedmoor's best guess was that there were not fewer than three dozen, and probably not more than a hundred.

Before Creedmoor, Marmion had been borne by a con man called Smiling Joe Portis, who'd been arrested by men of the Line in Gibson City and dragged back to Harrow Cross to be hanged. In the last century, Marmion had been borne by a woman called Lenore Van Velde, aka Lenore the White, who'd stopped the advance of the Line over the Stow River by introducing plague rats into their encampments while posing as a cook. It was *possible* that Marmion had been borne by the legendary One-Eye Beck, who'd blown the bridge over the Tappan Gorge with a black-powder petard, sending the Archway Engine screaming back down to hell, from which it arose again two hundred years ago. That was all Creedmoor knew of his master's history; presumably it went back a full four hundred years, to Founding and the first western settlements. And before that—before humans woke it and gave it form—before that Marmion slept in the earth. Or in fire. Or the stars. Or elsewhere entirely. It was hard to say.

The gods of the enemy were easier to count. Their straight and constant paths could be seen on maps. There were exactly thirty-eight Engines in the world.

❋ ❋ ❋

His head spun in the smoke and he drowsed for a second. The crack and hiss of the fire began to sound like distant conversation. A voice in the back of his brain snapped him awake—

—Creedmoor! Listen.

Not his master—one of the others. The voice was the same but different. Which one was it? Belphegor? Barbas? Naamur? Gorgon?

—Creedmoor! We have work for you.

—Creedmoor! We have chosen you from among many.

—Creedmoor! You must go west, to the edge of the world.

And there were other voices beneath those, more distant, more alien—buzz and click and the off-kilter rhythm of gunfire. Part of the Guns was in the world, and they sang to each other across the continent in those distant echoes of violence. Part of them was always in their Lodge, which was—where? In the fires beneath the earth? In the dark beyond the stars? Creedmoor didn't know.

The walls of old Josiah's cabin were no longer visible. The room was made of smoke and fire and stink. Creedmoor didn't understand or care to understand the metaphysics of it, but he was now in what might be called an anteroom to the Lodge itself, and it turned out that others were there waiting for him:

—Hello, Creedmoor. Have you been enjoying your retirement? No rest for the wicked, is there?

—You cowardly dog, Creedmoor, I thought you were dead. Dead or gone to No-Town. Have you been skirt-chasing while we were fighting?

—Hello, John. Sad news! The young bucks have forgotten you. You used to be a name to conjure with, but I mentioned you to a promising young fellow the other day and he said, *Who?* They have no respect, no manners.

Those were the voices of his peers, distantly refracted through the fire. His fellow Agents, scattered all across the continent, each one no doubt looking into their own smoking fires, each one accompanied by their own master. Jen of the Floating World; Abban the Lion; Dandy Fanshawe. It had been so long since he'd heard their voices. And there were others, again, clamoring behind them. Creedmoor recognized Hudnall the Younger, Kid Glove Kate, and Big Fane. He closed his eyes to clear his head and said,

—Are we all here? Such a rare gathering. I'm flattered.

Marmion answered:

—Many of us are here. You will go alone, but there will be others watching over you.

—Go where?

—On the edge of the world there is a hospital.

—Yes?

—West of here. North of Greenbank, northwest of Kloan. East of the world that is not yet made, and the far sea. It is called the House Dolorous.

—And?

—Quiet, Creedmoor. Listen. There is a man there. We believe there is a man there. We do not know. We have gathered rumors in dark places, and scryed, and sniffed out trails.

—They mean my spies gathered rumors. My girls. Don't they always take the credit? The Guns are as bad as men, I swear.

That voice was Jen's. Jen of the flaming hair, Jen of the Floating World. It had been six years since Creedmoor had seen Jen—six years since he'd last patronized her brothel, the Floating World, which hovered in the hills over Jasper City like a wonderful filthy dream—six years since he'd heard her red lips whisper secrets. She would be sitting now in her office in the Floating World, which was all jade and leather and mahogany and sensual curves; in fact, she would most likely be lying lazily on the sofa by the fireplace. He wondered if she was still beautiful. Could the Guns have kept her young? Would they? They must have. It was impossible to imagine her old.

The voice of the Guns:

—The House is a hospital for the wounded of the Great War. It is neutral—it takes those who fought in our service, and those who fought for the enemy. It takes the maimed, and it takes the mad.

—Commendable.

—It sickens us. Listen, Creedmoor: the House is defended.

—It's only a hospital. It has guards?

—On the edge of the world, things are not yet settled. Unruly powers arise. Small gods. One of them protects the House.

—Some gulch-ghoul, some First Folk demon, some haunt of dry rivers? A poltergeist? A dust-devil with ideas above its station?

—It is strong, and old, and well-fed.

—Stronger than you?

—Listen, Creedmoor. The man we seek is there, in a hospital room. If our intelligence is accurate.

Jen interrupted, in tones of mock-outrage:

—My intelligence is *always* accurate.

Creedmoor said:

—Is it? Must have been someone else who sent me and Casca into that trap back in Nemiah in '63. So who is this fellow?

—An old man. He was once a General, but now he is mad. The noise of the bombs of the Line shattered his mind. He does not know who he is, and nor do his doctors.

—Well?

—Well what? You do not need to know either. Bring him to us.

Secrets! Creedmoor could feel the Guns buzzing and preening. How they loved their secrets!

—They can be *so* dramatic, can't they, darling?

That slow drawl was Dandy Fanshawe—the pomaded and silk-coated old Queen of Gibson City, who was so outrageous and self-indulgent that few ever suspected he was a first-class spy or that he had once killed over a dozen Linesmen with nothing but his ebony sword-stick and his own teeth. It had been Dandy Fanshawe who first re-cruited Creedmoor into the service of the Gun, back when Creedmoor had been young, and Fanshawe, well, not *young*, but not so scandalously old as he was now. They'd met in an opium den in Gibson City, and Fanshawe had been lying on silk cushions wreathed in smoke, with his jade-ringed hand idly draped on some young man's thigh. His nails had been painted. He'd been ethereal, mysterious, behind clouds of smoke made nebulous by candlelight. *Darling boy!* Fanshawe had said. *We've had our eye on you for quite some time. . . .*

Creedmoor remembered old days and smiled. He said:

—They certainly can, old friend.

—They're such whispering secretive girls. They won't even tell *me*. None of us are favored with their confidence.

Creedmoor instantly suspected that Fanshawe knew exactly what was going on, but he kept quiet, because a dozen metallic voices chorused:

—Enough.

Creedmoor shook his head. The smoke dizzied him. He could see nothing except a haze of gray, in which ghostly forms came and went like memories. He was suddenly angry. He said:

—An old mad General. An old enemy? One of our many, many old enemies. You want me to kill him? You want revenge? What's the point?

—We want you to bring him to us. He is worth more than gold. You must not kill him. On no account must you kill him, or allow him to be killed. A frontal assault will not work. The Spirit of the House is powerful, and will permit no violence within its walls. It does violence in return to those who bring violence to it. If we attack, the General may be killed.

—Oh, dear! If murder won't work, we are rather at a loss, aren't we?

—Shut up, Creedmoor. We have chosen you because you are personable, Creedmoor, you are charming. Worm your way in, past the Spirit, past the defenses. Befriend them. Seek employment if necessary. You pass for an ordinary man.

—Like I've always said, Creedmoor, you're no hero, but you'd make a good janitor.

—Ha! Fuck you, Lion.

That voice was Abban the Lion. Abban, like Creedmoor, had not been born in the West; but where Creedmoor came from damp and misty Lundroy and was prone to grumbling and joint aches, the dark and eagle-nosed Abban came from the sands of Dhrav and was passionate. He fancied himself a warrior, wore his dark hair long, dressed all in black, and sometimes went so far as to affect a sword. At this moment he was probably staring into a fire in a camp somewhere in some distant hills, surrounded by the bodies of enemies. He said:

—I'll be behind you, Creedmoor. In the hills. Whether you want me or not. Watching. You won't be alone.

Fanshawe's voice again:

—So will I. Like old times, Creedmoor!

—Not sure I trust you behind me, Fanshawe.

—I've never heard *that* one before, darling, well done.

Jen said:

—I will not be joining you. I wish you gentlemen well at the ends of the earth. My spies will be working in your behalf back in Jasper City. Come find me at the Floating World when you're done.

—You should travel more, Jen. You used to go everywhere. Tell me—are you still young?

She laughed. Abban spoke:

—Don't think you can betray us, Creedmoor. Don't think if you run away again, you will be forgiven.

—Fuck you, Lion.

A gray shape that swirled through the smoke looked remarkably like the blade of a curved sword swooping at Creedmoor's head, and he ducked, and immediately felt foolish. He said:

—Listen. What's this about? Why do we care about this old General? There's no shortage of Generals in this world.

Marmion answered:

—He was caught by the bombs of the Line—the bombs of terrible noise, that shatter the mind with fear. His mind is gone. He will be one among many with minds like children, rotting away in the cells of the House Dolorous. They do not know who he is or what he is. There are secrets hidden in his mind.

—What secrets?

—Bring him to us.

—What secrets?

—What do you think, Creedmoor? A weapon. What else?

—A weapon.

—Yes.

—What kind of weapon?

—A thing of the First Folk. It could mean victory.

—An end to the War? Peace at last?

—Not peace. Victory.

—What weapon? What does it do? Who is he? Who was he? What have the Folk got to do with it?

—You know enough already. You are not trustworthy, Creedmoor. None of our servants are trustworthy. Bring him to us.

—Hmm. Fanshawe?

—Yes?

—Have the young bucks really forgotten my name?

—Afraid so, dear boy.

—Serve us well now and you will never be forgotten, Creed-moor. *Pay attention.* . . .

They began to talk tactics, logistics. One voice interrupted another, and again. A disagreement on a point of precise timing emerged, and they began to squabble and snipe. The unity of the Guns never lasted long. Ambush and volley and countervolley of words . . .

The smoke thickened. Billows of it crossed the room back and forth like cavalry charges. Voices echoed and overlapped. What always unnerved Creedmoor was that though each voice was different, they were also the same. They sounded in his head and they sounded in *his voice,* with only a crude approximation of Abban's accent or a mockery of Jen's lilt or Fanshawe's drawl or an echo of the thud and snarl of the Guns. It was horribly unpleasant, and enough to make a man wonder if he was mad.

When he threw open the door and let the smoke pour out, it was nearly morning, and Josiah was muttering in his sleep. Creedmoor walked away quickly before his master could decide the old man needed to be killed after all.

CHAPTER 5

Sᴍɪʟᴇ Tʜʀᴏᴜɢʜ Aᴅᴠᴇʀsɪᴛʏ

Dr. Lysvet Alverhuysen's coach traveled west, through Koenigswald's farmlands, and across the border into Sommerland, and along a high cliff road that looked over the vast gray Northern Ocean, and south across the moors, and up into the pines. Other travelers came and went—businessmen, widows, scholars, doctors, couriers, the idle rich on tour. Sometimes there was pleasant conversation; sometimes Maggfrid sat in deep silence and Liv read, or stared at the passing skies. Mail was picked up and dropped off. The coach bounced along the dirt roads that cut through the forests, narrow channels between dark walls of pine. A few logging towns and the occasional inn disrupted the green immensity. It got colder as they slowly gained altitude. They changed coaches twice, and both times Liv was convinced she was going to lose something vital from her luggage, though she couldn't think what; already most of what she'd brought seemed unnecessary. She'd taken to wearing her hair down.

There was a certain casual and vaguely decadent camaraderie on the coaches, and Liv spent several of her nights drinking wine by the fireplace of a drafty log-built inn with young men of business, or a certain eager young student of Natural Philosophy on his way to a symposium. On those nights, Maggfrid sat protectively nearby, or stood with the horses, or went walking alone in the woods.

Liv wrote a letter to Agatha—*Agatha, my dear, I have become quite daring! You should see me. . . .* But the coach bounced and she spilled ink on the page, and anyway decided she would prefer to keep such matters to herself. Some days she and Maggrid were alone, and she wrote in her journal, and the scratching of her pen and the clatter of hooves and the ticking of the golden watch passed the time.

The road ran farther south and west, and wound through the mountains, the blue-white peaks of which rose on either side like a wall built by God at the end of the world—like ghostly fairy-tale giants charged by God with guarding the border of creation.

That was what they still called them—the World's End Mountains—though for four hundred years there had been another world beyond them. And one afternoon they turned a corner and the trees parted and Liv looked out west across golden plains, spread out far below her and out beyond the horizon. She gasped as she made out forests and lakes and even toylike towns and out beyond in the north the stark black scrawl of the Line. A distant eagle soared overhead. Her heart surged with mad excitement. Maggfrid leaned suddenly over her and stuck his great head and shoulders out the window and yelled a nonsensical echoing shout of joy. The coach rocked on the edge of a steep drop and Liv, laughing, tried to pull him back in.

✻　✻　✻

The mail coach left them in Fort Sloten, a tiny way station up in the foothills of the World's Ends. From Fort Sloten, riders took the mail off along steep trails north and south and west.

Liv and Maggfrid followed the trail down into Fort Blue on foot. She'd had the forethought, before leaving, to consult with Professor Woch of the Botanical Institute, who was a keen hiker, and consequently she wore quite excellent fitted boots. Even so her feet quickly blistered and her legs ached. She had Maggfrid break off a sturdy branch for her to use as a stick, and felt quite pleased at her own resourcefulness.

From Fort Blue they traveled on the back of a cargo barge down the river to Burren Hill. The barge was laden with a heap of bleached animal bones, from which antlers poked out like stripped fingers. Liv turned away from that horrible cargo and sat with her hands in her lap and watched the white World's Ends dwindle behind her.

She arrived in Burren Hill in the late afternoon. It was a town of the border countries, a sprawl of low clapboard houses spilling down the hillside to the banks of a wide silt-brown river. There was a crumbling, ramshackle dock, to which Liv's horrible barge tied off, and onto which, with Maggfrid's help, she carefully climbed.

An imposing stockade sat on the hill overlooking the town. The warehouses by the river were fortified, too, and Liv had never seen so many armed men. The place hummed with industry—teams of men worked stripped to the waist digging ditches and erecting more stockades. Their backs were burned red. In the ditches and stepped earthworks, they bobbed and swayed like a thousand red flowers in a muddy garden. Bony shapes that Liv assumed must be the Hillfolk worked in chain gangs, and she wondered how they didn't cook under their long black manes. Already the sun was hotter and fiercer out here.

Director Howell's letter had promised that regular riverboats went west from Burren Hill, and had provided her with a letter of introduction to a Captain Canin. She showed the letter to a group of sunburned dockworkers, who regarded it with distaste and confusion, as if it might have been an arrest warrant.

"Captain Canin," she said. "If you don't mind, I have a letter of introduction to a Captain Canin, and I would be very grateful for your assistance in finding—"

"Dead," the foreman told her.

"I beg your pardon?"

"Dead six months or more. They killed him and took his cargo and burned his boat."

She put her hand to her mouth in horror. "How awful! Who did?"

Sunburned shoulders shrugged. "Bandits? Hillfolk? The Gun? Who knows? No one goes down the river these days."

"No one? I need to go downriver."

"Not these days."

"Why not?"

"Three boats lost these last six months, just a few miles west of town. Boats burned, throats slit, the bodies wash up in towns down-river. Something's taken up in those hills."

The foreman said *something's taken up in those hills* in the same resigned way farmers of the North might grumble about bad weather. It made Liv's skin crawl.

On the other hand, she thought, they were probably lying to her. Somehow this story would probably end in them asking her for money, in which case, so be it. "I can pay extra," she said.

"Well, good luck to you, then, ma'am." The foreman hefted a crate of bones and walked bowlegged away.

"Don't worry, Maggfrid," she said, though he hadn't spoken.

She found a room for the night in Burren Hill's one hotel—a two-story structure huddled under the wooden walls of the Fort, a maze of tiny wooden boxes. She shared a chaste bed with Maggfrid, and the huge warmth of his body kept her awake. Already she itched from the heat and the flies. For the first time in years, she remembered the flat mad smile on the face of the man who'd murdered her mother; it surfaced suddenly from her memories and made her gasp. She took a measure of her sleeping tincture, and it turned the water in her cup a soothing green like the peaceful gardens of the North.

✳   ✳   ✳

Her problems compounded themselves, as problems tended to do.

In the morning, she approached the overseers of the town—who she identified by the fact that they wore shirts, and in the case of one young man, a Mr. Harrison, a suit.

Liv found Harrison confusing. He had the long greasy hair of a pauper but the manner of an aristocrat or a popular and prosperous administrator. He sat on the hillside under the shade of a black canvas and watched the ditch-digging and wall-building going on below, and consulted his maps and blueprints, and gave orders to runners, and appeared busily content. He drank water with lemon in it—"For my health, Doctor. A healthy mind in a healthy body!"—and was apparently delighted to sit and make conversation with an educated lady traveler from the North—but his news was not good.

"No one goes down the river these days, Doctor. It's not worth the risk. Boats are expensive things to lose."

"Are there no police on the river?"

He laughed. "No police but what we might raise from these men. And we're brave men in Burren but not soldiers. And maybe there are Agents or wild Folk in the hills. Who knows?"

"Agents, Mr. Harrison?"

"The servants of the Gun, Doctor. We try to stay neutral out here, but the Gun's Agents get everywhere. Nothing we can do about it, is there? Just have to wait till they move on, that's all."

"I've heard stories—the Gun's Agents are said to be dangerous men, but they are only men, are they not? Is there nothing you can do?"

Harrison smiled and said, "You didn't learn much about this country before you set out, did you? First thing a businessman learns is to know the country he's traveling in."

"Enlighten me, then. Please."

"There are greater powers than the human out here, Doctor. The earth here is haunted."

She frowned. He called himself a businessman but talked like a mystic, or a lunatic. Under happier conditions, she would have found that interesting; now it just annoyed her.

He pointed out over the maze of ditches and earthworks and foundations. "It's not so bad out here. Burren Hill was settled two hundred and thirty-some years ago, and our soil's old and steady. But I still worry when we have to dig what we might dig up. What we might wake up. You just never know. Gun and Line had to be born somewhere, didn't they, in some town that was only going about its business? It'll only get worse as you go out west."

"How *do* I go west from here, Mr. Harrison?"

"That's the question, isn't it? That's the ten-thousand-dollar question. Someone might sell you a horse, but I couldn't in conscience advise you to ride alone. The river's closed, and it's slow and so damn expensive to send caravans, and our cargoes are rotting in our warehouses, and our investors aren't happy. This, too, will pass, of course—if we keep faith. But how? You tell me, Doctor. We are building fortifications, as you can see, but will it help? Shall I have a boy bring us more water?"

"I was told to get to a town called Gloriana, and from there I was told I could take the Line west."

"Gloriana's a Station, not a town."

"A town of the Line, yes. Is there a difference?"

"You'll know the difference when you see it. *If* you see it. It's in Line country. We're neutral here. No one's going to want to take you near it."

"I see." She couldn't think of anything else to say. Most of what Harrison said seemed nonsensical to her, and a number of sharp questions rose to her mind, but she didn't want to risk offending him. The horizon was a red-brown haze in every direction. Irritably she brushed away flies as Harrison sipped his water.

"Adversity strengthens us, Doctor."

"Does it?" she snapped. "I would be interested to see your evidence."

"Ten years in business and still by and large prospering is my evidence, Doctor."

"I'm sorry, Mr. Harrison. I'm not used to the heat here."

"Are you a Smiler, Doctor?"

"I'm afraid that's another question I don't understand,."

"The New Thought, Doctor. The practice is a great help in times of adversity. Would you like me to have a boy bring you a pamphlet?"

"Thank you, Mr. Harrison. Thank you. I'd like that."

He stood and bellowed, "Boy!" in a suddenly coarse voice. He sat back down, apparently pleased.

"I'll tell you what, Doctor. Talk to a man called Mr. Bond. He's taking a party out soon. A trading caravan. They're not headed to Gloriana, but they'll get you close. Maybe he can use a doctor. Who knows? The world is full of curses but also full of blessings, if you just keep on smiling."

❋   ❋   ❋

She took lunch at the hotel, in a dark dining room under the mounted heads of antlered beasts. There were stags in the forests of Koenigswald, but their counterparts here seemed more profoundly, more complexly, more savagely antlered than in the civilized world—antlered beyond utility, she thought.

She tried to explain their situation to Maggfrid; he was confused. Twice, he stood suddenly and proposed simply to *walk* west, and protect her from whatever got in their way.

He was full of energy these days, and restless. She wasn't sure whether it was a good thing or bad. On the walk down from Fort Sloten, she'd tried to explain to him how to walk with a stick and at first he hadn't understood the principle of the thing, and had used the stick to strike the ground with each step as if trying to beat the mountain flat.

To calm him, she played a very simple card game with him. Then she went to her room to lie down and read. She was entirely too tired to read any of the scientific journals she'd brought with her, so instead she opened, for the first time, *The Child's History of the West*.

* * *

The *Child's History* was apparently the work of one General Orlan Enver, of the Red Valley Republic—the severe-looking uniformed gentleman who glared from the frontispiece. It was written in tones of stiff enthusiasm. It alternated between accounts of battles, which Liv found dull, and advice regarding exercise and cleanliness, which she found duller. It struck Liv as a well-meaning but unsubtle piece of propaganda—when she skipped impatiently to the final chapter, she learned that the Red Valley Republic had established peace and liberty and democracy, forever and ever, that the last holdouts of irrationalism and oppression and vice would soon learn from the example of young men and women of virtue and decency, that the turbulent history of the half-made world was at an end, and that the West was now made whole and ready to take its place among civilized nations.

But of course, she reminded herself, with hindsight everything seemed absurd; no doubt her own publications would look comical to later generations.

She tried to read chapter 1, "The First Colony at Founding," but quickly fell asleep.

❋ ❋ ❋

She woke and washed her face with water from the jug. There was
no mirror, so she looked blearily in the window for her reflection;
and she screamed. The jug fell and shattered and cut her bare foot
but she hardly noticed, because the white face suddenly at the narrow window pressed up against the glass and—

For a moment the face had reminded her of that madman's face
from her most terrible memories, that face as it came running through
the willows, and she had been transported back to childhood. But
that face had been round and sweating and spectacled, and this was
angular and jagged; and the eyes were ruby red; and though the
killer's face had been pale, it was nothing next to the inhuman chalk
whiteness of the face at the window; and what hung around that
face was not the green branches of the willows, but a filthy black
mane of hair.

It was one of the men of the hills, she realized, one of the aboriginal people of the West, who had lived in the land when it was still
formless and unmade.

The expression on the face was solemn, still.

She calmed her breathing. Her foot started to sting.

She was in her underclothes—but then the figure at the window
was apparently naked, under his mane, and it seemed silly to stand
on ceremony. She said, "Good afternoon."

He reached out a hand. The arm—beneath that black mane—
was long, stick thin, and oddly articulated. The fingers were like a
necklace of bones. With one black fingernail it began to tap on the
glass.

Perhaps the expression was not *solemn,* exactly, but simply
unreadable—stiff as a crudely carved statue. Now she noticed that
his jaw and the protrusions of his throat were quivering, as if with
tremendous excitement. She wondered if he was able to speak.

The black fingernail drummed a rhythm on the glass. It was not
simple tapping; it had the quality of music, or language, or ritual. It
grew quickly faster and faster and more complex, and a second nail
joined it, developing surprising polyrhythms. Then it stopped; then
it began again. The red eyes continued to watch her. The sound was

oddly lovely. A song, always repeating. She stepped closer to the window. The finger struck a hard beat, and the glass cracked—

She shrieked and jumped back. In the same moment, a big man in a white shirt came into view and struck the Hillman on the back with a stick. "Hurry up! Move on! You leave her alone!" He yanked on the Hillman's chain and dragged him stumbling away from the window. "Sorry, ma'am." He tipped his hat. "Won't happen again."

They moved away, and the rest of the Hillfolk gang came into view, half a dozen of them, and almost at once she lost track of which had been the one at her window.

What had he wanted from her?

The golden pocket watch ticked quietly on her bedside table, where it sat on top of her copy of the *Child's History* and beside her flask of nerve tonic. She picked it up, more for comfort than for anything else, and was shocked to see that the whole strange communication had taken place in a matter of moments. It had felt like hours.

✳ ✳ ✳

Negotiations with Mr. Bond went poorly.

He was a big man, aggressive, with a bald and sunburned head and a boxer's body stuffed into braces and a sweat-stained shirt, and he looked entirely out of place sitting at a desk in a little warehouse office doing bookkeeping, but that was how Liv found him. He barked:

"Don't need passengers. Going to be a hard trip. Where do you think you are?"

"Yes, Mr. Bond, everyone tells me the journey is dangerous. That fact has been more than adequately impressed upon me. I can pay."

He named a sum that was quite outrageous, and when her face fell, he laughed.

"They say you're a doctor—know anything about horses?"

"No."

"Can you set a broken bone, at least?"

"I'm not that kind of doctor, Mr. Bond."

"Then we don't need you."

✳ ✳ ✳

Maggfrid was waiting outside Bond's warehouse. He looked so down-cast when he saw Liv's face that she laughed and impulsively hugged him. "Smile, Maggfrid! Mr. Harrison says good things come to those who keep smiling."

She'd read Harrison's pamphlet in her hotel room that after-noon. It didn't take her long—the print was large and the thoughts it expressed simple to the point of vacuity. It was titled *Samson Smiles' Commonplace Book, Or, The Book of the New Thought*. Mr. Smiles himself, pictured in black-and-white on the frontispiece, was a well-dressed and muttonchopped gentleman whose face bore an expression of almost holy serenity. His *Commonplace Book* con-sisted of short repetitive maxims on the virtues of confidence, enthu-siasm, perseverance, self-help, and moral character. *Hope is the mother of success, for who so hopes strongly has within him the gift of miracles.* Liv had found it inane. *The world smiles on a man who smiles!* Was this what passed for thought out here? *Seize the day!* Was this what passed for religion? *The world is what we make it.*

She'd tried to think of something nice to say about it, should Harrison ask; she'd decided she could more or less honestly say, "Charming!"

Now she walked with Maggfrid through the town and watched the teams of men at work, digging up their town, rerouting its streets, erecting new walls, and driving new canals, all of them sweating and red-brown with mud, and she thought: *The world is what we make it.* The notion was at once intimidating and encouraging.

"Smile, Maggfrid! We'll find a way."

She walked down by the bend of the river, where half a dozen men swung their picks in ditches, waist deep in muddy water. The river was slow, placid and sleepy—hard to imagine danger waited along it. *It was meant to be peaceful*, she thought. *It*—

"Fuck are you smiling at, lady?"

She started. One of the workmen had lowered his pick and was watching her with a vicious grin.

"You want to get down here with us? You want to get wet?"

Another of them laughed and shouted, "Harrison sent us a whore! Come on, get down here."

The chant went up: "Harrison sent us a whore! Harrison . . ."

She turned away. "Maggfrid, come away. Back to the hotel—"

Maggfrid let out a tremendous bellow of rage and leapt down into the ditch. Muddy water splashed and the diggers fell back in shock as Maggfrid reached out and struck the first man to speak hard on the side of the head. He tore the pick from the hands of the second man and hit him in the gut so that he doubled over in the water. He wrestled with a third man and a fourth; they thrashed in the mud and he threw them aside. The shaft of a spade hit his back with a terrible dull smack and he didn't seem to notice. Roaring, he held a man's head under. . . .

"Maggfrid! *Maggfrid!* Stop at once. Maggfrid, *please!*"

At the sound of her voice he stopped. He turned to her with an uncertain smile on his face. "Maggfrid, that's enough." She held out a hand to him, and he pulled himself dripping and filthy out of the ditch. The other men crawled away, moaning. "Oh, Maggfrid. You're not a violent man. Maybe I shouldn't have brought you here, Maggfrid. Oh . . ."

She heard a slow clapping behind her. She turned to see Mr. Bond, shirtsleeves rolled up, clapping as he came briskly down the hill. Two of his employees followed behind him.

"This one yours, Doctor?"

"Yes, Mr. Bond. This is a friend of mine, and a patient. I apologize for any injuries to these men, if they were your men, but they—"

"Fuck 'em. Not mine. Harrison's. Your big friend got a name?"

"His name is Maggfrid."

"He gave them what for, all right. One hell of a show, that was. He's a fighter, your friend."

"He's not a fighter, Mr. Bond."

"Strong, too. Fierce. I could use a man like that when we go west."

She shook her head. "He's not a fighter, Mr. Bond." He *could* have been a fighter, she thought; he could have been a monster. He had been prone to rages when she'd first found him. Years of work had made him gentle.

Bond looked Maggfrid up and down. "Well, why don't we let him decide that?"

Maggfrid met Liv's anxious eyes, then looked away. Then he smiled broadly and nodded his great head.

"Maggfrid," Liv said, "Are you—?"

"Course he's sure," Bond said. "Excellent." Bond clapped Maggfrid on the shoulder. Big as Bond was, Maggfrid towered over him. A great eager-to-please smile split Maggfrid's white moon of a face. It made Liv uneasy. But she saw no alternative.

Bond rubbed his hands together. "Let's talk about your fare, Doctor."

"First let's talk about my friend's wages, Mr. Bond."

"That's the spirit, Doctor. Let's talk business."

CHAPTER 6

KINGƧTOⱲN

Lowry looked out the window once on his journey west from Harrow Cross to Kingstown, and regretted it immediately. He was used to the Southeast, and the lands around Angelus, where the Line's grip was strongest, where the landscape was properly shaped by industry. Out on this farthest western extremity of the Line, there was nothing to be seen for a hundred miles across flat plains and rolling red hills but meaningless empty sky and dirt. A formless land, waiting to be built. The matchstick figures of a pack of Hillfolk loped along a ragged hillside and lifted their heads as the Engine passed by. . . . Awful. Lowry shuddered, closed the blind, sat in the gloom of his passenger car, and waited.

He had nothing to do. The work of the Engine went on around him, and he was not needed. He was left idle as any civilian. He hated idleness. Twice an hour, his thoughts switchbacked from sweaty-palmed nervous hope—because he might be traveling toward some unexpected, unimaginable promotion—to despair—because he might equally well be traveling to his own court-martial, for any one of the countless sins of which he was, he didn't doubt, entirely guilty.

After a while, he removed a volume of the Black File from his suitcases and passed his time studying it: the names and faces and the modus operandi and the long, long lists of crimes of his enemies, the enemies of all civilized people. . . . He told himself this study was useful work, but in fact he just found that the fog of self-righteous loathing that rolled over him whenever he opened the Black File soothed his nerves.

✳ ✳ ✳

He'd never visited Kingstown Station before. However, the Station's physical and hierarchical organization was almost identical to that of Angelus Station—as one would expect, since both were designed according to the same principles of efficiency and good order. The two Stations, though they were thousands of miles apart, differed only in that Kingstown's outer ring of fortifications was rather thicker than Angelus's, and bristled with a gteater density of barbed wire and machine guns—but of course, this was wild, unsettled country.

He quickly found his way to the relevant Desk where he was assigned a room and a temporary office, which was identical to the one he'd had back in Angelus.

He waited to be summoned.

✳ ✳ ✳

They came for him at midnight. Two Privates of the Army of the Kingstown Engine banged on his door, waking him from dreamless sleep. When he answered the door, they turned smartly on their heels and disappeared down an unlit corridor, gesturing for him to follow. He did. Their boots echoed dully down the concrete hallways.

A midnight summons almost invariably meant court-martial, or more often discipline without formal process, and so he didn't even bother to ask the two Privates where they were leading him. They probably didn't know, anyway. He trudged along in dismal silence, preparing himself for the worst, reminding himself that the Line's wisdom was greater than his own.

They led him into a windowless room, and left him there.

The floor was gray tile. At the far side of the room was a steel table. Behind that were three chairs and an electric lamp. Behind the chairs and the lamp, there was another door.

Presently three uniformed persons came through that door and sat at the chairs. Two of them were men. One of them was, Lowry guessed, a woman. With the light at their back, he could not make out their insignia or rank. Their faces were unremarkable, except that one of the men had only one ear, and their expressions told him nothing.

He folded his hands behind his back to stop them shaking.

One of them said, "Please sit, Lowry."

He looked around. There was nowhere obvious to sit.

"*Sit*, Lowry."

Slowly, not sure whether this was the proper response, he sat cross-legged on the cold floor.

"Do you know why you're here, Sub-Invigilator (Third Class) Lowry?"

He stared blankly at the tiles. "I submit myself to the judgment of the Line."

"You don't know why you're here."

"I'm sure there are reasons. I have not been informed of them."

One of them grunted and made a note on a piece of paper.

The one Lowry thought was probably a woman said, "You have a long service record, Lowry."

A pocket of stubborn pride surfaced in him, like stomach acid, and he said, "I believe my record of service is exemplary."

"It's adequate," she said. "No more."

The one-eared man said, "Repeated indications of pride."

"Inappropriate sympathies," said the other man. A deep and monotone voice.

"Blunders," the woman said, "Leading to the loss of men and matériel, and the slowing of progress."

"Yes," Lowry said. He didn't know what incidents they were referring to, but he was instantly quite sure they were correct. His face flushed and he continued to stare at the floor. "I regret my inadequacies."

"Very good." The one-eared man made another note.

The woman said, "Don't despair, Lowry. Despair is not productive. Your record is not disgraceful. For instance, you've survived an unusual number of encounters with the Agents of our enemy. I understand you have made a special study of their habits. What are your feelings regarding them?"

"Feelings?" Lowry shook his head. "Dogs. Vermin. Criminals. Scum. I don't know. I do my job. They have to be put down."

She said, "Why?"

He had no idea how to safely answer that question, so he remained silent.

"What do you know about their masters?"

He shrugged. "Monsters. Or delusions."

"You're not curious about them?"

"No, ma'am. In my experience, it makes no difference which demon they serve, or say they serve. If you need to know their individual peculiarities, their behaviors, you only got to look at the man himself. Or the woman. That's all you need to get the job done."

"Their masters are real," the woman said. "They are not delusions. The Agents are irrelevant. Criminal flotsam. Any lunatic will do. It's their masters who are our enemy, their masters who make them dangerous."

Lowry shrugged again.

"And their masters," the woman said, "are immortal. Killing the Agent, smashing the vessel, only sends the master briefly back to their Lodge. Do you know that term?"

"I've read it." He'd seen it in interrogation records, in the pages of the Black File.

"Immortal," the woman said. "Much like the Engines we serve."

The comparison was so shocking, so unexpectedly foul, that Lowry could not stop his lip curling back in a snarl.

The woman made a note. While she wrote, the man to her left spoke up. "Ever had any encounters with the First Folk, Lowry?"

The snarl faded from Lowry's face. He looked up, utterly confused. The question was bizarre.

Clearly this was no ordinary disciplinary hearing. He tried not to look hopeful.

"You mean the Hillfolk? No, sir."

"No?"

"No—sorry, sir. Yes. I forgot. Yes. Ten years ago, when we razed Nemiah. There was a nest of Folk in the hills, had to be cleaned out. They were messing with our supply lines. Don't know why. Stupid of them, really."

"You went in personally, I believe."

"That's right. We used noisemakers aboveground, then gas in the tunnels, but someone had to clear out what was left."

"Into their tunnels. Were you afraid?"

He looked from face to face. "No," said. "They're only savages."

"You're unimaginative, Lowry. That's for the best."

"Sir—"

The one-eared man interrupted, "Do you study history, Lowry?"

"No, sir."

"How old are you?"

"Thirty-two."

"Do you remember the Red Valley Republic?"

"Yes, sir. A little. An enemy."

"What do you know about them?"

"I was at the Battle of Black Cap Valley, sir."

"And?"

Lowry shuddered, remembering. In the last days of the Line's war against the Republic, the Engines had determined, in their infinite wisdom, that the situation called for one great final push, to put an end to the Republic's insolence and to free the Line's forces for operations on the western front, against the true enemy. This required full mobilization of all possible personnel. The children of the warrens under Angelus Station had been rounded up, packed into locked carriages, transported in the belly of the Engine without explanation halfway across the world, and delivered into hell. Lowry had been attached to a unit that had laid barbed wire, under cover of night, under fire, across the slippery black muck of the valley. He'd been ten years old.

Lowry said, "I did my job, sir."

"Good. Good." The man pointed to the scar he had in place of a left ear and said, "I was there, too. Does the name *General Orlan Enver* mean anything to you?"

"He was one of their ringleaders, right? Dead, I suppose."

"No. Wait a moment, Sub-Invigilator (Third Class) Lowry."

The three officers put their heads together and conferred. Lowry waited. It seemed unlikely now that they would discipline him; so what did they want?

✳   ✳   ✳

The woman said, "Lowry. You are one of thousands who might equally well have been chosen for this task."

"Ma'am."

"You're adequate. That's all."

"Ma'am."

"This is to be kept in the strictest confidence."

"Of course."

"In the morning, you are to travel north from here. You will accompany the expedition of Conductor Banks of the Kingstown Engine and assist him in all endeavors. On a probationary basis, you may immediately consider yourself and act as Sub-Invigilator *Second* Class. The paperwork will follow."

"Ma'am—of course—but under what authority?"

"We speak for the Engines themselves."

The one-eared man rapped his pen on the table. "Listen, Lowry. The General Enver is not dead. He disappeared after the fall of the Republic, and made an obstruction of himself for a decade, until finally a noisemaker shut him up. We don't know exactly where or when. No records. Apparently he had the bad luck to survive, if you can call that survival. He was picked up off the mountainside where he should have died and transported through various hospitals, where apparently no one had the good sense to just stop feeding him. His trail gets unclear. For some years, we've been aware of rumors that he's been seen, by now quite mad, in a little hospital in the very far West, about four days' drive northwest of this Station, calls itself the House Dolorous. Ever heard of it?"

"No. So, he's alive—we go in, kill him."

"No," the one-eared man said. "Not so simple. You'll read the file, Lowry. The hospital is protected. Hillfolk stuff. Listen, Lowry. The General must at all costs be extracted alive."

"Why?"

"The proper question," the man said, "is, *Why now?* And the answer is this: One month ago, the forces of the Dryden Engine occupied a town called Brazenwood, away back east."

"There was oil beneath it," the woman interjected. "Its development had been planned for decades. So what we are telling you, Lowry, is not a matter of chance and contingency, but the inevitable unfolding of Progress. Do you understand?"

Lowry nodded, but said nothing. That seemed safest.

"One of the locals," the one-eared man continued, "a pawnshop owner, currying favor, tried to sell the commanding officer on-site a letter. It appears to be the General's last letter, to his daughter and granddaughter. Not clear yet how it ended up in the pawnshop. The family are dead. It contains intelligence of great importance. We'd thought the General irrelevant. Not so. He must be questioned."

"Yes, sir. What?"

The woman said, "You don't need to know."

"Apparently," the one-eared man added, "the damn fool pawn-shop owner had been holding on to that letter for years, and he would have been better off holding on to it forever, because of course he had to be shot. Yet despite these precautions, I'm sorry to say, we have reason to believe that Agents of the enemy may have acquired the same intelligence we possess. If so, you will face opposition. You're to advise and assist Conductor Banks in that regard."

"And the hospital itself," the other man said, "poses additional strategic complexities. Listen, Lowry. . . ."

CHAPTER 7

THE LONG ROAD WEST

The sun was fierce all day, every day, and unrelenting, and Liv was glad of her broad-brimmed hat, though its whiteness and floral pattern seemed out of place in this dusty country.

The caravan worked its slow way up and down the rocky hills, and she rode alongside.

"Can you ride?" That had been Mr. Bond's first question to her. She could—up to a point—at least, she'd had a horse as a child. She'd used to go riding in the woods behind the Academy. That changed after her mother's death—but she saw no need to tell Bond that sad story. She was happier riding than sitting in the wagons. The caravan was slow and the horses placid, but she was all bruises anyway.

"Can you cook? Can you sew?" Less welcome questions. The answer was no. She was a scientist, not a homemaker. She had never lived without servants. Her mother, who had been Emeritus Professor of Psychology, had had many virtues, but domesticity was not one of them.

"Huh." Bond had shaken his head. "Not looking for a husband, then?"

"I had a husband, Mr. Bond. He was a Doctor of Mathematics in Koenigswald. He died two years ago, of a heart attack. He was, incidentally, a man of roughly your size and age."

"Huh. Can't cook, can't sew, can ride a little. A scientist, is that right? Can you count?"

"Of course I can count, Mr. Bond."

"I used to have a lawyer, but he got himself shot in a duel. Can you read a contract?"

"I expect so. I can certainly endeavor not to be shot."

. . . so she rode into Monroe Town alongside Bond, and a week later into Barrett, and helped him haggle over the sale of animal bones and pelts and silver, and the purchase of food, water, credit. They negotiated in smoky rooms with local merchants in mustaches and battered top hats and threadbare waistcoats. Bond blustered and shouted and banged tables with his great ham fists; Liv was patient and polite. It seemed to unnerve the opposition. Bond declared that she was good luck. He offered to pay her; she declined. He squeezed himself into a suit and took her to the best restaurant in Monroe, where he bought her the best steak and the least vulgar wines Monroe could offer. "A business dinner," he said. "To business," clutching a wineglass in his huge hand as if to crush it. "To a fruitful partnership." In Barrett Town a week later, they closed a deal at a very favorable percentage, and in the afternoon he showed her the sights, which were a shooting gallery, a boxing ring, some big black horses of apparently exceptional quality. . . . And when, two days out of Barrett, the caravan reached the top of yet another nameless hill, and the rolling plains were spread out below, in all their dusty rugged beauty, he came up beside her and said, "Gonna be sorry to see you go."

She lowered her fan and looked at him in surprise. "We're not there yet, Mr. Bond. Are we?"

He pointed west, down the valley of a meandering stream. "Just one day more to Conant. See?"

She didn't see what he was pointing at. Everything in this country looked the same to her.

"Conant," Bond said. An odd note of apology in his gruff voice. "Last stop. Then we turn back."

"And Maggfrid and I go on to Gloriana."

Bond spat. "Fucking Line." He looked over to where Maggfrid— who couldn't ride—sat on the back of a wagon, eyes closed, head resting drowsily on his chest. "Sorry to lose that one, too. He's earned his passage."

※ ※ ※

Bond's men had at first not taken to Maggfrid—some of them teased him, some of them considered him bad luck. But then Maggfrid distinguished himself in defense of the caravan against Hillfolk attack, and after that they adored him; the more superstitious crewmen kept shaking his hand for good luck, which he thought was a great game. . . .

The attack had come when they were two days out of Monroe Town, as the caravan made its way down a high-sided valley that was strewn not only with rocks and brambles, which were bad enough, but also with bales of old rusted barbed wire, scattered like a mockery of vegetation.

"Linesmen leave it," Bond said. "The wire. There was a battle here some thirty years ago. They put this stuff round their camps, for defense. Then it just rusts, forever."

"Thirty years ago. That was when the Line was fighting the Red Valley Republic?"

The *Child's History of the West* was full of lengthy accounts of the Republic's battles against the Line—a progression of victories that Liv doubted were so glorious or so easy as the General made them sound. She couldn't keep the details straight.

Bond shook his head. "That was south of here, and west. Republic never got out as far as us. This here was just some stupid local thing. Conant declared for Gun; Line came out here to show them what that meant. That was when they built Gloriana."

"Who won?"

"Who do you think? Line always wins."

The coils of wire had to be moved off the trail with long poles and ropes before the caravan could safely pass. They drifted slowly but ceaselessly back into place as if some fragment of the Engines' relentless will still was in them. It was hot and frustrating work. The hands of Liv's golden watch turned slowly.

The Folk attacked at sunset, while the men were still working.

There were half a dozen of them, tall angular shapes suddenly standing on the hillside, charging helter-skelter down, long legs springing and bending in odd ways. They didn't speak or call out. They rustled and clattered. Their black beards and manes streamed out behind them as they ran. They threw stones and scared the horses, and one of Bond's men fell backwards, screaming into a tangle of wire. Shouting "Form up, form up, wake the fuck up!" Bond drew his pistol and fired. . . .

Liv crouched under a wagon and watched. The Folk closed on the caravan at once. They didn't seem at all afraid of Bond's pistol. Most of Bond's men were armed with shovels or poles or picks, and they swung wildly at the attackers, whose emaciated bone-white bodies were like springs; they bounced and spun and dodged. The shadows concealed them; the dust they kicked up blurred Liv's vision. She saw long arms snap out and snatch picks from Bond's men's hands, she saw long white fingers close around Bond's pistol and tear it away. Their bodies were painted or perhaps etched in glittering bloodred designs—abstract, mathematical—spinning and whirling. They kicked and lunged and knocked men in the dirt. On spiderlike legs, one of them crouched down by Liv's hiding place, and then deep red eyes were staring into hers, steady, unblinking, as if fascinated by her.

She froze. Beneath the red eyes there was a long nose, oddly angled, as if not broken but formed according to a looser plan. Beneath the nose there was a wide mouth, which opened wider, as if it was about to say something to her. It seemed that it must be a communication of such great importance that every word had to be chosen with utmost care, or else there might be some error that could never afterwards be mended. . . .

With a great roar, Maggfrid appeared behind the Hillman's shoulder and pulled him away, yanking him by his mane. Maggfrid held a shovel in his hand and he swung it like a bat and the Hillman's head cracked open.

Still roaring, Maggfrid charged into the midst of the caravan's attackers. They dodged. He caught one on the elbow, and bones broke; he shattered another's kneecap.

They scattered as quickly and as silently as they'd come, and Maggfrid was left turning in circles, mouth working soundlessly, still tightly clutching the bloody shovel.

Liv approached Maggfrid slowly, whispering to calm him. She took the shovel from his hands.

No one was badly hurt except the man who'd fallen in the wire.

One of the attackers lay dead in the brambles. It was the one Maggfrid had hit in the head—the one that had nearly, it seemed, *spoken* to Liv. She knelt to study him. His brains, she noticed, looked like any other person's.

"It won't last," Bond said. His shirt was torn, and his broad face was red with exertion and anger.

"What won't?"

"They come back. They get up again."

"So I've heard. I'd like to see it."

"Well, I don't plan on waiting around."

The body looked nearly weightless. The long limbs were like a bundle of sticks. She found it terribly moving, and tears pricked her eyes.

"They didn't hurt anyone," she said. "They didn't even have weapons."

"Sometimes that's how it is. Sometimes they have spears, and they kill every fighting man and torture the rest for days. Sometimes they have some real nasty tricks with the wind and the stones. But then again I know a man who swears on his mother's soul that a pack of 'em found him injured on the trail and brought him water and set his leg and carried him home."

"Why?"

"They're not like us, Doctor. They do things that don't make sense. Sometimes they bring storms, floods, hurricanes, dust storms. You'll call me superstitious, but it's true. They were here first, and if you ask me, they're just waiting for us to fuck off, and this is how they play in the meantime."

"It seemed he was about to speak to me."

"They don't speak. And look at 'em—would you understand 'em if they could?"

At last he saw the expression of pity on her face, and his voice softened. "There are worse things than these, though. And what do I know anyway? I'm just a businessman."

"I understand, Mr. Bond." She turned away from him. Her hands shook as she reached into her case for her nerve tonic.

He called after her. "Hey—your big friend there did well, that was one hell of a job."

She looked where he was pointing. Maggfrid was pacing back and forth with his head in his hands. . . .

✳   ✳   ✳

There was hardly a single mention of the Folk in the *Child's History*. One faded illustrated plate showed representative scenes from the West: an Engine slumbering on its tracks, twisted wind-carved rocks, and a Hillman perched on a craggy peak, obsidian spear in hand. And the Folk appeared also in the first chapter of the book, which told the story of the first colony, at Founding. A handful of sentences: *Relations between First Governor Samuel Self and the aboriginal Folk of the Woods were uneasy, and not always honorable. . . .*

Otherwise, the Folk were effaced from the history of their country. Perhaps, Liv thought, if they'd fought more battles . . .

Most of Bond's men were illiterate. One night, one of them asked what she was reading, and soon Liv was reading to all of them. They were a rough lot, bearded, yellow toothed, broken nosed, but they listened to her like children. Most of them knew less of the history of their own world than she did.

Chapters 2 through 22 were a litany of disasters and battles. Founding was abandoned—lost years, a hard winter, plague, bad omens. The colonists spread west and south. Line rose in the south, where the colonists struck oil, and where the first Engines were built to travel between the outflung cities of the dry plains, and men quickly realized that they had built something larger and more terrible than could be comprehended on any human scale, something that had its own mind and its own will to expand. . . . Gun rose in the ragged West, among exiles, drifters, criminals fleeing the law. They hated each other at once. They were defined by their hatred. Line spread relentlessly, with its Engines and its machines and its speed and its masses of men. Gun cheated and schemed and poisoned and blackmailed and ambushed; it raised armies of mercenaries, mobs of deluded peasants. . . . And Bond was right: Gun was always losing. Three hundred years of defeat and bitterness. Why did they bother?

The *Child's History* condemned the Line as tyrannical and the Gun as anarchistic, and solemnly proclaimed the virtue of the Red Valley Republic—by whose Department of Universal Education it had been printed. The virtues of the Republic were Democracy, Reason, Self-Government, Property, and Ordered Liberty. There was a brief homiletic chapter devoted to each.

The Republic had arisen on what was then the edge of the world—a new idea. A loose alliance of freetowns and border states, that had become an Alliance, then a Federation, then, with the signing of the Charter on the banks of the Red Valley River, some forty years ago, a Republic. There was an illustration: several dozen dignified old men standing on the banks of a river, brandishing papers and pens, delivering speeches. The Charter itself appeared to be something intermediate between a code of public law and a sacred text, and in the illustration, a shaft of heavenly light fell upon it.

There was a history of the Republic's battles—glorious triumphs against both the armies of the Line and the pirates and mercenaries of the Gun. The Republic recognized no gods, no masters.

On the fifth night out of Monroe Town, the men were all busy mending broken axles and torn canvas, and so Liv sat on a rock by the edge of camp and read alone. Bond, who'd stayed away on previous nights as she read to his men, swaggered and looked over her shoulder.

"He's dead," Bond said. He pointed at an illustration of General Enver, rallying his troops at the battle of something-or-other.

"Dead," Bond added, as if he expected Liv to be astonished by this news. "Him and his Republic. They kept winning battles until they lost one, and that's all there is to say. Dead and lost and forgotten."

"So I've heard."

"Books are good for keeping accounts. You can't learn much else from them. The world changes faster than words can make it stick."

"The past doesn't change, Mr. Bond."

"They say the General was friends with Hillfolk. They say he had one for his adviser, a caster of stones, and that's how he won his battles. I heard he married one, but I don't believe that one, myself. Is any of that in there?"

"It's only a children's book, Mr. Bond. It's very simple."

"Huh. Books are all right for children, I suppose."

She snapped the book shut. "Well, thank you *very* much for your insights, Mr. Bond."

He flushed—he looked embarrassed.

"Mr. Bond, I apologize—"

"No offense, ma'am."

"The heat, Mr. Bond, and the lateness of the hour . . ."

She felt oddly attached to the silly little book. In a way, it was something from home, and it made her sentimental.

"They say," Bond said, "I mean, I've heard it said." His tone was unusually quiet and thoughtful. "I've heard some folks say that the War will go on until it chews up the whole world. The Republic tried to stop it, but look what happened to them. Wherever there's oil, Line will thrive. Wherever there's bad men, there's Gun. Forever."

"A horrible thought."

"I've heard it said that the Folk know how to end it. They were here first and they know this world and what's meant to be here and it stands to reason they could put Gun and Line back down, if they wanted to, don't you think?"

"Reason seems to have very little to do with it, Mr. Bond."

"A friend of mine used to say, if there's hope for peace, it's with them, not us."

"How shameful for us if that's true!"

"He died. Someone shot him. Doesn't matter who. I don't know. I don't know. It's something to think about, isn't it? Something to think about. I'm not a stupid man, Doctor."

"Of course not, Mr. Bond."

✳ ✳ ✳

Her husband, the late Professor of Natural History, Doctor Bernhardt Alverhuysen, had indeed resembled Mr. Bond in size—though beneath Bond's fat there was muscle, and Bond was sunburned where Bernhardt had been pale, and he was physically deft and sure-footed where Bernhardt had been clumsy. In fact, there was only the faintest shadow of a resemblance. Why *did* Bond remind her so of Bernhardt? Perhaps precisely because he was so different from all the men she'd known in Koenigswald; deep in alien territory, she sought out whatever traces of the familiar she could find.

Bond's arrogance, rudeness, and self-certainty reminded her of Bernhardt, too. And his lecturing—Bond had seemed taciturn back in Burren Hill, but out in the silent open spaces of the trail, he loved the sound of his own voice. Plants, weather, business, how to ride a horse and mend a wagon. He turned out to be surprisingly well informed and passionate on the industrial processes for which their cargo of bones were intended. Bernhardt had liked to talk philosophy. Bernhardt had had something of a romantic side, though deeply buried under bluster; did Bond?

What she had told Bond was true. Bernhardt had died of a heart attack two years ago, at the dining table, in the middle of a peevish diatribe on Faculty politics, during the soup course.

He'd been much, much older than her. She'd met him almost the very day she'd emerged from the Institute at Tuborren, where she had spent the greater part of her adolescence in treatment for shock, and certain related nervous conditions, arising out of the tragic death of her mother—a topic she most certainly did *not* intend to discuss with Mr. Bond. She'd been a pale, wan, sheltered little thing, uncertain of her place in the world—and Bernhardt been a great and substantial authority in his field, who had found her pretty.

She'd been very fond of him, albeit in a distant, irritated sort of way, and had mourned him for an appropriate period; but afterwards she rarely missed him.

It was a point of professional pride for Liv that she never deceived herself as to her own feelings.

Bond sounded out those feelings one evening as they rode together beneath the cedars. He stared fixedly at the path ahead as he spoke, and he somehow managed to be rude and coy at once—

"You won't find a husband in that hospital of yours, Doctor."

"I'm not presently looking for another husband, Mr. Bond."

"None of us have forever to wait, Doctor."

—but she was touched anyway. "It's a big world, Mr. Bond. Sometimes it seems as if we *might* have forever."

He was silent for a long minute. Then he said, "It does. Sometimes it does."

They talked about politics and history for the rest of the night.

✳ ✳ ✳

"That's Conant," Bond said. They came down a steep hillside, and a blazing sun was behind them and they cast long shadows. Spread out below was a little town in the bend of a river. Its walls were painted white, and it gleamed like a scatter of diamonds. The colors of nature around it were lurid, wild: the trees were brazen, the river muddy gold, the sky lush violet.

"Not much of a town," Bond said. "But you'll get a horse there, and you and your big feller can find someone who knows the way to Gloriana."

"I think I know the way." She shielded her eyes against the sun and looked south.

"I guess you do."

She could see it for miles, across the grasslands. She'd never seen anything like it, but there was no doubt what it was. The black spires, the smoke. Gloriana, easternmost Station of the Line.

"Watch yourself, Doctor. Some things are worse and weirder than Hillfolk."

CHAPTER 8

The Net

What left Kingstown the next morning was not, as Lowry had imagined it might be, any small or secretive adventure into enemy territory. Conductor Banks's Expeditionary Force consisted of 420 men; a commensurate number of troop trucks and staff cars; seven Heavier-Than-Air Vessels of both the rotary-wing and the ornithopter variety, lightly armed and stripped for scouting; eight Ironclads; two trucks containing wireless telegraphy equipment, one of which was redundant in case of emergencies; one truck containing five fixed guns; one truck containing mortars, rockets, noisemakers, gas; three trucks containing nothing but fuel and food; six trucks containing canvas, concrete, wire, and other parts and materials for the construction of a Forward Camp; and that wasn't even mentioning the clawed and treaded earth-moving machinery that went ahead to clear mudslides and deadfalls, to widen narrow roads not made for the Line. The expedition roared into the hills like a chain saw, in a haze of dust and noise.

Lowry found the noise an enormous comfort. If he kept his eyes down and didn't look at the horizon, he might still be safely at home.

※　※　※

Lowry had had one and only one face-to-face encounter with Conductor Banks, as the expedition gathered on the vast tarmac fields just outside Kingstown's fortifications, shortly before it was due to set off. He approached the window of Banks's staff car and waited patiently until the window at last wound down, and Lowry's reflection was replaced by Banks's face. As it turned out, Banks was a man of about Lowry's size, little more than Lowry's age, and with much the same sort of drab shapeless round-spectacled ghost of a face—except for the tracks of exhaustion and stress that invariably came with high command in the Line, which were more deeply cut on Banks than they'd ever been on Lowry.

Banks's lap was buried under a heap of reports, which he was studying through reading glasses. Large sections of text were blacked out.

"Yes?"

"Sub-Invigilator (Second Class) Lowry, sir."

"Right. Right. One of the advisers. The experts. The intelligence people." Banks took off his glasses and rubbed his eyes. "Do *you* know what we're doing here, Lowry?"

"No, sir."

"No, sir. No, sir—I bet you fucking don't. I don't. Why should you? What's your expertise in, Lowry?"

"The enemy, sir. The—"

"Who isn't an expert in the fucking enemy, Lowry? What do you think we do all day? Let's see—Can you talk to the Signal Corps, Lowry?"

"Yes, sir. I've worked with Signals—"

"Good. I can't make head or tails of any damn thing they say. I understand artillery, wheels and motors, fuel, supply lines, fortifications—not Signals. Report to S-I First Morningside, who's another so-called *expert* all the way from Archway. He's responsible for intelligence here and is acting in the absence of clearer orders as my second. Assist him with the Signals."

"Yes, sir."

"Lowry, come here. Lowry."

Lowry leaned closer.

"Are you here to spy on me, Lowry?"

"No, sir. My orders are to assist you in any—"

"Four hundred and twenty of us. Another two thousand coming

behind, Lowry, but no time to wait or fully mobilize or organize. Precipitous action. Seize and control each shitty little town in a patch of worthless red wasteland. Form a net, a circle. Why? It must be done *immediately*. No answer. Precipitous action; thirty years of service and never known *precipitous action*. Deliberation is what we *are*, Lowry, deliberation and control. Someone somewhere's in a panic. A blunder? Maybe. Not mine. Not mine, Lowry. I do my duty. Forward-progress! Right into the wasteland if that's where it's going, not my business. Not my blunder. I don't complain. Tell them that, Lowry."

It could be advantageous to Lowry's career to be taken for an informant for higher authorities; on the other hand, it could be dangerous to lie. He therefore stayed silent.

"Get to work, Lowry." Banks grunted with effort as he wound the window up.

✳ ✳ ✳

Sub-Invigilator (First) Morningside assigned Lowry to ride in the back of the Signal Corps' second truck, alongside the backup telegraph machinery and the senior officers of the Expeditionary Force's Signal Corps. A Subaltern thrust a stack of files into Lowry's hands.

The files were hastily prepared. The machinery was all brand new. Brass sounders and copper wires and bulbous vacuum tubes were still polished and glittering. Rows and rows of keys rattled with what sounded like enthusiasm as the truck bounced and rolled down dirt roads.

The senior officers of the Signal Corps were named Scale, Ditch, Benson, Collier, and Porter. Lowry introduced himself curtly, then sat in silence on the hard wooden bench and read the files.

THE "HOUSE DOLOROUS": INTRODUCTION

As of Year 292 at the latest, reports place the General, see principally B.140.1–B.140.310, at a hospital on the farthest northwestern Rim, known as "The House Dolorous" aka "The Doll House," hereinafter "The Hospital." See C.12.21.iv–x. These reports are considered of uncertain but generally actionable reliability. See C.12.34.iii.

The following report on the Hospital has been prepared in haste and is of limited reliability.

The Hospital was founded in Year 281 by one Winston Howell II, father of the Hospital's present director, and former resident of the town of Greenbank, see L.170.6. The Hospital has a very substantial endowment, provided primarily by Howell personally, out of the profits of the various silver-mining enterprises along the western rim with which his family was associated. The Hospital's name is apparently derived from a romantic poem popular in the southern Baronies, and is of no significance.

Howell II claimed in a Y285 memoir that he founded the Hospital after a dream in which a number of Hillfolk appeared to him in his office in Greenbank and led him into the hills to the Hospital's future location. See infra 4. This account cannot be verified. See infra 5.

The Hospital takes in the wounded from various conflicts over much of the western rim. A number of jurisdictions pay subscriptions to the Hospital to relieve them of their defectives, and this supplements the Hospital's endowment. The Hospital maintains a strict policy of neutrality, and refuses equally to do business with us or the enemy.

Its staff have few notable medical qualifications. However, the Hospital claims to be located on a site sacred to a spirit of the Hillfolk, which has healing properties. The extent of those healing properties cannot be verified, but the spirit appears to exist. It is most likely one of the minor aberrations that occur from time to time on the western rim, where human settlement is still recent and the conditions of creation unfixed. Cf. the "Red Plains Dust Devil," N.7.1, the "White Rock Werewolf," N.7.3, and the "Logris River Weeping Angel," N.7.4. Like them, it is likely soon enough to dissipate under the pressure of its internal contradictions. In the mean time, however, it is capable of significant extensions of physical force in defense of the boundaries, personnel, and inmates of the Hospital. According to eyewitness accounts, see infra 10, it remains generally dormant, unless violence is used within its zone of influence, at which point it responds to the perpetrator with overwhelming force.

In addition, the staff of the Hospital are reported to be intensely conscious of their security and defensive of their neutrality, and while their capacity for physical resistance is negligible, their irrational mindset is likely to complicate attempts at infiltration or negotiation. See infra 6–7.

In the event that it should be necessary to execute the General (or other inmate), aerial bombardment is advised. In the event that it should be necessary to extract any such individual alive, nonviolent means, though challenging, will be necessary. See infra 8.

The Expeditionary Force set up a temporary camp two miles south of Greenbank, on a broad expanse of rock and dirt. Weird rock formations towered overhead, fluted and curving like gigantic red flowers. They gave the camp a certain amount of shade from the constant oppressive sun, not to mention high lookout points, but they were hideous, and Lowry would happily have dynamited them flat.

They circled the trucks. They sent out the Heavier-Than-Air Vessels to scout in a wide radius. They unloaded and set up the fixed guns and the telegraph machinery, which instantly began to clatter and buzz with messages, the gist of which was *FASTER. FASTER. CLOSE THE NET.*

Sub-Invigilator (First) Morningside, who turned out to be a thoroughly insufferable prick, tasked Lowry with organizing the distribution of the men of the Signal Corps and their listening devices to each of the towns that ringed the Hospital.

"Anyone strange comes through town," Morningside said, "we have to be the first to know." As if that wasn't obvious.

"Yes, sir."

"Wire this whole slagging wasteland up. *Organize* it."

"Of course, sir."

✳   ✳   ✳

Lowry dispatched four men into Greenbank, two into Gooseneck, three into Fairsmith, three into World's End.

The little town of Kloan warranted only two sentences in the official files, and a faded and ancient photograph of a street with sad little buildings and some ragged bunting stretched from the rooftops. Something about it made Lowry uneasy, and he dispatched a dozen men to Kloan and made sure they were well armed.

CHAPTER 9

KLOHN

Creedmoor rode hard and fast, north and west out of the Delta Baronies, through the high cold passes of the Opals, north of Jasper
City, across the heartland prairies through thick green grass, leaping fences and waterways, day and night. His horse died beneath
him. Another was ready for him, tied to a post at midnight in a little
town south of Gibson that he never got a chance to learn the name
of, because Marmion instantly said:

—Move on.

That horse died, too. Creedmoor thought he might die himself,
that his old heart would give out, like a rat shaken in a terrier's
mouth. Every muscle, every joint, was constant agony. Marmion said:

—Faster.

Men of the Line might travel that distance in the belly of their
Engines, on soft leather seats. No wonder they were so fat! But an
Agent of the Gun couldn't travel by Line, of course—he'd be sniffed
out at once, by some damnable machine or snoop or other—and so
it was the old ways for Creedmoor, the back roads, the hills, by day
and by night. He caught a glimpse of himself in a dusty window-
pane once, as he thundered down the Main Street of who-the-fuck-
knew where, scattering women and children, and he was shocked
by how *old* he looked, how red and lined in the face, how gray his

hair was and how wild and ragged. It wounded his vanity. He always was a vain man.

—You'll kill me, old friend. I swear you'll kill me at this pace.

—Not yet. Faster.

He swung wide north around Kingstown Station, though it added two days to his journey, because he feared their spotlights and their search parties and their tollbooths and checkpoints, especially in his rapidly advancing condition of decay and exhaustion. Therefore he approached the Doll House from the east, just north of Kloan, and so he happened to see the posters nailed to trees every half mile alongside the road north of town, which were already fading and wilting like vivid blue-green flowers in the awful heat, but which still cheerfully promised the arrival in Kloan of DR. SLOOP'S TRAVELING EMPORIUM OF PHYSIC AND PATENT-MEDICINES, that very morning, once and once only, special-featuring "PROFESSOR" HARRY RANSOM AND HIS INGENIOUS ELECTRICAL LIGHT-BRINGING APPARATUS. . . .

—Medicine. Physic. Lights and amusements. A fair. Drink. Showgirls.

—No time, Creedmoor. Pass the town by.

—I shall die if I ride another hour without rest.

—No, Creedmoor. Too dangerous. We believe the enemy is present in this area. You may attract their notice.

—Fuck the enemy. I need medicine, by which I mean drink. Put the Goad to me if you like.

—One hour, Creedmoor.

—No more. On my honor.

—We will remember this.

※　※　※

There were few towns out there on the continent's still-uncreated edge. None were more than twenty years old. Greenbank, which was a ways southwest of Kloan, was the biggest and the richest of them. Supposedly—if Creedmoor's masters had not lied to him, which might or might not be the case—Dandy Fanshawe would be waiting there, worming in among the drifters of its bars and whorehouses. Abban the Lion and Drunkard Cuffee and Keane and Hang-

'Em-High Washburne would scout the hills south of Greenbank. Together those five Agents—a mighty force—would be ready to meet
Creedmoor once he emerged from the House and conduct him and
the General away east.

There was Gooseneck to the west, which was poor, but it had a
bank; and there was also World's End to the northwest, which was
ugly and sickly, but it had a mine.

And then there was Kloan, which had nothing special, except,
apparently, Dr. Sloop and his medicines, and "Professor" Ransom
and his apparatus.

Kloan was a few long straight dirt roads lashed together roughly
crosswise, with a lodging house and general store and similar in the
dust where they joined; a sprawl of small constructions knocked
up out of tin and wood surrounded them. There was a market square
with a kind of rickety stage, which was no doubt the most exciting
thing for miles around. It was peaceful and dull and drowsily
drunken.

Creedmoor rode in slowly, smiling and nodding. He left his horse
at a hitching post and wandered into the market.

The whole rough mess of Kloan was dressed in sun-faded bunting,
strung from the eaves of the big houses, nailed over the doors of lesser
structures. All flounced up like a whore's skirts. Dressed up soft and
pretty for market-day—it implied a town where women had consid-
erable say in the running of things, which struck Creedmoor as a
promising situation. The idling crowd was composed largely of farmers, but also of pleasant-looking young women. He turned to the
young lady next to him and beamed broadly at her and winked. She
went pink and hid her pretty face in her fan.

—Most promising!

—No, Creedmoor. One hour.

Kloan bobbed like driftwood in a dull sea of flat brown fields.
The fields were still but not empty. Hillfolk worked them, chained
in gangs at the ankles, shuffling under the tuberous weight of black
hair and beards. Probably their overseers were among the youths in
the crowd or sprawled drunkenly on the dirt. The pretty young girl
was arm in arm with a crop-headed barn-faced blacksmith-bicepped
boy, who had the look of a young man handy with a whip.

—You know, the first man I ever killed was a slaver. Before I came to your service.

—We know.

—I had passionate views on the matter. Back when the blood was younger and hotter. Marching and speechifying for the Liberationists. That was after they kicked me out of the Knights of Labor, of course.

—Leave him be, Creedmoor.

Dr. Sloop was whooping and hollering up on the stage. He wore top hat and tails, even in Kloan's awful heat; his face was red and his shirt was soaked and sweat ran from the ends of his long mustaches. One of his eyes was painted glass and it seemed to roll, glaring madly at the blue heat of the sky one moment and down at the dust the next.

—Oh, don't worry, my friend. I long since stopped caring.

Sloop rolled his hat deftly down his arm and handed it to his bosomy showgirl; he rolled up his shirtsleeves and let his wild dye-black mane shake free. "Oh let's get down to business, ladies and gentlemen. Let's take a look at Sloop's Tonic Water. It'll cure what aches ya; who here has aches and pains? It'll give ya vigor; who here's a strong man? Ah, I know, I know, Kloan's men are strong, I'm not blind! But who'd like to be *stronger*? It'll keep ya young. You pretty girls of Kloan; who'd let such flowers fade?"

—How long must we suffer this absurdity, Creedmoor?

—You'll be sorry if my health goes and my youth and my vigor go. When my eyesight goes and my heart fails out there in the dust one day.

—You can be replaced. Besides, your health cannot fail. We will not let it.

—Perhaps I have more faith in human science than in your will, my friend.

—That *is* absurdity.

The crowd filled about half the square; the women with their parasols and fans, the men sweating red-faced in their shirtsleeves and suspenders. At the back of the square, a single immense baobab tree curled out its broad dry branches and gave some shade. It was the most impressive structure in Kloan by far. The crust of obscene carvings on its trunk went all the way back to *Fuck Mr. Howell for bringin us out here, Big John, 1875*, and it looked to Creedmoor like it was Kloan's greatest cultural achievement.

Creedmoor stood half a head above the crowd—Kloan's men were short. The young men had a pretty good drunk on and sprawled on the hard earth with bottles and jugs, or sat in the branches of the baobab tree and hooted.

—Pointless, Creedmoor.

Behind and to the side of Sloop's stage, a clever-looking young black fellow in a somewhat stained white suit was working on a complex apparatus of tubes of colored glass and spools of copper wire and things that resembled cymbals and other things that resembled organ pipes. Creedmoor imagined that this was "Professor" Harry Ransom. Every so often he stopped, scratched his head, and looked baffled at the obstinate refusal of his apparatus to do whatever it was supposed be doing. . . .

—Creedmoor, this is pathetic.

—Look, I'll gather intelligence. Will that shut you up?

—Careful, Creedmoor.

—I'll take that as a yes.

At the edge of the square was a long log bench where the town's old men sat, all in a row. Creedmoor sat down among them, with a grunt, and joined in the grumbling. He agreed with them that the weather was dreadful, that prices were outrageous, and Sloop was nothing special, not like the medicine men of the good old days. Which was true; these days the Line's factory-produced drugs flooded the markets of the heartlands and drove out the more inspired and entrepreneurial type of chemist, such as Creedmoor hoped Sloop might be.

The old men grumbled about the War. A pox on both sides— that was the general consensus.

Gently Creedmoor steered the conversation to the House Dolorous:

"Ever heard of it?"

"Of course!" The wrinkled fellow on the bench next to Creedmoor rolled his eyes, as if to say: What *hadn't* he seen, in his long life in Kloan? "I've been there. Not far north of here, as far west as any sane man goes. Friend of mine died there, as a matter of fact. You look well enough, sir, what do you need to go there for?"

"Maybe I'm just looking for work."

"They don't take just anyone. They're unfriendly types, for healers. These are dangerous times, so who can blame 'em?"

"That's too bad."

"They say there's a Power watches over 'em. They say it loves peace and hates the War and if any man strikes another man there, that Power strikes 'em right back."

"A mothering Power! Who says that?"

"Everyone does. *They* do."

"Men from the House? You know them?"

"They come through town every now and again."

"Who does?"

"Men from the House. They go walking all over the country, looking for wounded and mad. You'll see 'em on the trails in these parts—a dozen men lame or mad walking, walking, one man of the House leading them, town to town and home to the House. Towns'll pay to get rid of the mad folk, often enough. Or the old folk. Maybe it'll be my time soon!"

And the old men started wheezing with laughter, and Creedmoor said,

—An idea occurs to me.

—Yes, Creedmoor.

—Our way in. Our disguise.

—Yes.

—Aren't you pleased we came to Kloan? I've done my day's work. Now it's time for my medicine.

✳ ✳ ✳

When Creedmoor rejoined the crowd, the pretty girl had moved closer to the stage, and her boyfriend had put an arm around her. Creedmoor stood quietly behind her and admired the view.

Professor Ransom's mysterious apparatus was still not cooperating, but Dr. Sloop and his hurdy-gurdy man and his feather-clad showgirl were putting on quite enough of a performance to hold

Kloan's attention. They strutted and clapped and roared and jiggled across the flat boards of the medicine wagon's stage. The backdrop behind them was a huge canvas painted with blue skies and clouds and soaring mountains and mighty forests sweeping horizon to horizon. Kloan and environs were flat as dirt from farms to cattle markets and the panorama was likely the most exciting thing they'd ever seen. The showgirl moved before that painted world like a beautiful colossus. Sloop worked the crowd up into clapping and stomping and hooting like apes.

Then Sloop brought out the muscleman.

Five foot five and practically square, bowlegged, clad in bearskin, and hairy chested: the muscleman pranced and bounced and hefted two huge anvils that were surely hollow inside. "Ladies and gentlemen of Kloan," Sloop screamed, "such are the benefits of Sloop's tonic water!" The men in the crowd clapped, and the women sighed and swooned.

—Fools.

—They know it's horseshit, my friend. They are only bored, and looking for amusement.

Sloop seized the muscleman's hairy wrist and held his arm up in the air, to applause that started mild and trailed off. Sloop had let the muscleman go on a little too long; the crowd was losing interest.

Creedmoor clapped loudly and cheered. He favored Sloop with a wide encouraging smile. Out of the corner of his eye, Creedmoor noticed the pretty girl noticing him. He noticed, too, her big blond boy standing possessively beside her, glaring. He smiled at them both.

"You sir," Sloop said, pointing at Creedmoor, "you man of Kloan, will you come up and test your strength against my good friend here? Would you see firsthand what Sloop's tonic water can do for a man's vigor?"

—No, Creedmoor. Do not draw attention.

But the pretty girl was smiling at him with interesting and interested eyes, waiting to see what he would do, and the dumb animal glare of her boy was intensely amusing, so Creedmoor laughed and stepped up onto the stage. He saw Sloop's one good eye drop sharply to his gun belt and to Marmion's gleaming grip, and he began to think twice, but it was too late to back away.

From the stage, Creedmoor could see all of Kloan and the flat land that stretched off into the haze of the uncreated West.

The stubby muscleman flexed into view, just under Creedmoor's chin. He stank of whiskey and sweat. He posed his bulgy body for the crowd. He seized Creedmoor's hand, and they arm-wrestled.

—Huh. Aren't you going to help me?

—Of course not, Creedmoor.

The muscleman slammed Creedmoor's hand down almost at once. Creedmoor smiled and took it with good grace.

"That's no man of Kloan!" The big blond boy was drunker than he'd looked. His sweaty face had gone from red to near purple. His neck veins bulged. "That old drifter's no man of Kloan! Why don't you try a real man, Sloop?"

Creedmoor offered the crowd a guileless and ingratiating smile. They looked back at him, and at the blond boy climbing the stage, with no hostility, only a bored curiosity.

—Look there, Creedmoor.

—What?

—There in the door of the boardinghouse, in shirtsleeves and spectacles.

—Ah. I see him.

A small fat man in the distance at the edge of the market, just by the boarding house. Pale-skinned but sunburned, soft-featured, in a dirty gray shirt, his blinking gray eyes fixed on Creedmoor; on Creedmoor's belt; on Marmion. The man's eyes flicked up and met Creedmoor's, and he flinched and ducked quickly back indoors.

—A man of the Line.

—No uniform.

—Nevertheless. As we said: The enemy is present.

—This far west? No Engines run this far. He's far from his masters.

—As we said: The enemy is present. The Lion and Fanshawe reported movements south of Greenbank. They were correct.

—Are they on the same trail as us?

—We do not know the plans of the Engines. They are mad. Creedmoor! Where there is one Linesman, there are many. *Go.*

Creedmoor smiled and moved to the edge of the stage. "Excuse me, Dr. Sloop, good ladies and gentlemen of Kloan, it's been a fine afternoon, but I must—"

But the stupid blond boy lunged out of the crowd and grabbed Creedmoor's arm with a drunken crushing grip and would not let go. Creedmoor looked into the oaf's dull eyes and saw there was no reasoning with him; so he flashed one last smile at the oaf's pretty young lady, wide-blue-eyed in the shade of her green parasol, and he twisted the oaf's arm—and there was a burning in Creedmoor's blood and there was cordite and sulfur in his nostrils as *now* Marmion's dark strength flooded his veins—he twisted so that the big boy spun like a ballerina and went down on his back with a wet snapping sound and a limp arm flopping at his side.

Creedmoor shrugged and jumped down from the stage. The girl met his eye again and recoiled; his eyes were shot with blood and darkness and he was not smiling now, not at all.

The oaf had friends; they shoved through the crowd at Creedmoor and instantly his thumb was in one man's eye and another man was kneeling on the dust clutching his bleeding nose.

Behind him, Sloop and the showgirl and the muscleman were frantically packing their clanking, sloshing stock of tonic water away for safety, and Ransom dismantled his apparatus.

The crowd cleared around Creedmoor, and he broke into a run for the boardinghouse door, kicking up dust with his boots.

When the boardinghouse door opened, he shot the first man to come through it in the head, but the body was at once trampled down by two more men, both of whom were dull and pale and doughy and glassy-eyed in the way of the mass-manufactured men of the Line. To either side of the door, the windows broke, and the ugly muzzles of machine guns poked through. Creedmoor lurched to a halt and turned on his heel back into the crowd as the guns opened up: the whir of the Engine first and the chatter of the feeding belt; a sound of threshing Engines and a gathering storm. He called out *MARMION!* and a dark rush of blood pounded through him and the world went gray, and he veered sideways and dove between bullets that swam past him in stately slow-moving procession. One scraped his leg, ripping his trouser, and the pain let loose another burst of black blood in his brain, but it was only a scrape, and

Marmion knitted the flesh closed even as he ran. He ran, thinking: *I'll need needle and thread to be presentably dressed for the House Dolorous.* Then he ducked for cover in the crowds of Kloan's market.

The hideous machines churned up the crowd. Kloan was a peaceful town, out here far to the west of the War; its people had not the good sense to drop—so they made excellent shields for Creedmoor. He darted between an old woman in a lacy dress who went down in a bloody spray and a dumb young farmboy who shrieked like a girl as the bullets hit him; between the two, Creedmoor fired a single shot that caught one of the Linesman gunners between the eyes; the Linesman's mechanical weapon fell from the window still automatically firing and thrashing like an iron snake until the belt was empty.

They were men of the Line for sure, of course; no one else had access to such hideous machines.

One of the Linesmen in the boardinghouse knelt in the doorway. He snapped open his black chrome-clasped briefcase and removed a black lump of iron, the size of his fist, and he bowled it through the air toward the crowd and Creedmoor. Creedmoor, darting from behind a screaming gaggle of girls in blood-spattered dresses, caught it on the wing with one careful shot (*time froze; the world became gray and cold and precise; Marmion guided his hand*) knocking it back like a billiard ball into the boardinghouse through the open door.

The boardinghouse immediately burst into flame. The curtains went up and the glass shattered and sparks and smoke poured forth from the windows. The shooting stopped briefly.

—Was that a firebomb? An unusual weapon for the Line.

—Remember Logtown, Creedmoor. They burned Logtown.

—How could I forget?

—It might have been a noise-bomb. Or gas. You broke it, Creedmoor, so now it burns. Who cares what it was made for?

—Now it burns. Who cares what it was made for? That should be your motto. I should have it *engraved* on your grip. Oh, look at it burn! That should keep them busy.

—There may be more nearby.

—What do you think they were doing here?

—Spying. Establishing their hateful spying machines. Laying claim to territory that is not theirs.

Two more men, short, hunching, coughing, staggered out of the blaze, smoke streaming from shabby black suits and howling mouths, ugly stub rifles held loosely and rattling away.

—Finish them. Smash their machines. *Go.*

✳ ✳ ✳

On his way back from the boardinghouse—his clothes somewhat singed; mopping ash, dust, and blood from his face with someone else's neckerchief—Creedmoor stopped by the stage and what remained of Sloop's medicine show. The crowd was long dispersed from the square; even Kloan's cow-slow folk had figured the score by then. Sloop was dead of a bloody chest wound. The muscleman lay beside him with the back of his head open. Professor Harry Ransom was laying out the bodies and cleaning them up, but he up and ran at Creedmoor's approach. Ransome's white suit was ruined, of course, and his apparatus didn't seem to have fared much better, because the stage now was scattered with broken glass and wire.

—Never know what it did now, I guess. Shame.

The showgirl was on her knees sobbing, her feather boa trailing in the blood and glass. Creedmoor paid her what seemed to be a fair price for two bottles of her dead master's tonic water.

—It is grain alcohol and curry powder. I can sense it. You will be lucky not to go blind, Creedmoor.

—Nevertheless.

The showgirl's trembling fingers half closed over the bills.

He said, "You keep your clothes very nicely, considering the rough country you travel in. Do you have needle and thread?"

The baobab tree was a blazing crown like some awful prophecy.

Over by the burning boardinghouse, half Kloan's folk were passing up buckets from the well. Mostly the women. Their efforts were not going well. The fire spread to another and another house, and meanwhile many of the men were eyeing Creedmoor angrily, nervously—this interloper who had brought down horror upon them—this dealer with devils, this Agent of the Gun. Some carried pitchforks and knives and hatchets; a few clutched old muskets; one or two had hunting bows.

He could have killed them all. But what would be the point? Kloan was a pretty town. And besides, one lucky shot might always end him. It happened, sadly, even to Agents of the Gun—only last year, Red Molly had died in similar circumstances. Though she had, of course, been ragingly drunk.

Creedmoor's horse was dead, slumped and bloody by the hitching post to which he'd tied it. The animals nearby were panicking and screaming and rearing against their ropes. He took another from over the other side of the square.

The men of Kloan edged closer, murder-minded. Creedmoor stared them down from horseback. "Your town is burning. See—your women are fighting for it. Go help them, you fools." And he spurred the horse round and thundered out of town before Kloan's folk—not so peaceful or simple anymore!—could start shooting.

The War had been bound to come to Kloan sooner or later. Still, Creedmoor felt just awful that he'd been the one to bring it, and he rode out in grim silence. Naturally his master, sensing his mood, set out to worsen it.

—We warned you, Creedmoor. You defied us.

—I did.

—Never again, Creedmoor. Next time you defy us, we will put the *Goad* to you. You have a *mission*.

❉ ❉ ❉

He went west into lands that were still peaceful—rough and hilly and broken but not yet marked by war. An hour later, he'd put some good miles behind him, and the smoke was no longer visible.

He spied a fast rider in the distance, tearing out of Kloan along a route southwest of and near parallel to Creedmoor's own, raising dust.

—Spare us embarrassment, Creedmoor. Keep this story from the newspapers.

Only a short detour was necessary to bring the rider within

Marmion's prodigious range—and Creedmoor didn't miss. He never missed.

A crack. The rider silently tumbled into the dust.

Creedmoor shook his head.

—Damn fool. Should have stayed home where they needed him.

—The Line knows we are here. Get to work, Creedmoor.

Creedmoor began to scour the trails and back roads of the hills. Twenty-four hours later, he picked up the trail of a procession—he could *smell* them—a dozen men and women, on foot, slow moving, some of them wounded, scents of pus and bandages and iodine.

—The House's men. And the walking wounded. A harvest of the sick and the mad for the House Dolorous.

—Yes. They will suffice. Finally we can begin. Faster, Creedmoor.

CHAPTER 10

GLORIANA

To enter the Gloriana Station was to leave the ordinary world behind. It was to enter into a world of noise and din and stink, in which even the light was different—because there was no real sunlight in the Station, only the cold glare of spotlights and the glimmer of industrial fires, and those few shafts of natural light that crept through the filthy windows and the dust-laden air were altered by their passage, stripped to the bone. To descend the broad black iron staircase onto the Concourse was to enter the bowels of the earth; to walk out onto the white stone of the Concourse itself, beneath the high arched roof and the sweeping acetylene searchlights, was like walking on the moon. Liv held tight to Maggfrid's arm, and breathed deeply, and clutched her ticket in her hand, and came into the presence of the Gloriana Engine. . . .

※ ※ ※

Gloriana was the most extraordinary structure she had ever seen. It dominated the horizon like a mountain; she rode into its shadow.

The Station itself was perhaps four or five times taller than the highest part of the Academy. Low sheds and warehouses sprawled to left and right, a mess of tin and concrete and wire. Pistons and windmill-sized gears rose out of the rubble. Chimney stacks vented. Gray blocky towers, some windowless and others bristling with blank eyes, buttressed the Station, whose black iron arches soared up at severe angles, forming distant peaks. It reminded Liv of a cathedral; it also reminded her of the vultures she'd seen here and there by the roadside, squatting inside the ugly arch of their shoulders.

It *moved*. From a distance it appeared to be rippling. Only when she came closer did it become apparent that the structure was covered in cranes, which swung monotonously back and forth from tower to tower, and in gears and cable cars and elevators and . . .

Behind Gloriana Station was the town in which the Engine's servants lived—a hive, a maze of shafts and towers. The populations of Burren Hill and Monroe and Barrett and Conant together couldn't have filled half of it.

The whole black mass sat on the open grasslands, roaring and smoking, casting a jagged sundial-shadow over the plains. It appeared to have been placed at random, or dropped from the heavens. Something about it suggested a vast indifference to the natural world. On all sides of it, as Liv approached, there were blue skies; only the Station itself was wreathed in smoke.

Gloriana was the northeasternmost endpoint of the continent-spanning network of the Line. Only one track left it—behind the Station, leaving high overhead on a raised iron bridge, and disappearing into the hills.

There were thirty-eight immortal Engines in the world. The Line bound them together—a great continent-spanning nervous system. Each Engine had its own Station, and its own anonymous masses of men and machines. Every few decades another was born—another demon risen from the earth to settle into a body of iron and coal. Gloriana was one of the smallest of the Stations, and the Gloriana Engine was one of the younger of its kind.

❊   ❊   ❊

To approach the Station—to approach the Station was to queue. For hours.

Liv and Maggfrid had walked south from Conant in the company of a local guide. A half day out from the Station, they had come upon the road. It was black, and wide, and straight, and the rolling grasslands appeared to have been flattened for it. They weren't alone on it. As they got closer to the Station, the road got more and more crowded. There were pedestrians like themselves, some carrying baskets of goods on their backs. There were horse-men and carts. And every so often, there was a great coarse *honking* sound, and the roar of motors, and a staff car or troop truck would come barreling down the road, stuffed with pale Linesmen in their black uniforms, bristling with rifles and bayonets, and every time Liv had to pull Maggfrid aside, because his instinct was to stand squarely in the road and not be moved.

And in the shadow of the Station itself there were crowds—shifting masses of men—and a number of roads led up to the Sta-tion's various gates. Little men shouted and directed traffic. *That way! You, that way!* Liv stumbled along with the crowd and pulled Maggfrid with her. She found herself in a long line, the distant end of which slowly moved through an arched gate in the south wall of the Station. She asked, "What are we—?" and the man in front of her answered with a grunt and a shrug. Someone pressed a ticket with a number on it into her hand. She said, "*Excuse* me . . . ," and was shushed, angrily. She'd never been in the presence of so many people, and it threw her badly off balance; she felt almost physically compelled to follow the slow-moving line ahead of her. She kept quiet and looked at her feet. The queue lasted for what felt like hours. When she got to the front of the Line and the clerk in the gate's little booth questioned her about her purpose, and her iden-tity, and her intentions, in the rudest possible manner, she was too cowed to answer back. Only once she'd been fed through into the interior of the Station was she able to stagger into a somewhat empty corridor and turn to Maggfrid and whisper, "These are the most *awful* people." But Maggfrid's face was flat with terror. . . .

※　※　※

The noise! Inside the Station there was a constant din of machin-ery. The roar of vast furnaces, the clatter of intricate clockwork. No wonder the Linesmen looked so pale and haunted! No wonder their eyes were so dull! After an hour, the noise was enough to drive Liv to tears—it *did* drive Maggfrid to tears. She was unsure of the long-term psychological effects, but she had no doubt they were unhealthy.

The Linesmen were gray-faced and short. They looked poorly nourished. They surged through the corridors as if they were themselves parts of the great machine, moving to the beat of the omnipresent clocks. Their ugly voices echoed from loudspeakers. They jostled and scowled and swore. They had no manners; they were too busy for manners.

Her golden watch worked erratically. She suspected it was the noise, and the grit in the air, and the constant shaking of the machines. Koenigswald's ornate and fragile workmanship was simply overwhelmed by the Line's monstrous operations. What did it do to the mind? What did it do to the soul?

Everything smelled of coal and oil and smoke. There was nothing natural in the Station, except the occasional rat. It was an ecology of machines. Somewhere at the heart of the structure, the Gloriana Engine lived, and its mechanical dreams shaped the world around it.

✳ ✳ ✳

The signs confused her, but eventually she found her way to the Ticketing Facility, where she was directed into a low-ceilinged dark room, lined with wooden benches and lit by whispering electricity. She sat and waited among her fellow passengers-to-be. An old woman wept silently, surrounded by black leather cases. A young couple clutched each other's hands and stared at the floor. Three fat nuns in the white of their religious order bowed their heads in prayer. Four bored Linesmen stared into space. The tick of a tall clock like a coffin filled the room and suppressed conversation.

An hour passed. Then there was another long and humiliating process of checking and double- and triple-checking of tickets and identification and questioning as to her business. Her questioners never looked her in the eye; they made constant scratching notes on their clipboards and they spoke in a bored contemptuous monotone. They read over and over the promissory note from the Academy that was her payment for the journey. She was not accustomed to being spoken to in such a manner. She swallowed her tongue; she could not stop her cheeks from flushing.

Each one of the men had gray dull eyes. They had a sort of shuddering glowing device like a—Liv wasn't sure what to compare it to—like a *mangle?*—a device with which they somehow reproduced gritty mirror images of all her papers. One copy was placed with some ceremony into a vacuum tube, and with a *thump* it ascended into the upper reaches of the machine. The rest of the copies the Linesmen indifferently stuffed into various cabinets and wire trays. One of them shoved a ticket into her hand and said, "Three days. Come back in three days. Nineteen hours. Don't be late."

✳ ✳ ✳

The Gloriana Hotel occupied six floors of the south face of the Station. From the outside, it was a concrete box. The interior, to Liv's surprise, was luxurious to the point of excess. Every surface groaned with food and drink—every corner was stuffed with sculptures—the walls were lush with paintings and tapestries and bronze and oak. A legion of servants whisked sheets away every hour, it seemed, and electric lights blazed ceaselessly. Humming electric fans cleaned the stench of industry from the air, and warmed and cooled the rooms. The only thing they couldn't keep out was the noise, which had Liv clutching her head and reaching for her sleeping tincture at night.

By day, Liv went out into the town, or at least she tried to; checkpoints turned her back, and half the corridors were sealed behind iron gates. Gloriana was secretive. But she saw enough to know that the Linesmen lived like rats in their tunnels, in squalor and privation, ruled by the clock and the bell and the loudspeaker. The Hotel's luxury was for show, for outsiders, for the travelers who were only passing through. Was it meant to seduce? Liv took it as a threat—it said, *Look how much our factories can make, and how easily. We could buy you. . . .*

"It starts to feel oppressive. Don't you agree?"

The fat white-robed women had turned out to be Abbesses of the White City Virgins. They were surprisingly worldly women. They went back and forth by Line annually on the business of their religion, and were no strangers to Gloriana. Liv met them in the hotel's oak-paneled lobby, under the great swaying chandelier. They leaned in and whispered, "The *smell* . . . wait till you try to get the smell out of your clothes."

"I can live with the smell," Liv said. "The noise is another matter."

"Wait until you see the Engine itself, dear. Try not to be afraid—remember, the journey won't be long. Where are you going?"

"To work in a hospital."

"God's work, my dear. God's work. Where are you going?"

"The House Dolorous, near—"

"Yes." The nuns shook their heads. "It's well known. They say there's a demon there, watching over it. You must be careful to remember that the demons of this land are not God."

"Here it seems they worship their Engines."

"They do."

"I can't say I like it. I feel like they're watching me, Sister. There's always someone looking, wherever I go."

"They are watching. They're always watching, my dear. You just have to get used to that. There's a file on every passenger. Everything in its place. Fortunately, they don't care very much about people. Try to be harmless."

"I'm a doctor. What could be more harmless? But they treat everyone here like criminals. They won't stop asking me where I'm going, what I'm doing, who I am, *why* I'm going, as if every word I say is a lie."

"Well, you're a long way from home. Why *are* you here, Doctor, if you don't mind my asking?"

On top of the usual din of motorcars and cranes, there was the sound of the crowd shouting outside, and the loudspeakers in the corridors were blaring news of a victory against the Gun in the Delta Baronies, and Liv couldn't think. She simply couldn't think of an answer to that question. The fat little nun kept blandly smiling, and Liv said, "Ah—"

The second nun tapped her on the shoulder. "Oh, my dear." The nun pointed out through the hotel's glass doors into the corridor. "Isn't that your big manservant—looks like he's in trouble."

It *was* Maggfrid—he stood outside, surrounded by half a dozen Linesmen, and he was shouting as they shoved at him. Liv ran, heels clicking on the lobby floor. He shouldn't have been out alone. He wasn't able to understand why he had to answer questions or show his papers—and anyway, Liv thought, the Linesmen instinctively disliked him, huge and defective as he was. If it weren't for the noise and her nerves, she wouldn't have let him out of her sight.

Liv threw her weight against the slow-revolving doors. She called out, "Wait—stop, please, wait!" just as Maggfrid swung his fist and knocked a Linesman flying, and suddenly whistles were blowing and more black-uniformed men came running, dozens more.

CHAPTER 11

SUB-INVIGILATOR LOWRY INVESTIGATES: KLOAN, AFTER THE FIRE

Lowry watched the messages come in by telegraph from the undercover personnel in Greenbank, Kloan, Gooseneck, Fairsmith, and World's End. Nothing of interest. He learned the details of every passing merchant or beggar. He learned about the comings and goings of the Hospital's staff, who went out into the world and collected up the wounded, mad, and dying and led them back to the Hospital to rot, as if suffering were a valuable commodity or fuel to be gathered, or as if the Spirit in the Hospital was *hungry*. . . . But nothing useful. No signs of the enemy.

The Forward Camp waited, unsure how to act. Lowry heard rumors that Conductor Banks had written to the Hospital, making a formal demand that the forces of the Line be permitted full access, and had been told in no uncertain terms to drop dead. Lowry presented Banks with a formal memorandum, urging a full siege of the Hospital's perimeter. Sub-Invigilator (First) Morningside opposed the plan, for no good reason Lowry could see other than spite. Banks was uncertain, indecisive. He told Lowry, "Precipitous action is worse than no action at all. Time is on our side. We can't afford errors."

"Sir, the Agents won't wait. They'll—"

"Don't make me report you, Lowry."

Lowry wired off his recommendation to Kingstown. He received no response.

On the off chance, he then wired off to Kingstown and to Angelus, asking for a list of all persons traveling west to Kingstown by
Engine who had indicated on their travel applications an intention
to proceed on to the environs of the Hospital. He was delighted to
receive back, only a few hours later, a message consisting of a long
list of names and destinations: a Mr. Joseph D'Avignon III, finan-
cier, in transit from Harrow Cross, en route to Greenbank on business; a Reverend Ed Kearney, traveling on Smiler missionary
business; a Dr. Lysvet Alverhuysen, in transit from Gloriana . . .

He wired back precise instructions for how each of them should
be handled.

He waited, imagining he might receive a response commending
him for his quick thinking.

After a while, one of the Signalmen—it was Portis, Private (First
Class)—pointed out that the telegraph in Kloan had been silent for
a suspiciously long time.

"Fuck," Lowry said.

✳   ✳   ✳

Within hours, Kloan swarmed with the men of the Line. Two of the
Heavier-Than-Air Vessels circled overheard like vultures, whipping
up Kloan's ashes. Morningside's men secured the area. Lowry
barged unannounced into the Mayor's office, sat down, and said,
"Our condolences on your recent tragedy. We expect your full co-
operation, sir."

✳   ✳   ✳

The Mayor of Kloan was a man of powerful body but only mediocre
intellect. He was also Kloan's main landowner and hotelier, its
lawyer and for most purposes its judge, and its poor excuse for a
preacher.

Kloan's folk were Smilers, one of the most persistent and ubiquitous of various small-town faiths based on self-improvement and
self-confidence and self-help. Lowry regarded it as nonsense at best,
prideful and blasphemous at worst. He could just imagine the big
oaf of a Mayor, every few months, pushed by some shrew wife's
nagging, trying to lead the Self-Improvement Circles, and making a

fool of himself. A strong handshake, a winning smile, could carry a man far out here; in Line country, the Mayor would be considered a simpleton, barely fit to shovel coal.

Lowry didn't have a high opinion of anyone from outside the Line, but his opinion of the Mayor was particularly low.

Lowry said nothing. He just stared at the blustering hick across the desk from him; he let the Mayor say it *again*: "I *said* you don't have no jurisdiction here, Mr. Lowry. We've suffered enough."

Lowry let the idiot start to say it *one more fucking time* then cut him off—leaned forward in his chair, snapped his fingers, and said: "My *bosses* think maybe your nice little town was *harboring* this villain. This man of the Gun. It's how they think, Mr. Mayor; they are *undiscriminating* when it comes to our kind. I told them, surely this man was just passing through; surely not *Kloan*. They're skeptical, Mr. Mayor. But perhaps if you'll let us have a little poke around, we'll find something to settle the issue. Don't you think that would be best?"

The Mayor's blue eyes twitched. He was twice Lowry's size, and thick necked and sunburned where Lowry was round-shouldered, pale, and bespectacled; but he wilted under Lowry's mild gray inexorable gaze.

It wasn't anything special about Lowry that made the Mayor wilt—feeling stirrings of improper pride, Lowry was quick to remind himself of that. It was the weight that was behind Lowry; it was the weight of *destiny* that was behind him.

By small-town western-rim standards, the Mayor was an important man, with powerful friends and solemn treaties and high-stakes business dealings, and all of that would one day soon be swept aside by the annihilating weight that came rushing at Lowry's heels. Everyone in the little room knew it.

The Mayor busied himself shuffling the letter opener around on his desk. In through the open windows came flies, and the stink of burned wood.

On the walls were mounted the heads of various mangy local beasts. Their fur frayed; they attracted the flies. Oh yeah; Lowry knew the Mayor's type. He'd be at home on the range, huntin' an' fishin', half-drunk, lordin' his mastery over the beasts. He was not made for sitting in an office trying to *think*. But there he was, and Lowry's orders left him no room for pity.

"Then we'll proceed, sir, and thank you. And my superiors want me to let you know that they regret, assuming you were *not* consciously harboring this Agent of the Gun, any loss of life and property caused by our personnel in what may have been in some sense our *overzealous* enforcement of our prerogatives. We hope you'll have no reluctance to host our men in the future. And to that end, there will of course be reparations."

The Mayor lifted his head hopefully. "And some of our men will be here shortly to assist you in the administration of the rebuilding efforts and in the disbursement of funds."

The hope was not quite off the Mayor's face. By the *Line*, he was slow! "And generally to put affairs in proper order here," Lowry added.

That did it; the Mayor made a tiny sound like a kicked dog.

Lowry waited for the Mayor to force out a broken noise of thanks. Then he put his broad black hat on his head, gave the Mayor a curt nod, and stepped out into what was left of Kloan, after the fire.

❄   ❄   ❄

Morningside and his men waited outside in the square. Four ranks of five, nice and proper. Kloan was warm and humid, and Morningside's men sweated in their unsuitable black uniforms, but he did not believe in deviations from protocol. Nor did Lowry; nor did their masters.

"All well?" Morningside said.

"All well."

"Took you long enough."

"Sir."

"All right, then." Morningside turned to his men. "You men, tear this pisspot town apart. Every stitch and fiber. Every print. If that stinking jackal pissed on a tree in Kloan, I want it broken down and bagged. You know the drill. Lowry?"

"Sir?"

"Question the witnesses."

✳ ✳ ✳

The girl's name—which Lowry carefully jotted down in block print in his big black ledger—was Susan. The one before that, the boy, had been sullen, hostile; before that, so-called Professor Harry Ransom had thought he was cleverer than Lowry; in both cases, it had been necessary to resort to a small show of violence. Susan was pleasingly quiet and docile. Insofar as Lowry was any judge, she was pretty, though her eyes were raw from tears and her skin was pale. Lowry made her nervous, which pleased him.

"He never spoke to you?"

"No, sir. He never did. He only smiled."

"A big smiler, you say. A happy man."

"Yeah . . ."

"How lucky for him. Your young man, the one who's dead now—oh, stop that, girl—your young man spoke to him?"

"No, sir, he never did."

"He never gave a name?"

"Who?"

"Who do you think, girl? Your stupid young man? Do I look like I'm here for him? No, the *stranger*. The *killer*. The *criminal*."

"Sir—he wasn't—it was like he was—"

"Like he wasn't a human being, is that what you mean to say, girl?"

"Yes, sir—"

"Better. Faster. Stronger. More daring. Never misses a shot. Handsome, was he?"

"I guess—"

"Of course he was. Tall, was he? Afraid of nothing. Worth twenty men like me in a fight, I'll bet. Like something out of a storybook. I bet he just smiled and your knees went weak."

"Sir—"

"All those daring crimes. Bet he's robbed a bank or two, but that hardly counts. Bet he's slipped right across Line lands a dozen times, over the wire, under the fence like a fox. Bet he's blown up a barracks or two or four or five, but that hardly counts, does it, because it's only soldiers. Only ugly bastards like me. Right? Bet you would have run away with him if he'd so much as winked."

"Sir, please—"

"How many men do you think he's murdered? No, never mind that: How many women? Pretty young things like you. Probably quite a few. Statistically speaking. More than none. That doesn't sound so romantic, does it?"

"Sir, I don't—"

"And for what? What's the point? They're losing. They're always losing. They're the past and we're the future. But they have to make it as painful as possible, because they're sick and they're mad. . . . All right, then. Never mind. Stop sniveling. Tell me what he looked like again. From the beginning."

The girl stuttered; Lowry jotted down notes.

A male, a white male, tall, blue eyed, leather skinned; well, that could be half of them. In his fifties at least; probably then an old and hardened one. The Gun took them young, as a general rule—in so far as the Gun *had* rules—and they did not generally live long. An old one was a bad one. Gray hair in a widow's peak; a *smiling* man. Sounded like *Rutherford;* but Rutherford had been sighted far down south, raiding supply lines, poisoning wells. One-Shot Luce? Reported dead.

Lowry sighed and flipped through the Black File, the several volumes of which lay open on the Mayor's desk; the cold eyes of killers and rogues looked up at him from every page. He waved a hand for the girl to keep going.

John Creedmoor? Creedmoor had an eye for the ladies, they said. Oh, Creedmoor was a bad one; his file practically stank of powder and blood. But he'd been reported dead by the Sub-Conductor of the Second Army of the Harrow Cross Engine, one Mr. Gormley. Lowry made a note to telegraph Gormley for details.

"You still here, girl? Right. Did he have a scar? Like so? No?"

No scar; couldn't be Slater, then. Dandy Fanshawe? Not if he was making eyes at the girls. Blood-and-Thunder Boch? Cantor? Red-Heeled Jack? Shit, they put one down and another two sprung up! Straight-Arrow Sussex? Thorpe, who'd brought himself to the attention of the Guns after the horrors of the Battle of Vezelay, horrors to which he, Thorpe, had been a great contributor?—but that was decades ago and Thorpe would be near eighty now, hard as walnut if he wasn't dead. Lowry kept flipping. So many of them. Sometimes he thought the Line's work would never be done.

"Go on, girl. Fuck off out of here. Send the next one in."

❋   ❋   ❋

He drafted a composite description of the killer, for circulation to all patrols and Heavier-Than-Air Vessels. Then he walked outside and leaned against a charred hitching post out front of the Mayor's house and watched Morningside's men work.

He had a headache. The Black File often gave him a headache. It was disordered; uncertain; full of suppositions and half truths and scraps of unverifiable almost-fact; facts that could not be put in their proper place; outright myths and stories and the most unpleasant sort of fantasies. The Agents of the Gun poisoned everything they touched, even unto the deepest recesses of the Line's most TOP SECRET files.

The boardinghouse was a charred ruin. So were several surrounding buildings. Most of the walls were gone, leaving only odd-angled and crumbling beams and struts, and Lowry could see Morningside's men at work in what had been bedrooms and bathrooms. It was eerie. Some Agents, the Black File speculated, could see through walls, which made them damnably hard to kill. . . .

Morningside's men carried wheelbarrowfuls of wreckage out of the ruins and laid them out on the street for analysis. Scraps of furniture, brass fittings, antlers, some charred and twisted painting frames. Kloan's residents stood by glumly at the perimeter of the activity. Professor Harry Ransom crept away down Main Street with a battered suitcase in either hand and a bloody nose, and Lowry couldn't be bothered to stop him.

Poor old Kloan, Lowry thought; it wasn't their fault, really. He'd exhausted his contempt on the Mayor, and now he allowed himself a moment of pity.

But what had to happen, had to happen.

He breathed deeply. He got a mouthful of ash and coughed, and it turned quickly into the bent-double coal-dust compulsive hacking of a Linesman born and bred. Some of Morningside's men looked up, shovels in hand, and glanced with concern at the Sub-Invigilator.

Lowry sent them back to work with a bad-tempered wave of his hand.

One of Morningside's men, deep in the ruins of the boardinghouse, called out, "It's here! I've found the telegraph, sir! It's badly—"

Morningside entered the ruins, clambering over heaps of ash and fallen timbers. "Right. Let's see. Let's see. Any last mess—?"

He stumbled and leaned against a charred beam of wood, which toppled under his weight. Wedged in the join of the beam had been a black briefcase, which had apparently dropped during the fire through a vanished upper floor, and which now fell the remainder of the way to earth. As it fell, it clicked softly open and its contents, which were the dead Signalmen's last weapons, tumbled out. As it happened, only one of them went off.

Moments before Sub-Invigilator (First) Morningside was wiped clean by waves of annihilating noise, Lowry had the presence of mind not only to dash for a safe clearance but also to throw his whole head into a nearby water trough, hands tight over his ears. He escaped with only a brief period of unconsciousness, from which he woke, somewhat disoriented, to learn that he had been promoted again.

CHAPTER 12

The Passage

The trek from the mountains through Burren Hill and west to Conant and Gloriana had taken weeks, and it had taken its toll on
Liv's body. She was sunburned, her hair was stiff and pale, and entirely unfamiliar muscles ached. Her standards of hygiene had been
somewhat relaxed. She had developed new nightmares. She had
seen violence. She had learned to ride and shout and haggle.

And all that journey was only the tiniest fraction of the distance
from Gloriana to the House Dolorous—a distance that the Engine
crossed in days. The Line reduced the world to nothing.

※　※　※

The cabin was small and dark. Outside in the Station's grand Concourse, the high steel arches threw angular shadows, and the sober
men of the Line went back and forth in shadow, in smoke, hard at
work, so tiny in their dark suits. There was so much empty inhuman space in the Line's places; dark spaces filled only with the
echoes of the machines.

Maggfrid heaved her bags into the luggage rack. He was clumsy.
The Linesmen had beaten him badly, and besides, the Engine made
him nervous. It made Liv nervous, too. They were inside the monster's belly. An ugly fairy tale!

She patted Maggfrid on his broad back and told him it was all right. The big childlike man whined gratefully. She sat down and folded her skirts, and gestured for him to sit down opposite her. She pulled down the blinds and breathed a sigh of relief.

The cabin was cold as a big black icebox, and the leather of the seats creaked stiffly. The Engines of the Line were always cold, she'd heard. She wrapped her shawl around her shoulders and shivered. She tugged on a thin silver chain by the window, and the cabin filled with cold electric light. She took out her journal and began writing. "Don't stare, Maggfrid. Why don't you sleep now? We have a long journey."

✳   ✳   ✳

She was surprised, after the altercation at the hotel, that they had not been thrown in some cramped and stinking Line jail to rot. Maggfrid had broken one Linesman's nose and hurled another bodily into a heap of rusting junk. It had taken seven men to bring him down. They'd held him and kicked him while she stood by, pleading. She'd tried to identify the officer in charge, but all Linesmen looked much the same to her. When they dragged Maggfrid away, handcuffed, she followed, and was not especially surprised when they decided to handcuff her, too, or when they sat her in a tiny claustrophobic concrete-walled cubicle and shone a light in her eyes and demanded that she explain—again!—who she was.

"My friend is sick," she explained. "Defective, you might say. He didn't understand your questions. He meant no harm. I can pay. . . ."

They confiscated her property, including the golden watch, and so she had no idea how long she sat in the cubicle.

They bustled in and made her sign more forms. Then they left her alone again.

She wondered if the Linesmen were discussing her case. Perhaps they were consulting the Engine itself about her. Perhaps they had simply filed away her papers and forgotten about her. She had no way of knowing.

She wondered if they were watching her.

She wondered if they would let her write a letter to the Academy. She doubted it. In any case, something in her rebelled against the notion of asking for aid; she had come here alone, and she would fight her own battles. Wasn't that, in fact, precisely why she had come here?

The cubicle was windowless, and the Linesmen did not feed her. Minutes became hours. The Engine would leave without her—perhaps it already had. She became light-headed, and then became angry. How dare they—how *dare* they? The Linesmen were ugly, ill-mannered, and vile, and their tin gods absurd. She stood suddenly and tried the door. It was locked, of course. The entire Station was like a great locked gate of iron—an ogre's castle standing across the road. How *dare* they bar her way into the West?

Her anger was both quite genuine and carefully calculated. *If I am to argue with these people, if I am to free Maggfrid and win my way past this place, I must be angry.* The proper manner when dealing with Linesmen, she surmised, was a haughty imperiousness. Linesmen were naturally servile and cringing. She was significantly taller than the average Linesman and markedly healthier. This was the first great challenge that had been set in her path, and she had no intention of failing it! She prepared herself, breathed deeply, and reached out to strike loudly upon the door.

She was quite astonished when the door clanged open and yet another Linesman, one of the pale stunted anonymous mass, reached in, tossed her watch back at her, and said, "Dr. Alverhuysen? Go on. No charges. On your way."

"How *d*—I, ah, hah." She collected herself. "I shall not leave without my friend."

✳ ✳ ✳

They let her go. She didn't dare ask *why*. Perhaps something was watching over her! They gave Maggfrid back to her as if he were just another one of her possessions. She filled out forms for him. "Sign here, ma'am, and here. Thanks. On you go." It was too easy; she was relieved and disappointed. *Not yet,* she thought. *The challenge will come, but not today.*

Then she hurried through the corridors, because she saw by her watch that she had been nearly a day in the cubicle and it was evening, and the Engine had returned, and was due to leave again. She could feel it in the walls of the Station: a sense of weight and expectancy. She ran across the Concourse and Maggfrid limped, laden with her bags, as whistles blew and gears ground and forces gathered, and so she caught only the briefest glimpse of the Engine before she boarded. And perhaps that was fortunate, too.

* * *

A note taped to the window of the cabin said REMAIN SEATED WHILE THE ENGINE IS STILL in an anxiety-inducing red typeface. It was, Liv assumed, a matter of respect for the occasion, like removing one's hat in church. She remained seated.

The seats were made of some deep black substance that resembled leather, and had, under the electric lights, an unpleasant oil-slick shine. They were made for persons shorter than her. Maggfrid had to squeeze sideways, with his legs under his chin, and looked the picture of misery.

The Engine sat still on the Concourse for what felt like hours. Liv sat folding and unfolding her hands.

"Don't worry, Maggfrid. It won't be so bad. Thousands or tens of thousands of quite ordinary people do this quite regularly."

He looked unconvinced.

The Engine wasn't *idle,* Liv thought, but coiled and ready to spring, a huge and oppressive potentiality; she sat tensed and ready for a sudden shock that would throw her from her seat. Pressure built up below her feet. There was a distant rattle and hiss, a constant low hammer-chatter, as the thing gathered its strength.

"Wait there, Maggfrid. Everything will be all right."

She nervously slid back the door; it resisted her. She stepped out into the narrow corridor that was the Engine's central artery. The door snapped shut behind her and she heard Maggfrid moan, but before she could go back to him, she was knocked nearly off her feet by a passing Linesman, and then another passing urgently the other way knocked into her and spun her around. She heard muttered fragments of conversation that meant nothing to her— *Ravenbrook. Refueling. Lowry. Torque. Diligence.* For a moment she feared she might be trampled as two more men came jogging side by side toward her, but they parted around her at the last possible instant, snarling contemptuously under their breath.

"Excuse me," she said. "Excuse me. Sir—excuse me. Please. When do we leave?"

The Linesman sidestepped left then right to avoid her, but she wouldn't let him. He glanced up at her and sighed.

"Sir. When—?"

"Twenty-four minutes ago. Go back where you belong."

His shoulder knocked her aside as he went past.

She stumbled back into her seat. Suddenly the floor beneath her seemed unsteady. She opened the blind a crack: the hills outside were a dizzying liquid blur of speed.

Oh—is that how they see us? Is that how they see our world?

Behind as the tracks arced inward and northwest, the Station obtruded onto the edge of her vision. It gathered distance like shadows but remained vast. Vast and hunched and complex and smoky, like a combustion engine or electric motor swollen to extraordinary size; as if the Station reflected its contents, and the world the Engines were making reflected their Stations; as if size and distance were nothing to the Engines.

The world was drowned by a wave of the gritty black smoke that poured from the mouth of the Engine carrying her.

Their boiling black blood, their breath!

Coal-dust fragments spun in the haze and reflected the electric light from her window. Liv let the blind fall, and she tried to busy herself in her puzzle again.

❊　❊　❊

Maggfrid was now thoroughly panicked. The Engine plainly terrified him. He darted his eyes from side to side as if expecting attack. Liv cursed herself for leaving him—not to mention for bringing him in the first place.

"Maggfrid. Come on, Maggfrid. Shall we play a game?"

She no longer studied his condition—she had accepted long ago it was congenital, and incurable. But he still enjoyed the motions of her analysis—the cards, the questions. It calmed him. He answered her questions with great seriousness, as if he were engaged in a project of enormous importance.

Why not? It would pass the time.

Maggfrid got the small medicine bag down from the compartment. Under the calipers and the various vials of brightly colored serums and powders were the cards.

The apparatus she used for the electric-cure was in the big black case overhead, safely cushioned in rags and old curtains. The applicator needles and plates, and the tongue depressors without which it was not safe, were all in the smaller bag.

She shuffled the cards and took the first one off the top of the pile. It was made of stiff wheat-yellow stock; it was printed with a complex dark pattern. "What do you see, Maggfrid?"

". . . a dog."

"Very good. And this?"

". . . a house."

"Excellent. Do you remember the name of the town we left this morning?"

". . ."

"It was called *Gloriana,* Maggfrid. But never mind. No, don't look so sad. Let's look at this card again, shall we?"

Time passed and outside the cabin the day wore into evening, though the monotone electric light inside never changed. At last Maggfrid slept, tired by his efforts. She tapped out three green smoky drops of her nerve tonic into a glass of water and soon she joined him, her bright hair lolling on the black of the seat back.

✳   ✳   ✳

The Engine rushed endlessly on, never stopping, seemingly never swerving—though in fact, Liv knew from the maps she'd studied that it was curving in a wide arc south and southwest through the lands of the Line and then west out into the wild lands. Green hills gave way to sage and rust red. If the stories were true, then ahead of them in the dark untamed hills of the night waited Agents of the Gun. Liv wasn't sure whether to fear them or not—she could hardly believe that any man could assault or even slow that dreadful Engine on which she traveled, no matter what sort of spirit or demon they'd trucked with.

The Engine obliterated space, blurred solid earth into a thin unearthly haze, through which it passed with hideous sea-monster grace.

The noise waxed and waned but never ceased. The chatter of pistons and hammers; low and sad moaning of steel under stress; the grinding of gears and the hiss of steam. The Song of the Line. What were they singing to each other? Orders and plans and schemes, no doubt. They planned in terms of leagues and multitudes. They sang to each other all across the continent.

Periodically Liv checked her golden pocket watch. It didn't work; it had stopped entirely soon after she boarded the carriage. She had no good idea how much time was passing.

※　※　※

She opened the blind and saw that they were passing through the foothills of gray and white-capped and distant mountains. They rushed through dark pines. She closed the blind. When she opened it again—an hour, two hours later?—the mountains were gone.

※　※　※

Liv wrote in her journal. Maggfrid closed his eyes and listened; he seemed to find the scratching of her pen soothing. He had a touching faith in science. His brow twitched.

I am aboard the Gloriana Engine, in Compartment 317C. Sometimes I am too excited to read, and at other times I am dreadfully bored. None of the other passengers come to talk to me. There is none of the camaraderie of a sea voyage, or of Mr. Bond's caravan. And I dare not intrude on them. It would seem sacrilegious, somehow.

The food is quite appalling. It tastes of ash and coal and dust.

What did the Engine look like? I saw it on the Concourse, but only in shadow, and besides, the memory fades. I cannot quite express it in words. I might try to sketch its machinery, as I have sketched in these pages the neuron, the cerebellum, the pituitary gland—but to do so, I think, would miss its essence. I can say that it was long, very long; it was four, five men tall. It was jet-black and it smoked. It was plated with extrusions and grilles and thorns of iron that might have been armor, and might have been machinery, but which in any case made it rough, uneven, asymmetrical, and hideous. It reminded me somewhat of the ink-blot tests devised by Professor Kohler. It reminded me also somewhat of storm-clouds. From the complex cowling at the very front of the engine two lights shone through the gloom and the smoke of the Concourse. The light was the gray of moths' wings or dirty old ice.

The carriages behind the Engine stretched out into the distance until the smoke and shadows of the Concourse swallowed them. I could not count them. A mile or more of carriages. Each journey of this thing carries the population of the town of Lodenstein back and forth across the continent. This world is mobile.

And the Gloriana Engine itself is more than a century old. It features prominently in a number of ancient battles recounted in Mr. General Enver's Child's History. *Its physical form was destroyed once, by the forces of its adversary, in 1800 or thereabouts. It returned. The black coal dust that gathers in its upswept corners, that I breathe in as I write this, is ancient dust. For all that time this machine has run in its tracks, back and forth, across the countless miles. What is my own journey in comparison?*

The lights went dim. The seats stretched with a groan of rust out into bunks. Liv closed her journal. The lights went out. In the darkness the Linesmen's black boots clanked through the corridors. So many of them! And all so much the same. Massing for war, or business, or some mysterious and complex project. She'd overheard them talking in the corridor outside; many of them would be disgorged at Ravenbrook, birthed back into the solid and sunlit world . . .

❋   ❋   ❋

Morning light streamed in through the cracks of the blind, making visible all the cabin's dust and dark slow-settling soot.

Liv pulled back the blind. They were racing across white salt flats that gleamed like a mirror; running like a black line across new paper; smoke tumbling from them like spilled ink.

Mountains in the distance again. So much *distance*. Habitations and cultivation became fewer and fewer as they went west—the world becoming crude, wild, unnamed, only half-made—closer and closer to that nameless Western Sea where, they said, unformed land became fog and wild water and fire and night. . . .

The world blurred, and a sudden and surprising mood of exhilaration seized her. Koenigswald and the Academy and her old life were ten thousand miles behind her, and the world was a blur, the world was a dream, the world was unmade. Anything was possible. Wasn't this what she'd come here for? She could hardly wait to step out into the world again and begin to remake it.

She noticed a shanty town out on the salt-flats. Little black dots of shacks—were those laborers bent double in salt-traps?—rushed up close and vanished at once behind. Perhaps the Engine had obliterated it with the boom of its passing, Liv thought. She let the blind fall again; the glare hurt her eyes. She blinked in the dark of the cabin, but the bright crude shapes of the world outside were burned into her vision.

Within the hour they'd left the salt-flats far behind.

✳ ✳ ✳

It never stopped; there was never a chance to deboard and breathe fresh air. Liv's mood of exhilaration came and went. She stepped out into the corridor sometimes, but the Linesmen who worked there looked at her with such annoyance and distaste that she soon retreated. Her legs and her back were stiff with disuse. No wonder the men of the Line were so stooped.

On the third night, someone came to her—she woke to a bright light in her face. She'd been dreaming she was before a blazing fire. She blinked slowly and in the glare, she could make out the vague shape of a man in black. He sat on the bunk opposite, leaning forward. He wore round reflective spectacles, a broad-brimmed hat; all else was dark. Maggfrid was asleep, slumped in shadows, and Liv herself was drowsy. She noted dispassionately a sharp glittering needle entering her forearm.

"Mrs. Alverhuysen? *Sorry* to bother you, ma'am."

He had an ugly hoarse voice—a Linesman's voice. Her head

lolled and his rough hand reached out to her cheek to steady her, to fix her gaze in the harsh light. He had very dirty nails.

"Steady on there, ma'am. The Line's got questions for you. About your *destination*. I hear you're a doctor. I hear you're headed out west."

Her whole arm was numb, and very cold. She found herself nodding, without intending to. A small part of her mind wondered with dispassionate curiosity what they'd drugged her with.

He spoke very slowly and patiently. It rather reminded Liv of the way she sometimes spoke to Maggfrid, and she disliked it, but she seemed unable to object.

"You're going to Kingstown. Then where?"

Her own words were a distant buzz in her ears. She wasn't sure what she'd said, but apparently it pleased him, because he favored her with an unappealing smirk.

"Good, good. Thought you might be."

He blurred. "Stay awake now, ma'am."

He reached out and pinched her arm.

"Dangerous country. Are you going there alone?"

She turned her head to Maggfrid, who remained slumped immobile on his seat. She realized that she would not have woken him to face this horrible apparition with her, even had she been able to call out, which it appeared she was not.

"Right. Him. The defective. Yes, he's on the manifest, we know. Disgusting. Anyone else? Anyone worse? Meeting anyone? A nice honest naïve young woman like you, a visitor to this part of the world, some handsome fellow talks you into helping him with something that doesn't sound quite right . . . Do you know what I'm talking about? No? No. All right."

Her head lolled. He snapped his fingers under her nose.

"Your purpose at this Hospital? Any particular patients in mind? Any . . ."

She drifted again. He slapped her and answers tumbled out. Then it seemed some more time had passed and he was hunched over, rummaging through her possessions. He sniffed at her flask of nerve tonic and snorted contemptuously.

"Opium-fiend, then. Unreliable. Oh, well."

He left dirty thumbprints on her journals and creased the pages of the *Child's History*. He lifted up her golden watch to the light and rattled it.

"Huh. All right."

Other men entered. Two or more—she couldn't count. Gray, black, indistinct. They opened briefcases and removed complicated metal instruments, pincers, spools of copper wire.

"She's watching us."

"Right. Sleep, Doctor."

Someone's hand reached out and pushed down on the plunger of the needle in her forearm. Something cold and annihilating rushed into the line of her veins, and she was flushed out of the light into silence and darkness. The black thundering singing monster these ugly men served carried them all through the night and along the silver web of the Line and across the dark continent into the West. . . .

✳ ✳ ✳

In the morning, Liv remembered almost none of it. She had a vague recollection that some passing Linesmen had disrupted her sleep and been intolerably rude. She put her stiffness down to her prolonged immobility on hard seats. Imperiously she *insisted* on walking up and down the corridors to restore the healthy flow of blood and humors; the Linesmen grumbled but tolerated it.

✳ ✳ ✳

They changed Engines at Harrow Cross. Three days after that, they arrived at Kingstown Station, the Line's westernmost terminus. After that it was horse-drawn wagons on roads then dust trails, then mules, then finally she followed her local guide on foot. Liv's watch started working again, and so she knew *exactly* how slowly they crawled over those broken red hills. Westward; out to the edge of things. There were ravens in the sky, and things stranger than ravens; in the distance she saw the heavy iron aircraft of the Line, droning and smoking, hovering like hawks. What were they hunting?

They descended a narrow slippery trail into a shadowed canyon, wide as the broad flat river that flowed beside the Academy, deeper than—well, certainly deeper than anything Liv could think to compare it to!

As they passed into the shadow of the canyon, there was a dark smoke-cloud on the horizon and she thought of war. Was the House safe? Of course not. Of course not! She had not come here to be safe. She ached, and she was tired, and she felt purposeful and strong.

※　※　※

Her guide pointed. "There."

There was a fence strung from side to side of the canyon, and a gatehouse, and behind it loomed what could only be the House. It hid in the shadow of the canyon's walls. It was a sprawling five-story mansion, painted in fading eggshell blue, with accents of a sickly white. Broad eaves like white eyebrows on an old man's face stretched from side to side. Its upper windows gleamed bright, its lower windows were shadowed. Beneath it there were gardens, out-houses, and distant matchstick men performing what looked like healthy exercises.

There were guards at the gate, dressed in white. They straightened up as Liv approached, and reached for their rifles.

There was an echo of footsteps down the ravine. She looked over her shoulder; behind her a little group was approaching on foot. Some of them were dressed in rags, wild-bearded and blank-eyed. A handsome gray-haired gentleman led them. More visitors to the House? Patients, possibly. They looked like they'd had a hard journey. She wondered what their story was; she doubted it was as strange as hers!

CHAPTER 13

CREEDMOOR AT WORK

It had taken Creedmoor some twenty-four hours—after departing Kloan, in embarrassing circumstances—to find a suitable group to which to attach himself. It was a procession of the walking wounded, the mad, the blind, and the lame—mostly the mad. They were being escorted through the deep ravines by a weather-beaten man in a dusty white jacket, with a rifle on his back, who held the rope to which they were all bound wrapped loosely round his right arm. They were *en route* to the House Dolorous, and doctors, and the healing balm of the hospital's mysterious *Spirit*—about which Creedmoor remained skeptical.

First he caught their scent. The mad were not great observers of hygiene. He stalked them. He crouched behind a red rock at the top of the valley and watched them shuffle along the trail below.

✻ ✻ ✻

—Damn it, will you look at these people. Will you just look at them. Did you ever see such a slack-jawed and sorry bunch, shuffling along in the dust, in the heat? Moaning and mumbling: oh, look at their faces! This is no way to live. Oh, will you look at them. I wonder what side they fought for, before the madness took them. Maybe no side at all. Innocents, caught in the deathly machine. What a terrible bill of indictment against us all these are; each one a count we can-not answer.

—They fell because they are weak, Creedmoor. Now they are only *things* to be *used*.

—Well, that's one point of view, certainly.

That sort of insincere agreeability irritated Marmion intensely, which was one of the few pleasures available to Creedmoor when he was at work.

Another was tobacco. He hunkered down behind the red rock, opened his tarnished tobacco case, and rolled a cigarette. He struck the match behind the rock so that the little procession below wouldn't see the flash, cupping it in his dirty hands though there was no wind. He tossed the dead match into a clump of thorny weed.

—Oh, but will you just look at this one, in the front. Look at his flat cow eyes and his inbred's weak chin and snaggled teeth and the way he shuffles. Look at the daft old bitch behind him with the hair like tumbleweed and the rags and the withered old gums in her mouth that's sucking the air, look, like it's sugar-candy. Fuck, will you look at the one with the *smile*. Look at these addled and ruined shufflers. This is so very sad.

—Never mind the madmen. Keep an eye on their leader. He is armed and watchful.

—Oh, sure, and he's the worst of the sorry bunch. Look how proud he looks! Do-gooder. Who does he think he's helping, run-ning these people all over the backcountry, holding their hands and wiping their asses? Taking them to rot in hospital? No one will thank him. Kinder to kill them.

—For now we need them. Later you may kill them.

—I was joking, my bloodthirsty humorless friend.

—Were you? Good. We like our servants joyful.

Creedmoor smoked. The tobacco was stale and unpleasant. In the ravine below, one of the mad folk had fallen over, pulling his neighbors with him, and their white-jacketed leader was trying to help them to their feet.

—An ugly business. No words can hide that.

—But we do not like self-pity, Creedmoor. Go to work.

—One moment.

—Go to work.

—One moment.

—You are disrespectful, Creedmoor.

—Do you know, my friend? They say that the Engines of our great enemy communicate with *their* servants only at a distance, by telegraph wire, by electric cable. *Their* Song is too terrible for any man to hear nakedly, not without ending up like these poor bastards down below. *You* natter and nag in my ear like a badly chosen wife. What does it say about man, do you think, that we have such an easy rapport with your murderous kind? Nothing good. What does it say about *you*?

It did not respond. It was sulking, he thought; he'd offended it. They had a remarkable capacity for sulking. Their pride was easily stung. Sometimes Creedmoor imagined the dreadful and unearthly Lodge of the Guns as a windowless Old Folks Home where bitter old men sat in the dark and sucked their gums and moaned endlessly about forgotten wrongs, meaningless slights, ancient pointless feuds and grudges.

His master sulked and throbbed darkly until the little hiding place behind the red rock grew uncomfortable and close. There was a stink of sulfur. It was almost audible, like the place swarmed with wasps. And besides, the shuffling party on the dust road below was moving along, out of sight. He took a last bitter drag on his cigarette, put his hat back on his head, patted the pockets of his long gray coat, and stepped out into the glare of the red hills.

✳　✳　✳

"Good day to you, sir. Now, now, put that rifle down! I'm no bandit; would a bandit walk out like this, alone, in the midday sun, no gun in his hand? Well, on further consideration, I guess a bandit *would* try to stop you here, at this narrow ravine, among these occluding rocks, and so I applaud your caution. These are bad times. I suppose the evidence on both sides of the question is finely balanced. I must throw myself on your mercy, on your trust in human nature. I don't believe a man such as yourself will shoot me. I'll wait here while you make your mind up."

The walking wounded shuffled like nervous cattle. A long rope bound them all together by the ankle. The rope was looped loosely round their leader's arm, in which the rifle sat.

He was a short man, balding, in dusty whites. His weathered face was full of suspicion. He held his rifle badly.

The rifle was a cheaply made thing. Nothing significant inhabited it.

Three black birds went overhead in the silence. Three ugly black crows in a ragged flock, framed in the sky for a long hot moment. They passed behind the red rock.

—Do crows *hunt*, do you think? In packs, like men or dogs? They have a predatory aspect, would you not say? Would you acknowledge them as brothers, my friend?

—Keep an eye on this man, Creedmoor. Be ready to kill if he blinks.

One of the madmen broke the silence with crying. Great snotty echoing sobs into his tangled hobo beard. The leader of the troupe of fools lowered his rifle and turned back to the sobbing man, said gently, "Quiet, William. This man means us no harm." He turned again to the stranger before him and shrugged. "What do you want, mister? We are on medical business. These are wounded and shell-shocked men and women, from Homburg and Monkton. I'm bringing them to the House Dolorous for healing. We are an *ambulance,* you see? The walking wounded. We are neutral, and harmless. We have no money."

"Who does? Who does, I ask you, these days?"

"That's a fine gun at your side, mister, for a poor man."

"This?" Creedmoor moved his hand slowly to his side. He took the Gun, not by its dark grip, but by the leather of the holster. With the other hand, he unbuckled his belt. He stooped to toss the twisting thing in the dirt. The silver and gold of the Gun's inlays and the polished darkwood of its grip gleamed in the sun.

Creedmoor kicked it aside into the rocks. Marmion's voice screamed in his brain, scratched at his skull. He gritted his teeth and ignored it. In the glare and the flies, he hoped no one would notice.

—We must all bear some indignity for the cause. Shut up, will you? Shut up.

The fools' leader softened. He put down his rifle, leaning it against

a rock. "Quiet, William," he repeated, and the fool stopped his sobbing, looking expectantly at the stranger.

—Bright empty eyes like a bird. Will you look at him. Will you
look at what's been done.

—How dare you.

—Will you stop your whining, please?

Creedmoor extended his open hands and smiled. "That weapon's
a mere precaution, sir. There are bandits in these hills, though I'm
not one, and perhaps Agents of the Gun, I've heard, about their masters' wicked business; and every traveler has warned me that the
Hillfolk in these parts are savage."

"The Folk round here keep to themselves, stranger; we've seen to
that. Agents have no business out here. We are neutral. It's plain
regular bandits that concern me."

—See, my friend? He's talking to me, man to man. This is how
things are done among decent men. This can be done cleanly. No
need to spook these cattle.

"Let's introduce ourselves. I am widely traveled and well let-
tered; you, if I am not mistaken, are a man of medicine. We are both
civilized men; let's introduce ourselves accordingly. My name is
John. You are?"

South-by-southwest, echoing over the hills, the distant *tump-tump*
of an ornithopter. In the hot and torpid air, sound traveled strangely;
the noise echoed close round Creedmoor's head. *Tump-tump-tump*
in his ears. All those present looked up; Creedmoor's eyes alone
could pick out the smudge of coal smoke on the horizon. Marmion's
voice screamed in Creedmoor's mind,

—The Line! Do you hear? The Line! They are close on our heels!
Take me up again! Be ready! Be ready!

—*Please* shut up. *I* am in control here.

The fools' leader shook his head as if to clear the last echoes of
the distant machine from the air. He held his hand over his brow,
squinting in the sun and flies. He came forward, his hand extended
in greeting, and he named himself: Elgin. Creedmoor smiled and
didn't listen. The name was not important. The man was not important. Creedmoor's plan required the fools, not their leader. All
Creedmoor needed was for the man to come closer, out of sight of

his charges. Creedmoor said, "I've come from Greenbank, Elgin. You're bound for the hospital? I know the road ahead of you, and you know the road before me. Join me under the shade of this rock here. We can share our stories."

Under the shadow of the rock they could not be seen. The rest was quick work.

※　※　※

The madmen had wandered a little, but their ankles were roped. Creedmoor rounded them up.

The one with the bright eyes, the one who'd been sobbing into his scraggly beard, the one who went by William, was the least damaged of the procession; his faculties were those of a slow but eager child, and he would not shut up. Would not stop asking where they were going. Would not stop asking what had happened to Mr. Elgin.

—Why doesn't he just forget him? Has he no sense?

—No, Creedmoor, obviously he does not.

The victims of the Line's mind-bombs weren't talkative, in Creedmoor's experience. Perhaps William had only just barely been caught in the blast. Perhaps he was a medical miracle! That'd be very exciting for the doctors at the Doll House, but for now it was a damn nuisance.

Creedmoor looked him very firmly in the eye—which was rheumy and muddled. "Easy, William, easy. Mr. Elgin had to hand you over to me. He was very sick, do you not recall? Do you not recall it, William? How he stepped on that snake? How his foot swelled up and went black? Yes, William, that's right, well you may go white. There are *snakes* in these hills. Rattlers, William. William, my friend, stop shuffling: you can stand your left foot on your right, or your right foot on your left, but not both at once. Gravity won't stand for it. You must choose a foot to put on the earth and take your chances."

—They believe everything you tell them.

Something like curiosity crept into his master's metallic voice, something like amusement. Human weakness was a mystery to them. He answered it:

—Yes.

And he touched William's shaking shoulder. "The poor man had to go back to town, do you not recall? You were lucky I found you. Could you have drawn the poison from his wound, William? Could you lead these folk? Could you lead them through these hills, these ravines and ditches and yawning canyons, with the snakes, with the big metal birds of the Line in the air? Could you, William? Now don't cry. *I'm* here to lead you."

The dull murky eyes. The ruined architecture of the face still had some grandeur. A human face is a beautiful habitation, Creedmoor thought, even when left empty. Solid bone structure. Now a yellow mucus curdled in the pools of William's eyes and in his stringy beard. Flies dabbled in it and he had no sense to swat them away. He stank; he'd pissed himself. They all had.

The mind-bombs that had done this to them were not the cruelest of the Line's weapons. Not nearly the cruelest thing in this war; Creedmoor personally had done crueler things, and would again. Still; still. There was a special horror to madness.

The terrible thundering noise of the Line's mind-bombs bred terror first, then despair, then the mind cracked and what was left was not really human anymore. Of this little group, childlike William was the luckiest. Others were mute, more puppets than men. One old woman at the back was like an ill-natured organ-grinder's ape. None could string together a sensible adult's sentence. Something about those husks made Creedmoor sentimental, which made him angry. William's eyes were wandering up and down Creedmoor's face, inspecting it with eager confusion, as if trying to read something in its lines and scars. Creedmoor did not know what to feel. The voice spoke in his mind with the finality of a hammer falling:

—You are wasting time.

—You're the boss. All right. All right.

"All of you ladies and gentlemen," he called out, "take up your ropes and your bonds. Let us begin again. I know, I know, it's hot and we're tired and there are snakes, oh there are *snakes* if we step out of line, do not forget it. But there's rest at the end of it. The House Dolorous awaits us. One foot in front of the other, ladies and gents."

Through the rocks and the ravine. This land was broken badly, like a china plate hurled by a *very* angry woman. From cool shadow to the hot sun and back again, again and again. Down in the ravines, the air was still and hot and fly-swarmed. Up above the hot dusty winds fluted the stone into sharp curves—the skyline was quite mad as the red sun set. Creedmoor kept the rope coiled around his left hand and walked in front. He tugged on it—sharply but not unkindly—when his charges showed signs of wandering off. But they balked and went slowly. He didn't have the knack of it. He was no leader of men, or even of those half men. They were still walking by nightfall.

※　※　※

The ravines were lousy with caves and they camped in one of them. There were yellow old bones piled at the back of it, but whatever wolves or bears or worse had dwelled there were years gone. Faded blue paintings on the rocks—deer, bears, men, the sun, goats, serpents, manticorae—indicated that Hillfolk had once inhabited it, but they seemed to have moved on long ago.

There were scraggly trees and brush out the front—not that that would hide Creedmoor's sad little party from the forces of the Line. The forces of the Line would not come poking along down the ravine, craning their heads into caves and beating away brush: they would just flood the whole damn thing with choking-gas if they had so much as a notion where Creedmoor was, or send echoes of that terrible annihilating Engine noise.

Creedmoor tied the fools' rope round a needle of rock at the back of the cave and left them in the darkness. He sat himself against a flat stone at the cave's mouth, where the air was clear. He unbuckled his belt and placed Marmion on the ground beside him. He let his charges sob at the darkness until the echoes got too loud. When one of the boys got overexcited and started grabbing at the women, Creedmoor banged his fist on the rock and shouted until they cried, but at least they were quiet again. Soon after, they went to sleep.

Creedmoor didn't sleep. Marmion's voice in his head saw to that. Creedmoor watched the stars and listened to the scrape and shiver of

Marmion's voice. The Guns talked war in their Lodge. Distant echoes of that talk reached Creedmoor's ears—incomprehensible fragments—a meaningless murmur of death, defeat, revenge, glory. All across the continent, the echoes of Gun-shot carried the message. The constant distant sounding of Guns was a code, a hideous song. It had thrilled him once, years ago.

—Hudnall is dead.

—Hudnall. Which one?

—The elder. A phalanx of the Line cornered him in Lannon Town not two hours ago. They sealed the main street from both ends and closed in and ground him up.

—Poor old Hudnall.

—He acquitted himself well enough.

—Ah well, that's all right, then. Who will take his place?

—Someone will come forward.

—We always do, do we not?

Creedmoor removed a slim novel from his pack and opened its scuffed pages to the mark. The beautiful red-haired peasant girl from the green and mists of the old country was facing for the first time her lover, fresh back from the war and wounded, though handsome.

Creedmoor had a vague sort of taste for romantic novels.

He read it by scant starlight. The night-sight was one of the Guns' gifts to him.

—Pick-Up Wells has died.

—Who?

—Young. A recent recruit. You do not know him and now you will not.

—A bad night for the noble cause, to be sure.

—He succeeded in destroying the dam at Redbill Gorge before he died, but he stupidly let himself be caught in the flood.

—Ah. Good news and bad. The world is most wonderfully full of ups and downs, would you not say?

❋   ❋   ❋

William came and sat by him like an eager dog. Creedmoor ignored him for as long as he could.

"Mr. Creedmoor?"

"You should sleep, William."

"Where are we going, Mr. Creedmoor?"

"To the House Dolorous. A romantic name! I believe it comes from a song. I'll spare you my singing voice. To the Doll House, William. To a house of healing, where perhaps one day you, too, may be healed and whole."

"Why are you taking us there, Mr. Creedmoor?"

"Because I am a kindly shepherd, William. Because I cannot bear to let injustice stand or suffering be."

"You feel scared. Is someone chasing after you?"

"Could well be, William."

"Is there someone talking to you?"

"Don't we all hear the voice of conscience, William?"

※　※　※

He led them shuffling through the hills and westward. After five days' trek, they found a well-trodden trail that switchbacked laboriously down into a canyon of red rock. The canyon was deep as the ocean floor, wide and flat as the widest triumphal avenue in Jasper City or Morgan. It wound and curved, following the course of some long-dead waterway. The rock walls were rough, striated, and marked with signs of Folk carving and painting that Creedmoor didn't have time to inspect, because his master said:

—Faster. Quick. We hear the Enemy's wings overhead.

In the afternoon, they came round a corner and saw the House Dolorous spread out before them, hidden in the canyon, a weird freak of architecture, a huge homely sagging eggshell-blue monstrosity. . . .

A tall wire fence ran from side to side of the canyon, and the House was on the other side of it. The fence had a single gatehouse, a little left of center, with a gleaming brass warning-bell beside it. Half a dozen lazy crows perched on the fence around it.

There was a small group milling about at the gatehouse. Among them, Creedmoor noticed a number of men in white jackets, several of whom had rifles on or near their persons, and he took them to be the House's guardians. No sign of any mysterious Spirit, of course. There were also a couple of individuals who Creedmoor assumed were newcomers to the House, same as him: a big bald oaf with a simpleton's face, and an acceptably attractive and intelligent-looking woman in a white dress, with her blond hair tied in a bun. They had a large number of suitcases.

It crossed Creedmoor's mind for a moment that they might be fellow toilers for the Cause, in which case he'd be *extremely* unhappy to be dragged halfway across the world to be some other bastard's backup—but then as he approached, he caught the woman's eye, and her innocence was obvious, indeed almost touching.

He smiled at her.

The guards took one look at him and raised their rifles.

CHAPTER 14

The Guardian at the Gate

"Steady, gentlemen, steady."

Creedmoor spread his arms wide so that his dusty coat hung open. He stretched out and wiggled his fingers like a stage magician, but what he produced from his open coat was no rabbit; it was *nothing*. His belt was empty but for a small silver-clasped knife.

"My name is John Cockle. Hear me out."

The guards at the gate relaxed a little, but kept their rifles rudely trained in Creedmoor's direction.

There were four of them. They wore white: white shirts, white slacks, white belts. They had commendably neat hair and clean teeth. Each was in some way wounded—a missing eye, a missing ear, a hunch, half a leg. Their faces were shiny with sweat—Creedmoor imagined them sweltering all day in the guardhouse, going mad with boredom and duty. He favored them with his smile.

He gave a wink, too, to the blond woman in the white dress with the heavy luggage cases. She was a little too old for his taste, of course, and lacked the rosy-cheeked plumpness he liked, but one could never have too many friends in a strange place. She raised a skeptical eyebrow.

The guards said, "Who are you?"

And, "Where'd you get these people?"

And, "We're not expecting any *John Cockle*."

And, "What do you want?"

He turned back to them and stretched his empty hands even wider.

"I understand your caution, gentlemen. I applaud you, in fact. A man who is not wary out here in these days is a dead man soon enough. A case in point is your poor friend who was leading these men through the wilderness here to be healed; oh, he looked all around for bandits and Hillfolk and bloody-handed Agents, sure enough, but did he look *down*? He did not. And a snake got his ankle. There in the hot sun I found him, slumped against a red rock, raving."

The guards spat and swore and angrily kicked at rocks and dust. "Who? One of us? Shit. Who?"

"Mr. Elgin. He clutched my hand as I bent over to hear his last words and told me his name. Poor man. The black swell and the stink of his poor ankle, gentlemen! The flies, and the carrion-eaters overhead, circling!"

He whirled his hands dramatically to indicate the circling of vultures, and watched the guards go pale.

"I knew from a mile off I would see some horror beneath those terrible birds; I was not wrong. I am no doctor, and I could not save him."

He gingerly lowered a hand, to gesture at a bloodstain on his shirt, courtesy of Kloan, which he'd noticed the guards taking an interest in.

"I bled the wound, but I fear I may have only hastened his end. A blunderer like me is worse than no doctor at all; my respect for your vocation knows no bounds, gentlemen. I'd like you more were you to lower your rifles, mind."

They didn't.

"Here!" Creedmoor produced from his coat—moving slowly— the dead man's papers. He waved them in the air until one of the white-clad men snatched them away. "He clutched my arm and said, *Save them. Promise me.* I did. I could not in conscience leave these poor creatures out in the wasteland to die. What sort of monster would I be, to do that? What else could I do but to take up their rope and lead them to you?"

They remained wary. They whispered to each other.

"Where did Elgin die?"

He told them.

"Long way from anywhere. What were you doing out there?"

"Isn't it obvious, gentlemen? I'm a traveling poet. Song, jest, good humor, and so on and so on. A clown, I guess. I'd juggle this instant if I did not fear you might shoot me. And, being good with words, I also do a little lawyering—I'll draw up your contracts or argue your case if you're in the unlucky situation of needing me. And perhaps I'd been traveling with the good Dr. Sloop and his emporium, you may have heard of him, and Professor Harry Ransome and his electrical apparatus, and there'd been a dispute over the affections of the dancing girl, and I struck out on my own in unfamiliar country and frankly, gentlemen, got lost as all hell and—"

"What do you want?"

"I'll get to the point, shall I? I hope to be paid for my efforts. Your charges would have died in the wilderness if not for me. I am not a young man, and I've walked for days. Will you not at least give me a bed for the night for my troubles?"

❊ ❊ ❊

Liv stood close to Maggfrid. She did not know what to make of this strange man. He was handsome in an awful sort of a way, though not young. He unnerved her. His skin was leathered and his clothes were torn and filthy, and in Koenigswald, he would have been taken for a vagrant and accommodation would have been made for him in an institution. But out here, things were different, and who could say what he was? He had the confidence of an aristocrat. His eyes were laughing.

Liv noticed that her guide was not nervous, or even interested; he stood by the asses smoking a foul cigarette and idly counting the money she'd paid him. The guards at the gate were wary, but they had been wary of her, too. They were wary people here at the House Dolorous.

Cockle grinned at her; she nodded politely but guardedly.

She watched the men haggle over Cockle's payment. She coughed once, politely, to ask if she might perhaps be allowed to enter; they had already seen her papers. . . . Cockle threw up his hands and disavowed most fulsomely any desire to interrupt the lady's business; he assured all present of his basically chivalrous intentions, notwithstanding his desire to be *paid,* on which subject he felt regrettably that it might be best if he were to speak to these men's superiors, intending no slight to them, of course, it was only that . . .

Liv sighed and walked away. Her dress dragged in the dust and tore on a sharp rock and she nearly swore. She'd kept a white dress packed safely away all this time so that she could approach the House respectably attired; already it was ruined.

Weeks of travel, and her entrance had been entirely upstaged by this . . .

Cockle kept talking. Now the guards were laughing along with his jokes. His voice rolled and echoed. Some mad people of her acquaintance could talk like that—quite cheerfully, endlessly, without ever saying a meaningful thing.

She busied herself studying the poor souls Cockle had brought with him. Her patients-to-be, her new experimental subject matter. They looked half-starved, and their skin was peeling from the sun, but one of them gave her a lopsided smile. "I'm William, ma'am," he said. She offered her hand, and he stared at it blankly, then mimicked her gesture with his hand hanging limp like a dead fish. She gave him her name, and he issued a little wheezing giggle.

"William," she said. "Do you know where you are now?"

"The Doll House, ma'am."

"What happened to you, William?"

"Ma'am?"

"How did you get here?"

"A man came."

"Why are you here, William?"

"They say I'm not well."

"Why do you think you're not well, William?"

She was so engrossed in her subject matter that she hardly heard the approach of the Heavier-Than-Air Vessel. She didn't sense it until after even William's dull senses had caught it; she followed his nervous rheumy eyes up and saw it hanging in the sky. It was made of brass and iron and defied gravity and sanity. A man in black sat like an oversized fetus in a glass womb. The beating of its dreadful blades drove dust into the air and into her eyes, and she blinked away tears. The gate guards were shouting.

* * *

Creedmoor fell silent and considered the situation.

The Heavier-Than-Air Vessel hovered just within the rim of the ravine; the thrum of the spinning wing-blades and the rattle of its clockwork echoed from the rocks on either side. The black coal smoke from its engines climbed out of the canyon and into the sky.

The pilot leaned out from his glass-and-brass bubble and surveyed the scene through a spyglass.

Creedmoor bowed his head and tried to look frightened. It wasn't entirely a pretense.

His instinct was to reach for his belt; but of course, there was no weapon there—he'd given it to William for safekeeping, strapped under William's rags, for what gate guard would bother to search William? That was more or less the whole of the plan, in fact, now whirled away like leaves by fucking 'thopter blades. Now what was he supposed to do?

If he took back his Gun and fired on the Vessel, he had little doubt he'd be able to bring it down. But then the guards would know what he was; and, if the stories were true, then the Spirit, which did not tolerate violence, would strike him down.

The Vessel hovered, apparently suffering the same indecision as Creedmoor.

He risked a glance at the pilot, trying to read the man's intentions. Did he know who Creedmoor was? Had he followed him here from Kloan, or was this merely a chance encounter? It was useless. Creedmoor never could tell what, if anything, Linesmen were thinking.

He turned to the guards and shouted, "Busy day!" They smiled nervously.

He thought: the pilot wouldn't open fire. That was for sure. The Line's intelligence was at least the equal of the Guns', and they would know what happened to those who brought violence into the presence of the Spirit of the House. If this was a chance encounter, the

Vessel would move on soon enough. If, on the other hand, the pilot knew who Creedmoor was, then unless he was a fool—and Linesmen were dull, but they were not fools—he would simply wire back for assistance and wait, and soon Creedmoor would be surrounded. . . .

*   *   *

With no warning but a high buzzing whine, the gun in the Vessel's undercarriage spun into action. It looked like a mosquito's nasty blood-spike; it cursed in lead. The guards scattered into the gatehouse. William and the mad folk milled around in panic, the rope at their ankles tangling. Rocks burst and red dust flew in the air and Liv fell to the floor and Maggfrid fell protectively over her, knocking the wind out of her.

It had fired thirty, forty feet clear of the gatehouse. A warning.

A voice sounded from the Vessel's loudspeakers. It echoed off the canyon's walls. It distorted and boomed.

"*GIVE UP THE AGENT. GIVE UP THE AGENT. GIVE UP THE SLAGGING AGENT.*"

Creedmoor threw himself behind a rock. His heart pounded, and he felt old and weak and exposed.

"*GIVE UP THE AGENT.*"

The loudspeaker boomed, and Creedmoor's master shouted in his ear:

—Now they will be looking for an Agent. The House will be on guard. You should not have dawdled, Creedmoor.

—Shut up. Let me think.

The loudspeaker boomed: "*I SEE HIM. GIVE THE BASTARD UP.*"

The Vessel opened fire. Lead cursed and roared and spat away on the other side of the rock, harming no one, echoing up and down the ravine's high walls. A pointless, ill-tempered display of power. One or more of the mad folk was screaming. Creedmoor uncorked a bottle of Sloop's tonic water and swigged down a mouthful of the acrid stuff. He waited with some curiosity to see if it would do anything for his nerves. It did not.

*   *   *

A whistling came down the canyon, subtle at first, then piercing. In the distance, the shutters on the House's windows banged wildly open and shut; even over the noise of the Vessel, the rushing and clattering were audible. Red dust rose whirling into the air.

There was a strong sense of *pressure;* it began with a prickling of the skin and progressed quickly to the point where sinuses and eyeballs and teeth ached. Blood thickened; the veins in Creedmoor's neck and head popped out, and his heart felt tight and heavy.

The Spirit in action! Creedmoor felt it rising, gathering. He hadn't expected to see it in action; in fact, he had hoped quite fervently *not* to. But he couldn't deny that he was curious. Hand on his hat, he poked his head over the edge of the rock.

✳   ✳   ✳

Little whirlwinds of dust swirled up, so that it seemed that long red fingers reached toward the Vessel. It reared back like a spooked horse. It hung in the whirling air, its gun silent for a second, and Creedmoor was able to observe it closely. Insectlike, yes; quite similar also to the rubber and glass and steel gas masks that the men of the Line sometimes used. The wings that spun above it were a blur.

The Vessel spun on its axis under the whirring wing-blades and rose slowly out of the ravine, but it was too late.

The air was full of dust and roaring; the whistle was now a howl, rushing past Creedmoor's ears as if he were falling. He clamped his hat brim down over his ears.

A fist of dust struck the Vessel from the sky.

With a dreadful noise, the Vessel's blades buckled. The dust cloud burst around the Vessel's blades and lost its illusion of form and solidity, dissipating upward into the blue sky. The Vessel spun down into the side of the ravine, where it tumbled into flame and broken metal. Its belly tore and clockwork guts tumbled out; toothed wheels and gears glowing red-hot rolled out into the canyon.

For a long moment, the billowing dust clouds over the canyon seemed to form a vast human shape, squatting protectively over the House. Dust swelled like sloped shoulders, heavy breasts, rolls of fat, thick haunches—*How* fat *it is,* Creedmoor thought, *how greedy, how old!*

It burst. A rain of sharp rocks, whipped up by the winds, now fell, as if hurled, on the Vessel's wreckage. That struck Creedmoor as spiteful.

The gate guards were shouting: "Who did this?"

"A machine of the Line?"

"Why would the Line attack us?"

"We're *neutral*! What do they want?"

"They said there was an Agent of the . . ."

Creedmoor thought:

—They want an Agent. They won't rest until they find one. So let's see that they do.

He stood and cried out—"There he is! I see him!" And he vaulted the rock he'd been hiding behind and sprinted full-tilt through the howling winds and the dust and the sharp rocks toward where the mad folk stood, still bound by their ankle rope, cowering in a circle. One of them, the old woman, was messily dead—the Vessel's gun had caught her as it spun and fell. "Your fault," Creedmoor muttered. "Your fault, Spirit, not mine."

He grabbed William by his shoulder. The poor bastard turned and smiled in relief to see Creedmoor standing behind him. He drew his silver-clasped knife and inserted it under poor William's ribs.

He turned away, not wanting to look at William's eyes, and saw that the Spirit's rage was slowing abating. The form that squatted over the canyon was gone. The dust was settling. The shrieking winds subsided.

He waited for a tense moment for it to strike him down. It didn't. It appeared distracted, exhausted, sated. . . .

The gate guards lifted their rifles again. Creedmoor reached into William's rags and tore out the glistening silver blackness of Marmion: he held the weapon up and shouted, "I saw it! I knew I saw it! The Gun! *This* is the Agent! This Agent of the Gun brought that mechanical monster down on us!"

The gate guards lowered their rifles and shook their heads in awe.

"An Agent. A fucking Agent."

"Here, trying to sneak in."

"Dead. An Agent, dead . . ."

Creedmoor wound back his arm and hurled the weapon away into the rocks. "Filthy thing!"

Then he was ostentatiously and tearfully sick. The clever-looking blond woman, whose white dress was now tattered by the winds and the dust, came and stood beside him and encouraged him to breathe deeply. He took great sobs and told her, *"I never—I never— oh, I killed that man! Oh, what have I done?"* She patted his shoulder and told him he had done the right thing; he had done the brave thing; he had done the only thing a decent person could do; he should not be ashamed. He told her she was very kind.

The winds had settled and the canyon was silent.

The gate guards fanned out, looking for the weapon. They didn't find it.

✳ ✳ ✳

That night, Creedmoor was freshly showered and shaved, and fairly compensated—and in fact, feted, cheered, slapped manfully on the back by damn near every one of the House's men, applauded and adored by its women, for he had saved the House from infiltration and done what few could boast: He'd killed an Agent of the Gun! It was pure luck, he said, pure good fortune. He went to bed drunk. And lying on a narrow bed in the little white-walled garret they'd found for him, he woke to a headache and a familiar voice. He rose on his arm; he leaned over the sleeping shoulder of that pretty young nurse. . . . There on the little nightstand, under the shuttered lantern, silver glinting in the moonlight, was his master. He looked Marmion in its yawning black barrel.

He reached out across the girl's body and lifted the weapon. It was heavy, and at once his arm ached.

—Well done, Creedmoor. Here we are.

—Yes.

—We are pleased with you.

—An ugly business.

—What do you mean, Creedmoor?

—The killing. Ugly.

—No. Daring. Clever. Lucky. Ruthless. Be proud, Creedmoor. We like our servants joyful.

The girl murmured. He brushed his lips softly across her shoulder.

—Never mind.

—Forgiven. Forgotten. We are pleased with you.

—The Spirit will make trouble. Did you *see* that thing?

—It is strong, but we are cunning. Are we not? First murder the Spirit. Then seize the General. What he knows, Creedmoor, what he has seen! The weapon! Victory!

—Peace.

—Victory.

—What does it do?

—It can end the Line, Creedmoor. It can kill them. It can prick them like a bubble, it can wake us from them like a bad dream, quickly forgotten.

—Really? And you? Can it kill you, too?

—Shut up, Creedmoor. Go to sleep. Tomorrow we begin.

CHAPTER 15

LOWRY

The ground where Kloan's boardinghouse had stood had been cleared. Now one large gray tent stood there, and one small one.

The large tent was used by Conductor Banks for meetings of senior staff. The small tent was for the telegraphy equipment. The neighboring buildings, including the Mayor's house and the Smiler meeting room and the offices of a small transportation business, had been requisitioned by the Line, and were in the process of conversion to barracks. The trucks had been brought in and now slumbered along Main Street like great black primeval beasts.

Lowry worked in the telegraphy tent among his Signal Corps. They had formerly reported to Morningside; now they reported to Lowry. It was hot, crowded, noisy, and dark. Signals came in. The telegraphs chattered. The Signal Corps dutifully decoded and transcribed their utterances and presented them to Lowry, who either circulated the information to Banks, or ordered whatever response was necessary himself, in Banks's name, and in the name of the Engines.

Signals came in from the device that had been placed in the Doctor's golden watch. In theory, the device should have transmitted every word that was spoken in the Doctor's presence. But the world was only half-made, and had not yet attained the perfection of theory. The signals were weak and tremulous. Much was lost in transmission. There was a delay of at least several hours between the moment when those signals arrived through the ether and quivered on the copper receivers of the telegraphy equipment, and the moment when the Signal Corps had translated them into something intelligible, and typed up a transcript that could be placed into Lowry's hands. It was therefore not until early the morning after, while he was shaving, that Lowry learned that (*a*) one of the precious Heavier-Than-Air Vessels had been lost, due to the criminal recklessness and idiocy of its pilot, and (*b*) a person matching the description of the Agent who'd massacred Kloan had entered the Hospital.

He sent a report up to Banks, and he sent a report back to Kingstown.

Banks did not respond.

❉   ❉   ❉

That evening, Subaltern Thernstrom of the Signal Corps interrupted Lowry as he was eating his dinner, alone at the end of a long table in what had been the house of the Mayor of Kloan.

"Sir."

"What is it, Subaltern?"

"Sir. A signal. Urgent, sir."

Lowry sighed, abandoned his dinner, and followed the Subaltern back to the telegraphy tent, where Subaltern Drum showed him a brief typed transcript. It began: FOR MORNINGSIDE ONLY. FOR MORNINGSIDE ONLY.

"Sir . . ."

"Morningside's dead, isn't he? I'm Morningside now. Let's see the rest of it."

> . . . FOR MORNINGSIDE ONLY. OUR ADVERSARY HAS
> ENTERED THE HOSPITAL. UNACCEPTABLE. CONDUCTOR
> BANKS HAS PROVED INEFFECTIVE AND IS TO BE REMOVED.
> YOU ARE TO TAKE ACTING COMMAND, MORNINGSIDE.

"It came via the restricted device, sir."

"I know."

"The Engines, sir."

"Yes." The transcript tailed off with a long, long signature, the names of each one of the thirty-eight Engines themselves:

ANGELUS. ARCHWAY. ARKLEY. ARSENAL. BARKING. COLLIER HILL. DRYDEN. FOUNTAINHEAD. GEORGIANA. GLORIANA. HARROW CROSS . . .

Lowry's hands shook. In decades of service, he had never, never once, had any direct communication with the Engines themselves. The fact that this communication was merely accidental, being intended for Morningside, only very slightly tarnished Lowry's pride or reduced his terror.

"Thernstrom."

"Sir."

"Wire back."

MORNINGSIDE DECEASED IN ACCIDENT ON FRONT LINE CAUSED BY OWN CARELESSNESS. SUB-INVIGILATOR 2 LOWRY ACTING IN MORNINGSIDE'S PLACE. WILL ACT AS YOU COMMAND. LOWRY.

There was no response for three hours. Lowry waited by the telegraph, moving only when his nerves got too bad and his stomach revolted and he was forced to go dry-heave outside.

At last the response came:

FOR LOWRY ONLY. FOR LOWRY ONLY. LOWRY, YOU ARE TO TAKE ACTING COMMAND. YOU ARE NOT SIGNIFICANTLY LESS ADEQUATE FOR THE TASK THAN MORNINGSIDE. BANKS MUST GO. ACT WITH OUR SANCTION. ANGELUS. ARCHWAY. ARKELY . . .

BOOK TWO

The Doll House

CHAPTER 16

EARLY DAYS

The Director of the House Dolorous had arranged for Liv to stay in an upstairs room, on the fifth floor of the East Wing. Maggfrid and two porters brought her bags up. One porter was missing an ear and an eye. The other was mercifully unwounded, though he had very nearly no teeth. She thanked them profusely, and asked them to escort Maggfrid down to his quarters—a bunk in a shared room on the second floor, West Wing. She asked for dinner to be brought to her. For two days, she hardly left her room.

The House terrified her.

"The aircraft," she told the Director, "The incident with the—what's the word?—the Agent—the thing at the gate—it rather shattered my nerves." He was very understanding.

But the truth was that she simply couldn't bear to face her new patients. There were too many of them. Their wounds, physical and mental, were too various, too terrible. She couldn't tell the patients from the doctors—they all shared the same vague and haunted expression. Most of the doctors and staff were old wounded soldiers themselves. The House echoed with sobbing. There was no organization that she could discern. And a demon slumbered in the walls and under the earth. . . .

She felt herself falling back into the bad habits of her youth, of the dark years following her mother's death. She despised herself for it.

On the third day, she woke early in the morning. She took three drops of her nerve tonic, which numbed her very helpfully. She spent an hour breathing slowly and deeply. She spent several minutes looking in the mirror, critically assessing her flaws, and her weakness, and her selfishness. Afterwards, she spent another few minutes practicing a confident unruffled smile. She placed the golden watch in her purse because she found its tick comforting, and she went to visit Director Howell in his office.

The Director's office was at the back of the House, on the third floor, and its wide windows looked out over the gardens, which decades of painstaking effort had somehow made moderately green. Sunlight flooded the office. Everything in it was white and clean. In the gardens below, a dozen mad persons with wild and filthy hair sat stiffly beside the paths like dead trees.

The Director himself was a little dark-skinned man with round gold-rimmed spectacles, and a neat black beard, and a mild and reasonable smile. As Liv entered, he rose from his chair with a look of concern on his face.

"Good morning, Director!"

"Dr. Alverhuysen, are you sure you're well—?"

"Of course!" She smiled. "Of *course*. Entirely too much work to do for us to waste time, don't you think? I intend to begin with a study of the victims of the Line's mind-bombs, the noisemakers. Uncharted territory, not yet visited by science—that's where I can be of most use. We must all do what we can, don't you agree, Director?"

"Fresh thinking, Dr. Alverhuysen. What a pleasure!"

❋   ❋   ❋

The West Wing housed patients whose injuries were (primarily) physical, while the East Wing housed those whose injuries were (primarily) mental. The victims of the mind-bombs were housed on the East Wing's second and third floors. Liv and the Director toured the cells, and she selected two to be her first subjects. She opened files on them under the names *D* and *G*.

❋   ❋   ❋

D is a woman in her early twenties. From her features, which include a prominent forehead and pale, freckled complexion, I would judge that she is descended ultimately from settlers from Lundroy. Her pupils are abnormally enlarged, which gives her an appearance (likely false) of being quite fascinated by whatever she sees. She is 5' 2" and somewhat overweight, though she is more physically active than is the norm among victims of the bombs—she is often found running heedlessly down the corridors or through the gardens. She has many bruises and scrapes.

She sings to herself constantly, generally love songs, most frequently something called "Daisy, My Dear," an irritating composition that I am told is the work of the fashionable tunesmiths of Swing Street in distant Jasper City. The staff have therefore nicknamed her "Daisy." In fact, her name is Colla Barber. She is the only daughter of a prominent Land Baron in the Delta, who is not incidentally a significant donor to the House. Four years ago, while out riding with a young man, she stumbled across a long-forgotten minefield.

She returns again and again to those songs. Based on my observations to date, this is typical of the victims of the bombs. Most of them have one or two fragments of conversation or knowledge remaining, quite arbitrarily; rather like the way in which (so the *Child's History* tells me) when the Line bombards an ancient city with explosive rockets, whole districts may be flattened, but sometimes a single fine old church will be left standing.

Otherwise her responses to communication (words, gestures, touch) appear almost random. Nevertheless she is more active than the average sufferer, less closed off from the world. I have some access to information on her life before the bombs (whereas the lives of most sufferers are a mystery). I propose to begin with conversational therapy.

––––––––––

G is a man of uncertain age, most certainly very elderly. I judge him to be of mixed descent, primarily Dhravian. He is more than six feet tall, and very thin—in fact, I suspect that the House's staff have neglected his feeding, and I have instructed that that is to cease. When I first found him, he had an immense and filthy white beard, which I had trimmed. For a man of his apparent age, he is remarkably healthy. Perhaps the victims of the bombs, being only half-alive, age more slowly than we do?

How he came to the House is uncertain. He has been in the House for at least seven years, probably more, and no records were kept of his arrival. This is quite typical. It is impossible at this point to determine when in his life he ran afoul of the bombs. If he speaks at all, which he does infrequently, he babbles garbled and nonsensical fragments of fairy tales, which makes me suspect that possibly he was damaged in infancy.

The staff have nicknamed him "the General," for no clear reason; perhaps because there is something grand and military in his posture and the fierceness of his eye? I would not assume from the name that he was, in fact, an officer or even a soldier. The staff have given at least seven other patients the same unimaginative nickname, for equally trivial reasons. (There are also four "Barons" and innumerable "Princesses.")

At first G seemed a hopeless case. He responds to nothing, and hardly moves. But his eyes are intelligent, and sad. Where we know nothing, we must admit that we know nothing, and trust to intuition. I propose to begin with the electrical therapy.

✳   ✳   ✳

She took Daisy—*Colla,* her name was Colla, but it was terribly difficult not to think of her as Daisy—out into the garden. The grass was a hardy desert species, sharp to the touch, and the flowers were battered and dusty and harshly colored, and the garden was full of large red rocks. Still, the girl seemed to like it.

Through gentle motions, Liv encouraged her to sit.

"Colla," she said. "It's nice to get outside, isn't it."

Those huge eyes darted to the band of blue sky visible between the canyon's towering walls.

"You like to ride horses, don't you, Colla?"

The eyes fixed intently on Liv then darted away.

"Colla—"

"Oh, Daisy, my dear, had I only the flair, to pen you a verse that's as fair as your hair, or the perfume you wear, then I wouldn't be in such a state of despair over you. . . ."

"Yes, Colla. I wonder where you first heard that song. Did someone sing it to you? A young man? Do you—?"

Daisy lurched suddenly to her feet. Still singing, she ran madly down the garden path, fell, cut her scalp on a rock, and lay there grinning and bloody, curled like a baby, and always still singing.

To Liv's chagrin, Dr. Hamsa had been leaning against the back wall of the House, smoking and watching the whole affair.

"Bravo," he said. "A triumph of modern science. Whatever would we do if you weren't here to show us the way."

❋   ❋   ❋

The West Wing of the Doll House held a number of doctors and surgeons. They were a crude lot. Nearly all of them were military men, and they approached disease and injury like an enemy, to be cut out or bludgeoned into submission. They liked to be called "Doc" or "Sawbones" and Liv could never keep their names straight. The distinction between *surgeons* on the one hand and *guards* and *porters* and *handymen* on the other was not rigorous, and seemed to depend mostly on who'd happened to have brought a saw with them when they drifted into the House's shadow. That they didn't kill more people was surely a tribute to the healing power of the Spirit below.

The East Wing, where the mad patients were kept, had only two doctors, not counting Liv. One was a Mr. Bloom, who wasn't really a doctor at all, but a Smiler, who bothered the patients with pamphlets and meeting circles and encouragement to "buck up." The other was Dr. Hamsa, who claimed proudly to have studied at Vansittart University in Jasper City. Liv was only passingly familiar with the institution. If Hamsa was typical of its graduates, she was not impressed. She suspected he might have been expelled. He was unshaven, slovenly, seedy. He abused medications for recreational purposes. He had a simple and rigid theory of psychological correspondences, according to which each patient's psychic wound was supposed to mirror some physical wound sustained at some point during their lives, the soul-stuff being composed of the same matter as the body: so that aphasia was a sign of an injury to the jaw; hysteria, of course, arose from damage to the womb; and mania was connected for unclear reasons to injuries of the hands. When he first explained this to her, Liv gently offered obvious counterexamples. He never forgave her.

Both of them regarded the victims of the mind-bombs as hopeless.

"The cause is very simple," Hamsa said. "Engines did this. Their noise brutalizes every part of the body and soul at once and leaves nothing behind. Therefore the Spirit is powerless to heal them, because there is nothing to heal; and because, though the Spirit is strong, the Engines are stronger. Cleverer. I know you think you're cleverer than us, but are you cleverer than *them*?"

"Buck up," Bloom said. "Some things aren't meant to be. The trick is to keep on smiling."

❊　❊　❊

Maggfrid helped her move the General—G—down from his cell and into her office.

Maggfrid wore the white uniform of the House staff, and seemed delighted by it, though it didn't fit: the shoulders were tight, and the collar simply had no hope of contending with his neck. He was already popular among the staff—a great deal more popular than Liv, in fact—in part because of his good nature, and in part because he could lift and carry as much as any three ordinary men.

He carried the General in his arms like a baby.

Liv's office was on the first floor, at the front of the House. It was still—despite her complaints—unfinished and largely unfurnished, and it smelled of sawdust. Still, it had a couple of chairs. Maggfrid sat the General in one of them.

The General quickly arranged himself in a posture of fierce erect attention, bony brown hands gripping the armrests, and stared out the window onto an expanse of rockscape and wire fence as if it contained something of enormous significance.

Maggfrid leaned against a half-constructed bookshelf and watched curiously as Liv unpacked the electric therapy apparatus from its leather case. It consisted mostly of leather straps, plates of copper, bands of wire, and a wooden box with dials and two meters of mercury. It was the most advanced and experimental thing at the Academy in Lodenstein, and there was certainly nothing like it for a thousand miles around the Doll House.

The General appeared to glance at it, then glance away. "Once upon a time," he said, very gravely, "a peddler came to the beautiful palace of bone with a magic box. It contained all the feathers in the world."

He seemed to have nothing more to add.

Outside the window there was a small, ancient portable

generator—the only source of electricity in the House. It was Line manufacture. One of the patients had brought it with him; he'd claimed it from a battlefield, where he'd been fighting in behalf of a Free City that had, without his knowing it, been fighting in behalf of the Gun. He'd stolen some valuable machinery but lost an arm.

"Maggfrid," Liv said. "The generator, please."

He began to climb out the window.

"The door, please, Maggfrid. Go around."

While she waited for him to find his way, she studied the General. Now that he was trimmed and cleaned, there was something familiar about him. He vaguely reminded her of some of the old professors at the Academy, the ones who'd been ancient back in her mother's day, when she was only a girl.

"Yes!" Maggrid shouted. "Yes! Right!"

"Like I showed you, Maggfrid."

He leaned forward and threw all his weight onto the generator's rusty mechanism. It roared into life, and started to smoke.

She attached the apparatus to the General's forehead. His skin was paper thin.

"This may hurt a little," she said. "If there's anything in there to be hurt. But it may spark some life into the embers. It may build new connections. It may—oh, well."

She turned a dial.

Nothing happened.

She turned the dial a little farther, and the General's eyelid twitched.

He continued to stare silently out the window.

"That's enough, Maggfrid."

She sighed. Of course, she hadn't *expected* a miracle, but part of her had *hoped.* . . . She made a note in G's file:

Not immediately promising.

✳   ✳   ✳

She went walking.

In addition to her studies into the victims of the mind-bombs, she was also responsible for a number of more ordinary patients, who suffered from simple shell-shock, depression, stress, and trauma. In fact, it was something of a relief to have a break from her studies, which were not going well.

There were no men of the Line among the House's patients. There were plenty of men who'd lost limbs and eyes or the like in the service of some border state that had pledged itself to the Line, but no true-bred Linesmen; none of those born in the shafts and tunnels of Harrow Cross, or Dryden, or Kingstown, or Gloriana. There was no particular policy against it, the Director said; the House took anyone who needed it, so long as they would respect its peace; Linesmen just didn't end up there. Rumor was the Line had its own unnatural surgeries.

Nor were there any Agents of the Gun. There were many soldiers from the ruins of Logtown or Sharp's Hold, or other places that had thrown in on the Gun's side in the War, but no Agents. Hardly surprising—by all accounts, the Agents were not in the business of being *wounded*. They fought until they were dead.

There was a one-armed man on the fourth floor who claimed to have fought with the Red Valley Republic, decades ago, in the days of that Republic's brief glorious flourishing—and who, accordingly, held himself aloof from common soldiers of lesser causes. And there were men who'd fought under no flag at all, but only to defend their little homesteads from the great clashing armies of the world. And there were two men who'd fought in the tunnels of the gold mines under Harker's Mount, on opposite sides: one for the Zizek Extraction Co., one for Jared's Limited. They'd lost their legs together in the same tunnel collapse: now they were the best of friends.

Despite their varied allegiances, the inmates never fought each other. There was rarely a harsh word exchanged, even. Liv wondered how much of that was due to fear of the Spirit that slept below.

She stopped in on the room of Mr. Root Busro, on the fourth floor, who was by far her least depressing patient. He was unwounded—in fact, physically quite healthy. He didn't sob or claw at his hair. Apart from the disconcerting way in which his gray eyes stared right through you, he wasn't unpleasant to be around. His one peculiarity was that he was quite convinced that the world as it appeared was all in his own mind, and in particular that the warring forces of Line and Gun that crashed back and forth across it were merely the opposing forces of his own diseased will.

"I feel just awful about it," he said. "But it's not my fault. I'm not well."

"You may rest assured that no one blames you, Mr. Busro."

"Of course, you can't help me, Doctor, since you're only a thing in my mind, too, and it's the mind that's the problem."

"Well, perhaps we can both do our best."

"I do enjoy your visits, though."

✳   ✳   ✳

After Busro, she visited a young girl called Bella, who'd lost her family and a leg to a stray rocket, and who was (again) on the verge of suicide. As Liv and Bella talked, Dr. Hamsa passed outside, in conversation with one of the House's guards—Renato, she thought his name was—and she overheard them talking gravely of "news of a massacre at Kloan . . . agents of the Powers . . . many dead, no one apprehended." Her blood ran cold. Bella just stared glumly at her feet and shrugged, as if to say, *See?*

✳   ✳   ✳

On the way back, she got lost. In her early days in the Doll House, Liv was forever getting lost. Its corridors were narrow and not well lit. They seemed impossibly long and labyrinthine. They were identical everywhere, painted either a funereal white, or a soft eggshell blue, which could be sometimes soothing and sometimes sad. The corridors were never empty, but the people one met were generally even less certain of their whereabouts than Liv was.

She turned a corner and bumped into John Cockle. He appeared to be replacing the hinges on one of the patients' doors.

He gave her a cheery wave. "It creaks," he explained. "Can't have that, can we? Will give the little ones nightmares."

"Good afternoon, Mr. Cockle."

"Good afternoon to you, too, Doc."

"You're supposed to be finishing my office."

"Hasn't slipped my mind even for a moment. When I'm done, you'll have the finest office any doctor ever enjoyed. Your friends from back East will come visit just to take a look at it. As it happens,

I myself am a Lundroyman by birth, no native of these parts, so I know what it's like to be far from home—"

"Well, you seem to have made yourself quite at home here, Mr. Cockle."

He grinned.

Cockle seemed ubiquitous; one bumped into him *everywhere*, except, it seemed, where he was supposed to be. After his heroics at the gate, he'd been instantly welcomed onto the House's staff. He wasn't a very good carpenter, and he wasn't a very reliable handyman, but it seemed that was what he wanted to be, and he certainly gave an impression of hard work. He was friendly with everyone. In particular, it seemed that all the doctors who most resented and disliked Liv thought Creedmoor was just the swellest fellow ever. . . .

She found him unnerving.

"Good-bye, Mr. Cockle."

"John, please. Otherwise I get confused. If you're looking for the stairs, Doc, it's left and left again and then, and this is the trick, *right*. . . ."

※　※　※

The *Child's History* said:

> Worst among the weapons of the Line is something you may not think of as a weapon at all: their noise. Yes, strange as it seems, their noise! The noise of the Engines is the noise of fear and submission. All those who hear it are diminished. This is why those who live in their grimy, awful, soot-choked Stations are so terribly stunted in their growth. Wickedly, though ingeniously, they have learned to focus it into a weapon. The bombs consist of hammers, pistons, sounding-plates, and amplifiers. The noise is said by those few who've heard its echoes and survived to be senseless and mad. It crushes the mind. What it destroys can never be rebuilt. This is a good lesson: What is destroyed is gone forever. This is why you must always strive to build, never to destroy.

Gone forever. After two weeks, she'd made no progress with D or G. She felt under a great deal of pressure, and it was necessary, each night before bed, to take two drops of her nerve tonic in a glass of water. It was a great comfort simply to watch that smoky green fluid unfurl itself into the water.

✳   ✳   ✳

Liv took tea with the Director at noon. They sat on wicker chairs in the House's herb garden, under the shade of parasols. A few patients listlessly wandered the garden's paths—one of them in particular had a wound in his face like a—well, she tried not to stare. She focused her eyes instead on the Director's neat black beard. She watched it enclose and devour a biscuit.

"Perhaps you were hoping I would report some wonderful success," she said. "I'm afraid I have to disappoint you."

"Early days yet, Dr. Alverhuysen," he told her. He neatly dabbed the crumbs from his beard with a lace napkin. "Early days. This House has stood here for many years now. It outlived my father, and I expect it to outlive me and my sons. We do what we can; no more. So long as there is war, the work of the House Dolorous will never be done."

"You are, of course, correct, Director."

"Call me Richard, please."

"Richard, of course, you're correct. But after coming all this way . . . the risks! I think I was a little mad to come. Sometimes strange moods seize me. I confess I hoped I might achieve miracles."

Her hand was shaking; she had spilled her tea. The Director was looking at her with concern. She flushed a little and dabbed with her napkin at her dress, muttering, "Early days. As you so rightly say. Oh, you must think me very foolish, Director! I am simply tired. And I suppose it was vain and foolish of me to hope that I could accomplish so much, so quickly, where others no less able have failed."

"Oh, but my dear! Where would we be without foolishness and vanity!" The Director's eyes twinkled, and he dipped another biscuit in his tea. "Hard work must be leavened with hope. This is a serious house and a sad house, but also a house of wonders." He raised a finger to cut off whatever she was about to say. "I think you need a break from your work, Dr. Alverhuysen. Get some rest. And come see me tomorrow morning. I want to show you something."

CHAPTER 17

TELEGRAPH COMMUNION

For a full day, Conductor Banks refused to emerge from his command tent or accept messengers, even after Lowry had the tent's electricity supply cut. In the end, Lowry had to organize the ten men of the Signal Corps and march on Banks's tent.

He told the guards, "Stand aside. Sanction of the Engines." They stared at their feet. They didn't seem surprised.

He sent in Subaltern Thernstrom first, just in case Banks was, in the extremity of his despair and humiliation, inclined to do something criminal. Who knew what a man might do when he knew—as Banks surely must—that the Engines had withdrawn their sanction from him?

Thernstrom said, "Harmless, sir." Lowry went in.

The interior was crowded with shadows. Banks sat at his steel desk, typing.

"One moment, Morningside."

"Lowry. Morningside is dead."

Banks looked up. His eyes were bloodshot.

"Right. One moment, Lowry."

Lowry glanced at Banks's desk. It looked like the Conductor was typing up a very long justification of his actions, or lack of action. It seemed to be mostly about the inevitability, regardless of individual human failings, of the progress of the Engines' plan for the world.

"That's enough, Banks."

"One moment, Lowry."

"No one cares, Banks."

"For the record, Lowry."

Next to the typewriter sat an empty mug and Banks's pistol.
Lowry said, "Mr. Thernstrom."

"Sir?"

"Watch him. Let him finish. Give him till evening shift."

✳ ✳ ✳

So there were a few more hours before the moment when, at his
desk and under Thernstrom's eyes, Banks shot himself, and command formally passed to Lowry. Lowry was deeply glad of those
hours. He was already being deluged with reports, queries, demands, problems. He stood firm. The attention of the Engines was
on him.

One of the first things he did was to order that the natives of
Kloan be organized. They annoyed him, the way they hung around
the outskirts of the Forward Camp, looking miserable and idle.
Some of them had taken to begging. He ordered that they be put to
work on construction and other menial labor, which freed up some
of his forces to add to patrols, and to the siege of the Hospital. Additional forces were supposed to be *en route* from Kingstown but
had not yet arrived, and manpower was short.

"Besides," he told Thernstrom, "it'll do them good. The Line's
here to stay now, and they'd better get used to it."

After Banks shot himself, Lowry had a team of Kloanites, which
he was amused to see included the former Mayor, remove the body
from the tent, scrub everything clean, and dispose of Banks's meaningless report. Then he moved in.

✳ ✳ ✳

At midnight, he wired to Kingstown:

CONDUCTOR (ACTING) LOWRY, KLOAN FORWARD CAMP,
ACTING IN PLACE OF BANKS, DECEASED. PROBLEM: SAFE
DISTANCE FROM HOSPITAL UNCERTAIN. RANGE OF HOUSE

DEFENSES UNCERTAIN. SITUATION COMPLICATED BY
AGENT'S SUCCESSFUL INFILTRATION OF HOSPITAL DUE TO
NEGLIGENCE OF BANKS

Lowry's finger hovered over *A* for AS I PREDICTED. He thought
better of it.

AGENT'S PRESENCE LIKELY TO RESULT IN CONFLICT, MAY
CAUSE LOSS OF TARGET. THEREFORE IMMEDIATE SIEGE
NOW DANGEROUS. RECOMMENDATION: WIDE, LOOSE NET,
MINIMUM SEVERAL MILES FROM HOSPITAL. ROADS TO BE
BLOCKADED AND TRAVELERS SEARCHED. GREENBANK,
GOOSENECK, FAIRSMITH, WORLD'S END TO BE EXPECTED
TO COOPERATE. NET TO BE PROGRESSIVELY CLOSED AS
ADDITIONAL FORCES ARRIVE. PLEASE ADVISE.

The machine churned and rattled and sparked briefly, and the
message was off to trouble the ether. Lowry dismissed the operator.

He sat back and breathed deeply. The telegraph machine sat
heavy and still. The Engines waited on his word. Soon they'd get it.
There would be a change in the rhythm of their pistons and wheels,
too subtle for gross human senses to perceive but nonetheless real,
and that would be their thoughts, their Song, turning to him. To
Lowry. Then they would cast their presence across wires and air
and all the vastness of the continent, and spark the telegraph into
life, and the tent would echo with the Song of the Line.

Subaltern Drum brought Lowry a tin cup of cold coffee, and he
sipped it gratefully. He planned to work through till morning.

CHAPTER 18

PLEASANT INVESTIGATIONS

Creedmoor stood near the top of the second staircase in the East Wing. He was surrounded by buckets of blue paint, and his white work clothes were stained with dribbles and splotches of blue. He was painting the wall with great cheerful messy swings of the brush. He whistled and grinned at passersby.

He said to himself:

—Last night I got talking to a *very* charming young nurse.

—We know you have, Creedmoor. We were with you.

—She tells me little things. She is talkative, afterwards.

—What you know, we know.

—If only it worked the other way around. Who is this man you are looking for?

—A General. The enemy destroyed his mind.

—I know. You told me. A name, please? There are half a dozen inmates here who the staff call *General*. Dozens more who have no names at all. Play fair. Are we looking for a black fellow or a white one? Fat or thin?

—He is darker-skinned than you. He is old. All men look much the same to us, Creedmoor.

—Very helpful. There are a great many old dark men here.

—Creedmoor, finding the man will do us no good; first we must find a way to kill the Spirit that guards him.

—Killing will come. Meanwhile, my friendly young nurse tells me that the Alverhuysen woman, the Doctor from the north, has taken a dusky bearded old man into her care. She is repairing his brain. She has strange and terrible sciences from the north, electric cures, drugs, mesmerism. Perhaps he is the one?

—Possibly. You must investigate. Creedmoor, if he is the one, and she extracts the secrets buried in his memory, she must be killed.

—We'll see. But with my luck, the man in question will be in the last place we look.

—Not true. You always have been lucky, Creedmoor. It is why we have tolerated you for so long.

Creedmoor slapped a last wide streak of fresh blue across the wall.

"Good enough," he said. "I think I'm due a break."

✳　✳　✳

He'd joined a game of cards. Not purely for recreational purposes— his fellow players were important men in the House. Sichel was Head Cook. Renato had for fifteen years wandered all over the northwest, collecting patients for the House, and now ran security at the south fence. Hamsa was a doctor, one of the few to have a real education, being a graduate of Vansittart U, back in Jasper, which Creedmoor understood to be quite fancy.

On his way down, he stopped by a dormitory on the second floor.

—A whim occurs to me.

A young man lay on his back on the bed by the window. He had only one leg. While the right side of his face was exceedingly handsome, the left had been melted, kind of like ice cream. His remaining eye stared up at a pipe in the roof with vicious intensity, as if trying to burst it.

Creedmoor leaned against the window.

"Kid. Hey, Kid."

"Fuck you."

If the young man had a name other than the Kid, it wasn't known to anyone at the House. That was what he'd written in the ledger, and he answered to nothing else. In fact, he hardly answered to anything at all. He'd come in on the last ambulance party to arrive, three days after Creedmoor. He was intensely bitter about something, presumably something related to his injuries. He rarely left his bed. When he did, he limped down the hallways, shouting and snarling and threatening nurses, and was generally thought to be a hairsbreadth from doing something that would cause the Spirit to flatten him once and for all, and he would not be missed.

"Hey, Kid. You play cards?"

"Which idiot are you? Cackle, right?"

"Cockle. John'll do. You play cards?"

"What's the point?"

"What's the point of anything?"

The Kid turned his head to glare at Creedmoor.

Creedmoor shrugged. "Some of these idiots have money for the taking. But if you're busy . . ."

—Why, Creedmoor?

—I like him. He reminds me of me at his age.

—He is maimed. Useless. We would not take him.

—Not useless. Not useless at all. Just not sure how to use him yet, that's all.

❋ ❋ ❋

They played down in one of the basements under the East Wing, in a vacant operating room. The afternoon was cool down in the tunnels—the walls were moist and prone to lichen, which had to be scrubbed off. Sichel brought whiskey from the kitchens. They sat on hard wooden stools, around an operating table.

"Bad news out of Kloan," Sichel said.

"A tragedy," Creedmoor agreed. "I blame the Line. Naked aggression. But no changing the subject, Sichel, my friend; let's see what you've got."

Sichel scowled—which made his scarred and empty left eye socket crumple in something like a wink. He tossed his cards on the table. His hand was mostly Engines, bad numbers.

"Curse the day you came here, Cockle."

"Now, now. This is a welcoming House. The Spirit forgives all. Even luck with cards."

Creedmoor reminded himself to start losing again. They talked more freely when they thought they were winning.

"It certainly does," Renato agreed, dealing. "It forgives every-thing." Solemn as ever. Renato slurred his words because parts of his jaw were gone; he wore a red domino over his face. His hand was mostly Guns, Creedmoor thought, and pretty good.

"It does at that," Sichel said.

"Bullshit," said the Kid, who sat on the far end of the table, by himself.

"Now, now." Renato shook his head. "Now, now. You just need to give it time. Lie back. Let the Spirit work on you and—"

"I got nothing to forgive," said the Kid. "It's those fuckers who did this to me who need forgiving, and I don't plan on forgiving them. I don't plan on sitting around here like a coward and rotting. I'm going to—

"That way you'll get yourself killed," said Sichel.

"So what?"

Renato said, "Listen. You were a soldier, right? So there's some-thing to forgive right there. Doesn't matter what side. Let me tell you a story. So twenty years ago . . ."

Creedmoor stopped listening. Twenty years ago, Renato had fought in the army of one of the richer and more inbred southern Barons, a Baron who'd allied himself with the Gun and whose lands and, more important, oilfields now belonged to the Line. Re-nato was a great storehouse of war stories. All of them had a moral at the end about forgiveness, and healing, and above all of the im-portance of turning to the Spirit, which would take up one's burdens onto its own metaphorical shoulders and bear them away. . . .

Creedmoor caught the Kid's attention and rolled his eyes.

Sichel started in with his own story, something about a woman, a camp follower, who'd died at the battle of Gabbard Hill. . . .

Dr. Hamsa interrupted with a confession about how, as a stu-dent back in Jasper City, he'd had problems with drink. The old soldiers didn't seem too impressed, but let it pass.

To keep himself in practice, Creedmoor told some lies about his own old soldiering career. He pretended repentance for unspecified and imaginary sins at the battles of Pechin Drift and Huka's Mill. Renato and Sichel listened solemnly.

The Director of the House Dolorous was a Smiler. He believed very strongly in the virtue of open and honest talk and confession; and though the House's staff were not required to share that faith, the Director's habits trickled down to them. Sometimes the whole House was like one big meeting circle. So much *talking*!

My name is John Creedmoor, and I would like to confess my crimes. Hope you all weren't going anywhere this week. . . .

He'd invited the Kid mainly in the hope that the other players would want to lecture him, which they were, but it was taking altogether too long, and Creedmoor had an appointment with a pretty nurse.

". . . and sometimes I still see their faces," Sichel said. "But the Spirit took the pain from me, same as it took the pain where my arm had been, and now—"

"Bullshit," Creedmoor interrupted, hoping to get the conversation to its point, which was the Spirit.

"Kid," he said, "I don't know what these fellows are talking about. I'm a simple man. In my experience, it's only time that heals wounds: forgetting and time. Try drink if those don't work."

Renato shook his head patiently. "There's healing here, Cockle, if you'll ask for it."

"Ever heard of a place called No-Town?"

"Sure, Cockle. Drifters talk about it. Old soldiers, too. Of course I have."

"Where it rains whiskey, and the women are easy, and no one has to work, and old soldiers and the lion and the lamb and even old Agents can find peace." He drew a card from the table. Engines. Useless to him. No-Town! He hadn't thought about No-Town in years. "And my point is that that's bullshit, too. No such thing. You'd have to be desperate to believe in it." Well, that was the truth, wasn't it?

Renato wouldn't be goaded. "You've never seen the Spirit. It's the real thing."

"I saw it smash a Vessel from the sky. I saw it guard our gate. I'll admit it exists. I don't know about healing. Where's the proof?"

Renato shrugged. "You just have to feel it."

The Kid snorted and threw his cards across the table. Engines, Guns, Folk, Women. "I'm done with this shit." He remained sitting.

"Not sure whether I do or I don't," Creedmoor said. "Tell me this, then: Why does it do what it does? What's in it for the Spirit?"

"Not everything has a reason," Renato said with infuriating priestly solemnity.

"I'm out, too," Sichel confessed.

Hamsa stood. "I have patients to see."

"Everything's got a reason," Creedmoor said.

"Maybe," Renato said. "Maybe not."

That was all Creedmoor could get out of him. Soon Creedmoor was out, too, and Renato took his winnings and went back to his post.

That left just Creedmoor and the Kid sitting at either end of the candlelit table.

"Well," Creedmoor said.

"Fuck you," the Kid said, and limped away.

※　※　※

The House had a fair number of female nurses. Most of them came from nearby towns, mainly Greenbank. Quite a few of them were pretty. It seemed the Director liked them that way.

—I could stay here forever, my friend. I like this work.

—Most of the other men here are cripples, Creedmoor. No wonder they like you. You have no reason to be proud.

—I like the company of nurses. I need a lot of care in my old age.

—You will get bored soon enough.

—Never!

—Question them.

He met Hannah in the afternoons in the bushes behind the herb garden; he met Ella in the north tower in the evenings. Other assignations were less regular, but not infrequent. He charmed them with stories of the cities back in the world. He had, it was true, a certain animal vigor that was rare in the House, and much appreciated. So far he had somehow managed not to make any of them hate him.

"The Spirit keeps us safe," Hannah said. "That's all I know.

Good thing, too, or what would I be doing here alone with a bad old man like you?"

"I don't like talking about the Spirit," Ella said. "It feels so sad. I didn't come here to talk about the Spirit."

On matters relating to the patients, they were more forthcoming—after all, what else did they have to gossip about?

Hannah told him about a fierce old man on the fourth floor of the locked wards who raved about the Battle of Pechin Drift. Ella told him about an old man on the third floor who never spoke, but compulsively stole pennies and bottle tops to make himself medals. They sounded promising, and so Creedmoor stole Ella's keys while she slept and investigated; but when he crept into their cells and looked into their faces, Marmion said:

—That is not the man.

. . . to them both.

—Oh well.

And Ella seemed a little awed by Dr. Alverhuysen, and had nothing to say about her, no matter how cunningly Creedmoor hinted and pried; but Hannah was full of rumors about the stuck-up northern bitch and the mad experiments she was doing on poor simple Daisy and that poor old General. . . .

※　※　※

Cards again in the afternoon. Creedmoor, Renato, Sichel, the Kid. It was getting expensive to keep letting them win.

This afternoon, Creedmoor was being argumentative. It seemed to be working well.

"Listen, Renato, I've traveled widely out here on the edge. I've seen a dozen little spirits in little towns, corn spirits, pray-for-rain spirits. They're common out here as two-headed calves or bearded ladies. None of them are much brighter than a candle. And most of them don't exist. And the ones that do are busy when it comes to taking sacrifice but idle when it comes to doing any good. This House is full of maimed people. I don't see much healing happening here."

"It *heals*," Renato said.

The Kid snorted. "That's a fucking lie."

No one liked the Kid, but he didn't seem to care; and they couldn't turn him away, not given the mission of the House.

"I haven't seen it," Creedmoor said.

"Nothing's easy," Renato said. "Everything takes its time." He touched his scars with a kind of reverence. "I was angry for a long time, you know? I used to be a handsome man. Why didn't it take these away, too, you know?"

Sichel nodded gravely. Creedmoor maintained his expression of skepticism.

Renato went on. His voice was muffled by his domino and his wounds, but he spoke with passion. "But that's not what it does. It takes away pain. It makes it so you can go on. It makes you at peace. It lets you *endure*. It's a wonderful thing."

Renato stopped to swig his whiskey.

Sichel grunted. "Too good for those hairy Hillfolk bastards who were squatting it."

"Folk?" Creedmoor was interested. "There were Folk here?"

"This canyon was one big warren."

"And? What? The Director's father forced them out?"

"*Shit*, no!" Renato shook his head. "You've seen what the Spirit does if there's violence in its presence."

Sichel leaned forward and whispered. "Once I saw a nurse in the West Wing, an orderly, dealing with one of the mental cases; well, this patient'd been giving him trouble all day. Calling him names, you know. Calling his mother names. Well, this orderly, Gregor was his name, he snaps; he reaches out and he cuffs the idiot. And we all call out, *Don't!* but it's too late; there's a pounding in our heads and the windows rattle and *something* surges up from the floor, through our feet, and *pow*."

Sichel clapped. The Kid started; the Kid was jumpy.

"Gregor's out the fucking window. Three stories up. One less nurse, one more patient. No, Cockle, my friend, violence here is a dicey proposition. That's how the House's stayed safe all these years, against bandits, against Hillfolk, against little border-state barons, even against the Line. No violence; not even against pigs or chickens. Why do you think we eat nothing but rabbit food?"

"It seemed impolite to complain," Creedmoor said, "but I won't say the question hasn't concerned me."

"Can't so much as slit a pig's throat. No violence. Not even against Hillfolk. No, he *bought* 'em out. He *built* 'em out. Slowly, bit by bit. Filled the canyon with our iron and our noise. They can't stand it, right? But they couldn't kill *him*, either. He built right over their paintings and their rock mounds and all that kind of thing, and they just gave up and went away."

"Poor old Hillfolk," Creedmoor beamed. "And now—"

The Kid spoke. "It's a vampire, I heard." He stared intently down at his cards. "It feeds on pain. Don't go to the Doll House, they told us. Better to get killed clean. It takes your manhood, they told us. It needs you to suffer, to be weak, forever, like little *dolls*. That's what it feeds on."

Renato glared at the Kid. "Don't be a damn fool."

"No one ever leaves, do they? You all just stay here and scab over and rot."

Renato sighed heavily. "We're doing good work here. Where else would we go? Kid, you came here by choice. No one made you. You know it was the right thing to do, Kid. You don't have to be so tough here. You know, maybe someone should take you to see it, take you to sit by the waters. That'll change your tune."

"Maybe we should at that," Creedmoor said. "So tell me, how does one get in to see the Spirit?"

"When the Director says."

"Which is when?"

"When it's right."

✳   ✳   ✳

He walked into Dr. Alverhuysen's office that evening as if he owned the place, tools in hand. "Evening, Doctor," he said, and before she could respond, he was already hammering away at the rickety half-made shelves in the corner.

She was sitting at her desk, in the light of a single candle, reading out loud from a little green book with pictures of ivy curled round the cover. Daisy was cross-legged on the floor, rocking from side to side, and the General sat ramrod-straight in the chair opposite. The Doctor's giant oaf Maggfrid stood by the window like furniture.

"Don't mind me, Doctor."

"You work odd hours, Mr. Cockle."

"Odd place. Odd times. Odd old world."

Creedmoor had to admit that he was doing a terrible job. He was losing his patience for honest labor.

She kept reading in a quiet murmuring voice, between blows of his hammer.

". . . 'Yes,' said the wolf, 'your mother is here.' And the woodsman's sons looked at each other, and they looked at the wolf, and they thought about how tired they were, and what a long journey it had been through the woods; and so they did a very foolish thing, and they followed the wolf into the little house on the edge of the woods—"

"Fairy tales," Creedmoor said. "When I was a boy back east in Lundroy, my mother used to read me fairy tales."

"I'm sure she did, Mr. Cockle."

"That was before my poor father died, of course. Never the same after that."

In fact, Creedmoor's father was, for all he knew, still alive. Certainly the bastard had been in rude health when he clouted young John Creedmoor round the ear for the last time and threw him bodily from the house. Creedmoor had lied on a sudden hunch that had told him that the Doctor herself had some damage of that variety; and it looked like he was right, because for a moment there was a flicker in her eye.

"Fairy tales," he said.

"Yes. The book belongs to Director Howell. The General seems to have a fascination for fairy tales. At least, if the patterns of his speech are reflective of any inner mental process, and not simply arbitrary. Who knows? It may catch his attention. And Daisy won't mind."

Maggfrid said, "I don't mind either."

"Nor does Maggfrid, of course."

"Good for you, Maggfrid! Nor do I. Does it work?"

"Not in the slightest."

Creedmoor said, "That must be frustrating." He thought:

—Well? Is it him?

—Possibly, Creedmoor. He is old enough.

He noticed the little bottle of green nerve tonic on the desk next to her glass of water and smiled. Ha! Old Dandy Fanshawe had been a devil for opium, too.

"Yes, Mr. Cockle?"

"Nothing, Doctor. Just enjoying the story. I'll work quietly."

"Be as loud as you like, Mr. Cockle—they won't hear my voice, whatever you do."

—Examine him more closely, Creedmoor.

"You sound tired. I can take over for a spell if you'd like."

"That's very kind of you, Mr. Cockle."

"I like a good story, Doctor."

He sat on the edge of her desk, next to the old man.

"Maggfrid, old fellow, come closer. Come on. Join in."

He looked idly through the little pile of her books. Scientific texts, mostly. His eye was caught by a little red book, which looked out of place; and when he picked it up and flipped through it he saw that it was something called *A Child's History of the West*. Some piece of pious propaganda left over from the old Red Valley Republic. How they'd loved to preach to children! Creedmoor flipped with amusement forward past pompous condemnations of the depravity of the Agents of the Gun. He flipped back . . .

—No.

He stopped at the frontispiece, which showed a severe and sharp-nosed man in a splendid red uniform. Dark skin, silver hair.

—No. Surely not. Is this who we're looking for?

—Perhaps, Creedmoor.

—But he's dead.

—Perhaps not.

—Is this him? I can't tell. It might be. Thirty years have passed since this was printed, and the picture flatters him and he has not aged well but the resemblance is there. *Is* it him?

—We cannot be sure. Possibly.

—The Doctor doesn't know.

—A stupid woman.

—Some said he died at Black Cap Valley. Some said he went bandit and died under the Line ten years after Black Cap. No one ever
said he survived mad in hospital. Is it *really* him? Hah! You sent me
here to find the General Enver. Why? What do you want him for?
Tell me your secrets—I'll find out anyway. I'm lucky, after all.

They reached out and stung him—a tiny taste of the Goad. A
gesture of pique. He'd annoyed them. His sinuses burned, and one
eye went bloodshot.

"Are you all right, Mr. Cockle?"

"Quite all right, Doctor. Quite all right."

She held out the little green book of fairy tales. "You were going
to read to the patients."

"Right. Of course." He put down the *Child's History* and read
them fairy tales.

※　※　※

He read them a fairy tale about a message in a bottle. Meanwhile,
the voice in his head whispered to him:

—Listen, then, Creedmoor. We give you our trust. Do not betray it.

—How could I?

—Late last year, the Line seized a town called Brazenwood.
They drilled there for oil. Among the wreckage, in a pawnshop, in
the pages of a girl's ridiculous journal of flowers and fancies, they
found the General Enver's last letter, to his granddaughter, who is
dead, recording his last journey into the mountains. Which mountains, and where? We do not know. The Line does not know either,
or so our spies tell us. The letter speaks of the First Folk, and a
weapon, which lies *somewhere. . . .*

CHAPTER 19

The Spirit

Liv went to the Director's office in the morning. She found him making notes in a journal. He put it aside, stood to greet her, and instantly resumed their conversation as if it had never been interrupted.

"I have something to show you, Doctor." He put on a tweed jacket and folded his glasses and put them in his pocket.

"So you said. And here I am, Director."

"Excellent. Now, you have never asked about our Guardian, I think. About our Guardian; our Spirit; our familiar; our *genius loci*. Our Egregore. Or what have you."

"I suppose I haven't. I think I saw enough of it."

"You're from the North, of course. The old world. Where reason and science are respected. Where things are made and ordered. Where men are ruled by *men*. And by women, too, of course. Such things as our Guardian must seem very strange to you. Almost barbaric, perhaps? No, no; that's all right. Will you take my arm?"

"Of course, Director."

"Walk with me."

They walked into the halls of the West Wing, and downstairs.

"My father," the Director said, "was a medical doctor by training, and a mine owner by inheritance, but an anthropologist by vocation. Like Dr. Hamsa, he studied in Jasper. He was once fortunate enough to visit your *alma mater*, Doctor, in the very far distant north; did you know that?"

She said, "I did not."

"A beautiful place, I hear. We must talk about it sometime. One of these evenings." He smiled at her. It occurred to her that he was unmarried, and probably lonely. However, she could see no polite way to withdraw her arm from his.

They passed through the kitchens.

He cleared his throat. "Anyway. Doctor. Have you met the Hill-folk of these parts?"

"The Folk?" She preferred not to discuss the attack on Bond's caravan. "I suppose so. I've seen them working as slaves in the fields. I believe I saw some watching me from the hills as our coach passed along the roads. They are so very thin and pale and hairy; their long manes remind me of trolls from a children's story. That fierce red paint all over their bodies."

"The red markings are signs of seniority and wisdom. And seniority in the case of deathless reborning creatures is not to be sniffed at. . . . *Free* Hillfolk, you say? Not chained in the fields? If you saw them, then they wished to be seen. The red markings are not paint, incidentally. What they *are* is not clear. They turn to dust quickly under the microscope. I suspect a paste of mica, indigo flowers."

They left the kitchens and passed into a maze of low-ceilinged corridors. She said, "You've made a study of them."

"My father did. The proudest moment in my father's life, after of course his visit to your country, was when he persuaded one of the Folk to allow him entry into their tunnels and he was able to inspect their paintings—I know this from his journals, in which the subject is discussed at . . . Excuse me."

A patient had just emerged from a corridor into their path. The Director let go of Liv and held her patient's hand very firmly between both of his and looked into her wide bruised eyes and said: "Are you well? Do tell me. Do tell me everything."

The girl looked panicked.

"In your own time." He patted her hand and instantly took Liv's arm again, as if switching dance partners, and he whirled Liv away down soft blue hallways.

"The Folk were here before us, of course. Before all our border states and towns. Out here on the western edge of the world, where things are strange and not-yet-made. To them this land is sacred. To them it is the center of all things: the place where the Spirits are born in the earth, where dreams walk. Some people say that the Folk are not fully made men themselves, and that is why they do not die. If that's so, then are they any the worse off for it? Perhaps civilization has not *reduced* them as it has us."

"You're a romantic, Director."

"And you're not, Doctor? You came a long way to be here." He spun suddenly on his heel and withdrew a set of keys from his pocket. "My father studied their ways. Their rituals. He produced a number of monographs. He published a memoir. Through here."

He unlocked a door and stepped through into darkness. His voice echoed back, "Their ways are more complex than perhaps you might imagine."

He struck a match. He was standing in a short corridor ending in stairs down into the basements. He took a gas lamp from a shelf and lit its flame. "Down here."

Liv followed him down into the tunnels.

"The truth is that they welcomed him in, Doctor. The truth is—and I would not tell this to just anyone, but I very much respect your judgment, Doctor—that he recorded that they visited him in dreams; that they crept into town; that they *called* him to this place. That they showed him what I am about to show you. It's quite common, of course, for sufferers from schizophrenia to believe the Folk speak to them in their dreams, but I do not believe my father was mad. It does happen. They can do things we can't. They operate according to different and in some ways looser rules."

She remembered Mr. Bond saying, *Sometimes they bring storms.*

"So. Previously it had been undiscovered. Once it was theirs. Then it became his. He had money, of course, which they did not. Did they know what would happen? He thought they did, or so he wrote. They willed it to be, and it was. But what possible purpose—?"

He suddenly passed her the lamp. "Take this. There are steep stairs here. Be careful." He walked down ahead in the dark, as if he knew each step by heart.

When she rejoined him at the bottom of the stairs, he was smiling again.

"So. Doctor. Where were we? More to the point, where *are* we? Very nearly on the farthest western edge of creation. Out west of us, there's Gooseneck, I suppose, then a few farms, then nothing at all that's ever had a name. Nothing that has been *made* into one thing or the other. Unborn land. And this hospital is scarcely twenty years old, and Greenbank is little older, and before that—this too was nowhere."

"It feels older than that. It feels as if it's been here forever."

"It does." He put a hand on her shoulder, directing her down the passage.

"They say," he said, "that if you go far enough, then the distinctions between land and water and air and fire break down, and there is a churning Sea of sorts, from which the most extraordinary things might emerge, things that make no sense in the made world, but here . . . Egregore is the technical name my father coined for such Spirits, from I believe some unpronounceable word of the Folk." He suddenly hunched over the lamp and attempted to look menacing and wild. He barked "Ek-Ek-Kor! Kek-Rek-Gok!"

He straightened and adjusted his cravat, and gave a small smile. "Or something like that. A technical term for something that hardly admits of technicalities."

He unlocked another door and stepped down into deeper, cooler, subbasement tunnels. The corridor ended in a heavily barred door, which the Director unlocked. On the other side, the tunnel was made of rough red rock.

"The natural caves go very deep here," he said.

The rock beneath their feet was worn smooth. The rock of the tunnel walls was traced with red veins, the work of the Folk. It was all abstractions—whorls, spirals, sharp-edge intricacies. Complex; obsessive; beautiful. The Director moved too quickly, still talking, and she had no time to inspect them.

"My father," he said, "was the first hairless man ever to be taken down here."

"Hairless?"

"Yes. Ah." He stroked his short wiry beard. "I imagine the Folk think of us as *hairless*. Stands to reason, don't you think? Even your very long and fine hair is nothing next to the long and wild manes of the Folk. Of course, we don't live long enough to grow such manes, do we? We die. They come back. Forever and ever. Imagine: they must see us as tiny and fractious and ignorant and hairless and naked children."

"I have no idea, Director. Possibly."

"Possibly? Certainly. Stands to reason. A Hillman is not an adult until he's lain once at least in the dirt and risen again. Lacking that talent, we may never win their full admiration."

He stopped with his hand on a door.

"My father," he said. "They respected him. He was a strange and distant man, and he and I were not close. But this is what it says in his journals. The Folk brought him here. There were three of them. Their names, insofar as it is meaningful to name them, were Kek-Kek, Kur-Kur, and Kona-Kona. They showed him what I am about to show you, and he felt what you are about to feel. He sat down by the water and he cut his arm open from his wrist to his elbow with Kek-Kek's stone knife. Such strength of will! A risk-taker; how could he be sure it would work? How did he know? He did not. He only believed. The Folk respected his ability to bear pain, he wrote. They respected *endurance*. They respected *will* and *belief*. And he bound the wound with his shirt and he slept there in that cave for seven days. The wound did not grow infected. The blood thickened and did not spill. In seven days, he was all but healed. Afterwards there was the most terrible scar and he never recovered full use of his fingers; but he had proved what he set out to prove. Later he came back with iron. There was no place for the Folk here anymore. It was wasted on them, he used to say. He had a vision. He built this House."

The Director opened the door.

"My mother had been injured," he said. "A stray bullet. The Spirit could not give her back the use of her legs, but I believe it eased her suffering. Of course, she's dead now."

"Oh! I'm so—"

He smiled wanly. "I would be very interested, Liv, in your opinion as to whether he acted correctly."

"Director, I—"

"As an outsider, I mean. I really don't know. Please don't answer at once."

He blew out the lamp. The cave ahead of him glowed with a warm red light.

❊ ❊ ❊

The Director stepped aside into the shadows to let Liv pass.

The cave was womb deep and womb dark. The ground was smooth damp earth, which sloped steadily downward to a still pool, as large perhaps as the Academy's duck pond. Tall rocks surrounded it, like women taking laundry down to the river to wash; or, Liv thought, like supplicants coming to be baptized in some very old-fashioned religion.

The water glowed with a soft red light.

The cave's walls were painted with designs of a strangely delicate character; they hung in the misty half light like the branches of the willow trees that hung over the Academy's river.

Self-consciously, she sat cross-legged on the floor.

The light emerged from *below* the surface of the water—like, Liv thought, when one held one's hand in front of a candle, and the light passed warmly through it.

"The light is very beautiful," she said.

She felt a little flushed, and she fanned herself with her sleeve. The cave was oddly warm.

"Director Howell?" She turned around, and was surprised to find that he was no longer visible. The cave was larger than she'd realized, and its depths were in shadow, from which the red markings glittered like stars.

She turned back. Something immense and invisible rose from the water and held her in warm arms and she cried out. There was a smell of earth, blood, tears. It surrounded her, and she could see nothing. It forced its way hungrily inside, probing, reaching. It found, near the surface, a knot of humiliation over her failures with her patients D and G, and a vein of misery and loneliness and resentment of the House staff's general coldness to her. She gasped as those things were brought into the light. It took them from her and lapped them up and she sighed with relief. Her nerve tonic, in all the years she'd been taking it, which suddenly seemed a simply *absurdly* long time, had never been so swift, so powerful, so *determined*.

It found and quickly devoured a nightmare concerning the Line's Heavier-Than-Air Vessel and its hideous insectile gun. It remained unsatisfied. It probed deeper, looking for deeper wounds. . . .

CHAPTER 20

The Wound

~ 1871 ~

The front the August Hall of the Academy of Koenigswald presented
to the outside world was dignified, imposing, severe—a closed face of
gray stone. At its rear, its square form collapsed slowly into a chaos
of arched buttresses, exposed plumbing, conservatories, shadowed
verandahs and cloisters, experimental greenhouses, a surprising pro-
fusion of gargoyles, a cluster of tool sheds where pale students might
at any time be found smoking—though not today—a pen for Dr.
Bey's goats, and down to gently sloping lawns.

The lawns were rolled and tended by old men in bowler hats, each
of whom Liv knew by name, each of whom she greeted on her way
outside with a *Good morning, Mr. _____*, just as she did every morning. One by one, the old men smiled and took off their caps to her.

She wore a white dress in a plain style. She had a book under her
arm, as always. She had a sun hat when she came outside, but she
left it perched on a hedge; she liked the summer sun on her skin.

Sunlight is essential for a growing child, her mother always said.
Healthy body, healthy mind. (Only she said that in a strange old
dead language, which Liv had not yet begun to learn.) She therefore
made sure that Liv's tutors sent her out into the grounds for at least
two hours each day, though Liv's inclinations were bookish.

Her mother was the Emeritus Professor of Psychological Science.
Liv had a great many tutors, because the students were always eager

to curry favor with her mother, and her mother was always busy, and her father was No Longer With Us—an ill-defined state he had inhabited for as long as Liv could remember.

Liv passed the croquet lawn, where the hoops were rusted and spiderwebbed and the balls grown tuberously over with dirt and grass. She walked around the edge of the pond—saying good morning to Dr. Zumwald, the ichthyologist, who leaned over the water, taking notes, conducting observations. The fish were exotics, bright blue: they flickered in the weeds like hot young stars. She crossed the rose garden, where Mrs. Dr. Bauer was cutting samples.

There was a famous oak at the end of the lawns, in the gnarled wood of which a less sophisticated child might have seen faces. Past the oak, the grass ran wild and unweeded as the garden sloped down to the river. Liv broke into a run, panting as she jumped the oak's twisted roots and vanished into the violet of the wild jacaranda. She always started running at the oak. The old men watched her go.

❋ ❋ ❋

Liv always started running at the oak; but that day she had particular reason to do so, because the book under her arm was *stolen,* and she'd imagined, as she passed under the oak's vast shadow, that she'd heard her mother's voice calling angrily after her. (It was, in fact, only two students from the Faculty of Metaphysics debating the Logical Necessity of Other Earths in raised voices.)

Her mother's rules were very clear. The books on the north edge of her mother's library: Liv was *Too Young* for those books. Criminal and Deviant Psychology—her mother's area of principal concern—was not a healthy interest for a child.

The stolen book in question was Gross's *Criminal Psychology,* third edition. Liv sat on her favorite log down by the water and opened the book, but she was quickly lost and bored, and she put it aside with a scowl.

The Academy was built on a bend in the river. This clearing was on a pond that she thought of as *the River,* but in fact, it was only a tiny side-trickle. The great water itself rushed past half a mile away, looping around by the bridge and the road, and down through the town and on to the capital, and south into the Principalities of

Maessen, about which Liv knew nothing at all, except that she once memorized a very strange chart of heraldic devices of the Princes, all eagles and lions and gryphons, which were both eagles and lions at once. . . .

The actual river thronged with barges and noisy boat races, and its banks were paved and crowded with carts and dray horses. This silent clearing was *her* River.

The water was still and green. Willows hung over it. It rained in the night, and the wood all around her was wet and lush and swollen. Her dress was already spattered with mud.

For a while Liv simply closed her eyes and listened to the sounds of the water and things growing wild. Then, very suddenly, very seriously, she cracked open the book again at a random page and began reading out loud:

"The question of homesickness is of essential significance and must not be undervalued. It has been much studied and the notion has been reached that children mainly, in particular during the period of puberty"—about which Liv knew nothing at all, except that she had once studied a chart of physiological changes—"and idiotic and weak persons, suffer much from homesickness, and try to combat the oppressive feeling of dejection with powerful sense stimuli."

Liv paused to consider this. She had never gone more than two days' travel from the Academy, and found homesickness hard to imagine.

"Hence they are easily led to crime, especially to arson. It is asserted that uneducated people in lonesome, very isolated regions, such as mountaintops, great moors, coast country, the West's red barren plains, are particularly subject to nostalgia."

Crime, arson—Liv pronounced the words with ghoulish happy relish. She closed the book again as her mind wandered to thoughts of lonely plains and mountaintops and wild people.

※   ※   ※

The library from which Liv had stolen *Disorders of the Criminal Classes* was Liv's mother's own personal library. It was on the uppermost floors of August Hall, nestled in under a low arched ceiling. It was just down the corridor from Liv's mother's office, where she met her subjects. She believed that the light and airiness of the upper floor was good for their minds. She said: *Blows away cobwebs!*

That morning, when Liv stole the book, her mother had been with a subject. She kept the door to her office open at all times, and encouraged the subject to sit near it. Once Liv had asked why, and her mother had explained:

"It keeps the poor young men from feeling trapped, dear. No one likes to feel trapped, but they especially do not. It prevents them from doing something they might regret."

"What would they do?"

"Raise their voices, dear. Embarrass themselves. Run along."

The significance of this irritating habit, from Liv's point of view, was that her mother sat with a view of the corridor, past which Liv had to creep to get to the library. So she waited at the end of the corridor until she judged that her mother was deeply engrossed in her work. She listened to the subject becoming agitated, his voice rising to a high-pitched quavering sniveling whine, *I don't know how much longer it's the dreams you see I don't know how much longer I can.* She heard her mother's voice, deep and calm: *Collect yourself. Collect yourself. Begin again.* She seized her moment and dashed—

She was safe in the library's dusty silence. No sound but her own panting. A faint pleasant smell of cigarette smoke, her mother's and the subject's, still lingered.

Books lined every wall. Liv ran her fingers along the dust of the spines. She lingered on some of the case studies—arsonists! thieves! women of ill repute—a concept that she understood only dimly— and even murderers. Even something slim that was supposedly a study, from interviews, of an Agent of the Gun, which she understood to be a kind of supernatural monster from the far West, where the world was in the process of making and distinctions between the real and the monstrous were not yet fixed. Something like a vampire? And there was—tucked away on a low shelf—something hand-scrawled on yellowing paper that purported to be a study of the madness of the Engines themselves. The library was like a fairy-tale cave, full of dark and grisly and wonderful treasures.

Liv screwed up her face into an expression of great seriousness of purpose, passed by those frivolous entertainments, and settled on Diamond's *Disorders*.

The subject in her mother's office had gone quiet, so Liv waited for a moment before making her escape. She took a second to flip through the book for the word *thief*.

> It is often intriguing to see the points at which the criminal seeks his "honor." What is proper for a thief, may be held improper for a robber. The burglar hates to be identified with the pickpocket. I remember one thief who was inconsolable because the papers mentioned that he had foolishly overlooked a large sum of money in a burglary. This would indicate that criminals have professional ambitions and seek professional fame.

Only a very stupid thief, she thought, would want her crimes to be famous! Then she slipped the book under her arm and fled, past her mother's office, and through the laboratory and its tables full of glass jars, in which floated the brains, pickled in solutions of various beautiful hues, of criminals, fallen women, apes, and—tiny, intricate, jewel-like—*rats*.

✳ ✳ ✳

The willow shook in a sudden breeze and loosed rainwater shimmering across the green of the pond. Liv, who'd fallen into daydreaming, suddenly started—

There was a rustling in the trees. A *crashing*. There were deer on the grounds, and peacocks; Liv turned hoping to see the puzzled face and gorgeous purple tail of one of the Academy's birds. Instead she saw a man, emerging from the bushes, blundering and snapping through branches.

He breathed in heavy short bursts and his pale moony face was slick with sweat.

On seeing her, he stopped short and stood there blinking. He seemed to be enormously surprised by her presence.

Liv was clever enough to be quite discriminating as to the ages of adults—among whom she spent most of her days anyway. She judged the intruder to be a young man. Hardly more than a boy himself. About the age of the more junior students. He wore an old suit, the sleeves of which were far too short, and a frayed red necktie. He was quite fat.

His pupils were remarkably tiny, making him appear rather alien; Liv wasn't sure what to make of that.

He dabbed at the sweat on his brow with his necktie.

Liv folded away the book and stood with her hands on her hips. He was short, not a very great deal taller than she. She resented his intrusion.

She said, "Are you a student?"

He held up a finger as if to indicate that he'd heard her question, but didn't answer. His peculiar eyes darted all round the clearing. His finger shook.

"My mother is Dr. Hoffman. She's one of the Professors here. In fact, she's very senior. Are you a student?"

The strange young man started a little at that name. "In my dreams," he says, his pale brow furrowed, "I've seen this tree. And this water. This clearing."

"I don't think that's very likely. I'm sure you've never been here before; only I come here.

"It's very lovely. It's very calm. I wish . . ."

He went silent and lowered his finger.

"My mother says that no one *really* sees things in dreams. They only think they do. She says it makes them think they're being spoken to by the universe. As if they're special. If they're weak-minded. Do you often think you see things in dreams?"

He focused on her for the first time. "In my dream, you're weren't here. There was no little girl in my dreams."

"But I *am* here. Do you see? This isn't a place from your dreams. I really rather prefer to be alone here, *actually*."

He blinked at her.

"Are you someone's subject? If so, you shouldn't be here anyway."

He stepped closer to the water. His suit was stained, Liv noticed, spattered with something dark. Many of the subjects—which was, she was increasingly sure, what this poor young man must be—were prone to stains. They could not take care of themselves.

He looked back from the water to her. He studied her, up and down. There was something damp and despairing in his eyes.

"Aren't you scared of me?"

"Not really."

"Most people are scared of me." The rising edge of panic in his voice was familiar; she realized that he was the subject who'd been talking to her mother that morning. "At least a little bit. Most people find me odd."

"You're only not well. That's all."

He started crying—slow trickles at first, then deep sobs, his throat working as if vomiting.

Liv had a handkerchief, lace-edged and monogrammed with her initials, in her pocket. She wondered whether to offer it.

There was a crashing sound again in the trees. Much louder than before. Suddenly there were shrill whistles blowing and the sounds of men shouting and calling.

Fear flooded her. At first she didn't know why, but then moments later, the shape of things became clear. And as the men burst out of the bushes, the old men, their bowlers left behind to reveal shiny sweating scalps scraped by the thorns of the wild garden— and some of the students with them, and a man in white stained overalls from the kitchens, clutching a wooden rod like a club—and as they called out, *"He's here! The bastard's here! I've got him!"*— and as they fell on the strange young man and wrestled him, still sobbing, into the mud—through all that noise and commotion, her heart beat so loud, she could hardly hear anything else.

One of the old men approached her, his eyes red with tears, to tell her what she refused to hear, and she ran.

She ran through the undergrowth and over the tangling roots. She ducked under sharp-thorned branches. She ran up the lawn. The lawn was full of people; the whole Academy had spilled out onto the grass, as they did for festivals or fire drills. They watched her go by like so many tall faceless statues. A few tried to reach out to hold her but she twisted past. She ran through the cloisters, the wet slap of her feet echoing on the cold stone, and into the corridors, through the chapel, through the lecture halls, through the General Library, up through the Experimental Facilities, up through

the Rooms, whirlingly dizzyingly fast round the iron spiral staircase and up past the laboratory, where someone had blundered
through and the jars were spilled, broken, the brain matter dead and
ruined: and one of the old men finally caught her and held her by
her shaking shoulders just outside her mother's office, where for an
instant, before the old man pulled her away and close to his dusty
old chest, Liv saw her mother slumped loosely in her green leather
armchair, her head lolling, blood soaking her chest and her shirt
and her lap, a dark blot tangling sickly through her white hair,
soaking the dome of her skull, the shape of which Liv had never
thought she'd noticed—she'd never thought of her mother before
now as a *body*—the skull now *dented,* a shape as unsettling and unfamiliar and pathetic as a missing tooth in one's mouth.

❋ ❋ ❋

After that, the world stopped making sense to her. It became a place
of meaningless shapes and broken forms, moving through empty
spaces.

When it became clear, after six months, that this condition was
likely to persist, perhaps indefinitely, the Academy made arrangements for her. She was placed in an Institute in town, where she
was given a clean white room, books, and a regular course of nerve
tonic. Her neighbor was a harmless young man with a congenital
deformation of the brain by the name of Maggfrid. She made a slow
recovery. Books helped. After a while, she was strong enough again
to keep a journal, which became a record of her progress toward
health, which became a cold and precise examination of her condition, according to some of her father's theories, and then according
to some of her *own* theories. Eventually her doctors pronounced her
recovered, an analysis with which she was happy to concur; in fact,
not long after that, one of her doctors considered her sufficiently recovered that he thought it not inappropriate to introduce her to his
friend Dr. Bernhardt Alverhuysen, Professor of Natural History,
who was looking for a wife. Sometimes, though, she thought she
hadn't really begun to recover until shortly before the day Director
Howell's letter arrived, inviting her out West. Maybe not even then.

CHAPTER 21

WEAKNESS

The water's radiance faded, until there was barely enough light in the cave to see by. It grew cold. Liv stood up and looked around.

The Director had left her alone. She hadn't noticed him go.

By the entrance to the cave, there was a bench with three gas lamps sitting on it, one of which worked. She went back along the tunnel alone.

She felt the most extraordinary sense of relief. Her body felt light, hollowed out. Initially there were symptoms of mild euphoria, which made her heart beat faster and her hands flutter and a smile rush to her lips. It resembled the euphoria associated with her nerve tonic, or something postcoital. It quickly subsided, leaving only a steady calm joy, which she was unable to describe or compare to anything else she'd ever had the opportunity to experience.

She'd spent two hours with the Spirit, and missed her morning appointments. She took lunch with Maggfrid, and in the afternoon she met with Daisy again, and she found herself trying to describe to them what the Spirit had done for her, but of course, they were both quite incapable of understanding.

At one point in their session, Daisy suddenly reached out and hugged her, which was a new and possibly significant behavior.

✳ ✳ ✳

Her new condition lasted for two days. After that, shadows began to return. A patient's flat and sweaty and pale face reminded her for an instant of *that* face, and then suddenly that old wound was back. It settled in comfortably, like a toad. Every other wound that followed from it was back, too. There was a fracture at the base of her being, and everything built on it was unsteady. She took her nerve tonic before bed and had nightmares anyway—worse, now, than ever before. . . .

She saw the Director again in the morning.

"Well, Doctor? Was it—?"

"Too early to say, Director. It was certainly . . . interesting. Whether it was effective or not is another question. I think I need to return."

He smiled ruefully and gave her the keys.

"I shall have to cancel my morning appointments."

He shrugged. "Of course. Daisy won't mind, I'm sure."

She went down into the cave.

She went back again two days later, and the day after that, and the day after that.

✳ ✳ ✳

The day after that, when she entered the Director's office, she found him standing by the window, with his hands folded behind his back and a distant and formal expression on his face.

"No, Doctor. I'm terribly sorry, but I must say no."

She was utterly astonished.

He seemed unable to prevent his formal expression from giving way to an apologetic smile, and after that, he unfolded and folded his hands again as if not sure what to do with them.

She adopted a reasonable tone. "Director Howell, I have only just begun my study of this phenomenon. It's never properly been examined or understood, as I'm sure you'd be the first to admit; why else would you bring me out here? Its risks. Its benefits. Its potential. Does it truly heal or only *appear* to—?"

"Liv. Doctor. The answer remains: no. I shall have to be firm."

"Why?"

"The Spirit's strength is not unlimited, Doctor. That much we know; that much we do understand. It takes on too much. There is too much suffering in the world. Others need it. Our patients must be our first concern."

He steepled his short brown fingers under his chin and looked at her with concern. "Do you understand?"

She paused.

"Of course, Director. Of course I understand."

"Good. Oh, good." Theatrically, he took the keys to the Spirit's cave down from their hook on the wall, and locked them in his desk. He placed the keys to his desk in the pocket of his white linen jacket.

One more of those regretful little smiles. It made her angry.

"Frankly, Director, my observations so far lead me to conclude that this entire place, and this entire enterprise to which your father and you and hundreds of other unfortunate individuals have sacrificed yourselves, is *entirely* pointless and *entirely* abominable and quite probably quite mad."

His face fell. She turned and walked out, nearly bumping into Mr. John Cockle, who stood in the corridor just outside, cleaning a window.

"All well, ma'am?"

She didn't bother to answer him.

She went straight back to her office and administered to herself four drops of her nerve tonic. She fell asleep in her chair and dreamed of the House and its oppressive heaviness closing in on her, its dampness and must and sadness, and the dark warrens of alien Folk beneath, and the wild emptiness of the hills outside, and the War.

✳ ✳ ✳

That night Creedmoor slipped silently into the Director's private quarters. In contrast to the neatness of his office and his public persona, his quarters were a slovenly chaotic mess, suggestive of some emotional distress, regarding which Creedmoor didn't give a shit. He found the linen jacket slung over the back of a chair and took the keys from it.

He entered the Director's office through the open window, and unlocked the desk with the keys from the Director's jacket. Inside was another set of keys, older and heavier and somehow more serious: the keys to the tunnels.

He went down into the cave. He took no lantern; he needed no light to see by.

—The paintings are Folk stuff.

—It is one of their Spirits. Weak.

—Strong enough.

He came to the glittering pool and knelt by its waters. He ran his fingers through it and felt them tingle. It was warm. He flicked the water idly into the shadows.

He leaned back against one of the painted rocks and contemplated his problem.

—No violence! A terrible handicap for a man in my line of work.

He stared into the pool's light and it shone back blankly.

At the corners of his vision, those red lines on the walls shimmered and slunk in the half light, half-seen, like the stripes of one of those sneaking jungle cats of the far East.

—It is stupid, Creedmoor. Or it would have killed you already.

—A creature of simple appetites.

He considered lighting a cigarette; he thought better of it. Best to leave no trace.

—It wallows in weakness and pain and suffering. It disgusts us, Creedmoor.

—We made it out of our misery. Just as we made you out of our hate, and we made the enemy out of our fear.

—Careful, Creedmoor.

He touched the water again. Water dripped from the walls like rain, a sleepy gentle rhythm. Circular echoes spread out across the pool.

—How do we kill it, do you suppose?

—It is immortal spirit, Creedmoor. It cannot be killed.

—Except by the General's wonderful long-lost weapon, which can kill the enemy and can kill you and presumably this poor misbegotten thing, too.

—Presumably.

The water lapped at Creedmoor's fingers.

—It has limits. When I killed poor William at the gate, it was distracted.

—You were lucky.

—Can't kill it. But I know how to get around it.

—Yes. We know.

—It feeds on pain. So what happens if we *choke* it?

CHAPTER 22

FORWARD CAMP
AT KLOAN

Lowry knocked back three of his gray bitter-tasting lozenges with a glass of water. They made him cough, and his eyes watered. He waited, clutching the edge of his desk with white knuckles, for the surge of energy that would kick his exhausted body into life again. He had not slept for—he didn't recall how long. Ever, possibly. Too much to do. Only science and the will of the Engines kept him plodding forward.

There it was. Yes.

⁂ ⁂ ⁂

"Thernstrom. Drum. Nickel. Slate. To me."

He burst out of his tent into the blazing afternoon sun and the smoke and din and minutely ordered chaos of Kloan Forward Camp, which was gearing up for an assault.

"Come on, come on. Time's wasting. Act fast. No second thoughts or turning back. Come on."

He plunged into the crowds and they followed.

Old Kloan was nearly gone now. *Poor old Kloan,* Lowry thought. *Too late now.* The Line had done to Kloan what it did wherever it touched.

A city of tents surrounded Lowry, heavy, gray and black, squatting on Kloan's remains. Black-clad soldiers emerged, formed into lines that pressed together into squares, rifles at the ready, gas masks dangling loosely round their necks, eyes forward. Lowry shoved through.

"Yes. Yes. Drum? What the fuck's wrong with these idiots."

Drum stopped to shout at a line of men who appeared uncertain where to go. *Pick it up, pick it up, you idiots.* Lowry pushed on.

Over the last month, nearly a full division of the Line's forces had moved in. They came from Kingstown, Angelus, Gloriana, Harrow Cross, Archway, elsewhere. They came grumbling and cursing, blinking in the sun. They were far from any familiar Stations, and they hated the big sky and the hot sun and the bare earth and the thin air, which lacked the *texture* of air into which the Engines had exhaled. So Kloan had been rebuilt for them. Tents; then a *city* of tents; then iron shacks; hastily erected iron hangars and vaults; smoking chimneys and forges and foundries. The Line was mobile. Industry could be brought in on the back of trucks, assembled in days. . . .

An error. He stopped short, wheeled around.

"Slate? Where are these men's gas masks?"

"I don't know, sir."

A rank of Linesmen, maskless, looked dead ahead, avoiding Lowry's furious red-eyed gaze.

"Where the *slagging fuck* are their gas masks? Who's to blame? Mr. Slate? Eh? They'll die without masks. Serve 'em right. Take care of it, Mr. Slate."

He strode on, through slick oil puddles, past ranks of throbbing machinery. He didn't even know what it was. He passed the Signal Corps tent, where several shiny new telegraph machines had recently arrived, just barely keeping pace with the new volume of communications.

A Signalman emerged from the tent and came running up with a transcript in his hand. "Sir—Acting Conductor, sir—the woman has been talking to the target again. The device captured the conversation with better accuracy this time, sir, near twenty percent—"

"The *potential* target, Signalman. Make no assumptions. Anything new?"

"Unclear, sir, as you know he talks in nursery rhymes and we're uncertain how to decode—"

"No time now. Assault under way. Mr. Nickel, go with him."

Lowry and Thernstrom pushed on. Residents of old Kloan, under the eyes of Linesmen, loaded gleaming newly made gas rockets onto the back of trucks. Lowry nodded in approval. The Kloanites were looking pale and sickly now, they didn't take well to the new air, but they were tolerably hard workers when properly directed.

Lowry put his arm round the shoulder of a Kloanite boy.

"Walk with me. The rest of you, get on with it."

Lowry pushed on through ranks of Linesmen who struggled under the weight of machine guns, two men each and one to hold the ammunition case. Their insignia said they were from Gloriana. They staggered to one side as he passed and lowered their heads in submission.

"See that, boy? That's good order, that is."

"Yes, sir."

The forces now at Lowry's disposal had doubled since the day he'd taken Banks's place. More had been promised. But the Enemy was active now in the South and in the East. Agents had destroyed tracks, fomented uprisings, poisoned, burned, committed acts of sabotage and terror. Good; the Enemy was afraid. It meant that Lowry's reinforcements were delayed, but Lowry was willing to make do with what he had.

So far, he had not been removed from command. No doubt he was being watched.

There were cranes overhead. They lifted concrete walls off flatbed trucks and slowly lowered them into place around Lowry and Thernstrom and the boy, like a city exploding in reverse. Lowry squeezed the boy's shoulder. "Wouldn't have seen *that* in Old Kloan, would you? Wonderful, isn't it? Progress."

He passed by a row of Linesmen bent over the innards of black motorcycles. His mood was much improved now, the bustle and fear and respect of his men had put him in good spirits, not to mention the chemicals were now having their full energizing effect. "Good work, that man. Well done. Will they be ready?"

The Linesmen snapped to attention. *"Yes, sir. Yes, sir."*

"Good, good. Forward, forward."

Lowry modeled his good-fellow manner on old moving-picture

images of Mr. Clay, the old Master of Angelus Station. They used to pack the children into the moving-picture vaults, back in Angelus, when Lowry was a boy, to learn the Line's Purpose in glorious pure black-and-white. There little Lowry saw Clay: that jerking gray screen-phantom in muttonchops and long black tailcoat striding through the halls and shadows and shuddering machines of Angelus with a glad word for every busy soot-black worker.

"GOOD FELLOW, GOOD FELLOW"

. . . the moving-picture title card had read.

MASTERS OF INDUSTRY.

Stark white block letters on deep inky black.

Of course, Clay was long gone, *removed,* and all those moving-pictures gone, too, burned probably, and his name forbidden, and quite right, too; it didn't do for a mere man, even a man like that, to get too popular. Still, in secret, Lowry remembered him. Clay had a useful way about him. *"Good fellow, good fellow, strong arm there,"* Lowry said, just as Clay used to. *"Keep it going. . . ."*

A Signalman came running up, disturbing Lowry's daydream.

"Sir."

"What? Good fellow. What?"

"Scouts report they're moving, sir."

"Do they know we know their location?"

"Not clear, sir."

"Which way?"

"Northeast. Across open country, parallel to the road."

"Good. Fine. Good. Then we have them. As you were."

❊　❊　❊

Lowry realized that he was still holding the Kloanite boy, who was trembling and staring at his feet.

"Hey. Hey, boy. Look up."

"Sir."

"Do you know what's going to happen here?"

"Sir."

"We're going to kill a bunch of the Enemy. But that's nothing to do with you. Let me tell you what's going to happen to Kloan."

. . . because Lowry, he explained, was only the point man. That was how the Line worked. Military forces went ahead to scout the path, clear out enemies. Behind them come and will come and will *keep* coming the factories. The smokestacks and forges. The silent soot-smeared foundry men straining in their hundreds and then thousands as the towers of iron and concrete go up and the drills go deeper and deeper down, relentlessly in search of anything that might smell like oil.

Along with the factories would come the gray-haired women of the assembly lines, endlessly grinding up the earth and spilling out goods and necessities.

"This *will* happen, boy. It has to happen. The Line does what it does. First, after the soldiers, they'll send the merchants, the traders . . ."

In fact, the traders were already there, like they were waiting in the earth all along and the Line's passage had ground them up from it, spilled them out like slag or mine tailings. They came in classes and grades like standardized engine parts. Some of them were low nervous men in shabby patched coats, trading shoddy and damaged goods out of battered suitcases; they would get sent out to Goose-neck, and to the farms around Fairsmith, where the hicks would be thrilled to see so much as a dented tin kettle, or maybe a sharper kind of plow or something. Lowry didn't know the details. Some were sober men in gray suits already poking around Kloan's streets, teams of surveyors and engineers in tow, site-scouting for the coming workshops and factories. A few were flamboyant. Strange as it seemed, the Line sometimes had to produce flamboyance and color, because the hicks loved it so: so a few of the traders sported silk ties, silver watches, tall black hats, waistcoats in purple and gold. They brought with them little bright flocks of showgirls. They'd go out to Greenbank and World's End and put on a song and dance to sell medicines, and watches, and eyeglasses; or ephemeral factory-milled luxuries like cigarettes or chocolates. Or spun sug-ars and ices, dyed bright unnatural shades of gold and cobalt blue and cadmium red, refined in the processing towers of Angelus Station or Arsenal.

"How does that sound? Sounds good? Well, boy, the factories aren't built yet. In time. For now, the goods come by Engine and by truck. Bulk. Cheap. Cheap as we care to make 'em. The smallest youngest Station of the Line produces more goods in its factories in an hour—produces more goods *by mistake* every day—than Kloan and Greenbank and Gooseneck would ever have produced in ten years, in *twenty*. You can't compete. As you are to the Folk, we are to you. Right where you're standing, boy, there's going to be a moving-picture vault. I marked the spot personally. Things you'll never have imagined you might see."

Lowry crouched to look the boy in the eye. "So it's time to decide, boy, whether you'll stand in the way and be ground down, or go forward. Join up. Think about it. You have to choose, boy, and you have to choose—"

The boy slipped Lowry's grasp and ran off across the fields.

A gray numbness descended on Lowry's vision.

※   ※   ※

Thernstrom coughed.

Lowry got to his feet. "What are we waiting for? Let's move."

He strode out across the fields. The crops were dead. Now Kloan's fields sprouted huge new tuberous growths: motor trucks and flatbeds and earthmovers and Heavier-Than-Air Vessels and armored cars of various hulking kinds and the jutting stalks of heavy mortars.

He climbed into a truck. Thernstrom followed. He banged the sides. "Let's go. Let's *go*."

※   ※   ※

He watched the assault through a telescope, from an elevated position, at a safe distance, under heavy guard.

The day before, one of the Heavier-Than-Air Vessels had reported sighting a camp in the hills a few miles south of Greenbank. It contained at least two men and one woman. They were concealed from casual detection by the shelter of a tall arch of rock and a stand of pines; they were not well hidden from aircraft. Each of them was armed. They had no cattle, no cargo, no other signs of legitimate employment.

Lowry had not doubted for a second that they were Agents of the Enemy.

He ordered no further approach. Nothing that would spook them. He'd dispatched troops and Ironclads to cordon off the roads in all directions, at a distance from the camp of a mile or more. He'd had Heavier-Than-Air Vessels moved into positions where they could strike quickly at all possible points in a mile's radius around the camp's location. He'd had mines and barbed wire laid, mortars readied.

Now the targets were on the move, heading northeast across open country, and Lowry watched them. They were specks on a vast empty red brown landscape, until he tightened the scope's focus and was delighted and revolted to see them close up—he could see the sweat stains on their clothes.

They suspected nothing. They strolled idly through the hills as if out on a holiday. There were four of them. He recognized two from their photographs in the Black File. The tall Dhravian hook-nosed arrogant-looking bastard was the Agent who went by "Abban the Lion." The leathery young spike-haired woman was Keane—just Keane. There was also a surprisingly fat man in a double-breasted brown suit, with long greasy blond curls; and there was a wiry vicious fellow in battered blue denim, with a bald scalp and long lank white hair in back. Keane was arm in arm with the fat man, and laughing.

Lowry said, "Begin."

It began with the Heavier-Than-Air Vessels. Four of them approached, two from the south and two from the north, converging on the enemy's position. They roared in at all possible speed, leaving huge black trails of smoke across the sky. The Agents, of course, heard, spun, opened fire. Two of the Vessels went down before they could launch their noisemakers, smearing themselves in flame all across the hillsides. Two made it into range and delivered their weapons. They wheeled around and fled. One made it to safe distance.

The Agents ran as the noisemakers landed. They were impossibly fast. Lowry had a glimpse of the woman, Keane, bleeding profusely from her nose, hands clamped over her ears, before she *leapt* directly up and out of his view. . . .

"One down, sir. There."

It took him a moment or two to find the body. The fat Agent, lying still on the dirt.

"Good. Someone better know where the others are. I have no fucking idea."

They were three dots on the red hillsides, diverging west, east, north, at such speed that they raised clouds of dust behind them. The mortars launched more noisemakers, but they landed harmlessly in the Agents' tracks, or were shot from the sky.

They launched poison gas, too. The noisemakers arced and fell like thrown stones; the gas rockets were more complex in their operation, and Lowry preferred them. They climbed into the sky with a tense shriek until their fuel was nearly exhausted—at which point, they used their last strength to silently burst, stabbing sharp white lines of lethal dust down to more or less random locations on the ground below. Soon it looked like there was a white dawn mist hanging over the hills.

"There, sir."

Lowry had the pleasure of seeing Keane down on her hands and knees in a cloud of white gas. Black trucks surrounded her, disgorging dozens of shadowy masked Linesmen.

She staggered to her feet.

Lowry felt a moment of sick terror and, quite irrationally, lowered the telescope, as if somehow it made him vulnerable to her. By the time he'd pulled himself together and found the position again, there was nothing left to see but burning trucks and Linesman corpses and the survivors surrounding something on the ground and bayoneting it over and over.

Distant sounds of artillery and smoke on the horizon indicated that either Abban or the white-haired denim-clad Agent, or both, had encountered one of the cordons. Lowry didn't get the satisfaction of watching those fights.

In the end, all four bodies were recovered.

CHAPTER 23

The General in His Retirement

Creedmoor and Renato stood out in the rocks and dirt, south of the south fence. They leaned on their shovels, panted, and sweated. They were grave-digging.

"You've got a gift for this, Cockle."

"I've had practice."

"I bet you have. You'll have more. These are bad times."

Five of the House's patients had died in the last two days. An infection had swept the East Wing. Renato had volunteered to dig their graves. He seemed to regard it as a kind of penance for his various sins. Creedmoor had offered to help.

He was about ready to make his move, any day now, and he was wondering if there was some way he could arrange things so that he wouldn't have to kill Renato, who he'd discovered he rather liked. He thought it unlikely.

"I've known worse," Creedmoor said.

"Not in these parts. What happened at Kloan . . ."

News of the massacre at Kloan had reached the House a few days ago. Fortunately, no coherent description of Creedmoor had emerged. The House had sent out parties to collect the wounded, and been turned away by Linesmen. Rumor had it that the Line had entirely devoured Kloan. Worse, it was said that the Line was asserting its authority over Greenbank and all the House's other neighbors; and Line forces were patrolling the roads, searching and harassing all travelers to or from the House.

"Where the Line is," Renato said, "their enemy won't be far behind. And the War will come here."

"And it will move on. We've seen it happen, you and I. The House will survive."

Creedmoor happened to know for a fact that there was at least one Linesman up on the canyon's edge as he spoke, hiding among the rocks, looking down at them with his long spyglass. They knew that he knew they were watching him, and he knew that they knew. He couldn't kill them and they couldn't kill him, but his shoulder blades itched, waiting for the sniper's bullet. . . .

He laughed. "Bad times. Good times. Even the good times are bad somewhere. Where'd you learn to dig a grave?"

Renato thought for a moment. He rubbed at the red domino that covered his maimed jaw.

"The Hawsy Range," he said.

"For me, it was the siege of Huka's Mill," Creedmoor lied. "I wasn't there as a soldier; I'd quit soldiering, in fact. On private business. But no one was neutral when the armies came. An infection arose from the shit-pit; you could almost see the black stink of it rise like a dark Power. They gave me a choice: shovel or rifle. Dig graves or fill them. I chose the shovel."

Renato nodded. "Right. Good choice. So. We were chasing a force of men from the garrison at Fort Hawsy, and *they* were chasing after some Agent's band, who were chasing after one of those armies from the old Red Republic that went bandit after Black Cap, who were chasing after who knows what. I tell you, I don't even remember anymore. And we went up into the mountains. . . ."

Creedmoor stopped listening.

Together they lowered the white-wrapped bodies into their graves. Creedmoor held the legs.

"A day's wages," Creedmoor said. "That old Mrs. Fraction in the South Extension goes next."

It was impossible to tell if Renato was smiling, but his eyes looked amused.

"With that cough? No bet, Cockle. Tell you what, I bet you old

Root Busro wakes up one morning and finds he's vanished up his own fundament and gone from this world at last."

"Busro's the gentleman who tells us all we're all just figures in his dream? Infuriating. I bet you someone shoots him, Renato, before he learns to vanish himself."

"No chance, Cockle; the Spirit preserves his infuriating ass. Now here, I got one: a week's laundry duty says the Kid shoots *himself* before the year's out."

"Ha. Could be. Could very well be. How about . . ."

—Creedmoor.

"How about the old General, surely he's due for retirement at last."

"The world would be a better place without Generals. But which one, Cockle? Narrow it down."

"Ah, you know the one I mean. The old—"

—*Creedmoor.*

—What?

—Abban the Lion is dead.

—What?

"Cockle? What's wrong?"

—Abban the Lion is dead.

—Impossible.

—Abban the Lion is dead. Keane is dead.

—Who the fuck is Keane?

—Was. She was with Abban, they were preparing—

—I know who she is. Was. One of the new ones. A child. I knew Abban for thirty years, the things we saw and did together—

—He is dead. Keane is dead. Hang-'Em-High Washburne is not dead but lost to the noisemakers. Drunkard Cuffee is dead. Abban took by far the greatest number of the Enemy with him. Drunkard Cuffee fled and nearly escaped.

"Cockle? Are you listening? Are you sick?"

—What do I care how many he killed? They were to be our protectors on the road home. Now we must go alone.

—You will not survive alone. Not taking the General with you. The Line's forces are very strong here. They have moved faster than we anticipated. You have taken too long, Creedmoor.

—I've taken too long? Fuck you. Fuck you all.

—Fanshawe remains alive in Greenbank. We have more Agents not far from here. Tonight in darkness they will move. Soon they will join Fanshawe. You must be patient.

—*You* tell *me* to be patient? What—?

"Cockle!"

"Yes! Yes. It's the heat. Excuse me. A touch of . . ."

He let go of the corpse's legs and walked back to the House.

✳   ✳   ✳

The truth was, Creedmoor thought, that he *had* been idle in the House, too comfortable, too slow to move, enjoying his clever little puzzle and his card games and his lies and his pretty rustic nurses, and now a trap had closed around him. He could not bear to be trapped.

He stalked back through the corridors of the House. He made for the kitchens and took two bottles of whiskey from a shelf.

Sichel the cook said, "Cockle, what—?"

"Put it on my account. Get out of my way."

He felt like gnawing his own leg off.

He headed up to the roof.

On the way, he bumped into the nurse Hannah, who put a hand to her mouth in shock and said, "John, what's wrong?"

He looked her up and down critically. She seemed a great deal less pretty and pleasant than he'd previously thought. He pushed past her without a word.

In the upper corridors of the House, he passed Dr. Alverhuysen's pet idiot Maggfrid, who stood in his way and seemed too confused to get out of it, and it took all Creedmoor's strength to restrain the urge to kill him.

"I *beg* your pardon," he said.

He climbed out a window onto the roof and started drinking.

Linesmen watched him through their spyglasses from the edge of the canyon. They hid among rocks and anthills. No ordinary man would have been able to see them, but Creedmoor could.

—They may fire on you. Go back inside.

—They will not risk it. Battle here might awake the Spirit; might kill the General.

—We would risk it.

—They are not us.

—No.

He drank and watched the sun slowly turn red and set.

—It was Black Casca who introduced me to Abban. This was back in Gibson City, thirty years ago.

—We recall.

—I loved her then. What happened to her?

—She died, Creedmoor. In the destruction of the Tilden Ship-yards. Many years ago.

—So you told me. I was not there. We were enemies by then.

—She died. One day, so will you.

—She loved Abban, too, and therefore I tolerated him.

—He was stronger than you, Creedmoor.

—He probably was. Dead now, though.

—I remember once we fled together into the southern swamps at Black River—'63, '64. Cypress and slime and shadows and black muck and stink. We hid together in a half-rotted hut that I would swear once belong to a witch. Why were we there? Yes. Yes. We were hiding a letter, I remember. A perfumed letter. It was to be used to blackmail a wealthy Smiler gentleman in Jasper City. Aircraft hunted us. Hot wet rain. Alligators. We ate snakes. Abban hated it, he was a desert creature. I cannot say it was a great pleasure for me. Two weeks together. We did not kill each other. That's almost a friendship, isn't it?

—We know all this, Creedmoor. We were there.

—Your servants are too good for you.

—You are drunk, Creedmoor.

—Yes.

It was dark. He stood and threw the bottles from the roof.

—I am drunk. Steady me.

He dropped clumsily from the roof, clutched hold of a drain-pipe. He swung loosely for a moment. Something warm in the night air closed around him and steadied him.

—Thank you.

❊ ❊ ❊

He climbed in through the window of Liv's office.

He slumped down in her chair and rifled through her papers. The General's file was one of the thick ones.

—She's been busy. Look at all this. What does it mean?

—We do not know.

—Not bad-looking, either. No life for a woman, this.

It might as well have been in code. Perhaps it was. *Day 17—Card A-3; "church spire" (father? Cf. Card E-2, Day 9).* Rubbish! *Day 20—constant on axis 1, axis 2. Naumann's Conjecture?* Cant! *Day 22 - 3 bursts f. current at .5 = min. seizing; exc. sp. re: "horses" (cf 9, 12)* Gibberish!

"Please, Dr. A.," he said. "I am a simple drinking man; can you not write in a simple honest tongue?" It was only thanks to a heroic effort of will, and Marmion hissing in his mind,

—Control yourself, Creedmoor.

. . . that he was able to resist the urge to rip the absurd things to shreds and scatter them petulantly around the room.

He caught sight of himself in the little polished desk mirror and realized that he was becoming unattractive. He pushed his sweaty hair back behind his ears and breathed deeply.

He stole the keys from Liv's desk and stalked down through the empty corridors into the patients' cells. He unlocked the door to the General's cell and stepped inside.

The old man sat awake in the corner of the cell. Erect in his chair, dark liver-spotted hands folded on his lap in the moonlight. He fixed gray-green eyes on Creedmoor, who closed the cell door silently behind him and stood there panting, glaring.

He said, "Well?"

The General did not respond. And slowly Creedmoor realized that the General's eyes weren't focused on him, but on a point slightly to his left—the door handle.

"You want to get out of here, old man? Well, maybe. Maybe soon. First we talk. We talk about you. Look at me. *Look at me.*"

Creedmoor lunged across the room and held the General's jaw tight in his hand, and jerked the old man's face up so that he could glare into those empty eyes.

The old man began talking, grandly, gravel voiced, as if addressing a lecture hall: *"Once upon a time, there was a—"*

Creedmoor cupped a hand over the old man's mouth. He moved slowly, gently. He had not forgotten the Spirit hovering everywhere with its sticky maternal oppressive attention.

"No nursery tales today. Instead let me tell you a story of the old times, old-timer. There was once a man who everyone called the General, because he *was* a fucking General, a great man, unlike you, *sir,* rotting feebly in this piss-pot all day and all night. You who can't wipe his own ass much less command an army."

Speculatively, he let go of the old man's mouth. No further babble came out of it.

"Good. This General. I don't mean you, old man. I wouldn't insult him by comparison to you. This *other* General commanded the forces of the Red Valley Republic. A bunch of ragtag border states and freetowns with big ideas. This was long years ago. Decades, I suppose. I was barely full grown back then."

Drunkenly he paused to count on his fingers. The General's eyes watched him.

"Yes. A boy. Only recently arrived in the West from Lundroy. I was not there at your battles. I was, in fact, a pacifist back then and a sometime sermonizer for the Penniless Brethren, or the Liberationists, or the . . ."

He stopped again. He had unpleasant memories of his time with the Liberationists.

"Yes. I was a different man then, too. I would have read in the newspapers the stories of your bloody southward course of conquest and clucked with disapproval, and shook my head and said, *Violence solves nothing; what fools.* I know better now. You will appreciate the irony, sir, a sophisticated gentlemen like yourself."

He pulled up a chair and sat facing the General, leaning in close. "You were magnificent, sir! In the name of what cause was it— independence from Gun and Line and all domineering Powers? Constitutional and tricameral self-government, yes? Suffrage of all freeholders? Plunder and spoils? Virtue? Enlightenment? Women and wine? Art for art's sake? I forget. Does it matter? You may feel free to answer me, sir, if it *does* matter. Friends of mine died today, and I do not know the reason, if there ever is a reason. Speak up!"

He held up his fingers in front of the General's face and began to count down. "You conquered *first* Morgan, and *then* Asher, and *third* Lud-Town, and then . . ."

He ran out of fingers. "And then all the lands between Morgan and the Delta. I think you fought for a President, yes, or a parliament, or something; would you care to say which? I am not a political man anymore, and I was never a man for the fine details. They are *dust* now, sir, as is your Republic." The General turned his face away to the window. Creedmoor held his jaw and pulled him back.

"Never mind politics. I have a better memory for battles. Your eldest son died on Hekman Hill. Died from a belly wound before reinforcements could arrive. Was it worth it? Was it worth it? From Gloriana and Victory and Harrow Cross, the Line came rolling across the land. And Gun came creeping by night. And your little Republic could not stand, sir, caught between those two great forces. But then there was that one last great battle. In Black Cap Valley, you held the Line back; you checked them. You trapped three divisions of the Line in that poisonous place, the muck and those evil flowers soft underfoot and sick-sweet and deadly and moist; and you flooded the valley with blood. You fed that valley so well with blood! Are you not proud? Were it not for lack of horses, at the end, they say, you might have outmaneuvered them; you might have *escaped;* you might have saved your forces. But no cavalry rode to your rescue, and so the dream died in blood. That was where your other son perished, is that not right? Damn you, answer me. I may break your spindly old neck if you do not. Nothing but the trickle of blood in that valley, the moans of the dead, the slurp and suck of mud. I would be very eager to know how you yourself escaped. And had you saved your own forces, perhaps you could have repeated the trick again and again. Who knows? Perhaps you could have held back the Line. There is a Station now in Red Valley. Arkely. Young but vicious. Does that not sadden you?"

Creedmoor had long since let go of the General's face. The old man's eyes were wandering idly.

"So you lived to fight another day and to lose another day, and another, and at last to fall to the mind-bombs and end up here, an *animal*. What need my masters have of you, I cannot imagine. What is it you know? What is it you *know*? We planned to bring you back home, back to our hidden places, where we could question you at leisure. The girls of the Floating World. Would you have liked that? But now we are under siege. Without you, I might be able to flee. I'm old, but I'm fast. But with you . . . Impossible. I am stuck here. Trapped. Do you know how I hate to be trapped? I shall go mad. So."

He angrily unbuttoned his overalls and withdrew Marmion and pointed the heavy Gun's barrel at the old man's distinguished brow. "Tell me your secrets or I will simply destroy you now."

—I will not fire, Creedmoor.

—Perhaps I will use my hands.

—If he dies, you die by the Goad, Creedmoor.

—Tell me what you want from him. What you know. Why they died.

—This is how you ask us to trust you? *No*, Creedmoor.

Creedmoor watched the General's eyes wander. He watched them flick to the Gun's black mouth and away again. *Oh yes,* he thought, *you know this*. He kept his grip steady.

And eventually the General's eyes drifted down and down and locked onto his and the General's ancient sticklike throat quivered and his mouth worked and he spat in Creedmoor's face.

Creedmoor lowered the gun and laughed. He wiped his face.

—He remembers. Oh, he remembers *us* all right. There's something in there. I should be a doctor.

—Never do that again, Creedmoor. He is ten thousand times more precious than you.

The General looked away, and when he turned back, his eyes were distant again, fixed on some point on the far wall.

"Once upon a time," he said. "There was a . . ."

Creedmoor frowned.

There were footsteps in the hallway outside.

—This problem is beyond your abilities, Creedmoor. Now flee. Do not be found here.

He left by the window.

CHAPTER 24

BREAKING COVER

—Black Roth.

   —I beg your pardon?

   —Black Roth, Creedmoor. And Stephen Sutter. And Dagger Mary.

   —Who the fuck are these people? Why are you waking me with this?

   —Control yourself, Creedmoor. Your fear is beginning to disgust us. They are your brothers and sisters.

   —I know none of these names.

   —So? We do. They will be in Greenbank in two nights. They will join Fanshawe.

   —Fanshawe! I know Fanshawe. Four, then. Only one I trust. They will help us? They will bring us to safety?

   —We do not know. The Line is so strong. But they will only get stronger. This is our last and best chance.

   —You are afraid, too.

   —Get out of bed, Creedmoor. Go back to work. You are beginning to arouse suspicion. Be ready to move.

✳ ✳ ✳

The next day, Daisy died. She died attended by shrieking nurses and one very badly shaken doctor.

It happened during Liv's morning session with her. Daisy quite suddenly interrupted Liv and said: "Oh! I am so, so, *tired* of questions!"

Liv was astonished and delighted. "Daisy—Colla, I mean—Colla, are you talking to *me?*"

Daisy didn't answer. Instead, she took a deep breath and held it. And held it. Her broad simple face went red and then purple and then blue. Her eyes remained quite clear and calm. Then she fell from her chair, and Liv rang the bell and summoned the nurses, who forced open Daisy's mouth but were unable, even by pounding on her chest, to force her to breathe. The poor girl's eyes remained quite calm until—and it seemed to take a terribly long time—Daisy finally expired.

Liv took three drops of her nerve tonic, and when she felt sufficiently recovered, she went to the Director's office.

"It's quite impossible," she said.

The Director smiled sadly. "Nevertheless, it appears to have happened."

"It is simply impossible, Director, for any person to . . . to injure themselves in that fashion. If it could be done, every sulking child in creation would have done it. The mind will not allow it."

"Their minds are broken. Some vital self-preserving part of the mechanism may be gone."

"*Quite* impossible."

"You seem shaken. Please, don't imagine anyone thinks this is your fault."

"Dr. Hamsa has already told me he considers it my fault."

"Other than Dr. Hamsa. Please don't let this discourage you from your studies."

They held Daisy's funeral the next afternoon. The House's entire staff attended, all dressed in black. No one was sure what faith Daisy might have belonged to, if any; in the end, they sent her off with a plain wholesome Smiler ceremony. The Director, who was dressed all in black, save for his gold-rimmed spectacles and a dapper golden tie-pin, gave a long, long speech on the sadness of life, the inevitability of death, and the importance nevertheless of a positive attitude; and he praised Daisy's simple love of music. Maggfrid began to bawl like a baby, and Liv had to lead him discreetly away.

※   ※   ※

—Say what you like about Daisy. She had good timing.

—Quickly, Creedmoor. While the staff are busy. We make our move.

—You don't need to tell me twice.

He ran up to the second floor of the West Wing and called on the Kid.

※   ※   ※

Creedmoor had been working on the Kid for a while. Since their first card game together, in fact, after which Creedmoor had followed the boy as he limped back through the corridors snarling and cursing at nurses. He'd followed him all the way back to his room, and leaned in the doorway, saying, "Kid?"

The Kid lay back on his bed, reading a book. His lips were moving.

"Hey. Hey, Kid."

"I got a name, old man."

"Yeah, but you won't tell anyone what it is."

"I don't want to talk to them."

"Fair enough. My name's John Cockle."

"I know."

"Well, that's great." And Creedmoor came into the room and sat down opposite the Kid. The Kid put down his book—a cheap lurid and entirely false account of scandalous sexual practices among the Hillfolk, told mostly in pictures. He regarded Creedmoor with an insolent glare, which Creedmoor found amusing.

"Fact is, you don't have a name, Kid."

"What are you talking about, old man?"

"Not here. Names don't matter here. Here you're just a number. An entry in a ledger. A patient. A victim. No one gives a shit what your name is, Kid."

The Kid sneered. Creedmoor had to admit, it was a first-rate sneer. Admittedly, it was greatly aided by the scars in the Kid's face, but even so. The boy had character. He must have been something special when he was a soldier.

—A wolf. He deserves better than to sit here with the sheep. He won't get it, of course, but still.

"Get out of here, Cockle."

"Make me get out."

"If that damn *thing* weren't watching, I would."

"No, you wouldn't." He leaned forward and got close to the Kid's face. "You couldn't, and you know it. Maybe once when you were strong and whole. Not now."

"What's wrong with you, Cockle?"

He laughed, and stood up. "Nothing. Just saying. I know how you feel, Kid. Alone. Trapped. Nowhere to go. No hope. Well, a man should stand on his own two feet—no reference, Kid, to your unfortunate situation, I mean *figurative* feet. But a man should stand up on his own, and he should fight for himself, and he should go where he wants. Right? If I were your age, all over again, and I'd ended up here, I'd feel the same way you feel, you can bet on that, Kid. And maybe I did, once."

And he got up and left before the Kid could reply.

They talked again the next night, and the next. *Robert*, the Kid said, *it's Robert;* and Creedmoor told him that names sometimes had to be earned.

"I don't want to end up like the rest of them. Letting that *thing* feed on me. I don't want to rot here, Cockle."

"Not Cockle. Creedmoor."

"What are you talking about?"

"Let me show you something, Kid."

Creedmoor withdrew the weapon from his white overalls.

"This is *exactly* what you think it is, Kid."

The Kid's eyes were greedy, frightened, ashamed, proud, one after the other. He let the Kid trace Marmion's silver inlays with his finger.

"Here's real healing, Kid. Here's what's going to make you strong again. *Dangerous* again. I wasn't much older than you when I was married to this beauty. Many of us were maimed when we took up the Gun. We *heal*. Think on it, Kid. Think on it."

"Yes."

"Think on it."

"Yes."

"I'll need your help. But it's work you'll enjoy."

—We like him, too, Creedmoor. He hates well. But we do not take cripples.

—Poor dumb kid.

—What if he gives us away?

—He won't.

—He agreed too quickly.

—We're quick to corrupt. We come into this world that way.

—What if he has second thoughts?

—Oh, you give our kind too much credit.

By the time of Daisy's funeral, the Kid was as ready as he was ever going to be.

❋ ❋ ❋

Maggfrid was inconsolably distraught. Apparently he'd taken a liking to Daisy; the funeral was too much for him. Liv sat with him in his room and made soothing noises while he sobbed. She brought down the *Child's History* from her office and read him stories of battles, which sometimes cheered him up—not now. Eventually she drew water from the sink at the end of the corridor and measured out five drops of nerve tonic into the glass; that was enough to put Maggfrid swiftly and surely to sleep.

She consulted her ugly noisy golden pocket watch: the Director would be talking for a while yet. She had time to check on her patients. She had time to check on her experiments.

With the help of Renato, who was strong and handy with a saw, and could be trusted not to be squeamish, she had removed Daisy's brain the night before the burial. What was being buried was an empty husk; everything that mattered of Daisy was pickling downstairs in a jar in Liv's office. She was eager to study it further. She had already identified some unusual bruising in the thing's folds. Poor Daisy—something might still be salvaged from her tragedy.

Liv left Maggfrid snoring and slumped mountainously on his

narrow bed, and walked out into the silent corridors. She slipped the *Child's History* into a pocket of the black jacket she'd borrowed for the funeral.

Unusually silent. At first she put it down to the funereal mood of the day, but as she walked through the corridors and down the stairs—Maggfrid's room was on the fourth floor—she began to feel uneasy. So many empty rooms. Where was everybody? They could not be walking in the gardens; perhaps they were all in one of the common rooms, but then would it be so quiet?

The legless blond boy in room 320—rolling his chair indecisively back and forth between window and door of his cell—shook his head and told her he didn't know where anyone was. She left him be.

His neighbor was more forthcoming. "Downstairs, ma'am. Try downstairs." He refused to say more—but that already was as much conversation as the man was capable of on any typical day, so she left him be.

She took the stairs down and stepped out into the second-floor corridors just in time to see John Cockle emerging from the General's cell, leading the old man with him. Cockle had his arm around the General's shoulder and was gently urging him forward on his unsteady legs. Cockle had a heavy kit bag slung over his shoulder. He met Liv's gaze, and his eyes were terribly cold for a second; then he smiled. "Taking the old man for a walk, Doctor. Fresh air's good for the lungs."

There was a tension in the air that Liv did not understand.

"He's not due for a walk, Mr. Cockle. We don't want to strain him."

The General smiled vaguely. Cockle's own smile stiffened. Liv's late husband Bernhardt had been a Professor of Natural History and an amateur taxidermist; Cockle's smile was now like the glint of the glass eye of one of Bernhardt's stuffed foxes.

"Please return him to his cell, Mr. Cockle."

"Can you begrudge an old man fresh air and light, Dr. Alver-huysen? On this day, when we are reminded of death's constant shadow, can you begrudge him that? He's heavy to hold, though; will you help me with him?"

"I will not, Mr. Cockle. Please return him to his cell."

"No, Doctor."

"I will call for assistance."

Cockle sighed theatrically. The next second—she did not see Cockle move at all—the General was slumped against the doorframe, and Cockle was pointing at her an implement that she realized—it was not immediately obvious to her—was a gun.

"Come here, please, Dr. Alverhusyen."

She considered her options. She said no.

Cockle scowled.

"I don't know what you think you're doing, Mr. Cockle. I suppose you've gone mad. But you can't menace me with that thing. You *cannot* harm me. The Spirit of the House will not allow it."

"I wouldn't be so sure of that, ma'am."

She took a small step backwards. Cockle seemed to think for a second. Then he ran at her. He was terribly fast; he had crossed the length of the hallway and clamped his rough hand over her mouth almost before she could scream; but not quite.

❋ ❋ ❋

—You should have killed her, Creedmoor. She has raised the alarm. Things will be bloodier now.

—A whim. I'm rather surprised myself, to be honest.

—Kill her now, then.

—No. I think not. She may be useful to us.

❋ ❋ ❋

He wrapped a surgical rag around her mouth and dragged her by her arm. When she struggled and moaned, he took a little green bottle of chloroform from his pocket and waggled it significantly in front of her eyes. She stopped struggling. Dragging them by their arms, poking them in their backs, he herded Liv and the General down the hallway.

The stooped form of Mr. Root Busro stepped into Creedmoor's path from an adjoining corridor and turned sad eyes in Creedmoor's direction. Busro looked neither frightened nor particularly surprised. Creedmoor gestured him out of the way, and he stepped mildly aside.

Creedmoor stopped in passing. "If I shot you, Mr. Busro, what would happen to me? And all the other things in your head? Where would we live if I unhoused us?"

Busro shrugged.

"To break the world. It's a tempting proposition."

—Kill him or don't, Creedmoor. We have places to go.

"Ah—go on, then, Busro. Keep yourself well, for all our sakes. Come on, Doctor."

Busro wandered away, and Creedmoor dragged Liv and the General down the stairs, down the hall, and toward the stables.

✳   ✳   ✳

Aha! Footsteps, rushing; then at the other end of the hall, a half dozen men came running or, in some cases, limping.

Renato was at the fore. He wasn't stupid, Renato: he sized up the scene quickly. Renato was an old soldier, Creedmoor recalled— Renato, too, had probably dragged more than a few women struggling away from their homes in his time.

"Cockle, have you gone mad? Let her go. The old man too."

"Or what, Renato? I am armed and you are empty-handed. I *will* be passing through."

Renato looked so disappointed! Or so Creedmoor thought; it was hard to be sure, with the scars on Renato's face, and the red domino covering his maimed mouth. But Creedmoor was well familiar with other people's disappointment.

Renato folded his arms and stood in the middle of the hallway. The other men stood beside him. Arms folded—those who had two arms—they blocked the hallway. They stood calmly.

Renato sighed. "You may've gone mad, Cockle. But you're not a fool. You know the rules. You know what would happen if you fired. But you won't. Put it down. Let's talk."

—Kill him.

—Must we?

—Of course. He is dangerous.

The gun fired, and the greater part of Renato's head burst bloodily across the wall.

—Did I do that or did you?

—It makes no difference, Creedmoor.

The other men fell to the floor, hands over their heads, and waited for the Spirit to strike.

Nothing happened.

*   *   *

Nothing happened—because of what the Kid had done, a little over an hour previously.

Creedmoor had given him the master keys to the House.

"From the office of the Director himself. Consider yourself honored. Now, go do it. As we discussed. Quickly."

"What about you?"

"Smashing their rifles. Administering sedatives to their horses. And so on. Two-man operation. Quickly, quickly, poor Daisy's funeral can't keep them busy forever, and it isn't every day a much-loved vegetable dies. *Run!* Or your best approximation. Go *on.*"

Panting, cursing, the Kid limped from door to door, knocking and calling the occupants out. The keys gave him a certain authority. Besides, the inmates needed little persuasion. They were always eager to see the Spirit.

Some of the near-catatonics and depressives had to be dragged out and damn near shoved down the corridor, but the Kid was determined; he was deadly keen to prove himself to Creedmoor.

The Kid collected some thirty or forty of them. Creedmoor had said that should be more than enough.

The Kid led them down through the hallways and the basement corridors and into the tunnels in the rock, where the wheelchair-bound had to be lifted and carried over the shoulders of their fellows.

As they neared the Spirit's cave, some of the more eager of them ran or limped on ahead.

The Kid *loathed* them: their crippled flesh—their craven need—their cowardice and ugliness.

They crowded past him and into the Spirit's cave. They sat or slumped in reverent silence around its pool. They bathed in its soft red light, the gentle *drip-drip* of the waters.

The Kid felt the Spirit's touch as a softening in his bowels; a coolness in his mind; a warming pleasant itch in his scars and his stump. He resented it; he was damned if he would let that *thing* feed on his essence, lap at his wounds, steal his bitterness from him. He gritted his teeth so hard, he opened the stitches on his face and his wounds dampened. He stood at the entrance to the cave, leaned on his stick, scowling, ready and eager to force his fellows back in if they tried to leave. They did not; they sat there. Most of them had their eyes shut. The light bathed them all.

"Get in," he said.

They looked nervous.

"Go on. All the way in. Why not? No one's here to stop you."

They waded in. Two of them first, then another, then another, then a stampede. They laughed and moaned as the water lapped at them.

After a while, the Kid thought maybe the light was dimming— guttering—thinning—sleeping. The constant drip of the water lost its rhythm, and then went silent.

It went dark. The Spirit was sated. It slept. The Kid turned and limped as fast as he could back up the tunnel.

✳ ✳ ✳

—Kill the rest of them.

—No.

Creedmoor strode right through Renato's men and past them, dragging the General with one arm, pushing Liv in front of him with the other.

—Do not do that again.

—Do not make it necessary, Creedmoor.

The stables were not far away; a left turn and a left again.

"Can you ride?"

Liv shook her head, then, looking terrified into Creedmoor's cold eyes, seemed to change her mind and nodded her head *yes*. Creedmoor wasn't sure what to make of that—and anyway there was only one undrugged horse left in the House—the others stand- ing now drowsy and trembling—and so he had her sit on the same big bay horse as him and the General. Creedmoor snug in the middle; the General in front, lanky bird-boned body held tight in Creedmoor's lap; Liv behind, holding tight to Creedmoor if she knew what was good for her. So awkwardly arranged—it would be bearable for just long enough—they rode out into the gardens, where the funeral was breaking up in confusion, and what was left of the staff ran for cover at the sight of Creedmoor's little band. One or two of them tried to shoot—they'd gone and grabbed their rifles from the armory—and their weapons clacked dully and did nothing.

They fled.

Creedmoor turned his attention to a purple-flowering bush not far from the fence, from under which poked out a pair of expensive and well-shined shoes that could belong only to Director Howell.

"Mr. Director, sir! Yes, you; come out of that bush, sir. You dropped your spectacles; take a moment to pick them up. There. There you go. Stand up straight. Will you do me a kindness, Director? Will you open the gates?"

Creedmoor tossed the keys; the Director fumbled the catch and picked them up off the ground. His face was scratched and his neat vest was torn from the thornbush he'd hidden groveling in. He hunched for fear of Creedmoor's Gun—*fair enough! fair enough!*—and scuttled over to the garden gate, the House's rear entrance, and unlocked the bars and bolts, and sidled crabwise away. Creedmoor considered shooting him—it seemed unfair that the man who made his career from the House Dolorous was himself unscarred. Marmion urged,

—Kill him. He may still organize a force to pursue us.

. . . and it gave Creedmoor enormous pleasure to spite it.

So Creedmoor rode out of the gardens of the House Dolorous, with the General and Liv balanced precariously before and aft. The hoarse and desperate shouts of the Kid echoed distantly in his ears—the Kid stumping along on his stick after him crying: "You promised! Take me with you! You promised!"

Creedmoor rode out and into the rocks and dust of the canyon. Not as fast as he would have liked, with the woman and the old man to hold on to; but he spurred on the horse a little anyway, in a moment of high spirits. Liv moaned but did not dare let go.

Behind them a wind was gathering and the dust was rising and the pressure was building. The Spirit was perhaps waking from its sated stupor, hungry again for *more* pain, *more* sorrow. . . .

✱ ✱ ✱

Liv looked back. Out of a blue sky, gray rain clouds formed over the House, and it seemed they swelled and settled into the form of fat haunches and shoulders and pendulous arms reaching out desperately after them. A sad giant; a baffled god. A wheeling flock of birds formed its hair. Its eyes were glimmers of sun, and it wept light as it reached for them.

It tries so hard, Liv thought. She felt it tug weakly at her soul, and her soul answered. *It tries so hard, but it cannot heal everyone, cannot protect everyone, not in this terrible world.* The horse jolted beneath her. *It cannot cure the world.* Creedmoor yelled something. We *woke it! We made Gun out of our spite, and Line out of our fear, and this poor thing out of our sorrow.* Liv was very afraid for herself, but for a second, as she prayed for it to reach out and save her, she was able to pity it.

. . . but they'd left it too far behind; they were too hard to reach, and it let them go, and recoiled into its lair. The clouds dispersed. The birds moved on. The gray form unraveled. And the overburdened horse came up over the edge of the canyon and onto the red plains. The sky was very wide and blue and cloudless; the sun hung so high and golden, it was like it was daring Creedmoor to steal it. He breathed in dusty air deeply.

"Once upon a time," the General said, "there was a high tower, where a young girl was visited by white birds. She . . ."

Creedmoor laughed and let the old madman ramble.

Two roads led off into the hills. From the west road there was the sound of roaring engines, coming closer. Wheels and shouting men and clumsy weapons being readied. No surprise; of course they had been waiting and watching for this moment.

Creedmoor felt Marmion's dark burning strength in his veins; he felt the world go slow and cold and brittle around him while he grew faster and hotter and more terrible with every second.

—Two motorcars; carrying at most twenty men; at most two heavy motor guns. More will follow, but for now there are two.

—Fair odds.

—Many more will follow.

—An honest fight. A clean fight.

—If you like.

BOOK THREE

WESTWARD

CHAPTER 25

FLIGHT

Liv kept her eyes firmly closed. She thought yearningly of the tonic for her nerves, which was behind them now—*far* behind perhaps—she had simply no idea how far they had come. She was thrown from side to side. She held on to Cockle's back as tight as a frightened child, hating him, fearing him, not understanding. The muscles in her back and shoulders and arms were in agony. Her gag smothered her, and she was light-headed. The horse's hooves were a mad, meaningless din. From behind, there was the sound of roaring motors, shouting men. Cockle turned and laughed and there was another noise, right by her ear, the loudest thing she'd ever heard in her life, so loud that for a moment all sensation left her. She felt herself floating in darkness; lifted up helplessly from her body and its aches and terrors; set aimlessly adrift in a cool no-place among black waves. The sensation somewhat resembled falling asleep.

A small clear part of her mind said: *This is the beginning of a dissociative state, the onset of fugue, occasioned by shock and trauma. You are going mad, Liv. Again.*

She disagreed. It was the world below that had proved itself mad—had proved itself to be, behind its rational façade, a world of broken forms, meaningless turbulence, terror and incoherence.

Another part of her analyzed her situation. *This is politics. This is history. Cockle is an Agent of the Gun. Therefore the men pursuing him are servants of the Line. Or perhaps vice versa. You are not important. Therefore, somehow, the General is. Plans are in motion. Oh, Liv, you have become involved in history.*

She disagreed. There was no logic to her situation.

And yet another part of her was wordless, long gone, dreaming of history, adrift across the red plains of the West, its wars, its bitter myths, lost in images of blood and battle and destruction and madness. The lies of the *Child's History*—progress, purpose, virtue— turned inside out, revealing horror. Four hundred years of the Great War. She dove deep, looking for meaning, past politics, past the bloody fall of the Republic, past the battle of *this* and the battle of *that* and four hundred years of cruelty visited on and occasionally by the Folk and back to the first colony at Founding, which now seemed like a mistake in itself, the frightened colony huddled behind its walls against the alien woods, mad and dark and shifting. . . .

✳   ✳   ✳

Cockle pulled her to the ground. Her legs gave way and she sprawled in the dirt. She opened her eyes. It was night and cold and they were among pines. Needles pressed sharply into her palms. She did not know how much time had passed or where she had been.

She tore at her gag, released it, and coughed and retched until a thin trickle of fluid ran from her mouth.

The horse was a huge steaming shadow at the edge of the pines. A few feet away, the General sat stiffly against the trunk of a pine. Cockle stood above her, smiling. He held out a hand. "Are you all right, Doctor?"

She looked him in the eye. He kept smiling.

She swore to herself that she would not beg.

She begged.

"Please, Mr. Cockle, let me go. I know nothing, I have nothing, I cannot help you, I will only slow you down. I am a stranger here and—"

"Doctor—"

"And no one will pay for my release. Let me go, Mr. Cockle, I will tell your pursuers whatever—"

"*Doctor—*"

"Please, Mr. Cockle."

"Call me Creedmoor. Cockle was a nice enough fellow, but he's gone now. Stand up. No?"

He lowered his hand and shook his head sadly.

"If you were caught by what's pursuing us," he said, "you wouldn't lie to them. Not that I doubt your good faith or your word as a doctor. But no one lies to them. Their methods of interrogation are more *methodical* than ours. And what would be left of you afterwards wouldn't be you anymore, which I'd regret. So we are in this together now, Doctor."

"In what, Mr. Co—Creedmoor. In *what*?"

He waved a hand vaguely in no particular direction. "Everything. The Great War. We're coconspirators, Doctor. No doubt it's obvious to you which side you find yourself on—I am far too handsome and charming to be a Linesman."

He sat down with his back against a tree, facing her, and began to roll a cigarette. He looked up at her and smiled.

"I brought my vices with me. I apologize for taking you without warning. I imagine you miss your nerve tonic. Not to worry! We're going to meet my very old friend Dandy Fanshawe in Greenbank, and he'll have all the opium you need to *float* all the way back east with us if that's what you'd prefer. One more reason to stick with me."

"The tonic is a medication, Creedmoor—"

"As you please." He lit his cigarette, took one long drag on it, then extinguished it between finger and thumb. "No light tonight," he said. "No fire, either, sadly."

"Why am I here, Creedmoor?"

"Why are any of us here? They don't tell me everything, Doctor. One of the things you think before you take up the Cause is that when you do, you'll be in on all the great secrets of the world; not so."

He pointed at the General, who was staring at his feet and quietly muttering nonsense.

"There's a secret in that old fool's head. He saw something, or did something, or went somewhere. There is a weapon. I can say no more. But anyway, the secret is buried under the rubble the enemy made of his mind."

He patted the gun at his side. "My usual methods of questioning are ineffective here. So I thought, Dr. A's a clever woman. I read your notes. Didn't understand a damn word of 'em, but they looked clever enough to a simple man like me. So I want you to heal him, Doctor. That's not so bad, is it?"

"I don't know how to heal him, Creedmoor."

"Try."

"I don't know how."

"I have faith in you."

The General suddenly shuddered.

"Cold night," Creedmoor said. He walked over to his bag and extracted one of the House's rough woolen blankets. He wrapped it around the General's shoulders.

"Sorry, Doctor. I brought only the one blanket. Unchivalrous of me; but I'm sure you agree the patient comes first."

He removed a rope from the bag, too, and tethered the General's ankle to the tree.

"In case he wanders off. Of course, there's no need to do the same for you. I wouldn't insult you by suggesting anything of the kind. Do be mindful, though, that I sleep lightly."

He lay down on his back with his hands behind his head.

"We're sleeping, Creedmoor? What about . . ."

He looked up. "The Line, Doctor. Say it out loud if you like, no awful consequences will follow; or at least nothing that wouldn't have happened anyway."

"The Line, Creedmoor. Are they not—?"

"We will be meeting friends of mine in Greenbank, at the Grand Howell Hotel. I can't vouch for most of them, but Dandy Fanshawe's a good fellow in his way. But we cannot ride down into Greenbank like this, three to a horse, you in your funeral clothes. A little way over the edge of a scarp to the south, over which I suggest you do not wander in the night, there are some farms. We shall resupply in the morning. Sleep while you can, Doctor."

He lay back and started snoring.

Liv had rarely seen anyone sleep so quickly or deeply. Had he no conscience?

But the Gun by his side, close to hand, that did not sleep.

Nor did Liv. She sat hunched against a tree with her arms around her knees. She listened for sounds of pursuit. It grew colder.

As it happened, she *did* have her nerve tonic with her, or at least a tiny three-quarter-empty vial of the substance, which she kept around her neck at all times in case of emergencies, for her patients or, if necessary, for herself.

She had no water with which to take it, so she let a slow greasy droplet of it bead on her fingertip, and she licked it quickly up. Under the sickly-sweet of the palliative, her finger tasted of sweat and earth and pine needles. Her tongue tingled and went numb. A numbness rushed up through her head. She'd never taken it unmixed with water before. A peaceful greenness washed over the world. She slept.

※　※　※

"Wake up."

Creedmoor shook her.

"Wake up."

It was still night. They were still in the pines.

"Do you hear that?"

"I hear nothing, Creedmoor."

"No. No, you wouldn't. But they're close." He stared off at something invisible in the distance.

"They're close. Move."

They staggered on through the night. She did not know where they were going or why.

※　※　※

In the morning, they went down into a village: a nameless scattering of houses and farms at the foot of a brown stony hill.

"We've lost them for now, Doctor. But there must be no alarms. Remember, Doctor, if we are caught, I will die and the Line will take you and so eventually so will you, and their machines will drill the poor old General's head for secrets. I very much want to live and be free. Do you?"

She nodded.

He smiled. "Excellent! Then I can trust you to make no sign of distress when we go into town. If there is any disturbance, if there is any violence, if I'm forced to bring bad luck to these folk, it will be on your head, Doctor."

He looked her up and down. "Perhaps we can say we're husband and wife, Liv. May I call you Liv? The General is your elderly grandfather from the less-blond side of the family. The rest will come to me. Come on."

Before they went down, she took a drop of the tonic.

※　※　※

Creedmoor purchased a horse from one of the farms in the valley, and a saddle, and a pack and blanket, and a dented kettle and a bent pan and tin plate; and the farmer's wife was not far from Liv's size, and so Creedmoor haggled for sensible country clothes for her—red flannels and breeches—while Liv herself sat silent in the corner, the unmixed tonic numbing her mind and flattening her vision so that the farmer and his wife and the horse and the kettle seemed all infinitely distant and toylike.

The horse was mostly brown.

"Not a bad animal, Liv."

"If you say so, Creedmoor."

"I know horseflesh. Can you ride?"

"Yes."

"Where did you learn? Back home? The old world, Koenigswald? Let me guess: a riding academy. Green meadows, flowers. Ponies? I'm not convinced."

"What do you expect from me, Creedmoor?"

"So Professor Creedmoor's School of Equestrian Studies is apparently in session. Come on."

Creedmoor set a pace that terrified Liv and left her so badly bruised and aching, she thought—when they finally dismounted—she might never walk again. Creedmoor held the General tight, and the old man mumbled and droned. Liv could think of nothing all day but staying on the beast's back. She barely noticed their course curving around—from northwest to northeast to east to southeast— as the afternoon wore on and the sun moved across the blue sky. But when they finally stopped for the night—only for a few hours, Creedmoor told her—then the fear came back.

She sat shivering against a rock as Creedmoor stood and smoked and looked out over the dark hills.

"Greenbank tomorrow," he said.

CHAPTER 26

GREENBANK

The Subaltern came around back of the armored car and knocked on the doors to indicate that it was safe for Lowry to emerge. Lowry took a last swig of his coffee; he gargled and spat half the cold gritty substance back into the mug. He adjusted his collar and removed his spectacles. Then he buckled on the heavy rubber muzzle of his gas mask, strapping it on tight and snapping on the round bottle-glass goggles. In theory, the gas had long since dissipated, but Lowry didn't like to take risks. Once he was fully ready, he opened the door and stepped out onto Greenbank's Main Street.

It was the early hours of morning, and the sky was flat and gray. Smoke shadowed the town. The Grand Howell Hotel and the Howell Bank and half the buildings on Main Street were crumbling ruins. Fires still smoldered here and there.

Lowry slipped for a second on a drift of loose ashes. He waved away the Subaltern's offer of a helping hand and stamped his way down Main Street, over the bodies, to the scaffold his men had erected in the square.

Three bodies hung from it, trussed up by bloody ropes like butchers' pheasants.

Two were dead. One Lowry knew from the Black File: Dagger Mary. The other was a woman, too. Red hair. No other remaining identifiable features.

It hadn't been possible to capture the women alive. The women had been the worst. They usually were.

The third was an old man. Face handsome but badly bruised now. Long gray hair wild and matted with blood. Mustache burned. He'd been wearing an elegant russet silk suit when the morning's operation began. After he'd finally been beaten to the ground, he'd been stripped of its torn and bloodied remains. He now hung naked, ropes cutting into his pale flesh. His torso was a ragged mass of wounds. An ordinary man would have been dead long ago. He looked ridiculous, vile.

There'd been a fourth and final Agent. Name unknown. He'd fled. Yet to be recovered.

"Fanshawe, right? You called yourself Dandy Fanshawe."

The old man lifted his head and grinned. His left eye was closed with blood. The right regarded Lowry with contempt.

"So I did. I was famous and that name will not be forgotten. Do you have a name, Linesman? Does it matter?"

A gesture of psychopathic dignity. Lowry said nothing.

The Agent laughed. Lowry was glad his own eyes were hidden behind the dull glass shields of the gas mask; he wouldn't want the Enemy to see him flinch.

Behind him, his men cleared away the dead.

Very little of Greenbank had survived the engagement. If it had been possible without alerting the enemy, Lowry would have preferred to warn Greenbank's people to evacuate.

"You did this," he said. "You made this necessary. Skulking among innocents."

The Agent rolled his good right eye. "Oh, *please,* Linesman."

The Agent's left eye was already starting to heal. His masters' hideous power still flowed into him, mending his flesh. Lowry could see broken bones writhing and knitting under the old man's skin. Within a couple of hours, he'd be as strong as ever.

"Show me your face, Linesman. Are you ugly? All Linesmen are ugly, of course, but *how* ugly are you? This matters to me. Show your face. Are you afraid of me? Still?"

He was. He'd never stood so close to an Agent. He had a stone of fear in his gut, and his skin crawled. He folded his hands behind his back to stop them shaking. He stared up at the Agent from behind his mask.

How many had Fanshawe killed? The Subalterns were still reckoning up the extent of the losses, but they were heavy. The capacity of Lowry's forces had been very significantly degraded. Numerous Vessels, Ironclads, and trucks lay broken and smoldering all around. Bodies filled the streets in every direction—many of them were Greenbank's former citizens, but more than Lowry would have liked wore the black of the Line. Dozens were dead at Fanshawe's hands, and that wasn't counting the tolls taken by the women.

"I won't ask your name, Linesman. It doesn't matter. Your kind have no names."

"Lowry."

"You're boring me, Linesman. You are a very ugly and inferior man."

"Fanshawe. We have a file on you."

"No doubt you do. Does it liven your dull life to read it? I imagine it does. I could tell you some stories, Linesman."

"A sodomite. And an opium fiend."

"What of it?"

"Creedmoor gave up your location, Fanshawe."

In a manner of speaking, that was true. Creedmoor had spoken his own name, and Fanshawe's name, and the name of the Grand Hotel in Greenbank, in the presence of the Doctor's signaling device. Five hours later, the Signal Corps had translated the information and brought it urgently to Lowry's attention.

Fanshawe lifted an ironic eyebrow and said nothing. Lowry had hoped for more of a reaction.

"Where's Creedmoor going now, Fanshawe?"

Lowry had hoped to catch Creedmoor with the rest of them. No such luck. The Agent had been taking his sweet time getting to Greenbank. Lowry had struck too soon. He was not yet sure whether he would or would not be punished for his error of judgment. Likely he would.

"I have no idea, Linesman. Creedmoor and I have not been intimates for many years. Do you want to hear all our gossip? Do you want to pry and sniff into our intimate secrets?"

It was possible to track the movements of the signaling device, but not with precision. The device could be tracked to within a mile or two of its location, depending on various conditions—bad weather interfered with the transmission, as for some reason did the presence of substantial populations of Folk. It had been dreadful in the House. And the signals, of course, took hours to receive and decode. Five hours ago, Creedmoor and the target had been a few miles northwest of Greenbank. Where were they now?

Fanshawe blinked his left eye. The swelling was nearly gone. "Are you a virgin, Linesman? Have your masters permitted you to mate? Do they consider you good breeding stock?"

Lowry clapped his gloved hands, and his attendants approached, carrying a low steel folding table. On the table, arranged neatly, were three Guns, grips facing Lowry, deadly muzzles facing safely away.

An attendant handed Lowry a hammer. It had a head of pig iron and a shaft that Lowry had to grip in both hands. He raised it over his head and crashed it down on the leftmost weapon, so that the table rang like a cracked bell and shook and sparks flew from the steel. Behind the ringing, there was something like *screaming* at the edge of Lowry's hearing. He drew the hammer back—and *again*—and again and *again* until he was red-faced and sweating.

Lowry tore off the mask and breathed heavily.

The table—and the earth around it—was littered with the bright silver coils and broken black wood of the Guns. Their demonic blood was a thin and sulfurous scattering of powder.

"There's an end to them, then." Lowry threw the hammer aside and gasped for breath. "Your master's gone, now, Fanshawe. Gone back to its Lodge. And left you all alone. It'll come back, I know, with some new servant. You won't."

There was a satisfying change in the Agent's bearing. Now that his master was gone, he hung limply. Now he looked frightened, old, weak. His bruises blackened, and his left eye began to bleed again.

"Cut him down. Harmless now. Not so clever now. Right. Let's get to work."

CHAPTER 27

OVER THE BORDER

They rode south toward Greenbank across open country. It was just before dawn, and the sky was banded red and gray. Distant trees were black silhouettes.

They rode along the crest of a steep rocky slope. At the foot of the slope, far below, were white rapids; beyond that, wilderness stretched out into the west.

The General rode with Creedmoor, lashed inelegantly to his back. Creedmoor was telling stories.

". . . so in those days, I was part of Fanshawe's circle back in Gibson City. Young and new to the Cause. We were the finest fellows in town. All Gibson's fashionable folk paid court to us."

Liv gave him no encouragement. She hated the sound of his voice.

"The banks all owed us a cut. No doubt it went to finance some struggle somewhere; I don't know. Fanshawe was the strategic thinker among us. But so one fine day, Liv, Fanshawe and Casca and I— Oh, Casca! So dark, so beautiful. This was after we'd fished Casca half-dead from the river, a suicide in her black dress, and recruited her into our number. . . ."

Liv's hands tingled on the reins. The urge to *break* and flee was so great that she could hardly resist it. Her hands twitched.

"Fanshawe and Casca and I paid a visit, listen, to a certain bank manager, I shouldn't name him, who had refused our cut; and Fanshawe, cool as you like . . ."

Would he gun her down? Perhaps, perhaps not. He would almost certainly *retrieve* her, slung over his back most likely, a humiliation she did not wish to endure.

"On *another* occasion, I recall, Fanshawe . . ."

She clutched the reins. Now, she thought; now or never. While he was lost in his horrible, ugly memories. . . .

Creedmoor fell silent.

The next instant, he yanked on his horse's reins so that it reared, and he *screamed*. Had the General not been roped in place, he would have been flung limply to the ground, and most likely rolled helplessly down the slope and into the rapids below.

Liv froze. She held her breath.

Creedmoor's face went red, and the veins on his neck bulged. He drew his Gun and he fired again and again into the rocks, shattering them into bloodred dust; he was screaming in rage and the Gun was screaming, too, in its way; she could not tell which one controlled the other.

Suddenly it was over.

❉   ❉   ❉

—What shall we do what shall we do? All of them dead! Fanshawe dead! First Abban then Fanshawe! And Keane and whoever-the-fuck else! They were to spirit us to safety what shall we do now?

The place inside Creedmoor's head where he spoke to his master was still again, dark again. It stank of powder, and the darkness echoed dully and throbbed with blood; but their rage was exhausted. The voice came back to him:

—We are thinking.

—You were supposed to have thought before we embarked on this venture my friend now where are your plans?

—We are thinking. It is hard. It is . . . noisy in our Lodge. Our siblings' bodies were broken. Belphegor, who rode Fanshawe. Yblis, who rode Mary. Gorgon, who rode Black Roth. Their spirits released in pain. You cannot imagine how we feel pain. Their spirits have returned to us; now they must be reborn in new hosts and rebirth is painful and noisy. We can think of little else but vengeance. The flames rise.

Creedmoor waited.

—Stephen Sutter fled Greenbank. He would not return to battle. We struck him down by the Goad, and he died in a ditch. We were angry and in pain. It was unwise.

—I don't care I don't give the least fraction of a shit what happened to Sutter what will happen to *me*?

—We are still thinking. For now, you must flee.

—The Line is all around me! My time is running out!

—You must flee west of here.

—There is nothing west of here.

—We know. You must go into uncharted lands. Nameless and unmade lands. Unsettled lands. It will be . . . strange.

—No.

—They will not expect it.

—And if they do? If they follow us? We will go farther and farther from any allies.

—And so will they. They will pursue you, but the western lands will wear them down. It will be hard for you but harder for them. You will not be coming home for a long time. It is the only choice. We have decided.

—West of this place is uncreated land you bastard the lights and the sea and the storms and the wildness and the nightmares and the monsters I will go mad I won't go.

—Of course you will go, Creedmoor. It is the only way out of this trap. Go now.

—You piece of shit Marmion you pieces of shit all of you I pray the Line destroys and devours you but only after I am gone safely to my grave so so be it then: west it is.

✳ ✳ ✳

Liv's horse had fled a little way when the shooting began. Not far. Now it waited nervously, and Liv waited with it.

She watched Creedmoor lower his Gun. He put his head in his hand and his chest rose and fell as he breathed slowly, deeply.

She didn't dare move.

At last he lifted his head and turned to Liv.

"Liv? Still here? Good. Our plans have changed. We will not be continuing to Greenbank and to old dear friends and east to civilization and to warm baths and a change of clothes and the councils of our betters. We will be fleeing west, into uncharted, uncreated lands. We will be pioneers."

He pointed with a grand flourish across the valley below, in a direction that Liv supposed was westward. He smiled as if he were trying to sell it to her.

The river below was wide and white-rushing. Its banks were stony and the river itself broke around sharp black rocks. Her heart clenched at the thought of fording it. Beyond the river were sandy plains of yellow grass and a dark forest of tangled oaks; hills and a forest of pine; sharp hills like broken teeth for miles and miles, under a haze of heat and clouds; blue mountains wreathed in white— And Creedmoor's grinning teeth were discolored and uneven, and his eyes bloodshot.

"Let me go, Creedmoor."

"No."

❈ ❈ ❈

Lowry got nothing out of Fanshawe. He worked Fanshawe over, and the old man just kept laughing through bloodied broken teeth. Lowry's satisfaction in the task didn't last long, and after it was gone, the job still stretched out ahead of him through a long, long afternoon in the ash and ruins of Greenbank. Eventually he got sick of the whole sordid business and handed it over to his professional interrogators. Unlike the Agents, he was not a sadist, he was not a pervert, he did not relish cruelty for its own sake.

He returned to Kloan, and to the warm noisy shadows of his communications tent.

He spent some time drafting a message to be wired back to Angelus and Kingstown.

THREE AGENTS OF THE ENEMY EXECUTED AT GREENBANK.

"FANSHAWE" TAKEN ALIVE. TARGET IN HANDS OF FOURTH

AGENT, BELIEVED TO BE "JOHN CREEDMOOR," LOCATION
PRESENTLY UNKNOWN.

They would punish him for losing Creedmoor. A message would
come, not to him but to some underling, Thernstrom perhaps, an
order that he go the way Banks went.

In hopes of saving his neck, he noted that

DR. ALVERHUYSEN IS STILL WITH AGENT AND TARGET.
SIGNAL DEVICE ENABLES PURSUIT OF TARGET. SIGNAL
DEVICE WAS PLANTED ON DOCTOR AT SUGGESTION OF
ACTING CONDUCTOR LOWRY.

It was a stroke of extraordinary good luck that the Agent had
taken her with him. Had he not, Lowry would probably have
shot himself hours ago, to save the Engines the expense of a telegram.

He tried to think of a way to suggest, without precisely lying,
that it had been part of his plan all along that the Agent would take
the Doctor with him. . . .

"Sir."

"What is it, Thernstrom?"

"The interrogators have finalized their report."

"Fanshawe. Yes. And?"

"In summary, sir: He was contacted two months ago in Gibson
City with instructions to—"

"No. Where's Creedmoor? Where's Creedmoor going? Does he
know that?"

"Southeast. He was to accompany Creedmoor and the target to
a place in Keaton called—"

"Have it destroyed. That's a thousand miles away. Where is he
going now?"

"Unknown."

"Execute him."

"Sir—"

"Execute him. We can't spare men to look after him. And look,
I've already stamped the forms."

* * *

He stamped the forms to authorize the disposal of the three Agents' bodies by fire. He stamped a series of further forms authorizing the payment of compensation for damage and loss of life to Greenbank, in return for permanent representation of the Line's interests in Greenbank's administration.

And then he had to deal with his Subalterns, who wanted to tell him just how severe their losses were: how many vehicles had been lost, how many men, how much matériel. . . . His stamp was needed on a whole weary afternoon's worth of forms.

* * *

The next day he reorganized the patrols, taking into account the recent degradation of his forces. He spread them out to cordon off all points southeast of Greenbank.

No signs of Creedmoor were reported.

The Signal Corps reported that the device was working poorly; Creedmoor might be anywhere in a thirty-mile radius.

No orders came that he should be relieved of command.

Nor the next day.

* * *

Thernstrom came rushing in again. It was the late evening of the third day after the Greenbank incident.

"What, Thernstrom."

"The Signal Corps, sir. The device is working again. It passed through some interference, but it's transmitting again with tolerable precision."

"Well?"

"Precise location unknown. But he's gone west."

"West?"

"Straight west. Fast, too."

"There's nothing west of here. Slag it, there's hardly anything *here*. Where's he going?"

"West, sir. He has several days' lead on us. He'll be out past the farthest outlying settlements and into wild territory."

"Then we follow."

"Sir? We're undermanned for any such expedition. Conditions will be unfavorable for—"

"We follow. No delays. No time for reinforcements. All presently available vehicles and men to be mobilized. Go on. Get out of here, Thernstrom. No one sleeps tonight."

Thernstrom stepped out. Lowry sat in the shadows with his head in his hands.

West. Unmade lands. Part of him was so terrified, he could vomit; part of him was so relieved, his sallow jaw kept creasing into a smile. . . . If the empty sky and frightening hills here on the western rim were bad, the lands beyond would be a nightmare. On the other hand, Lowry did not plan on waiting around in Kloan to be relieved of command if there was any respectable alternative. So west it was, then.

CHAPTER 28

The Rains

West of the western rim: the first thing that fell apart was the weather. It rained for ten fucking days, and all Lowry's motor trucks mired in mud. The Heavier-Than-Air Vessels were grounded. Even the tents were washed away in mudslides, and somehow dozens of Lowry's men managed to drown, to fucking *drown*, miles from any river or sea, on flat mud. So much mud, the Engines themselves might flounder and drown in the depths. The rain fell in shafts that hammered Lowry's skull; it fell in sheets that washed the world away five feet in front of Lowry's face. And the signal from the device in the gold watch the woman carried was weak; in the constant crashing rain, the ethereal vibrations of the device's delicate hammers and rods were lost—drowned—*damn* it. Four artillery pieces and two motor guns sank in mud. Two of the telegraph devices were ruined, and one of the two amplifiers, despite all efforts to waterproof them. Patrols went out and they came back days late, or not at all, as if washed away. Their weapons jammed so bad, it was a good thing they *couldn't* catch up with the Agent; he would have slaughtered them. They crept forward. Every foot they slogged forward, they slid six inches back.

After ten days, the rains broke without warning or apology—just plain stopped and the clouds parted and the sun came roaring on in, and within ten minutes the Linesmen were steaming and baking in their soaked uniforms. Some of the men put their heads back and turned their pale faces to the sun.

"Well, come on, then," Lowry roared. "Let's get moving again. Come on, come on."

Fuck the weather out here. It made no sense and it had no decency at all. That was how it was out there, over the border of creation and into lands not yet reduced to order. How Lowry longed to see all that land subdued and made sane.

※　※　※

The rains had come out of a cloudless sky without warning—a sudden madness of the heavens. Mud and rain came roaring downslope toward them. The first thing they lost were their horses. One was washed from its feet and broke its leg. The other fled into the rains and was lost from view. After that, Creedmoor and Liv moved on foot from shelter to shelter, caves and overhangs, as one rat-hole after another flooded. Very soon there was no shelter. "High ground," Creedmoor said. "High ground!" He slung the General's brittle body over his shoulder. Liv staggered behind, sliding in the mud; sometimes Creedmoor had to carry her, too. The rains seemed to pour down for years; they seemed to have been pouring forever. The drumming and pounding of it drove all thoughts out of Liv's skull except survival, and soon even that was beyond her, and all she could do was inch along in Creedmoor's wake. From time to time, Creedmoor was talking to her, but she couldn't hear his words; in the gray hell of driving water, she could barely see his mouth working.

She took the last of her tonic; cupping her shaking hands to keep the rain out, she drank down the dregs of the vial. She risked overdose, but she did not expect to survive the rains anyway. For some uncountable blissful period of time, she felt nothing at all; she believed she was following Creedmoor, but she could not be sure of it; the rains were gentle and their purpose clear and sane.

But that was the last of it. As it left her body, her joints racked with pain and her head burned; Liv lay in a cave, while the rains pounded outside, and the last of that sickly-sweet poison sweated out of her crawling skin. It seemed that Creedmoor stood over her and wiped the sweat from her brow. It seemed that her mother was there, holding her, whispering to her, scolding her for her weakness. Her very good friend Agatha from the Faculty of Mathematics offered to make her green tea, and stirred poison into it with a dirty knife. The cave's walls crawled and glimmered with the Folk red markings, and it seemed she was watched, from the cave's far shadows, from beneath a vast and wild black mane, by curious alien eyes in a deathly white face. She thought she was going to die, but she did not.

When she returned to herself, she was *not* in a cave, and perhaps never had been; she was slogging along through mud, Creedmoor's arm around her shoulder as he pulled her and pushed the General and yelled, "Faster, Liv! They're closing."

It was still raining.

※　※　※

A Line patrol blundered upon them.

They were slogging ankle deep across a plain of seemingly infinite mud and rain in search of shelter. Creedmoor forged on ahead, shoulders down, the General in his arms. Liv stumbled after him, screaming, "Creedmoor!"

He screamed back, "Keep moving!" One had to scream to be heard over the rains.

"Where are we *going*, Creedmoor?"

"How would I know? Forward. West or east or back, which way's the damn sun? Day or night? How would *I* know, just—"

And the patrol just stepped out of sheets of thundering rain ahead of them as if from behind a curtain. More than a dozen Linesmen in black uniforms rain-plastered to their bodies. They marched heads-down. When they saw Creedmoor, their mouths fell open with surprise and exhaustion. Creedmoor looked briefly stunned, too, as if the rains dulled even his keen predator's senses.

He shoved the General back into Liv's arms. The Linesmen lifted their rifles, struggling against the rains' downward force. She pulled the General down into the mud, where she lay prone beside him.

When she looked up again, Creedmoor was gone. She heard his Gun fire once, twice. Between washes of rain, she saw a red flash and something moving. The Linesmen shouted in panic. She saw bodies dressed in black falling—one, two, three, four—how many of them were there? The mud went slick and black with blood; it was quickly washed away. The General kept trying to stand. He was barking out nonsense orders—calling out, "To me! Forward for the Republic! Strike at their flank; damn their cannon!" Liv tried to hold him down for a moment; then she just let him go. He fell over anyway in the rain-slick blood-slick mud and lay on his back shouting orders at the sky. The noise of the Linesmen's rifles was tinny and rattling next to the deep thunder of Creedmoor's Gun. Then it stopped altogether.

She was crying. Rain washed mud and tears from her face.

Creedmoor pulled her to her feet. "Keep moving."

✳   ✳   ✳

The rains ceased without warning. The sky parted and sun burst across the world. Everything shone so bright, it seemed it could catch fire.

They were in a wide and deep valley. Before them the ground rose through bands of green and brown scrub, becoming a great hillside like a woman lying on her side, above which the sun burned through white clouds.

Beneath Liv's feet, the mud was already drying, turning red, cracking.

Creedmoor shaded his eyes, looked around. The air was beautifully clear, and it was apparent that there were no Linesmen for miles around.

"West," he said. "Soon we won't be able to trust the sun out here, but for now that way's west, so: Forward."

He lifted the General into his arms and set off up the hill.

✳   ✳   ✳

Again they stood on the side of a hill, among pines and hemlock, overlooking a valley. Below them, the hill was a slope of flinty scree that slid down into a dry riverbed. How was it possible that the riverbed was dry after those rains? This was a strange place.

Something sparkled and glinted in the sun, all along the riverbed far below: It might have been gold; it might have been diamonds.

The other side of the valley was a sweep of dense and dark forest. Liv could name none of the trees. She was dreadfully hungry and weak and she believed she was developing a fever.

Creedmoor scanned the distant forests, one hand shielding his eyes from the sun, the other on his Gun. "They say," he remarked conversationally, "that if one presses far enough to the west, there is a sea. The handful of madmen who've pushed out this far report it. A sea. Just as the ancient far East is bounded by old seas, and cooled and gentled by their lapping waters."

Creedmoor was not hungry or weak or sick; he never was.

"But the *western* sea is a mad and stormy thing. Indeed, those few who have seen it say that it is hard to know where the land ends and the sea begins, so changeable and stormy and foggy and swampy and generally foul the land out there is, so windswept and glacier-carved into sealike waves. And the sky, they say, cascades and pulses in green-blue waves of starlight, space-light. And the sea itself is cold and steams and rages like fire. I should think it is very haunted indeed. The world that is not yet made is where demons are born. The world unravels at its edge. But fortunately, I do not think we shall have to go so far. I believe our pursuers are lagging very far behind and soon . . . Aha!"

His Gun was in his hand and he fired at the far hillside.

He turned to Liv and smiled. "A deer! Fat days are here again, Liv! You stay here with our elderly friend. Talk things over with him. Remember your vocation, Liv—we want this poor old man up and walking and spilling his secrets."

"I can't, Creedmoor."

"Liv. Listen closely. This is what you are here to do. For all I know, it may be why you were put on this earth. What he knows might mean the end of the Great War. *Peace,* Liv. They'll build statues to you."

"I don't know what you're talking about, Creedmoor."

"Excellent. I'm glad we've got that sorted out. Get to work. I'll return shortly."

He picked up his pack and rummaged for knives and rope.

"It's *miles* away. What if some other animal steals it?" Liv hated the desperation in her voice, but she was so *hungry*.

He grinned. "What animal would dare?"

Then, hand on his head to keep his hat on, he slid down the scree. He went fast, recklessly, like a much, much younger man.

When he was far enough away—he was *never* too far away to see her, but she hoped he wasn't looking—Liv scrabbled on the ground for sharp flints. She snapped away a dry branch from the nearest tree. It was stiff; she was horrified by how weak she had become. She sat with her back to the valley and tried to sharpen a weapon from the wood. It snapped in her hands. She was too weak to cry.

She composed herself.

She sat cross-legged in front of the General, and she held his face—gently, firmly—so that his eyes were on her.

"Secrets, Creedmoor says. Spilling your secrets. What do they want from you, you poor old man?"

His eyes wandered again and she let go. She sighed.

"You must have been a very great General indeed, if they want you so badly."

Liv sat before the General and considered how to proceed.

"In the rain, you were giving orders."

He began to mutter nonsense.

"Wait; hush; listen. What did you remember? Where were you? What's still in there?"

He did not stop muttering.

With some self-consciousness, she sat straight; stiffened her spine and squared her thin shoulders; deepened her voice as much as she could; and asked, "What are your orders, Sir?"

Was that a flicker of interest, of recognition?

He began to urinate.

※　※　※

Creedmoor came running noisily up the scree slope, the deer slung over his shoulders. Its pelt was a striped red-black that Liv thought—not that she any great experience with deer—rather unusual. Creedmoor threw it down and rubbed his bloody hands with glee.

"Any progress with our friend, Liv? Has he said anything interesting?"

"No, Mr. Creedmoor. Do you expect results in an hour?"

"Call me Creedmoor. And you're quite right; early days yet."

Creedmoor made a fire. He looked at the General's rheumy eyes and reached into his pack, from which he produced a vial that Liv recognized as fever medicine stolen from the House. He dribbled it down the old man's throat. After a little thought, he offered the vial to Liv. She dosed herself with shaking hands.

Creedmoor drew a knife from his boot. "Well?" He waved it vaguely at her and at the trees. "Gather firewood." He dug the knife point in under the deer's hide and began tearing.

She went into the trees to gather firewood. It was a strange and unpleasant experience, about which she was too tired to think clearly.

She brought back dry branches and stacked them crosswise, according to his instructions.

He butchered the animal in front of her. Her mouth watered at the grisly sight. In a warm conversational tone, he explained just how it was done. He cut the meat into thin strips, some of which he hung to dry in the sun over the spiny branches of a tree on the edge of the slope, and some of which he cooked.

"To absent friends," he said as he gnawed on a strip of flesh. "My friends are all monsters and they should have been hanged long ago; nevertheless, I shall mourn them. Not because they deserve to be mourned, but because I do not deserve it either, but I hope they'll miss me when I go."

His head was bowed. "So: Black Roth. Dagger Mary. Stephen Sutter. Keane. Hang-'Em-High Washburne. Drunkard Cuffee. Abban the Lion. Dandy Fanshawe." His voice caught on the last name.

He looked up and winked. His sentimental mood seemed to leave him as fast as it had come.

"On the other hand, fuck 'em all; they're dead and I'm alive." He laughed. "Absent friends!"

Liv gasped and put her hand to her mouth; she realized that she'd quite forgotten Maggfrid, who'd be terribly frightened without her. . . .

❋   ❋   ❋

After they ate, Creedmoor sat himself back in the shade and re-moved a small paperback novel from his pack. He opened the pages carefully; the rain had forced its way into the pack, and the book was lumpy and swollen. The *Child's History* had fared no better.

"Someone must keep the flies from the meat while it dries, Liv. Would you mind at all taking the first shift? . . ."

Liv spent the remainder of the afternoon standing on the edge of the steep slope, swatting at flies with a pine branch. Her feet were blistered, and she shifted her weight uncomfortably. Her nerves flared and jangled and ached dully, and she could think of little else but her nerve tonic. There was no hope of obtaining more of it while they remained on their westward course. There were substi-tutes for it that could be extracted from certain herbs, but she had only the haziest idea how. In any case, she recognized none of the strange plants that grew out on the edge of the world. They seemed made according to no settled or sane rules of botany.

For instance—among the trees from which she'd cut firewood for their meal, there had been a growth of bristly greenish black weeds; and she'd been deeply disconcerted, on bending down for closer inspection, to see the leaves and petals surrounded by twitch-ing black segmented *legs* like those of flies, or bees; as if the distinc-tion between animal and vegetable was not yet clearly or regularly observed out here. She had very much disliked the way the green flowers turned slowly toward her.

Liv told herself to be strong: to maintain, by force of will if nec-essary, her reason. She swatted the branch back and forth, back and forth, and watched the dull meanderings of the flies. After a while, she forgot herself in the work.

Creedmoor fell asleep over his novel. Twice, he lurched up and fired a shot that claimed an animal in the scrub nearby. The first was a white rabbit; the second was rabbit-eared but otherwise mostly doglike. He cleaned and stripped them, too.

Shortly before he fell asleep for the last time, he looked up and waved to catch Liv's attention.

"Yes, Mr. Creedmoor?"

"I forgot to tell you. That old madman who pissed on you this afternoon is none other than the General Orlan Enver, architect and hero of the Red Valley Republic, greatest of the great men of Western history."

He grinned broadly and his eyes twinkled. He seemed to have hugely enjoyed revealing that secret.

Then he leaned back and fell asleep for good and was soon snoring like an Engine.

The General was asleep, too. Liv regarded him with astonishment.

※　※　※

The stars came out. They were different. A spiderweb of light hung over the western edge of the world. One bright star shot and burned out, then another; then a third; then the web dissolved into darkness.

※　※　※

In the morning, they went down into the valley.

CHAPTER 29

THE VALLEY

—Creedmoor.

—Yes?

—You talk too much to the woman. You should not have told her who the General is. We ordered you not to.

—Too late now. And how else can she do her job?

—And you let her poke around in the General's mind. If she succeeds, you know you must kill her.

—I understand your position.

—In the end, you must kill her.

—Suppose I refuse? I'm not saying I will or I won't. But if I did. What then?

—You are increasingly rude and arrogant. We should renew your respect for your masters.

—But you need me whole and healthy and fleet of foot.

—For now. Creedmoor, we must leave you for the time being. There are deliberations under way in our Lodge. We are making alternative plans. In the event of your failure. It is . . . difficult. Painful. Frightening. It demands our attention. We can leave you with strength; you will not have our wisdom.

—Somehow I'll manage without your wisdom, then.

—You have your orders. Flee west. Do not think we are not watching you.

✳   ✳   ✳

Creedmoor suddenly lifted his head and smiled at Liv.

"Courage, Liv. All will be well. We must go on alone as best we can."

They walked down the dry riverbed. It was their second day in the valley. The narrow corridor stretched through the hills and farther into the distance than Liv could see. She'd learned to tell by the sun that they were heading roughly westward.

"Above all, I regret the loss of our horses," Creedmoor said. "Noble beasts, the both of them. But the *important* thing is that there are no roads out here, and we'll avoid the plains, and so our pursuers' vehicles will be useless to them. They can't ride horses, Liv, the Linesmen can't—they are afraid of their muscles and eyes and teeth and wildness. And their little fat legs and blackened lungs will not carry them fast. We have a solid lead. I am quite optimistic."

The sun itself still blazed red-hot; however, it had set very early the day before, as if it was midwinter. Creedmoor had shrugged and told her not to worry about it: things would be strange as they went west.

There'd been dreadful winds down the valley all night, lifting the stones of the riverbed and sending them hurtling down. They'd sheltered in a river-carved grotto and listened to the echoes of the tumbling stones. In the morning, they walked on over the cracked red mud of the riverbed.

✳   ✳   ✳

Around midday, when the sun flooded the riverbed with terrible heat, they sheltered again under an overhang of rock. It had been hollowed out centuries ago by the river's passage. There was a trickle of water beneath it, which Creedmoor pronounced safe. He filled his water-skin and doled out the strips of dried meat and they ate.

It was hard work forcing the stuff down the General's throat, as he moaned and shifted and refused to swallow. He fouled himself, and Liv had to clean him as best she could. She felt very keenly the absence of nurses.

"It would be unchivalrous of me to leave the old man's care entirely to you," Creedmoor said. "Remind me to take my turn one of these days."

He settled in to read his novel with evident pleasure. He started to whistle.

Liv sat beside the General.

"General Enver," she said. He didn't look at her.

She felt ridiculous now, reading him fairy tales or talking to him like a fool, or prodding and poking him with drugs and electrical therapy.

"We are in the presence of history," Creedmoor interjected. She ignored him.

"General, I read your book," she said. She was aware that the General was a great figure in the West's troubled history; that meant very little to her. To her, the broken creature beside her was first and foremost the author of the *Child's History*.

He was humorless, proud, a little self-righteous, in many ways narrow. His lectures on *decency* and *fair play* and *democracy* and *moral cleanliness* were often unintentionally amusing. His system of virtues (seven personal, six civic, five martial, illustrated diagrammatically in an appendix) was closer to madness than to philosophy. And yet . . . the *Child's History* emphasized more than once that General Enver was *merely an ordinary dutiful hardworking citizen like yourself,* but it was clear that he was not, and knew he was not; he was a visionary.

He had been there in the Republic's first days, in Morgan Town, when it was a conspiracy of scholars and idealistic aristocrats, meeting in the upper rooms of taverns. He alone had dared to make their philosophies real. He had liberated Morgan Town, Asher, Lud-Town. He had turned the Red Valley Accord, which had been a kind of loose mercantile association of baronies and trading companies and city-states, into a military alliance, then a movement, then a faith, then a spearhead of conquering forces that had swept south, and west, and then east, toppling petty states and towns and self-styled dukedoms and kingdoms and forcing their rulers, at gunpoint if necessary, to sit at the great stone meeting hall in the Red Valley

and, grumbling, to cast their votes in the jury-rigged but rather remarkable democracy of nations they called a Republic. He had
purged the Agents of the Gun from his lands; he had held back the
Line. Liv knew little of politics and nothing of tactics, but it was apparent even so that he was a genius.

He had been present at the banks of the Red River for the signing of the Charter, but he had not signed; he'd said he was just a
simple soldier. He left that to the Presidents and the Senators and
their kind.

Liv removed the *Child's History* from the pocket of her baggy
red flannel shirt. It had been swollen by the rains and now by her
own sweat into a shape that was curved and gilled like fungus, and
decades of its story were now unreadable, but it had survived. It
was a well-made old thing.

"Do you remember this, General?"

He said nothing.

"Very well, then." She opened it and began at the beginning.

In the winter of the year 1482, representatives of the nations and trading companies of the East met to discuss the news that a pass had been
discovered in the World's End mountains, which had previously been
thought impassable. Indeed, it was commonly believed by scholars and
peasants alike that the mountains had been erected by God for that
very purpose—impassability. Perhaps He had changed His plans. Reports of initial explorers were of an ocean of dark woods. It appeared
that God's Creation was far larger than anyone had imagined. Some
foolish priests, who saw in change only the danger of decline, not the
hope of progress, fell into despair. Braver and more forward-thinking
fellows discussed exploration. From these discussions came the famous Council of Seven Nations—the Maessen Principalities, Dhrav,
Juddua, the Provinces of Kees, little Koenigswald. . . .

The General showed no interest.

"Try violence," Creedmoor interrupted. "I made progress when
I threatened him."

"You are disgusting, Creedmoor."

She'd been suddenly angry; the words had spilled out. She glanced at him nervously, but he only smiled.

"Cooler now," he said. "Positively chilly. Time to move on."

✳ ✳ ✳

All afternoon and all evening they trekked west down the valley. The sun seemed not so much to set as to *recede,* shrinking slowly in size and in brightness as if withdrawing from the world into the interstellar depths, until at last it was only one of countless dim stars. The moon, by contrast, grew and grew, larger and larger, yellow at first and then closer to red, until Liv could no longer bear to look at it.

When she tore her eyes away from the derangement of the heavens, she noticed that Creedmoor was looking intently around at the valley's dark walls, and appeared to be listening for something.

He put a finger to his lips.

She listened. She slowly became aware of sounds of distant motion—and snorting, and grunting, and what might have been barking.

Something howled.

"Not the Linesmen," she whispered.

Creedmoor shook his head. He whispered, "No. They are days behind us. Short legs, as I think I've said. I hear them only faintly, which is a relief; their conversation is dull."

"Then what is it?"

"I have no idea. Could be anything. I suggest you ignore it."

They continued.

✳ ✳ ✳

The next day was cool and pleasant. Nothing in the behavior of the sky was remarkable, and there were no disturbing noises. They stopped to eat and rest in the open air, in the gentle breeze that blew down the riverbed and rustled the willow trees on its banks. Creedmoor produced a battered tin cup from his pack and made a small fire. With a grand air, he also produced a bag of dark leaves, and he made tea. Liv shivered at the waste of water.

She had never before noticed a waste of water.

But the leaves had been spoiled in the downpour and the tea was not a success. "It's the effort that counts," Creedmoor explained, and he downed the bitter dregs. "As a representative of civilization, Liv, you will understand. Now you and the General sit for a moment; rest. Talk amongst yourselves."

Creedmoor jogged off up the wooded slopes. For food? To spy on their pursuers? Liv had no idea.

She sat under the willows and attempted to ignore the way the green fronds flexed and stroked the air as if they were trying to become fingers. . . .

She checked her golden pocket watch. It was still broken. It had broken days ago. It still ticked steadily, but some days the hands didn't turn, and some days they spun so fast, the mechanism shuddered, and sometimes they turned backwards—the land out here was not yet ready to be reduced to regular time. Useless though it was, she didn't quite have the heart to throw it away. Surely it would never be found, and that saddened her.

She made a search for weapons and was stunned to find, on the riverbed's floor, among the flat round river stones, a stone spearhead. Arrowhead, perhaps. She had no idea and didn't care. It was very sharp. She soon found another, and another.

Hillfolk's traces. So obvious, even she could see them—but of course, this far west they had no reason to hide themselves. Were they recent? Surely Creedmoor, too, had seen them, long before she had; why had he left her alone with these weapons? Was he watching to see what she would do with them?

That way lay madness, paranoia, ultimately paralysis: Liv shut the door firmly on such speculation. She selected the lightest and sharpest of the arrowheads. She slipped it under her clothes—under the shapeless red flannels Creedmoor had purchased from the wife of that farmer near Kloan; beneath the farmer's heavy belt that still felt so strange on her.

How she hated to wear the clothes he'd stolen for her!

It was not uncommon, Liv knew, for persons in her unenviable situation to form attachments to their captors. She had for an

instant felt that it was disloyal to plot against him. She had no intention of allowing that to go any further, either. She'd seen him
murder a man—*do not lose sight of that.*

✳ ✳ ✳

Creedmoor bounded up the sandy slope. He was happy. The simple
purpose of walking west was proving quite enough to entertain
him. Fresh air and exercise was, as the good Doctor and the General
would no doubt agree, the best of all medicines. More important, it
was days since his masters had spoken in his mind; it was days since
he'd had to do anything degrading or dreadful. In fact, one could
say he was engaged in a noble cause, shepherding the poor old man
and the young lady to safety from the Line. . . . It amused him to
imagine so, anyway.

When he stood on a high rock and cupped his ear, the Line's
blunderers were just barely audible in the distance. Their heavy
stamping boots were a remote echo. He had days of lead on them.

He found a freshwater stream and filled his water-skins.

He'd saved a handful of cigarettes from the long rain in a tin
case. Now was as good a time as any to indulge himself. He sat
against the rock and smoked and listened to the stream.

The rocks around the stream were marked with swirls of crimson paint. Flakes and facets of cobalt and red glittered in the sun
that fell through the trees.

The stream's water pooled between the rocks. Motion in the water
caught his eye, and he knelt to look more closely.

From the water's depths hands reached up. The pale white hands
of drowned men. Thin almost fleshless fingers waving nervelessly
like weeds on the tide. He could count three, four, ten: but counting
was beside the point. A single broken nail violated the water's tense
surface; a shock, an obscenity, as if his reflection had winked at him
in his morning shaving mirror. The dead flesh beneath the nails all
red and bloody. Thin arms receding down like a tangle of white
roots into the water—the water deep and dark as memory. Creedmoor recalled drowned men. Murdered men. Some women, too—
mostly men in his career, but inevitably a few women, murder being
no kind of exact science. All waving feebly beneath the water. Some

of them beckoning. The whistling of the birds in the trees around him, the trill of frogs in the reeds had gone silent.

This was Folk trickery. It was meant to threaten or communicate or warn or amuse or *something;* who knew with the Folk? It did not seem friendly, if Creedmoor was any judge.

It was all frankly unpleasant, but he'd seen worse. He'd seen uncannier things near every day in the whispering dark behind his closed eyes when Marmion spoke to him. If this was the worst the valley and the far farthest West could offer, he'd consider himself lucky. He stared into the water until the unsettling images went away; until, in the blink of an eye, they turned back into lilies and white water froth. The birds and the frogs regained their voices, like bar pianists starting up again once the shooting's over.

❋ ❋ ❋

The General stood and tried to wander off. Liv held him back; he struggled feebly, but she easily overpowered him. She sat him down on the dry earth of the riverbed, and she sat beside him.

The absurdity of it! Liv nearly laughed; she felt as though she *should* laugh. Creedmoor seemed to think she could mend the man in a matter of days, while they fled helter-skelter into the wilderness. Creedmoor had her confused perhaps, with a fairy-tale witch or fairy godmother. She *did* laugh, and she turned to the General and asked him, "Sir, do you have any stories about a fairy godmother? Anything to pass the time."

The General said nothing. He was shivering. She held him close to her. His breath and his heartbeat fluttered. She stroked his bony shoulder. She felt a great and ridiculous affection for him. For a moment, she felt close to tears.

Slowly she became aware that the General's eyes were wide and fixed forward, down the valley ahead of them.

Some twenty feet westward, the valley floor narrowed; two big rocks nearly met and pinched it shut. In the gap between them stood—what was it?

It was not a goat, but it was goat-*ish*. It was too large to be a goat; it had shoulders almost like a bull, but it had a goat's horns and legs and fur. Black fur. It had terribly wild and pained red eyes.

It stamped and pawed the earth with a hoof like a grave-digger's shovel. It snorted and whinnied. It smelled of—weeds? Stale water? Loamy earth? It smelled *terribly* of it.

"Once upon a time," the General announced, "there was a bridge over a river in a forest in a land ruled by three queens and in a forest in the mountains and over a river, and a goat lived under that bridge. In midwinter when the river was frozen and like a necklace of diamonds a traveler approached not in hopes of crossing the bridge but in search, you see, aha, of the bridge itself, the border itself, it having been foretold . . ."

The creature did not move; nor did Liv. She gripped her sharp arrowhead tightly and waited.

She was ashamed to hope desperately for Creedmoor's return.

The creature's fur was black, and the long hair that hung scruffily from its throat was stone-stiff with dirt. Its eyes were blazingly red. Its shoulders were huge and swollen.

"The traveler is driven forward by love of a woman," the General continued. "The goat is fixed by mute love of his place, of his bridge. Before there was a bridge there was a mountain, and before there was a mountain there was a great city of the First Folk, and before that there was nothing."

Liv wished she could silence the old man's ravings, but she did not dare make any sudden movement. The thing stared at her and she stared back. She averted her eyes—it occurred to her that the animal might take her fixed stare as a challenge. When she looked back again, it was gone.

There was nothing there but a dark rock; and a stand of reeds; and moss crawling across the rock; and two red circles painted on the rock—spirals, rather.

". . . the goat," the General explained—excited; something about the incident had him more voluble than she'd ever seen him— "attempts to explain itself to the traveler, who is uncertain. There is a murder, and a change of costume. Goat? It was said of Sam Self, first Governor of the first colony at Founding, that he was known to transform into a wolf. Secrets are lost with the death, with every death. Nothing can be atoned for, but errors can be corrected and sickness cured. The moral lesson of this story is clear. It teaches . . ."

He had not inhaled for some time. A word caught in his throat and he began to choke. He fell forward and Liv caught him. She held his head back until he began to breathe again.

"General Enver?"

His eyes were frightened. She kissed his wrinkled forehead to calm him.

He said nothing further all day.

She did not mention the incident to Creedmoor when he returned.

CHAPTER 30

LOWRY IN THE WILDERNESS

The Linesmen were beyond refueling range for the Heavier-Than-Air Vessels—which were ferocious guzzlers of fuel, which was a proof of their spiritual excellence. The motor vehicles had all been left behind; they'd struggled in the mud of the downpour, and were nearly worthless anyway over the roadless untamed hills and valleys. That meant leaving behind the heaviest artillery. They now had three motor guns, one of which no longer worked but might conceivably be repaired. They had two light cannon. It took half a dozen Linesmen to push and drag each one of those huge wheeled weapons across uneven ground. The rest of the Linesmen slogged on foot in two columns, each 160 men deep—160 men *on paper,* that is. In fact, there'd been bears, and a fever, and a rockslide, and the patrols that hadn't returned, and the actual numbers were rather lower, and uneven. Their marching form was decaying out in the wilderness. They were going ragged and wild. They looked like a bunch of slagging tinkers.

They'd marched through a field of tall grass, and the green stalks had followed them, straight-backed, in march formation, roots rustling and slithering, as if mocking them. . . .

And one of the riflemen had brought down a rabbit, and it had had the glittering glass eyes of a microscope, and the long black jaws of a spider, and it had gushed black blood and guts that smelled of oil. . . .

And last night when Lowry woke, gut twisting from bad food, bad water, to take a long runny painful shit behind a tree, the moon in the starless sky had been like a mirror, in which his yellow face was reflected, bug-eyed and straining, smeared, distended, hideous. . . .

And the *silence*! The empty sky swallowed sound so that even when Lowry shouted, it sounded like no more than a whisper. No noise but footsteps through muck and wind through trees—and that was another thing!—Lowry didn't like trees at the best of times, but the trees out here were entirely unprincipled, a nasty stupid joke. Some were crudely impossible, being five times the size of any natural tree, or no taller than Lowry's leg. Others were more subtle—the patterns of their branches was *wrong,* too complex, developed according to mathematical principles different from those that pertained in the more solidly made world, but in ways that Lowry could spend hours staring at and not fully be able to articulate; in ways that intruded on his sleep.

They were beyond reach of the Engines. They were so far distant from even the most remote Station of the Line that the Song could not reach them. Lowry had never been so long outside their Song.

❉ ❉ ❉

They'd gone into the wilderness with three telegraph devices, two spare. Three Linesmen had been selected to carry them; it was just about possible for each man to carry one telegraph strapped to his back, though they bent near-double under the weight, and lagged behind, and looked in silhouette on long evening marches like gigantic parasites were feeding on them, and were generally thought likely to die soon. Only the poor bastard who labored under Lowry's amplifier had it worse.

Two of the telegraphs were ruined by the rains. The third survived but soon proved useless anyway.

On the first day out, Lowry had wired:

AGENT FLEEING WEST WITH TARGET. ALL AVAILABLE
FORCES IN PURSUIT. LOWRY IN COMMAND.

There'd been no answer for nearly twenty-four hours, during which time he dreaded that he'd displeased them, but dreaded more turning back, and so kept going. At that point, there were still trucks, and he sat in the back of a truck with the telegraphs and waited for them to speak. He sat with a single translator and a pistol in his hand and wasn't sure whether in the event that the telegraph condemned him he would kill the translator, or himself, or both. At last, in the early evening, as the convoy was reversing itself to navigate a steep rocky incline, it spoke:

MORE FORCES COME BEHIND YOU. DO NOT SLOW. DO NOT FAIL. TAKE THE TARGET ALIVE AT ALL COSTS. HE MEANS VICTORY. DO NOT FAIL.

Then came the rains, which it seemed no signal could penetrate. When the rains were gone, he wired back again, on the one remaining telegraph:

DESPITE ADVERSITY WE GO FORWARD.

Six hours later, the telegraph began suddenly to clatter, knocking its unfortunate bearer to his knees. It stopped almost at once. The message simply read:

LOWRY.

Two hours after that, another message came: LOWRY. And another, an hour after that: LOWRY. And another, half an hour after that: LOWRY. And again. And again. LOWRY. LWROY. LOWWRY. LOO-WWWYRRY. LOW. YRWOL. LOW. WL.

Then it stopped. No further communications came.

Lowry attempted to keep this from his men but could not. Rumor got out. They were alone. Half a dozen men threatened to break ranks and go running back; one had to be shot. Better numbers than Lowry expected.

✳   ✳   ✳

But the wheel turns up as well as down! There was one good thing. In the clear silent air out there was nothing to interrupt the signal from the device the woman carried, and it came with exceptional clarity.

Two men of the Signal Corps carried the heavy receiving apparatus between them. Every now and then, they stopped and consulted the machine—which could be powered, in desperate and debased circumstances such as these, by a foot-wheel and a lot of huffing and puffing.

They'd bring Lowry the transcripts, and he had to admit: it was damn good stuff. They caught nearly every word the woman spoke, the bastard Agent spoke, the target spoke. Most of it was useless. The General talked nonsense, the woman was barely better.

But this! He held the transcript paper in shaking cracked and sunburned hands. There in the old man's ravings: *Secrets are lost . . . Errors can be corrected, sickness cured . . .*

"Is this it?"

The Signalman nodded. "He went silent after that."

"What secrets?"

"I don't know, sir."

"Who's Sam Self? Is that a real person?"

"I don't know, sir."

"No." If it was a real person, there would be a file somewhere, a thousand miles away back east, in the minds of the Engines. But what good was that to Lowry now?

"All right. Well? Fuck off, then."

Lowry thought for a moment. Then he called Subaltern Thernstrom over.

"Tell all the officers: We're going to go slow now. For a while. All right? We're going to stay on that bastard's track, right enough, but we're going to give him some room. See how some things work themselves out."

"Sir—our orders were to pursue with all—"

"You spying on me, Thernstrom?"

"No, sir."

"No, sir. The target may speak. Maybe the woman's not so useless after all. Maybe he likes her. No need to risk confrontation, then. We listen. We wait."

"Sir—"

"And the Agent speaks to the woman; we'll learn his plans. His secrets. Stay outside his sight, Thernstrom. He won't expect that. We'll see who's cleverer. We'll see."

"Sir, our supplies will run out in four days. We lost a lot in the rains, remember, sir."

"I remember."

"After that, we don't have enough to return."

"I understand. We're all in this together, aren't we?"

"Our orders—"

"Are silent. The Engines do not have access to this information."

Thernstrom looked shocked. Lowry was shocked, too. It had been a dreadful and blasphemous thing to say.

"You have your orders, Thernstrom."

Lowry watched the Subaltern walk away. He had no idea where the notion of waiting had come from. Much as he dreaded the wilderness, the idea of *watching* and *spying* had a strange appeal; so had he acted selfishly? Had he acted from pride or even viler motives? How would he explain himself if and when there was inquiry? He was suddenly terrified. Thernstrom had gone over to talk to Slate and Drum, and the three of them were gesturing and glancing back Lowry's way. Lowry turned his back to them, so they couldn't see his face turn green; he stared out over the hills, over the uneven forests, into the mountains and a livid sunset where in the distance an eagle was circling, searching, suddenly diving! It *looked* like an eagle—who the fuck knew what sort of monster it was in its guts. It swooped low and Lowry's gut lurched in time and he felt sick and lonely and shameful.

CHAPTER 31

The Games

In the middle of the night—her hands shaking at the horror of what she was about to do—Liv rose, held the little stone arrowhead like a dagger, and crept silently over to Creedmoor's sleeping body.

Creedmoor lay on his back, snoring. The rope around the General's ankle was connected to Creedmoor's belt. Creedmoor lay with his legs and his arms crossed and his head resting on a mound he'd made of dry river-mud.

Liv stood over him. In the moonlight she could count the tiny white scars on his face. She could see how thin and strawlike his hair was; in the moon, it was quite white and he seemed like an old man. She raised the weapon anyway, over his throat.

His eyes opened quite leisurely, and he smiled up at her.

"No, dear," he said. "Not tonight. Maybe tomorrow."

She dropped the crude blade and recoiled in horror.

"I take no offense. It is my fate to be hounded like a wild beast from every brief resting place. I have chosen it. I am well used to it." Creedmoor sighed; then he winked to show his good humor. Then he rolled over and was soon snoring again.

She thought that she would never be able to sleep again that night, but as it turned out, she was quite wrong.

✳   ✳   ✳

In the morning, some instinct prompted Creedmoor to shake out his boots; and indeed, there was a scorpion, glistening and white and red and heavy-coiled like a dead thing's intestines, hiding in the heel of the left—or, as he observed to Liv, the *sinister*—boot. "The world is very full of treachery," he said. She flinched, and he smiled to show he bore no grudge.

In fact, scorpions always reminded Creedmoor of his youthful days in a backwoods scorpion-handling cult in Gacy. (The trick was to be so unrighteously drunk, the creatures would disdain to touch you.) The little beasts now afflicted him, not with fear or distaste, but with a kind of affectionate embarrassment. He stamped on it anyway.

* * *

The river's empty gorge stretched on for another day, and they followed it. Dry mud gave way to a loose and shifting sand. The gorge narrowed and sharpened. The sun rose behind them; all morning their shadows stretched long and dark before them.

The hills on either side of the gorge were purple with heather and sage. Round rocks—strange molten shapes, the rock of ancient fires and eructations—swelled up out of the purple—like an army of trolls out of the myths of old Koenigswald.

At midmorning, Creedmoor—who was in fine form—called a halt to their progress. Two beautiful birds—white breasted, golden crested; powerful, regal, remote—circled and swooped across the valley. Creedmoor said that he wanted to watch them, for a moment, only for a brief moment. He seemed sincere. To Liv's surprise, he did not kill them. At first she watched, skeptically, Creedmoor's face; soon she, too, was watching the birds.

When she returned her gaze to the earth, Liv shrieked and put her hands to her mouth in shock.

The hunched rocks on either side of the river had faces and glittering red eyes; and they were looking coldly down on her.

Their shoulders were covered in long black hair that fell to the ground. Beneath the hair the rock was now bone-pale skin. They hunched and crept forward on through the heather. Their legs were too long, overarticulated, which should have made their gait awkward; somehow it was not. They carried stone spears, stone axes.

There were a hundred or more of them; their ranks stretched up into the distant hills.

Creedmoor put a hand on Liv's shoulder and said, "Steady." He drew his weapon. She flinched to cover her ears, expecting the flash and the thunder; but he did not fire. Instead he held the weapon by its barrel, at arm's length, as if it was a talisman.

Creedmoor called out—and now Liv did cover her ears, because his voice was impossibly, inhumanly loud—"We do not dispute your ownership of this valley. We do not wish to challenge its spirits. We are passing through. We do not want to do you harm. But if you try to stop us, we will surely destroy you. My demon is stronger than any of yours."

Creedmoor's voice rose in volume throughout this speech; by the end, it boomed and echoed off the rocks like an avalanche.

He spoke again, in a different language, guttural and choking; and again, in a deeper and harsher tongue that Liv recognized as Dhravian, and he boomed out the words yet again in the nasal Kees-tongue. Liv turned away, her hands clamped over her ears, and closed her eyes. When she opened them again, the rocks were only rocks and the valley was still and quiet, save for the wind and those circling distant birds.

Creedmoor was staring darkly into the middle distance.

"Were they really here or was that a trick of the valley? Will they let us pass?"

Creedmoor said nothing. She approached carefully.

"Creedmoor. Will they let us pass? Creedmoor—if they will not let us pass, we must go around them—you cannot take the General into—"

Creedmoor shook himself. His eyes cleared and he smiled. He gave her shoulder an avuncular pat and said, "They're only playing a game with us. I wouldn't worry yourself overmuch."

※　※　※

—The First Folk. These lands are not ours yet, so they're theirs still. I have never seen so many free and wild. If they decide to make themselves our enemy, it may go badly for us. Their powers will be terrible here, where things are loosely made already. The earth will serve them.

There was no answer.

—Listen. If they decide we are an enemy and they *should* decide we are an enemy if I were them I would decide we were an enemy then we are likely dead or dead if we are *lucky*; I hear tell that when they torture a man they have it in their power to keep him alive for eternity as his entrails are wound on a spear; they are very curious about our workings. They want revenge. I know you understand *revenge*. They will drag us down under the red rock where there is no time and no dying. They are before us and the Line is behind. What shall we do?

He waited.

—Your deliberations cannot take this long, or consume your attention so fully. You are not deliberative creatures. You lied to me. You cannot reach out here. Or you have abandoned me.

He was alone in his head.

—Well, then.

He reminded himself that he was happy to be alone.

※　※　※

There were no further incidents that day, or the next. Sage gave way to shimmering terraces of ash-white leafless aspens, then to a thick dark forest of some stout evergreen neither of them could name. The riverbed widened then narrowed again, and continued westward. There was a tremendous noise of rushing water from the south, over the hills, but the gorge continued dry. The sun set early the first day, and the moon was swollen as if it were crashing to earth. The next night, it seemed the sun would never set at all—though it seemed, even while the sky was still hot and blue, that the stars were crowding impatiently at the edge of vision.

The General did not speak all day, despite Liv's efforts. She read to him from the *Child's History,* she questioned him regarding his system of Virtues and his theories of politics, she criticized his tactics, she talked gently of nothing in particular—he didn't respond.

They had no idea of time. Liv's golden watch was still not working; Creedmoor was used to telling the time by the sun, which was proving itself unreliable. So they stopped when they had to—that is, whenever the General could take no more. It usually fell to Liv to remind Creedmoor of the old man's frailty. Creedmoor grumbled but deferred to her expertise.

Water came and went, according to no rhyme or reason that Liv could discern. Some days the valley walls glittered with a bright web of spring-water rivulets and there were clear pools at their feet. Some days the valley was dry as old bones, the parched earth hard as paving stones. Sometimes days went by waterless, and Liv could share just a few rationed sips of stale water each day with the General, who sickened. . . . Creedmoor's devil pact sustained him, it seemed, and he went without water with no obvious ill effects save, after the third day, a reddening and contraction of the pupils and a darkening of the skin toward the shade of old blood. But if they pressed on, the water would return, and there would be enough and more than enough, and plant matter to eat, and sometimes a rabbit or thing sufficiently *like* a rabbit. Water's secret currents pulsed and gathered in the earth, sometimes receding, sometimes surging with life. It came to seem as if *time,* too, surged and receded—the moon overhead sometimes full and ocean blue, sometimes a narrow slit of ice—as if sometimes the riverbed valley remembered its youth, and sometimes it sank into bitter old age. Some days it was a friend and some days an enemy. There was nothing to be done about it but to press on and hope for the best.

❋　❋　❋

"Interesting," Creedmoor observed.

Light spilled down the valley from a red sun in the west, risen early and hung defiantly low. Long mountain shadows lunged out to meet them. The dry riverbed burned like brass in the sun; the cracks in the mud were a stark lacework of shadow. Even Creedmoor, who could, in normal circumstances, stare into the sun till the damn thing set, had to cover his eyes to look down the valley ahead. "Interesting," he repeated.

Liv, eyes screwed half-closed and downcast, did not respond. Creedmoor appeared somewhat annoyed, and went silent.

It was another hour's trek before Liv could see them. First as four long black lines of shadow running down the valley floor toward them. Then as four bleached-white sticks poking up out of the mud in the middle of the valley. Lastly, when they were almost on top of them, as five rough wooden grave-markers.

The markers were wrist-thick branches, cut and stripped white. Three still stood straight. One tilted. One had fallen and was half-buried by dust. Beneath the markers were five shallow mounds of mud and clay.

Three were draped with medals, most of which had fallen on the ground when their ribbons rotted through. On one the words MOTHER and WIFE and DAUGHTER and TEACHER were carved; there was a silver necklace wound round it, held in place by rusting wire. An old yellow book, flayed almost to chalk or dust by time, lay beneath a fourth grave.

"These are not Hillfolk graves."

"No, Liv. We'll make a frontierswoman of you yet. In fact, the Folk do not exactly bury their dead as we do, but take them deep into their warrens under the rock; I do not know what happens next; I've had dealings with them, but no outsider sees the Rebirth." He lifted a medal off one of the sticks and tossed it up and caught it. "These are the graves of men and women of the Red Valley Republic. We passed another grave site a few days ago, but it was unmarked and I saw no reason to trouble you with thoughts of death. I imagine those graves were of the same party. We are not the first to explore this valley."

"Clearly not, Mr. Creedmoor. What were they doing here?"

"Deserters, perhaps. Though the Republic's was not an army much plagued by deserters. I suppose this valley recommended itself to them just as it did to us—as a clear path west, and away from the world and its wars."

"Maybe they fled the Republic's fall."

"Maybe. In the years after the fall, there were purges. I would have fled."

"When did they pass?"

"Ten, twenty years ago, perhaps?"

"Are you sure? So long ago?"

"Yes, Liv. I can *smell* them. Faintly, but I smell them. Many years and long gone. We are alone. Never fear." He smiled.

The General, shuffling, approached the graves. He knelt, creaking, and reached a shaking finger down to the book on the grave mound. He turned its ancient pages to dust. He whimpered.

Creedmoor came and stood over him. He rubbed the grave medal against his shirt until the brass glinted again. "But let's talk, old-timer: Do you miss your people?"

Creedmoor held the medal in front of the General's eyes and let it shine. The General flinched but did not pull away. "Do you miss your old empire? Locked away in that ruined head of yours, do you dream of the ruin of your empire? Does it hurt?"

Liv felt a sudden sickness; a sudden fierce rush of protectiveness toward her charge; an urge to strike Creedmoor's smirking face. . . . She swallowed it down bitterly and said only, "Do please leave him alone, Mr. Creedmoor. You cannot torment him into good health."

He shrugged, spun the medal on his knuckles and into his pocket. "You're the expert, of course, ma'am."

✳ ✳ ✳

Three days later, Liv saw, carved on the side of a white fang of rock in the riverbed, the words ONE HUNDRED DAYS OUT and the date *1870*. No other words; no other signs of life. Creedmoor shrugged.

✳ ✳ ✳

Creedmoor whistled a song, over and over. It was a pretty little melody, though his tone was flat.

"Do you sing, at all, Liv?"

"I do not, Mr. Creedmoor."

"Can you recite any poetry?"

"I do not believe that I can."

"The wilderness stirs nothing in you? No recollection of some words you treasured as a child? No instinct of song?"

"If you kidnapped me for my musical talents, perhaps you should let me go now."

"No going back now, Liv; we're in this together. But it will be a long journey if I must make all the music."

Liv stumbled over a dry root snaking through the dirt, and wrenched her hip. Creedmoor, in a generous mood, announced an early end to the day's trek. They watched the sun go down over the mountains and the valley flood with red shadows.

"Do you know this game, Liv? My name begins with R. Who am I? You must ask me questions, you see. I am someone of great renown; you'll soon guess me. It's a guessing game."

R proved to be Richard the Red Fox, who was a famous gambler, possibly fictional, of whom Liv had never heard. In fact, it turned out that Liv and Creedmoor knew hardly a single famous man or woman in common. The rogues and adventurers and killers and monsters and generals of Creedmoor's world meant nothing to her; while the statesmen and scientists and philosophers of the old North bored Creedmoor—even their names bored him. Hardly surprising, Creedmoor conceded; it was a very big lonely world, but marvelously full of strangeness and renown. "As it happens, Liv, I myself have a certain renown. I do not collect my clippings, that would be vulgar, but I was much noticed in reports of the Battle of Akeley Wood. There's a story the old soldiers still tell. . . ."

The sun was a long time setting. All Creedmoor's stories were horrible: battles, crimes, murders, cheap tricks, and lies. Liv paid no attention to his words, but listened to his tone, which was uncertain, flickering—a mixture of pride and shame, sentimentality and cynicism. He was performing—whether for her benefit or his own, she couldn't tell.

❋　❋　❋

"Creedmoor?"

". . . now, one story that's never been credited to my fame is the matter of the Keaton City mob, whose triumphs over the lawmen were written up in all the newspapers, but I appeared only under the alias John Circus, which I was using at the time—"

"Creedmoor."

"Yes, Liv?"

"Why should I help you? Suppose I can heal the General—which I cannot—why should I? What will you do with him?"

"You'll heal him because I told you to, Liv."

"If I refused?"

He looked genuinely intrigued. "I wonder. Who knows what I might do?"

"I don't believe you would harm me."

"I can't imagine why you think that, but you're the expert. Is that your diagnosis of me?"

"Yes, Creedmoor."

She kept her voice calm. In fact, she had no idea what Creedmoor might do. She hoped he might be convinced, or at least confused. Something about him seemed uncertain.

"Well, Doctor, I'm sorry but I can't pay you for it. How about this: You'll heal the old man, if you can, threats or no threats, because you are a healer, and a good person, or at least a conscientious one?"

"What would you do with him, Creedmoor?"

"You wouldn't? Cold, unfeeling. I misjudged you."

"What are you making me a party to? What would you do with him?"

"*I* would do nothing, Liv. Hand him over, wash my hands of it, go get drunk. I am no strategist."

"There would be war?"

"There's always War."

"But you think he would make you stronger. You've expended great effort to recover him. Why? Does he know something? Do you think he can lead you . . . but to what? You'll launch new attacks? You will raise new armies? You'll make new incursions into the Line's lands?"

"We are losing, Liv." Creedmoor flinched for a moment, as if expecting a blow. It seemed not to come. He continued.

"We are falling back everywhere. We have always been falling back. We were falling back when I"—he patted the grip of his weapon—"took up the Cause. Indeed, that was the year that the Line razed our stronghold of Logtown and dragged its Baron's body back to Harrow Cross, chained spread-eagled and still breathing, in the poison smoke, chained to the Engine's black cowl. It made an impression, believe me. It was in all the newspapers. So, no, I do not imagine that we will launch new attacks. Apparently this man once saw something important, or heard something, or knows something. Some secret. The world is full of secrets. Maybe—maybe—what he has in his memory could help us slow the Line's advance. Not stop it. That's all I would dare hope for. We did not come to the service of the Gun because we wanted to enjoy victory, but because we wanted to lose magnificently."

Creedmoor looked at the General—sleeping, bony legs curled like a dog, rope around his ankle, thinner and frailer now even than he had been when they left the House—and he shook his head. "Or this may very well be pointless. It would not be the first pointless mission my masters have given me."

Liv looked at Creedmoor in surprise. He shrugged and said, "The Guns are mad, Liv." Again, he flinched. Liv wondered if he knew he was doing it.

"Quite mad. Mad as anything in the world, bless 'em; madder even than the Line, whose purpose is at least consistent. Mad as snakes."

"Why do you serve them, then, Mr. Creedmoor?"

"I'm sorry?"

"Why do you serve them?"

"Because if I disobey my friend here, I get the Goad; you cannot *imagine* the Goad, Liv."

"No, Mr. Creedmoor, I mean—"

"I know what you mean, Liv." He sighed. "They told me"—he flinched again—"They told me that the secret is a weapon that can kill the Line. A Folk weapon. Something that can kill immortal spirits. Such as, for instance, the Engines of the Line, who for four hundred years we have sabotaged, and exploded, and destroyed, and sent to hell, and back they come inexorably five or ten years later, angrier and greedier than ever."

"A weapon."

"Of sorts. Something of the First Folk."

"Magic. Superstition. A delusion. Your problems are not so neatly solved. Your masters are a form of madness; you cannot *wish* them away."

"A cure, then, perhaps. A cure for madness."

"Perhaps. And your masters, too? Can it cure the world of them, too?"

He shrugged. "Maybe. Maybe not. Besides, they were probably just lying to me."

His expression was unreadable. Did he mean anything he was saying?

"Creedmoor. When you took up the Cause, how old were you?"

Creedmoor stared at her long and hard. Then he winked. "Oh no, Doctor. We will not be playing that game. I am quite healthy in my mind, thank you. Or so scarred as to be beyond your help, perhaps. One or the other. Time to sleep, I think, in any case." He lay down with his back to her.

❋ ❋ ❋

The General whimpered in the cold. She went to sit by him.

His stick-thin old limbs twisted uncomfortably. She held him and helped him settle into stillness.

His fierce eyes glared upward, as if challenging the stars.

"Too good for this world," she said, surprising herself; then she repeated it. "Yes."

There was dry mud in the General's tangled beard.

"This is a mad world," she said.

The General muttered, but she could not catch the words.

"How glorious your Republic must have been. I wish you could tell me of it."

She opened the *Child's History* to the chapter recounting the founding of the Republic. Much of it was illegible—swollen and smeared by the rains and now by black mold—but she was able to read:

> The signing of the Charter was an occasion of simple ceremony. No pomp or ritual was called for. The principles of the Charter, as you have learned, were derived from plain good sense, and from natural reason. There was no call for the blessing of any prince or priest or power. Therefore the signers met by the banks of the Red River, among reeds and rushes, in the clear light of noon on a quite ordinary summer's day in the year '46. "A jolly day for it," laughed President Bellow, as his manservant passed him his pen. . . .

The General fell asleep.

He was shivering; she lay against him to share their warmth.

❋ ❋ ❋

The next morning there was a great crashing from the south slope; the trees threshed and shuddered and tore. Birds barreled up from the branches in terror. And three immense bears—black and frothing at the mouth—a wedding-dress froth, thick and swaying and glistening—came roaring out of the forest.

They had the most terrible red eyes. They had claws like stone spearheads. They were covered in something that was not fur but long, swaying, heaving black hair, oily and liquid.

They were, but for the Engine that had carried her West, the largest and most terrible creatures Liv had ever seen. They could not possibly be natural-born animals.

She stiffened her spine and refused to look away—another illusion, another horrible trick of this horrible valley!

Creedmoor fired three shots.

The first caught one of the bears in its great head, as it reared. The skull was obliterated: the black body swayed and shuddered and flung ragged bloody ropey spew from its vacant shoulders. The second shot caught another bear in its side and opened up the architecture of its chest so that Liv could see the curve of its bloody bones and the bright pumping engines of its organs. It ran for a few yards farther then fell with a thud. With the third shot—it was as if Creedmoor, having experimented, had found the precise minimum of force to expend—though all three shots had been fired within a fraction of a second—Creedmoor caught the third bear in its left eye and that wild red orb burst into a brief neat spurt of blood, then blackness, and the body slumped limply to the ground.

It was all over before Liv could scream; so instead she breathed deeply and sat down on the mud.

Creedmoor holstered his weapon.

The bodies of the bears did not disappear. They did not neatly resolve themselves into rocks or shadows. They did not in any way confess their unreality. Instead they lay pouring out blood and stink and very quickly attracted flies.

"This game," Creedmoor said, "is rapidly ceasing to amuse."

CHAPTER 32

LIBERATION

The next night was freezing cold. Creedmoor built a fire out of stacked branches and stones, like the pyre he'd built for his dead comrades, and stared into it, hat pulled down over his eyes.

It had been some time since Liv had thought of her nerve tonic. She recalled the sweet metallic scent of it suddenly—something in the fire's smoke triggered the memory—and for a moment, she felt a deep sad craving. It passed quickly. She set the thought aside. Her nerves felt—oddly—quite healthy.

The General had been in good form during the warmth of the day. His tongue was loosening somewhat as they went west; Liv thought the fresh air and activity were doing him good. He'd even responded to some of her questions, albeit only to weave her words into the nonsense of the fairy story he was telling. (A bird; two squabbling brothers; an endless journey into winter.) It made Liv smile and laugh to see it; she held him and he wheezed with what seemed to be happiness. Creedmoor was distant all the day, lost in thought, and Liv and the General were alone, and almost happy. But when the cold came suddenly down, the General went silent. He curled himself up in simple animal pain and whimpered at the outrage of it. He flinched at Liv's touch, and her heart broke. She withdrew from him and huddled by the fire and rubbed her legs—which

were thinner now and wiry, like the legs of a stranger who'd led a
harder life than the one she was meant for.

This, too, is a trap, Liv thought. Her growing affection for the
poor old General was irrational. Its causes were obvious: first, loneliness and fear; and second, displaced guilt over her unintentional-
but-nevertheless-painful abandonment of Maggfrid. It would bind
her to Creedmoor's side, prevent her from running. She could not
stop it from happening.

She sat by the red wounded throb of the fire and attempted to
harden her heart.

She started a little when Creedmoor spoke.

"Have you ever heard of a place called No-Town, Liv?"

"No-Town? Never."

"No." He poked at the fire. "Why would you?"

He was silent for a while. Liv waited.

"You asked when I came to the Gun. When I signed up. That's a
short story. I was drunk at the time—the end. I'll tell you instead
about an earlier occasion, when I was still very young and innocent; the first time I set eyes on an Agent of the Gun, and as far as
I know the first time the Gun turned its attention to me. Or who
knows? Maybe they watched me in the womb. Their ways were
mysterious."

Liv stayed quiet. Creedmoor looked down into the fire and kept
speaking. "It was in a town called Twisted Root. Far east of here,
far north of the Deltas, on a dusty plain, away over the Opals, a
frozen range on which I once nearly died. There's hardly a wild
place left in the world where I haven't nearly died. This was thirty-
some years ago; when you get to my age, you lose count. Thirty-two.
I was there on behalf of—"

✳ ✳ ✳

The Liberationists. That was his cause at the time. The Liberation
from bondage and oppression of the First Folk, who never seemed
grateful for the Liberationists' attentions; but virtue was its own re-
ward, and futility only a spur to greater sacrifice. . . .

A stocky bespectacled young man, with a pale face and shaggy
black hair. He still had the accent of a boy from rainy and distant

Lundroy, which was the home he'd run away from. He stood on an upturned crate in Twisted Root's market square and shouted his message of Liberation in singsong Lundroy tones, his voice straining and cracking over the noise of the market.

It was the hot season, late in the day. The sun, descending, burned the world a raw-flesh red. The market was noisy with cows, and traders, and goats, and half a dozen blacksmiths, and occasional gunshots as gun merchants showed off their wares, and men on horseback—and red-coated *soldiers* on horseback—forcing their way through the crowds. And the buzzing of the flies!

John Creedmoor preached Liberation. The Hillfolk, the objects of his charity, stood silently in their pen, chained by their bony ankles, pale as bone and black-maned and stiff as pines. Iron chains; the Hillfolk could work stone like water, but iron pained them. Iron made them biddable. Iron shaped them into tools.

Ten feet away, a hunched old man of maybe forty-five stood on a tree stump hawking cheap yellow novels and ballads and picture books of the adventures of Henry Steel, Slavoj the Ogre, Springknife Sally of Lud-Town, and other rogues and killers and bank robbers and Agents of the Gun. And the slaver himself, a little rat of a man called Collins, in a tattered fur hat and a threadbare suit, stood by the Hillfolk's pen and shouted out the praises of his stock.

And Creedmoor raised his voice again, and scattered his own pamphlets into the crowd: copies of *The Chain-Breaker,* house organ of the Liberationists. No one moved to pick them up. The farmers of Twisted Root looked at him with dull dislike.

A man's voice shouted, "Go home, boy!" Not angry, yet—just bored. It wounded Creedmoor's pride. He was the kind of young man who'd rather be hated than ignored.

He read from *Chain-Breaker* Number 22, Volume 3. It was the text of a recent speech given by one Mr. Ownslow Phillips, back in Beecher's marbled City Hall.

Gentlemen, ladies, be not afraid of TRUTH; be not afraid nor too proud to look the monster SLAVERY boldly in its face. Be not too blind to see the cruelty you do to your brothers, to those simple folk whose land this once was. Is it any wonder that our earth sprouts the

monsters of GUN and LINE to rule over us, when we water it hourly
with the blood whipped from the backs of innocents, when we . . .

Liberationism was a new cause for Creedmoor. Six months ago,
it hadn't ever occurred to him to give a damn for the Hillfolk's well-
being. A year ago, he'd been a pious shaven-headed devotee of the
Virgins of the White City. And the year before that, it'd been Free
Love, and the Consolidated Knights of Labor. Cause after cause,
each one a disappointment. And until a few months ago, he had
frittered away his time on Self-Improvement, attending a meeting
circle of Smilers in Beecher City. *My name is John Creedmoor, and
I know that I have been a frightened man, a willful man. . . .* All
that shit. A meeting circle of two bakers, a wheelwright, three bank
clerks, and a haberdasher's assistant; the mediocrity of it embarrassed
him still. He'd given not one moment's thought to the Hillfolk, not
until he'd skipped meeting circle one morning and wandered by
drunken mistake into Beecher City Hall, where Mr. Ownslow
Phillips had been speaking. The grand speechifying and the organ
and the stern determined songs echoing from the rafters—
electrifying! And more electrifying still was the sight of Phillips,
that noble white-haired old man, being dragged from the podium
and beaten bloody by the thugs of some slaving-trust. Creedmoor
had charged into the riot, laughing, fists swinging, and broken a
slaver's nose.

And six months later, he was out in the backcountry, in Twisted
Root, all on his own, being ignored by dumb farmers. Laughed at.

And another voice called, *Go home!* and another, and the crowd
started up a dull hooting at him, which he struggled to rise above
with dignity.

The slaver Collins relaxed, leaned against a fencepost, and
watched the proceedings with a rueful smile.

Creedmoor had been dogging this slaver's steps for two weeks
now, from town to town. When Creedmoor and Collins first met, in
Far Peck, Collins had owned twenty-six Hillfolk; by the time they
got to Twisted Root, he had ten. Business had been good. Creedmoor's pure loathing of Collins had not diminished with familiarity.
Collins, however, sometimes got avuncular; he sometimes talked to

the younger man as if they were friends, casual rivals, players of the same rough game. He caught Creedmoor's eye and shrugged, as if to say, *Some you win, some you lose.*

Creedmoor kept preaching.

"It's a fine thing," Collins shouted, "that in the cities a young man has leisure enough to develop such tender feelings for these dumb brutes! Will *he* do your work for you, with his soft hands?"

Creedmoor kept preaching, and the hooting rose to an angry chant, and the first thrown stone came soon after. It hit him in the shoulder and even though he was expecting it, he still dropped his pamphlets. The crowd laughed as he bent to pick them up. Another stone, and a handful of dirt, and then a hail of stones and dirt and muck. Creedmoor shouted even louder, and the crowd hooted back, and the market's dogs started barking. Another stone hit Creedmoor on his forehead and he stumbled and the wooden crate tilted beneath him and he went down in the mud, on his hands and knees, looking for his spectacles.

※　※　※

A soldier of the Red Valley Republic saved him.

A shadow fell over him, and he looked up, and up, to see one of the red-coated soldiers astride his horse, looking down.

The mob withdrew.

The soldier's red coat—red was for the Republic's officers—was very fine. He had golden trim on his shoulders and a field of golden medals on his breast; a rifle on his back, a sword at his side; a proud black mustache and long black hair to his shoulders.

In those days, the Republic was at the height of its glory. Under its President Iredell and its great General Enver, it had won a sweep of brilliant victories and negotiated a series of grand treaties, and was carving out an empire in the heart of the West. It bowed to no inhuman Power—it fought the massed legions of the Line on one front and the mercenaries and bandits of the Gun on another. It was one of the few great causes Creedmoor had never been interested in; he found them self-righteous and dull. He didn't see the romance of them until a few years later, after the Republic was smashed at Black Cap Valley and the cause was doomed, and by then it was too late.

The soldier's arm was outstretched to help Creedmoor up.

"You're a long way from home, son."

Creedmoor stood without taking the officer's hand. The officer shrugged; smiled; rested his hand again on the reins. "By your accent and your aspect, I reckon you're a Lundroy-man, born and bred. Far, far from home."

Behind him the mob was watching, waiting.

"You're a long way from home, too, Officer. What business does the Republic have here?"

"No business of yours, son."

Hanging from the officer's saddlebags like strange fruit were three black iron canisters, roughly cylindrical, but jutting with sharp-edged protrusions: gears, teeth, wheels, hammer-locks. Bombs. Weapons of the Line, mass produced in factories, like the Linesmen who carried them. The officer must have won them in battle.

The officer wasn't much older than Creedmoor. Creedmoor envied and despised him and suddenly craved his respect. But before Creedmoor could say anything, the man leaned down and in a low flat voice told him, "Now, go home. Go to your lodgings. If these farm boys take it into their flat heads to show you violence, I ain't going to help you." He straightened again in the saddle. "It ain't my mission here to make trouble. Sorry, son. Go home."

❋ ❋ ❋

What home? Creedmoor passed the last of the afternoon out in the fields, under a tree—hiding, sweating, wretched. He stole back into town in the evening. The market was over.

There was one main street in Twisted Root and two bars: Kennerly's and the Four-and-Twenty. Kennerly's ran gaming tables for traveling quality and advertised wines shipped in from Juddua and the farthest old-world east; the Four-and-Twenty had sawdust floors and smelled like an outhouse. Creedmoor sat alone in the shadows of the Four-and-Twenty and drank, and drank, and shook with anger, and watched the door with eager dread for the farmers from the market to show their faces.

There was a card game going at the next table. He avoided eye contact.

He drank the cheapest stuff in the house—money was tight. His pamphlets were gone, trampled in the dirt. He'd paid for the printing of them himself, and he didn't have the money to do it again. Actually, he'd paid for the printing with stolen money—with money he'd borrowed from a trusting bank clerk from the Smiler meeting circle back in Beecher City, who'd been eager to invest in Creedmoor's new business plan, a plan that did not, in fact, exist. Creedmoor could be charming and persuasive when he was lying— it was only when he tried to tell the truth that he got himself into trouble. He'd told himself the money was for a good cause, and it was; but now it was gone.

None of the farmers who'd assaulted him came through the door. The whore who worked the house flounced her skirts over to him, saw the look in his eyes, and swished swiftly away again. She sat and laughed with the game-players. A couple of snaggletoothed grave-digger-looking gentlemen sat at their own table, silently staring past each other. Some old traveler in a long black wax-coat sat in the far corner, in shadows, under a wide-brimmed hat, in still silence—save that every few minutes, he muttered to himself. The bartender read—lips working slowly, one finger tracing the page—one of the hawker's lurid pamphlets: *Regarding the Bloody Adventures of the Agent Henry Steel (Who Carried Both Hammer and* GUN*) and His Terrible Death Ground Under by the Wheels of the Line.*

When the slaver Collins darkened the doorway, Creedmoor froze stiff in his chair.

Collins was alone. Weaving and smiling; already drunk—he must have been made welcome at Kennerly's, Creedmoor thought. He must have done good business.

Collins's eyes lit on Creedmoor and he winked and laughed. "No hard feelings, son." Then he sat down at the game table, put a hand on the whore's voluminous skirts, and waited to be dealt in.

Creedmoor half stood and loudly slurred, "Collins. Collins. You make me sick."

The bartender put down the pamphlet and reached below the bar. The man in the long coat in the corner mumbled something to himself. The two men who might be grave-diggers watched with what might have been professional curiosity.

Collins turned calmly to Creedmoor—"You're young, son. You'll learn how things are"—then turned back to the game.

Creedmoor clutched the bottle by its neck and leapt over the table. When the bottle connected with the back of Collins's head, there was an explosion of glass and whiskey and noise and a shock ran down Creedmoor's arm. Every nerve in his body sang. Whiskey and glass sprayed the table and everyone who sat at it. Collins fell from his chair. What was left in Creedmoor's quivering hand was a broken bloody bottleneck. Blood spread on the floor. It had an odd oil-thick sheen in the candlelight. It soaked into the sawdust and became a dark blot. A gathering stain. Irregular. A valley traced in the dust by the scrape of a chair leg flooded and became a river. Long cracks in the floorboards made lines. Creedmoor stared transfixed at the map of violence growing at his feet. He felt numb—frozen—drained, as if it were his blood on the floor. He looked up past a dozen shocked and outraged faces and saw the old man in the long black coat watching with a casual smile on his face, and sharp blue eyes, one of which winked. Creedmoor said, "What?" There was something so strange and familiar in the old man's eyes that Creedmoor hardly noticed the yelling of the mob, or the hands on his shoulders, two hands, four hands, more hands seizing his arms, a fist in his back, in his kidney, one in his gut bending him double, still staring numbly as they dragged him away.

※　※　※

The crowd dragged him out into the market, where there were stalls and poles and stages and the makings of a gallows. They hunted around drunkenly for rope. The bartender was with them, and the grave-diggers, and the cardplayers, and the whore. Creedmoor had daydreamed for years of what it would be like to hang, how he'd spit defiance and roar with laughter and make a speech that would make the crowd weep—now that it came to it, he was too astonished to say a word. He'd been a thief for a long time, but he was genuinely surprised to find himself a murderer. Two men held him roughly against a post and shouted in his ears, but he didn't care. They cinched the rope around his neck and pulled him up onto a box. He didn't struggle. The rope was looped over a crossbeam, but they couldn't work out how to make it taut, Creedmoor noticed, and they'd left his hands untied, possibly an oversight, certainly no kindness. They were still shouting nonsense at him. He looked around for the man in the long black coat—

Who came ambling quite leisurely down the street and across the red dust of the market. Now that he was standing, it was apparent that he was extraordinarily tall. He seemed to be keeping up a cheerful conversation with the night air. A shake of his head; a full-body shrug; a laugh. He took off his hat and held it in one hand, revealing long gray hair. With the other hand, he drew from his coat the most beautiful gun Creedmoor had ever seen, breathtaking in silver and black, heavy and ornate as a sacred icon. A thrill of fear shot through the crowd, who were suddenly only a handful of little men and women standing drunk in cow dung in an empty market square, fumbling with frayed ropes.

"A promising young man!" The man in the long black coat spoke in a booming voice, actorly, amused: a voice of utter command. "It's a lucky young man," he said, head cocked, over his shoulder, as if he was talking to the weapon in his hand, "who has a higher power watching over his shoulder."

There was a shot; Creedmoor didn't see the man's hand move. He fell over backwards. The rope was cut. The crowd scattered, stepping over him. Someone was foolish enough to draw a weapon and there was another shot, and more blood.

※　※　※

There was more shooting. The man in the long black coat—who seemed to ignore bullets as if they were flies—walked casually past the makeshift gallows and gave Creedmoor, who still lay in the dirt, an appraising glance, and said, "Not yet. But you've got promise. Maybe later."

Up close, it was obvious that the man was drunk.

Then he kept walking, past Kennerly's, where red-coated soldiers spilled out of the doors shooting at him, and down the street, and—kicking the doors open—into Twisted Root's little bank.

Creedmoor ran. There was fire behind him, but he didn't look back.

That was Creedmoor's first murder; that was how he first came to the notice of the Guns.

*   *   *

"I never learned the identity of the Agent who saved me. I imagine he died. We have a tendency to do that. But two years later, I walked full of pluck and resolve and despair into an opium den in Gibson City, where one Mr. Dandy Fanshawe was known to be a regular; I was drunk and angry, but that's no excuse; and I . . ."

Creedmoor was silent for a long time. Eventually Liv spoke.

"And?"

He glanced warily up. "And? And nothing. What happens after that is inevitable."

"You were an idealist."

He shook his head under the brim of his hat. "A very poor idealist."

"And did your service to the Gun—?"

"Liv. You're a fine listener, Liv. A professional skill, I assume. And I'm too fond of my own voice. I'm a vain man. I know it. It's not the least of my flaws. And the Guns are silent out here, Liv, the echoes of their Song cannot reach us, and so I have a great deal of time to devote to my thoughts, and so—"

He pushed back his brim and gave her a sudden unshadowed grin. "Dangerous notions, unsafe even to think. Good night, Liv."

"Creedmoor—"

"Good night. The General needs cleaning, I think."

CHAPTER 33

FORWARD THE GLORIOUS PURPOSE

If the Doctor's signaling device could be trusted, then it seemed the Agent had taken the low road west. There wasn't much out in the uncreated world that could be trusted, but Lowry's faith in Line engineering hadn't entirely deserted him yet; and besides, it seemed *right*. The Agent had found a valley—a cut, a cleft, a crevice, a ditch, a gutter—a *sewer*—and was squirming wormlike along it out to the Western Sea. Disgusting.

Lowry took the high road—that is, he led his men along the heights, the clifftops, high over the valley, where he hoped he'd be hidden from the Agent's wolflike ears and eyes. This required some self-sacrifice on the part of Lowry's men—the winds up on the heights were terrible. They froze, burned, stung. Sometimes they carried improbable scents—salt, spice, engine oil, fire—things Lowry couldn't name—things that woke powerful homesick emotions but, in fact, were only meaningless—misplaced and drifting scraps of creation.

Lowry slogged forward, left-foot-right-foot-*left*, and the wind blew along the ridges and whipped the dust up into mad shadow shapes and blew right through his fucking brain.

Lowry was falling apart. The men were, too.

A few days ago, Subaltern Collier came to Lowry and told him, in a whisper, that they were officially crossing the point of no return;

that if they pressed on, they would not have enough food in their packs for the return.

"We have our orders, Mr. Collier," Lowry said. "We'll hunt or something if we must."

"Whose orders, sir?"

"Orders, Mr. Collier."

No return. That was the last straw; that was the last fucking straw. That opened some cracks in everyone's casing, all right.

Shortly after that, Subaltern Thernstrom approached him to say, "The men are frightened."

And Lowry said: "Good. So am I."

Subaltern Collier came up with a plan: If some of them made camp, and some went back in shifts, came back with supplies, organized a supply chain of sorts, they could perhaps all make it back. Lowry waved him away with a grunt and a scowl. Two days later, Collier came back with a new plan, suitably tinkered with to take into account the fresh wilderness miles they'd stumbled across since last time. Under more normal operating circumstances, Lowry would have had a sneaking admiration for Collier's mechanical persistence, his careful calculating mind, though he would still have filed whatever reports necessary to have the jumped-up bastard demoted or arrested. *No one goes back.* As it was, Lowry just stumped on, hunched, lost in his own thoughts, which were bleak and gray.

The men chattered behind him. A general breakdown of discipline loomed. How many were still sound, and how many were broken parts, rattling loose? Lowry didn't know. He no longer trusted his Subalterns to keep him informed on the mood of the men. Collier had his own agenda. Thernstrom talked to himself. Gibb had a look of wild-eyed sweaty-faced excitement that couldn't be trusted. Lowry should have had *all* the Subalterns shot, but he couldn't spare them.

It was different for the men, who at least had Lowry to lead them. Lowry had nothing, was out there all alone. The silence of his masters' Song was more than he could handle.

He had no idea how much he muttered to himself all day.

✳   ✳   ✳

Lowry's one entertainment was reading the transcripts from the woman's signaling device. Every night, they camped in tents that didn't do a slagging thing to keep out the winds, and Lowry read in cold murk by the faint reddish light of an electric-bar lamp.

The typewriters were long since abandoned. The Signal Corps wrote their transcripts by pen, using shorthand and filling the margins to conserve paper, the supply of which was dwindling in a nerve-racking way, as Collier could be relied on to inform everyone. There were pages and pages of it every day. The Agent would not or maybe *could* not shut up. Sooner or later, he'd have dragged every filthy little detail of his filthy life into the light. Unveiling—unburdening—exposing himself, like a pervert. His first murder, in a town called Twisted Root. His adventures as a dealer of opium, and with the Keaton City mob. His very good friend Abban the Lion, who was dashing, and handsome, and brooding, and romantic, and who Lowry happened to know had murdered well over a hundred men. His days in various ridiculous religious orders, in his confused disordered pre-Gun youth, and a month in a cellar with the Knights of Labor in Beecher City, wiring up explosives for use on bankers. The first kill he made at the Guns' command—a kill that reignited a feud that threw Burnham Town and Olmsburg into chaos, and opened them up in the end for new Mayors under the Guns' thumb. *Jen of the Floating World; now* there's *a woman worth knowing. . . .*

Lowry had begun to imagine that he could hear the voices of the woman and the Agent and the General in his head. The woman's voice as he imagined it was sometimes high-pitched and shrill and imperious, and sometimes, when she was frightened, soft and quite touching. The Agent's voice was deep, theatrical, full of gloating gusto, fascinatingly horrible. The General sounded like a small boy.

He'd long since lost interest in what the General might say—it was Creedmoor who held Lowry's attention. Lowry had never before had the opportunity to get so close to an Agent. What would the next disgusting revelation be? Could it get worse?

What confused Lowry was that Creedmoor seemed to shift between pride in his crimes and something like shame—at least, he was prone to dropping little defiant remarks at his masters' expense. He toyed with the idea of disloyalty. Was he planning to betray his masters? Lowry couldn't tell. He suspected not—he suspected that Creedmoor was simply so vain that he demanded to be admired both for his loyalty and for his disloyalty, and for his oh-so-tortured indecision between the two—but he couldn't rule out the possibility. Did Creedmoor have unexpected allies hidden out here?

And what was the woman's angle? She was mostly silent. Sometimes she asked pointed questions. Did she share Lowry's mixture of loathing and fascination? Maybe. Did Creedmoor's stories disgust her? Impress her? Was she falling in love with him? Maybe. Lowry didn't have much sense of what made women tick. No sign of mating yet, though who knew what kind of significant glances they might throw at each other between the cold lines of the transcript?

Better than a moving picture.

✳   ✳   ✳

When Lowry stamped along in the morning's freezing fog, he kept thinking of the Agent and the woman, down in the valley where, for some reason, it was warm, *talking*. He resented them deeply.

No one ever asked about *Lowry's* life. Lowry's stories were, he was keenly aware, of interest to no one. No one gave a half-an-ounce of clinker for Lowry's stories. No different from any other man of the Line, was he? Competent, not exceptional. Angelus born, Angelus raised. Father unknown, mother irrelevant. Unschooled— you picked up things on the way. Tunnel-scrabbling childhood, in dust and rust and soot. Stunted, pale, rheum-eyed, coughing. Pale girls laughing at him. *Leery Lowry.* Filthy appetites, in later life suppressed not so much through *will* as through constant grinding exhaustion. When he first saw an Engine, still on the Concourse, he pissed himself in terror; that wasn't much of a story, was it? First uniform, ill-fitting on a child's scrawny body. Long barbed-wire nights at Black Cap Valley, long muck-and-blood nights, horrible but hardly unique, one of thousands of boys to fight, one of hundreds to survive. First posting to Gloriana. Two talents discovered: violence, mathematics—three if you count organization— four if you count greasing up and kicking down. Man of the Angelus Engine. Hardly the perfect model, but effective and cheap enough for mass production. Incapable of disloyalty; he lacked the parts.

❋ ❋ ❋

Lowry marched through thick gray fog. His men were flickering shadowy smears of black. What that reminded him of, when he got sick of his own self-pity and looked up, was a moving picture brought to life. The world was gray, no, black-and-white, grainy and ill-focused, and everyone marched with an odd lurching jerking motion.

Back in Angelus, the tunnel-children had been rounded up from time to time and herded into moving-picture vaults. The vaults were dark and cold and echoing and smelled of sweat and rust and leaking fuels. Lowry still remembered his first time: two hundred boys, shoveled in like coal—the doors had locked behind them, and the littler brats whined and pissed themselves then went silent. Even Lowry at first feared a trap—though it wasn't a trap, that would come a couple of years later when they shoved him into a lightless crowded car on the back of the Angelus Engine and it carried him off to the battle of Black Cap—in fact, it turned out to be the most wonderful thing he'd ever seen, though that wasn't saying much.

The huge screen had glowed softly—flickered—seemed to crack open with those shuddering black lines and sudden flaring of ink-blots—and then the cracks and blotches had resolved instantly into smoke—clouds of dark smoke, gray smoke, billowed across the screen—then *whoosh*: a pure black Engine punching through the smoke and pulling it behind as it rushed on along the tracks into the distance as the screen opened up to show a vast gray sky, gray plains, a world made of shadows, a terrifying emptiness that nearly made Lowry piss himself, too—and the title card, in white block print on black:

> **THE LIVINGSTONE ENGINE PATROLS THE NORTHERN BORDER. THE BORDER IS YET TO BE CIVILIZED BUT THE LIVINGSTONE ENGINE IS PUSHING THE PURPOSE FORWARD!**

Or something like that. The vault had been full of a noise that drove Lowry to his knees. . . .

✳ ✳ ✳

He marched through the fog for what seemed like days. The ground was uneven: he stumbled over low walls of rock. The shadows of his men moved all around him but didn't speak. That was normal enough, since there was nothing to say; but after a while, it frightened him anyway. He began to doubt that they were real. He began to imagine that they'd been replaced, in the nights or in the fog, with man-shaped hostile reflections of themselves. He swore and spat and told himself not to be such a slagging coward.

"Mr. Collier!"

"Sir?"

"There you are."

"Yes, sir."

"Begun to wonder."

"Yes, sir. I know—"

"Mr. Thernstrom!"

When Thernstrom didn't immediately answer, Lowry went stamping over, waving wisps of curling fog away from his face, to a knot of men that he thought might contain Thernstrom but didn't; then when he turned away from them, he grabbed at the shoulder of the first shadowed figure he saw before him. Instead of a uniform jacket, he got a fistful of greasy black hair. The figure spun round, and for a moment an inhuman face was pressed up against Lowry's own—bone white, odd angled, red eyed—then the figure twisted, effortlessly pulling its mane from Lowry's fist, leaving Lowry stumbling as that First Folk interloper scrabbled away into the fog.

Someone nearby screamed. Lowry drew his gun.

CHAPTER 34

KU KOYRIⱧ

A chill mist filled the valley, hiding its walls from sight. It coiled and shifted like cigarette smoke. It brushed damply against Liv's face. It was a thick whiteness shot through with the faintest, eeriest hint of red. Creedmoor strode through it confidently, and it flowed around him and drifted together again to put its fingers on Liv, struggling along behind him, her arms around the General's hunched and shivering body.

"Not too much farther," Creedmoor told her. "Bear up."

"I thought we were going to the ends of the earth."

"I hope not! I sincerely do. Our enemies lag behind. Some days I can hardly hear them. Soon the wilderness will grind them down. They're made of cheaper stuff than us."

"And then what?"

He shrugged. "Set up a little place together in the wilderness. I'll build it and feed us, and you can care for the young 'un. How is he today?"

"He's freezing, Creedmoor. We should stop, make a fire, if you're so confident the Line are lagging behind."

"We'll see." Creedmoor whistled for a moment, then lost the tune. "I am sorry to bring you out here, Liv," he added. "But these things happen. Great forces contend for our souls; we are dragged helplessly along. Is this not perhaps what you expected, when you came west? Perhaps even what you *wanted*?"

Was it? She could no longer remember. She listened to the meaningless tick of her golden watch and was unable to answer.

"You have no children, Liv, is that right?"

"No, Mr. Creedmoor. I do not."

"An enviable state. Unattached and without responsibilities. Free as a bird. You were married, were you not? I should have asked these questions sooner, I know."

Creedmoor was only half-visible in the thickening fog, and his voice was muffled. For the first time, she didn't want him to stop talking. Horrible as he was, he was better than the ghostly white silence.

"I was married," she said.

"He died?"

"He did."

"I thought so. No sane man would let you go, if he was not torn from you by death."

"*Please,* Mr. Creedmoor."

"Old habits. Beg pardon. May I ask how he died?"

"Of a heart attack. He was—ah—he was carving the roast at dinner, for the Dean of the Faculty of Mathematics and his wife, and the Bishop of Lodenstein, and others. And the effort, and the occasion, were too much for him. He swelled up in his shirtsleeves and burst. He fell with his mustaches in the gravy."

Creedmoor laughed and Liv felt ashamed of herself.

"He was an older man, then, Liv?"

"He was close to your age, Mr. Creedmoor."

"Ah, but I keep myself fit through clean living. You have no aged parents to care for? No grizzled father to feed and nurse? No poor old mother?"

"No, Creedmoor. None of those things."

"When did the poor old fellow die?"

"Three years ago. Three and a half."

"Alone and unencumbered for three and one-half years. I picture a perfect and respectable life, laboriously constructed, all fallen apart, and you alone. That soothing green fluid, your nerve tonic, you called it; I think you took it every day when I first met you. Did you take it every day during your marriage? I imagine your husband as very tiresome; pompous, gray-bearded, both fussy and slovenly. Am I unfair to him? I picture you making sacrifices of your health to maintain that wholesome and perfect life. Am I correct? Do correct me if I'm wrong, Liv."

Liv didn't answer.

"Some of us are not suited to domesticity. Some of us, fight it though we may, are not suited for reason; we must make our peace with madness. We can hardly be blamed for our defects. That's my diagnosis. You were bound to come out here in the end, I think. I recall the day I came out here. I was a Lundroy boy, as I may have told you, a boy of the mists and the bogs and the mire and the *songs,* Liv, the bloody awful old songs. . . ."

A wind had picked up, and the whine of it made Creedmoor increasingly hard to hear. Whatever he had been about to say was lost when a sudden whirling gust blew dust and damp leaves into their faces, and blew away the mist, and revealed a slate-gray sky and a valley that was greatly and magnificently transformed.

※ ※ ※

The dry riverbed had widened and was now interrupted by sharp black rocks, tree-tall, mountainous. The last ghosts of the mist drifted on the ground between them. The hills on either side sloped more sharply than ever, treeless and rocky, red and flinty and so sheer not even a goat would dare them, but—and it was no wonder Creedmoor had stopped, and tilted his head back, and back, and whistled and removed his hat—someone had *carved* them.

The scale of the work was magnificent, barbaric, inhuman.

Two immense statues stood on either side of the valley walls. They were hundreds of feet in height, and stretched so far into the distance overhead that their extremities were almost invisible. They had no legs; their upper bodies leaned forward from the valley walls far overhead, as if they were rising from water, or stepping through a curtain. One on the south slope, one on the north: two gigantic Hillfolk. Their manes seemed to stream out behind in steep slopes of flint. Their hands were empty, outstretched, reaching toward each other, meeting at the tips of long many-jointed fingers.

Eagles nested in the hollows of their eyes.

The slopes behind them were painted with swirls and arabesques and jagged angles of stark red. Each of those intricate swirls was— Liv reckoned—maybe five feet wide, maybe twenty feet apart.

It was perhaps the most beautiful and absurd thing she had ever seen. It thrilled and terrified her.

Creedmoor was pacing excitedly back and forth across the riverbed underneath the two giants. He had removed his hat and was swinging it from side to side, banging it dustily against his knees, and he was laughing.

Creedmoor's beard, it struck Liv suddenly, was growing quite wild now; he had been clean-shaven and impeccably groomed in the House, but out here, now, he was well on his way to savagery.

"Wonderful things! Wonderful monstrous things! Who would have thought we'd ever see the like! Look at 'em, Liv! Look at 'em, Marmion. Are you there, Marmion? Do you see these things? We've seen a thing or two in our time, but *this*—"

Liv thought: *Marmion. It has a name.* She knew at once who— what—the name belonged to. She was suddenly more scared of tiny capering Creedmoor than of either of the looming rock giants.

"This is a sacred place. This is one *fucker* of a sacred place. No wonder they've been trying to scare us away. No wonder! Who can blame them! Marmion, suppose strangers came blundering into your sacred Lodge—how would you deal with them? How much more bloodily would you deal with them than the spirits of this place have seen fit to deal with us! How . . ."

❋ ❋ ❋

—Creedmoor.

—How much more—? You're back.

—Yes, Creedmoor. We have found our way to you. It was difficult. This place is not yet ready for us.

—How do they manage out here without you, I wonder. Look at this!

—Shut up, Creedmoor.

Pain filled Creedmoor's head, and a stink of burning, sweat, gunpowder, fear. Red-hot fingers probed and dug into his memories.

—You do not know how we have suffered, Creedmoor. You do not know the agonies of terror and uncertainty, the screaming and weeping in our Lodge. Weeks in the wilderness. We did not know if you had failed us. Creedmoor, what's this?

—What's what?

—What have you been telling the woman? What lies about us? How *dare* you? You profane our mysteries with your chatter. You give up our secrets. You—

—It gets lonely out here. No harm—

—You think of betraying us.

—I do not!

—We know you better than you know yourself. You *coward*, Creedmoor. You must be brought to heel.

※ ※ ※

Creedmoor fell silent. His face flushed, and he clutched his forehead, and he grunted, suddenly stricken. He stood there, head in his hand, and his hat dropped limply to the dusty ground.

For a moment, Liv considered going to him—asking him if he was well, if she could help him, as if he were not a monster. . . . Instead she held the General by his arm and watched.

Creedmoor stumbled two steps forward, then half a step back. He shook his head and moaned.

Liv fumbled in her smock for the arrowhead. She clutched its shaft tightly and thought carefully.

A cold touch against her calf—something rough and wet scraping against her bare flesh—distracted her.

The mist drifted around her legs. Eddies of it thickened, congealed, acquired a strange slippery solidity. Only a few feet away from her—distracted, Liv let go of the General's arm—a white wisp of mist flicked fish-tail around a rock.

Another wisp slipped from behind and touched against her, and this time it was quite clearly wet, and scaled; and what was more, there was no doubt that it was moving. She shrieked and spun around to see it course past her, squirming over the dry earth, and it leapt into the air like a salmon at spawning, and shone for a moment, then blew away.

She turned back—the General was talking again, but she wasn't listening—and saw that the white mist poured now down the valley all along the miles of riverbed behind them and all the way back to the place where the river bent around a distant rockslide, two days back—and the mist rushed urgently past her legs, up to her knees now, leaping and full of purposeful pulsing shadow-life.

More solid now, flickering, sinuous, some tiny and darting, some of them heavy and long as her forearm. All white, save for their eyes, which—rushing past so quickly they were like shooting stars—were a pale blue. The tide was up to her waist now, and still leaping; one flicked just past her ear—she could see for a second the precise intricacy of its scales—and she gasped. The ghosts of all the life the river once held? They were weightless and insubstantial; nevertheless, she staggered and nearly fell.

Then they were gone; all gone past. Her legs, Liv noted with horror, were bleeding; whether from the rough touch of their scales or from the needles of their teeth, she could not say, but tiny trickles of blood ran down her calves.

There was no pain.

Blood trickled thinly onto Liv's boots. It trickled onto the riverbed, which was no longer dry cracked red earth, but was now mud. A loosening, thinning mud, in which her feet sank.

Water trickled up from the earth to meet her blood. It pooled, clear and glistening, at her feet. It pooled all around her, in the mud; the pools overspilled, and tiny rivulets crawled searching through the mud, joining in a bright tracery that was soon washed away as the water rose everywhere—there was a whistling sound, a rushing sound, a faint sound of drumming in the distance—and suddenly the river was rising all around her.

An inch deep. Soon it was two. The river's rock released its memories of water.

Liv, screaming, scrambled, feet slipping in the muck, for the nearest bank.

She was nearly there—just reaching out to pull herself up onto the rocks—before she thought to turn back for the General.

The water was maybe a foot deep now. It was still, but eddies of white froth swirled here and there on it. The General was on his knees and bending over; his hands were cupped and he seemed to be drinking from the water, or washing his face; his long gray beard dangled wetly in it.

She shouted, *"Creedmoor!"*—but Creedmoor remained frozen, useless. He stood some forty feet away, leaning against a rock, heel of his palm to his eyes, eyes closed, groaning hideously.

"Creedmoor—for once when you might have been useful—what are you *doing*!"

Liv forged back through the water—it was deep enough now to be a slog, and she kicked up spray with each heavy step—and seized the General by his bony shoulders. She tried to lift him to his feet, but he struggled; pulled away; and within seconds, Liv's own footing was lost in the mud, and she fell, and for a long moment her head was beneath the water, and everything was silent, and blue, and peaceful. Then she thrashed up, gasping.

It was a harder fight than it should have been. When she broke the surface, she saw that the waters had risen farther, were waist-height now, and there was the beginning of a tide. Slowly, sluggishly, the heavy waters were moving.

Liv held the General by his beard and lifted his head out of the water. He smiled blankly up at her.

She started out for the bank again, trying to drag him with her. The waters shoved rudely against her.

✳   ✳   ✳

—Creedmoor. Enough. You are forgiven. Remember that this pain we showed you was *nothing*. Remember we were only starting. Now go save your own hide, Creedmoor. We trust you to do *that*, at least.

✳   ✳   ✳

Liv heard the sound of Creedmoor yelling. She turned to see him take his hands away from his head—still balled into fists—and stare around him with wild bloodshot eyes.

Creedmoor's eyes met hers, as she thrashed through the water, and for a second, he looked terribly confused and old and frightened and mad. Then he gathered himself, and the thin smile returned to his face.

"Sacred space!" Creedmoor yelled at her. "Who can blame them if they are angry? But we have a sacred purpose, too, don't we? Yes, our purpose is no doubt very sacred and noble indeed—"

He drew his weapon, spraying water in a wide flourish. He raised it up into the gray sky until it was leveled at the mighty head of the giant of the southern slope. He faced Liv again for an instant and winked. Then he fired.

The valley echoed with it.

A cloud of dust and stone burst high up on the hill.

Slowly, slowly, the giant's vast face slid apart; the left side of its jaw sagging slowly down. It put Liv in mind of a stroke victim. Then with gathering speed, with a terrible grinding roar, the mass tumbled, broke, scattered in cascading dust and shards. The giant's shoulder leaned and then cracked and fell, taking the outstretched arm with it, breaking what it occurred to Liv might once have been a *bridge*, back when this was a wide fast living river. . . .

She screamed and turned and covered her own face and the General's as the crumbling mass descended.

Rocks fell around her. There was a sharp pain in her shoulder, and blood, as a fragment of flint hit her. . . . She screamed and held her hands over her ears and waited until the noise stopped. When she opened her eyes again, she moaned, because the madness was not over:

The river rose. It reared, as if wounded. The waters rose in an instant from Liv's hips to her chest; they pushed more strongly; slow, still, but implacable. Dark heavy shapes pushed through it, around her legs. Something sleek and sinuous shoved past her, and she stumbled. She was barely able to stand upright.

She would not make it back to the safety of the bank again.

"Creedmoor—*help* us!"

Thunder sounded overheard; drumming sounded from the hills.

Creedmoor, his face gray with stone dust, turned his weapon to the northern giant and laughed.

Then he returned the Gun to its waterlogged holster. He rolled up his sleeves and stalked forward. He passed Liv without looking at her, his eyes fixed intently on the water. He turned left—stalked left, searching—right again—and lunged.

He reached into the water with both hands. He seemed to have grabbed something—something that slipped and wriggled beneath the tide. Liv could see only a dark shadow, thrashing. Creedmoor set his shoulders firmly and held tight, and then, like a farmer delivering a breached calf, wrenched the thing up out of the water and into the air.

Creedmoor was holding by its throat something that at first Liv took—so sleek and long and black-haired was it—for an otter, or a large dog. It shook itself, and the long black hair and beard shook aside and exposed chalky flesh, red-painted; bony flailing arms with long, long nails that scratched at Creedmoor's face, long fingers that wrapped around Creedmoor's throat.

It was one of the Folk. Tiny, thin, pale, struggling. Wizened and ancient. Something in its lines, in its red sigils, under the hair, suggested to Liv that it was a female of the species.

Creedmoor held the wet Folk woman with his left arm, his elbow locked around her throat, just as her long white rootlike fingers locked around his. With his right hand, he held the Gun against her head.

There was a moment of expectant stillness. The waters stilled, too, Liv thought. The General was nowhere to be seen. Sobbing, she began again her struggle for the safety of the north bank.

Behind her, Creedmoor and the Folk woman held each other in tense silence.

※　※　※

—Monster.

—John Creedmoor to you, ma'am. What are you doing in my head?

—Your kind are not wanted here. Do not look on this place, do not name these things, do not make them into things they are not.

She spoke in his head with no voice, no accent, no sound or

illusion of sound—there was only the sense, an instant afterwards, of a memory of her meaning.

—Kill it, Creedmoor.

His master spoke with a noise like the drop of a gallows, the snapping of necks.

—This is very crowded and painful and confusing. I don't suppose either of you care.

—How dare you bring this thing here?

—*Kill* it, Creedmoor. Kill it at once.

—Fallen thing. Broken thing. Mad thing. Poisoned thing. We pity you. But you have no place here. Not yet. Go.

—Kill it and be done with it, Creedmoor, it mocks us—

—Go.

—Marmion?

—Your master has gone away.

—Forever?

—No. It will find its way back.

—How long?

—Long enough.

—I don't know whether to kiss you or kill you or run screaming.

Creedmoor slowly took the gun from the woman's head and pointed it back down the valley away from her.

The woman uncurled her long fingers from around Creedmoor's throat.

He didn't holster his gun, but kept it ready. The waters were now surging around his chest.

—What now, ma'am?

—Go back, monster. Do not look on these things, do not—

—What's your name, ma'am?

—It pains us to talk to you. It pains us to be named by you.

—I told you mine.

—Ku Koyrik. Do not misname me.

—Is that a name or a curse?

—Hound of the border.

—What border?

—Made; unmade. Fallen; free.

—Let us pass.

—No.

—Please?

—What?

—Please.

—You are strange.

—I mean it sincerely. I see no need for us to fight.

Creedmoor let go of the woman. She darted through the water and launched herself up with a flealike kick of her bony legs onto a rock, where she crouched, glaring. Creedmoor holstered his weapon and stood in the rising waters with his hands raised and empty.

—I have maimed myself so that I could stand before you.

—Have you? How? I'm sorry regardless. This place is sacred to you, and . . .

—Your word. Not ours.

—I'm sorry.

—Words.

—I talk too much, I know. A vain man, and not the least of my sins. If I were you, I wouldn't welcome me either. What about the old man? Who, you'll notice, is drowning.

She flicked her red eyes out across the water.

—He is the General Enver. Do you know his name? He was once a friend, so say the more scandalous and unreliable history books, of one of your kind, who went by a name that's on the tip of my tongue, *Kan-Kuk,* is that right? And in his head is one of your secrets, which I believe—

—We know all this. We planned it. We chose him. He promised to help us, he willingly took up the burden.

—Him and old Kan-Kuk made a deal, is that right? He was to take up your weapon, save his Republic, destroy his enemies, which are also yours, is that right?

—Stop prying, monster.

—*You're* in *my* head, ma'am. And why would you—?

—He may pass. And the woman, perhaps. She is sane and we may be able to save her. Not you.

—Without me, they'll die. I am terrible, ma'am, right enough, I disgust myself sometimes, but what's behind me is worse: the men of the Line. The servants of the Engines. Only I can keep the old man safe from them, and the good Doctor. Without me the Line may take what's in the old man's head and then I have it on good authority will be unstoppable, and that will only speed the day they come out here smoking and roaring and digging up your rocks and warrens and who built those handsome statues, ma'am, may I ask, while we're talking?

—Are you loyal to your masters?

—Not so loyal as all that, ma'am. Is there a better offer?

—I don't know what to make of you.

—I'm trying to negotiate, but I guess we don't understand each other well enough.

—We understand you well enough, monster.

—Would it help if I begged?

—No. It would be disgusting. Pass, then. For now. But we will watch you.

Without a further word, she turned her back and dove headlong into the water, her mane stretching out in her wake like weeds.

❋ ❋ ❋

Liv struggled at the bank. The rocks were slippery and she fell and bruised herself again and again before she could climb free of the water. When she was safe, she turned back to see Creedmoor standing alone in the water, looking around.

The water was at his chest.

It receded.

Within moments, it was at Creedmoor's waist. He strode through it—it was at his knees, now—and bent down to lift from the water the General's limp body. In another few heartbeats, the water was gone. Liv's clothes, which a second before had hung heavy and soaking, were dry again and dusty.

The General turned in Creedmoor's arms and mumbled through his beard, which was wispy and dry again. He was asleep.

With a nod of his head, Creedmoor beckoned Liv back over. She came laughing and crying in relief to take the old man from him.

✳ ✳ ✳

They left the giants behind in little more than an hour. The valley began to curve sharply south, and the giants were lost to view.

Ahead the sun was setting, and the valley flooded with red light. Creedmoor shielded his eyes from the glare and stared south down the valley ahead, then west up the jagged tree-lined slopes.

"What do you think, Liv? South, sticking with this valley where we've had such fun, or strike out west into the heights and the forests and who knows what?"

She stood behind him. The General hung limply on her arm.

"How would I know, Creedmoor?" She shook her head, too tired to think. "Where are the Line? For all I know, they never existed."

"I haven't lied to you lately, Liv. A few days behind us still. A little to the south."

She shrugged. "West, then, I suppose."

"I agree. West it is. We should be atop these slopes by nightfall. I'll take our friend."

"You certainly will." She passed the General like a sack of meal into Creedmoor's arms.

"Shall we go?"

"What happened back there, Creedmoor? Why did they let us pass?"

"We may have violated some by-laws of the locals. I had words with their representative. I told her, *I am John Creedmoor, how dare you bar my path!* And she turned tail and ran."

"Then don't tell me. And what happened before? When you held your head and—"

"My master is gone." The words came out abruptly, and his face closed behind them. He paused, as if waiting for a blow that never came.

"For now," he added.

"Creedmoor . . ."

He kept staring west.

"We'll talk later." He glanced back at her. "I have to think."

He started out bounding up over the rocky banks and up the

slopes and into the trees, the General slung over his back. Maybe he was telling the truth about his master's absence, and maybe he wasn't; what was clear, though, was that his horrible strength and speed were not significantly diminished. Liv followed as best she could.

CHAPTER 35

The Shadows

Lowry breathed deeply in the freezing fog, and clutched his gun with the same tight panicked grip one might use when riding on the outside of an Engine as it swerved hugely around high mountain passes. . . .

He counted the shadows around him.

"Mr. Collier?"

"Yes, sir. Sir, I—"

"Who's missing, Collier?"

"Don't know, sir."

"Come here. Stay close."

There was motion in the fog. Black and gray bodies, swinging arms and legs, waving arms, heads a vague bobbing blur. Shadows at work. Lowry thought again of motion pictures, like *We Too Play Our Part,* with its great scenes in the foundries of Harrow Cross, the screen a mass of moving black-and-white shadows, five thousand tiny soot-blackened men in clouds of smoke, moving like pistons. . . .

Five bodies came running up out of the fog and revealed themselves to be a bunch of privates Lowry didn't recognize—each of them unshaved and filthy and a general disgrace but under present circumstances a beautiful sight—and Lowry said, "You men. Stay close. Follow me."

And he thought of *Victory at Logtown!* which he hadn't seen for twenty years, but he still remembered vividly the battle scenes, the grainy flickering shadows of the screen hiding a thousand mercenaries of the Gun, who were, in fact, played by Linesmen as decent and upstanding as Lowry himself but who were transformed by the shadows into nightmares of depravity, savagery, and wickedness. . . .

He pressed forward. Two bodies came toward him through the fog, the first waving an arm as if the fog were smoke that could be cleared away, the second following a step behind.

The first figure proved to be Subaltern Thernstrom, who lowered his arm and met Lowry's eye with palpable relief.

"Sir, there you are—sir, this fog, some of the men—"

The figure that stood behind Thernstrom stepped forward, then, and though it seemed to emerge from the fog, it brought the fog *with* it, because where there should have been a face under a black cap with the plain honest features of a Linesman, there was only shifting gray dust.

Lowry stood and watched with baffled horror as the figure in Thernstrom's shadow reached forward and yanked Thernstrom's knife from his belt and—as Thernstrom said *some of the men are missing*—drove it up into Thernstrom's back. Thernstrom convulsed and jerked suddenly forward, and a good quarter pint of shockingly bright red blood splattered from his open mouth.

Lowry shot the thing behind Thernstrom in its head. It dissolved to the ground in dust. Thernstrom's body slumped beside it.

"Collier. You men." Lowry turned and scanned their pale faces. "Are you all men? All right. All right. You'll do. Stand back to back. Follow."

✳   ✳   ✳

He knew where he was now. A battlefield. This was enemy action; whether it was the Folk or the land itself or somehow some horrible trap the Agent had laid for them was beside the point. The field of battle was always the same, differing only in the particular arrangement of bodies and forces and fortified lines and vectors and inclines— details varied, but the problem posed was essentially invariant.

Two shadowy figures in Lowry's path were locked arm in arm, wrestling. Collier acted smartly and shot the shadowier of the two in its leg, and the whole eerie shapeless half-made creature burst into dust, leaving a very grateful Private (Third Class) Plumb alive and breathing heavily.

Moments later, Collier stumbled over another dead Linesman and fell forward onto his hands and knees. A figure came running up out of the fog and proved at the last minute faceless just as it swung an arm holding someone's pistol like a club down at the back of Collier's head—Plumb drove his bayonet into it. It fell apart. Collier got to his feet covered in a shower of reddish gray dust but otherwise unharmed.

Lowry barked orders, gestured. But in fact, discipline was already reasserting itself, with or without him. The men of the Line fell into their places unbidden, automatically. Weeks of exhaustion and disorientation and despair and confusion blew away like dust, and the steel beneath was revealed. Lowry's squad came stumbling out of the fog to find that Subaltern Slate had already organized some one hundred men into a line, back-to-back, fifty on each side, against which the shadows and dust devils that came running and sneaking out of the rock charged and burst harmlessly. Slate's line passed through, taking slow methodical steps, and Lowry's squad was wordlessly integrated.

Lowry, for a moment, lagged behind. He watched the line pass away into the fog. Muzzle flashes sparked in the gray, marking its path. The fog echoed with the crack of rifles. No screaming now.

By Lowry's side, the fog eddied, convulsed, and a brief tiny whirl of wind like a drain in reverse lifted dust and grit and shards of flint up from the ground and spun them like potter's clay into a form that was roughly human. Lowry shot it.

He hurried after Slate's line and fell in.

※ ※ ※

Afterwards, he wrote in clumsy longhand a report that would almost certainly never be read, but which he nevertheless felt was necessary.

The confrontation persisted for roughly two hours. In the first minutes with the advantage of surprise and disorder 110 casualties were sustained. However, the discipline of the Line could not be broken and only six men were lost in the following two hours, mostly to friendly fire. It is probable that this action was a tactic of First Folk who claim this wilderness as theirs. Their tactics are as always ineffective against good order and training and the will of the Line.

There are now 219 men fit for duty including myself. Subalterns Thernstrom and Drum were among the dead, and First Signalman Sinclair. Gauge and Mill have been promoted to Thernstrom's and Drum's place. No artillery or munitions were lost. However, the Signal device was lost to friendly fire. Therefore First Signalman Sinclair will not be replaced. We can no longer listen to or track the Agent. We now operate without orders or directions or realistic hope of success. Morale is low. Nevertheless we push west.

BOOK FOUR

A Land Fit for Heroes

CHAPTER 36

The Rose

Liv sat in a silent sunlit clearing, her legs folded beneath her, studying a rose.

The floor of the clearing was soft dirt and leaves, interrupted by occasional crests of grass. The clearing was about the size of a ballroom. It was bounded by a stream on one side, and on the other a fallen ancient oak, its shape blurred by decades of moss and decay. There was a low mound of earth in the middle of the clearing, and a single rose grew from it. The rose was the only thing visible anywhere that was neither green nor brown nor the blue of the vast sky overhead; it was only natural that it drew Liv's attention.

What color the rose actually *was* was unclear. At first glance, it had seemed to be an intense sunrise red. As Liv came curiously closer, its petals had flushed shyly, shifting down through the spectrum, purpling. By the time Liv sat beside it, it was a deep pulsing amaranthine. She suspected that if she turned her head away, it might change again.

It was also not strictly speaking a rose, though of all things of the made world, it most closely resembled a flower, and of all the flowers Liv knew, it most closely resembled a rose. It was more like a sketch of a rose, perpetrated by a person who'd never seen one; or, more precisely, it was like the product of processes that would, in the made world, have resulted inevitably in a rose, but out here were not so narrowly constrained.

Its petals formed a corolla that was roselike, yet iterated over and over, whorls within whorls, past the point of ordinary botanical possibility. Nor was its pattern simply a matter of spirals; there were regularities and irregularities and repeated themes within its architecture that Liv could not begin to describe. The whole thing was no larger than the palm of Liv's hand, but it appeared to have vast starlike depths. Liv had a sense that it might at any point slowly begin to turn.

It smelled of electricity, and slightly of motor oil; and in its heart, where a flower made more rigorously to the standard specifications would have had soft anthers and filaments, this one had a delicate crisscrossing of golden wires, enclosing something minute and fleshy that pulsed with a steady beat.

With each beat, the petals shivered as if in a breeze.

The thing was hideous. It was ridiculous. It was beautiful. All those things at once, and none of them. It was not meant for her, and her opinions of it were beside the point. It would have been both futile and insulting to classify it; it was neither a rose nor a relative of the rose. It was perhaps in part the *potentiality* of a rose, or an *alternative* to the rose, or more likely something with no meaning at all. . . .

There were gentle creatures among the oaks that in many ways resembled deer, though they weren't. She'd taken to calling them *deer* anyway.

"Name nothing," Creedmoor had warned her. "It's poor form out here to name things." She saw his point.

All around the clearing rose tall silent oaks. The light that fell through them was golden. Anywhere Liv looked, there might be something equally as strange and beautiful as the thing that she was conscientiously trying not to think of as a rose.

※　※　※

The oaks were peaceful—a surprise. Liv had expected, when she and Creedmoor and the General first struck out west beyond the valley, that they would be walking into growing chaos and horror. And indeed, there *had* been bad days—as they climbed through broken hills with ditches and ravines that ran with what smelled like blood and looked like bile—as they forced their way through thick yellow grass among which hid huge black ticks that beat like a heart—as they struggled through forests of bamboo, and mangrove, and trees that had no name but were nightmarishly immense, their branches riddled with hollows like big-city tenement blocks in which lived golden-furred monkeys that Creedmoor pronounced *good eating* but screamed like children when he shot them—and trees whose hollows were fleshy and vulval—and they had climbed cold rocky slopes into windy heights and camped for a night watching the stars fall and wheel and deliquesce in waves of green and blue that surged like a sea.

"The Western Lights," Creedmoor had said. "Or the Western Sea, toward which we are heading. Sea, sky, land, day, night, indistinguishable, not yet separated. Where creation begins, or maybe hasn't happened yet. How many explorers have come this far? Not many. One day we may come to the shore and make our stand there against the Line under the light of its mad energy. They should write a poem about us."

Then Liv and the General had caught a fever, and Creedmoor reluctantly let them stop for three full days, and Liv thought she might die, but didn't. When they were strong enough to move on, they went down again into forests and soon they were among the oaks, which were peaceful and beautiful and still and silent as a library and restful and seemed to go on forever, day after day, perhaps all the way to the ocean. So the western wilderness resisted her expectations again.

✳ ✳ ✳

Creedmoor returned to the clearing. He carried one of the animals-that-wasn't-a-deer over his back, and he threw it down into the dirt not far from where the General lay curled up asleep. He went and sat on the fallen oak at the clearing's edge, toying with his knife.

The not-rose closed itself. Liv sat up straight.

"Well done, Creedmoor. Give me the knife and I'll clean it."

"Thank you, Liv." He didn't move.

"Are we still alone?"

He waved vaguely. "Our friends from the Line are still behind us, of course."

She strongly suspected that he was lying; in fact, she suspected that they'd lost their pursuers days or weeks ago. Creedmoor had, seemingly without noticing it, let the pace of their westward flight ease, then come almost to a standstill. Hours would go by when he simply sat in silent thought, or walked off by himself into the forests to *hunt* or *scout* or just to *think*. It seemed that he recalled their pursuers and the need for haste only when he wanted to cut conversations short.

"And the creature?"

He shrugged. "Signs. Spoor. The usual. Nothing more."

Liv considered it symptomatic of Creedmoor's generally poor mental health that he didn't find the oaks restful. Even the General seemed happier under the oaks—but not Creedmoor. Peace and calm unsettled him. At first he'd insisted that the oaks were only the eye of the storm, that in a matter of days they'd be replaced by lakes of fire, or poison swamps, or something else equally awful. When that didn't happen, he became slowly convinced that they shared the oaks with something monstrous and predatory. He deduced its existence from claw marks on trees that looked to Liv like nothing at all, faded spoor-scents that Liv couldn't smell, the yellowing bones of not-quite-deer.

"And—"

"And my master has still not found its way back to me, Liv."

He continued to play with the knife. He quite clearly very much wanted to be smoking.

"And you?"

"The General is well enough. He talks but says nothing. Today I encouraged him to walk unaided."

"That helps, does it?"

"Probably not. He fell."

"Oh, well." Creedmoor sheathed the knife. He looked as if he were about to stand up, but didn't.

In fact, the General *had* been showing signs of improvement in recent days, or at least signs of change. He was calmer. He didn't shake so much, or roll his eyes. He talked more—it was nonsense, of course, but it suggested some activity going on within—and his voice was firmer. His movements were steadier. He struggled more when Liv fed him and cleaned him, which was tiresome but also encouraging. Sometimes his eyes fixed on Liv's and he seemed to be straining to speak sense. Liv liked to think this was because of her efforts; more likely, she suspected, it was because of the calm of the oaks; just possibly it was because of Creedmoor's frequent absences.

Creedmoor noticed none of this. He was occupied with his own thoughts. Liv didn't mention it to him.

"Liv," he said. "Is it possible that you *could* make the General speak his secrets, but you won't?"

"You overestimate me."

"Or maybe when I go walking or hunting, he *has* spoken to you, and you keep it secret from me."

"You're paranoid, Creedmoor."

"True. On the other hand, you did try to kill me once."

"Not lately." She walked over and sat beside the General, whose breathing had become labored, and put a hand on his shoulder. "Anyway, can you blame me?"

Ordinarily he might have laughed, to prove that he was above bearing grudges. Now he just kept talking. "If the General were to speak to you, if he were to reveal his secrets, would you tell them to me?"

"Yes, Creedmoor. Of course."

"Why?"

"What kind of a question is that, Creedmoor? Because I'm your prisoner, because—"

"You shouldn't."

She didn't know what to say, so she kept silent.

"The brave thing to do," he said, "would be for you to refuse; to flee if necessary; to take a knife to the General's throat or your own rather than give his secret into my hands. Why don't you? In fact, your guilt is worse in a way because you are free to make your choices while the rest of us—"

He paused again and collected his thoughts. "It's true that the secret, if the Guns obtain it, may slow the Line; at least that's what they told me. But who knows what else it may do? Who knows what the Guns would do unopposed? The present war is terrible; could it be worse?"

The General muttered. Liv shushed him.

"Suppose I promised you, Liv, that I would not give the secret into the hands of my masters; suppose instead we found someone loyal to neither Gun nor Line, who might turn it against both; or we sold it on the open market, perhaps, or published it in the letter columns of the newspapers, or took it to Jasper City and shouted it in the streets, or suppose we just stay out here in the wilderness like it's No-Town where what we do matters to no one and enjoy the harmless satisfaction of knowing for ourselves. . . . I don't know. What do *you* recommend? But what if. Would you help me then?"

"If I could heal the General, I would, Creedmoor."

"Would it make any difference?"

"I would probably believe you were lying."

He scowled. "I am, of course, used to distrust, to—"

"Stop pitying yourself, Creedmoor."

"Careful, Liv."

She pointed at the gun that hung at his waist. "You still carry that thing. It may or may not be silent; how would I know? If you want me to believe that you are no longer loyal—"

"I was never *loyal*. Am I a dog?"

"Then destroy it."

"I—" He looked genuinely shocked. His eyes widened. The thought seemed to appall him. He appeared so genuinely terrified at the possibility that for the first time Liv wondered if he might be sincere.

She got quickly to her feet. "Destroy it," she said. "Throw it away. That, Creedmoor, would be the *brave* thing to do, and then I might—"

His eyes narrowed and his expression went flat. "Do you hear that, Liv?"

"No."

"The Line. I hear marching feet, not so far behind. The roaring of motors. We must move on."

"Creedmoor—"

"We must move on. See to the General."

✳ ✳ ✳

Creedmoor strode through the forest. He kept his head down and his hand hovered, perhaps unconsciously, near to his weapon. Liv followed along twenty paces behind him, holding the General's hand and pulling him stumbling along like a wayward dog. Leaves rustled underfoot and twigs cracked.

"Creedmoor—slow down. The General—"

"No time. No time."

Overhead a thick canopy shifted. One moment Liv was in shadow while Creedmoor moved through a shaft of sun; the next moment Liv blinked in sudden light and lost sight of Creedmoor as he moved into darkness, and it was only the sound of him pushing violently through underbrush ahead that made it possible to follow. That was how they went on for hours. Leaf-drifts thickened like snow, ankle deep. Slowly the sun fell—or perhaps the canopy thickened—and moments of light became few and far between, and the forest filled with soft shadows. It was cool, windless, dry, and musty. At last Creedmoor said—

"Stop."

He stood at the foot of an oak, looking up. He held out a hand to warn her off. Then he changed his mind and beckoned her closer.

"Stay," she said, and let go of the General's hand.

She took a few steps farther, and suddenly became aware of a foul odor, which only grew as she approached the spot where Creedmoor stood. As she stood beside him her face was pale and she covered her face with her filthy sleeve. The odor was rot, feces, and something else, something oily, something metallic, something burned.

A half dozen bloody and mangled corpses were cradled in the oak overhead. Broken backs were slung over branches; gore trickled in the hollows. Liv's first thought was that the corpses were human— then she noticed a stripped leg loosely dangling, which ended in a cloverlike three-pointed hoof—and she noticed a head flung back, its throat torn, with the glassy round eye and delicate features charac- teristic of the local fauna, the not-exactly-deer—and then she turned away and retched.

"Well, well," Creedmoor said. "Do you smell that?"

"Yes, Creedmoor, of course I do, *yes*." She staggered away and leaned for support on a nearby tree trunk.

"I mean its spoor. Its piss, Liv. It marks its kills, see. Oils, acids. Not a regular creature at all, but something very strange and misbegotten indeed."

He paced back and forth under the defiled oak, stroking his beard. "Claws not unlike a bear. Habits of a mountain cat. Look, see, it kills for pleasure—these corpses are butchered, not eaten. Doesn't this interest you, Liv?"

"Monsters do not interest me, thank you, Creedmoor."

"How can they not?" He crouched and gestured out across the forest's thick floor of fallen leaves. "It slithers, Liv. It *slithers*. The motion is not at all that of a cat or a bear, but something snakelike."

She could see that the leaves were disturbed; she had no idea whether Creedmoor could or could not reliably guess at the creature's method of locomotion.

"Or possibly an eel. Something that crawled out of the Western Sea, onto mad shores, made neither of one thing nor another, a passing thought, a nightmare, one of the world's bad ideas, brought on by indigestion, perhaps—a monster."

He leapt to his feet. "A serpent. A serpent in paradise. Didn't I tell you there would be one?"

"You did, Creedmoor."

He drew his gun and grinned repellently. "Now there are two."

The thoughtful, uncertain Creedmoor of that morning had vanished. Instead of *thought* his eyes were full of low cunning. His grin was confident, cheerful, animal. The possibility of imminent violence seemed to be a great relief to him.

"Oh no, Creedmoor. No."

"Oh no *what*, Doctor?"

"You mean to hunt it."

"I do." He spun his weapon on his fingers. "I certainly do."

The General stumbled up, feet dragging through the leaves, and she put an arm around his shoulder to stop him.

"Would you rather wait for it to hunt *us*, Liv?"

"I would rather stay as far from it as possible."

"And you will. You will. You and the General. This will be no work for women or the elderly, and what kind of man would I be to drag you into it? We'll find you a hiding place, where you can await my return, with one hell of a glorious story, *John Creedmoor, slayer of the serpent of the western wilderness;* if that's the last story they ever tell about me, it wouldn't be too bad. . . ."

❋ ❋ ❋

They left the monster's kills behind and walked until sunset, at which time they came across a steep rocky scarp, a twenty-foot tumble of rocks and roots. A stream formed a very pleasant little waterfall and a deep clear pool at the bottom. Beside the pool there was an overhang of roots and a kind of shallow cave. The oaks stretched away into the distance, the stream winding on out of sight.

"Perfect," Creedmoor said. "You'll be happy enough here."

He filled his water-skin but left Liv with their bags and all their food.

"Hunger sharpens the senses," he said. "Bear in mind, Liv, that I am an *excellent* tracker."

"Where would I run to, Creedmoor?"

"Exactly. Take care of the old fellow. Keep yourself to yourself. The Line are a few days behind us, but they'll find us again; the bastards do not give up. Good luck."

He turned and ran back the way they'd come, leaving her alone among the oaks, save for the General, who was looking into the pool and talking quietly to his reflection: *"Once upon a time . . ."*

CHAPTER 37

OUT OF THE OAKS

In the morning Liv drank, washed herself and her clothes, and sat for a while on the rocks by the pool, warming in the sun. When she was dry, she dressed herself and returned to the cave.

The General had been energetic overnight, pacing and stumbling and muttering and gesturing as if giving commands, and so she'd tied him by his leg to a gnarled root. This procedure was by now so familiar that she had to make a particular effort to recall its oddity.

He sat on the floor and addressed the root in learned tones.

"Once upon a time there lived a miserly couple who had no children and expended their affections upon the serpents that slithered in the churchyard around branches and bones, when once upon a time a beggar . . ."

She sat before him and held his jaw open, so that his discourse devolved into wet guttural noise, and forced a strip of dried meat down his throat. With a little encouragement, he began chewing, and eventually he swallowed. She worked some water down him, then wiped his bearded chin dry.

"Are you well, General?"

He said nothing.

"The oaks seem to do you good. You talk more, and how can that be bad? Creedmoor's gone. We're alone. Will you speak?"

He fixed her with a glare of fierce command, as if about to pronounce a sentence of execution or order her to charge a motor gun emplacement. It was, of course, quite meaningless.

She sighed, and untied him. She picked up her bag and slung it over her shoulder, and with the other hand she led the old man down to the pool, where she began to strip him naked.

He struggled. She held his thin flailing arm up and tugged his shirt over his head.

"Do you know, General, one could learn a great deal about the operations of the mind by a comparative study of your kind. If the devastation were less total, if perhaps only parts of the mind were damaged, here and there, one could learn, from the ways the injuries might differ from subject to subject, how . . ."

She got the shirt off, exposing a sunken hairy brown chest. "This is how I pass the time, General."

She unbuckled his belt. His trousers were foul, and he was greatly in need of a wash.

"Creedmoor suggests that I should kill you, rather than risk your secrets falling into his masters' hands. Murder may be his answer to everything. Watching John Creedmoor attempt moral reasoning is a ridiculous and revolting experience, like watching a dog walk on its hind legs or a cat trying to give a sermon. Nevertheless, he may be right."

As she spoke, she removed the General's cracked and battered shoes, leaving him naked, and urged him gently into the water. He stood in it up to his waist, swaying in the faint current, and shivered despite the sun.

"It would be simple enough, and probably not even cruel. I could stop feeding you, or simply hold you underwater. I think he rather hopes that I will. It would relieve him of the burden of making a choice. He could run back to his vile masters and say: *The woman did it, blame her.* And perhaps they would forgive him and put him back to work and the world would go on again the same as ever, for ever and ever."

She sat on a rock and folded her hands in her lap. "I will not do it."

The General stood in the water and stared impassively up at her.

"Is that right or wrong, General? What would you say, if you could say anything meaningful? I've read your book. On the one hand, you were ruthless. You burned cities, torched fields. You had traitors executed. You told ten thousand young men it was virtuous to die in battle, and they did. You were quite willing to make necessary sacrifices."

He didn't blink.

"On the other hand, you were an optimist, despite all evidence against optimism. You believed the world could be remade. So perhaps you would say: *find* the weapon, take it back, *use* it. And risk letting it fall into the hands of the Gun or the Line, it would be worth the risk. Creedmoor's change of heart cannot be trusted; but what if it *could*? Because . . ."

She shook her head and smiled.

"I understand why Creedmoor would prefer not to make his choice. I would prefer not to choose, too. This is not a responsibility that should fall to me. It's quite mad. No sane person can consider such a question without laughing. Really, General, *you're* the hero, *you're* the legend, the great man of history, *you're* the one who should . . ."

He said nothing.

"I would prefer not to be alone here," she said. "That's all there is to it. I don't believe in any of the rest of it."

Still nothing. She sighed. After a while she opened her bag and removed the *Child's History,* or what was left of it.

It had never recovered from the rains. Its spine had warped and cracked, its covers had begun to rot and fray, its pages dried and stiffened and fell loose. A grainy black mold bloomed all over it. Whole centuries were missing and illegible. Between the first awakening of the first Engine in what was at the time the city of Harrow Cross, and the Tri-City Accords between Jasper and Gibson and Juniper, there was a 120-year period about which Liv knew literally nothing at all.

She had read the General the story of the signing of the Charter a dozen times—not to mention the stories of the making of the Republic and its early battles—and the chapter that recounted with diagrams its system of government and the democratic Virtues—and the discussion of the debates over tariff reform and the Nullification Principle and the Public Land Controversy—and a very long aside on the early childhood of President Bellow regarding his honesty and his courage and his simple kindness to a poor slave who might or might not have been one of the Folk (it was unclear from what remained of the text)—and the story of the Relief of Beecher City— and. . . . None of it had elicited much of a reaction. She was never sure whether he was listening or not.

She sorted among loose pages—smeared, worn and moldy pages—and settled almost at random on a few loose pages, which, once she'd scraped away the black mold, turned out to be from chapter 1: "The First Colony, at Founding." Her voice carried with great clarity in the silence as she read:

> There is a famous painting of Governor Sam Self. Perhaps you've seen it, or one day you will, for it hangs in the Museum of the Republic in Morgan Town. It shows a very fat man, with jowls like candle wax, golden rings on his fingers, which are seen in the act of signing a warrant of execution. The window behind him is open and the young fields of Founding are visible, and in the distance is a man being whipped on a cruciform frame. Behind that are the vast dark primordial woods. The artist has made Self's eyes almost yellow, not unlike those of a wolf, and perhaps this painting is the source of certain persistent and scandalous rumors regarding the Governor, which we shall not give credence here. (For while the world was very young then, and unsettled, and some things were neither one thing nor the other, the forms of *man* and *wolf* were well-made and distinct.)
>
> You may have heard that the Governor was a tyrant; that he ruled Founding cruelly; that he was known for the whip and the stocks and the headsman's axe; that his treatment of the Folk of the Woods was dishonorable. All of this is true. Nevertheless, this is where our world begins and

She heard the General splashing but did not look up. When his hand suddenly reached up from the pool and closed around her wrist, she cried out in surprise and dropped the pages. They scattered across the water and were washed away by the stream.

The General stood half out of the water, precariously balanced on the rocks of the pool, and his eyes were fixed fiercely on Liv's.

He had never before touched her intentionally.

His grip was stiff; it hurt. His mouth worked as if he were chewing, or about to spit up something that disgusted him.

Liv waited, watched. She put her hand over his and nodded.

He said, "Once upon a time . . ."

She sighed and let go of his hand.

". . . an old king a mad king white-bearded on a charging horse with a sword and flags and trumpets like in the very oldest oldest stories we learned in our nurseries and taught us to be brave there was an old king and a fallen kingdom and his wise adviser who was very old and wise and who talked to rocks and birds and the wind and his name was *Kan-Kuk,* madam, *Kan-Kuk* of the First Folk who saved me on a night when I lay dying under stars and on ash ash ash and we promised to aid each other for neither could stand alone—he stepped from the rocks and lifted me in his arms and his red eyes were sad and wounded—he told me: It began at Founding, the first . . ."

He shook as he spoke—the name *Kan-Kuk* tore itself from his throat like two sharp gunshots—and as he said the word *Founding,* he slipped on a rock and let go of Liv's wrist and fell back into the water. His head went under.

Liv waded in after him.

The General thrashed briefly, pulling her off her feet, then went still. She lifted his head clear of the water and pulled his limp form up onto the rocks. Fortunately, he was near weightless—and even more fortunately, he began to breathe again on his own, much to Liv's relief, because she had no real notion of how to help a drowning person.

He was silent again. She sighed and looked away.

※　※　※

She sat in the sun and waited. The General remained silent.

After a while she checked her golden watch—it was, as she suspected, still not working. Time was not reliable in the western wilderness. She snapped it shut and returned it to the bag.

When she looked up, she gasped in shock.

Three men stood under the oaks, not thirty feet from the rock pool.

At first, because they were in shadow, she couldn't make out their faces or their clothes. They might have been Linesmen, or Folk, though they were tall for the former and short for the latter—and something in their bearing suggested that they were almost as surprised to see her as she was to see them, which suggested they were neither Linesmen nor Folk. It seemed possible but unlikely that they were hallucinations, brought on by loneliness.

They approached. They moved slowly, stiffly, almost shyly.

They'd come silent as Folk, but they were clean shaven and sun-browned, dressed in bright clothes, holding steel weapons—they were *men*.

She inched her hand closer to her bag, and the knife within it. Not too close or too quickly, for the men held bows, arrows notched and straining. Bows! Like storybook fairies. Not Linesmen, then.

Two were bare from the waist up. The tallest, thinnest, and oldest wore a red jacket—a cavalry jacket—with faded golden epaulettes, and a few remaining black buttons. Beneath the jacket he, too, was bare chested. He wore rough deerskin trousers. He carried a cavalry saber at his waist. He had a fine-boned old face, long white hair greased back from a high scalp.

The other two were younger. Both were short and heavy shouldered. One fair; one dark. The dark one had a large wen on the side of his nose, from which hair sprouted. An unfortunate face but not an *alien* face. Liv could not, she thought, be imagining them—she would not have troubled to create that wen.

They came forward slowly, staring with such open amazement that Liv could not fear them, bows notwithstanding.

Liv stood, hands open. They were already lowering their bows.

"We are not alone," she told them.

The silver-haired man in the red jacket—where the jacket fell open, its buttons lost to time, the hair on his skinny old chest was white, too—saluted smartly.

He greeted her: "Madam." He nodded to the General, who appeared to have fallen asleep. "Sir."

Then he huddled and whispered with his companions.

She was so delighted to see the faces of human beings other than Creedmoor and the General that it was all she could do not to run up and put her arms around them and burst into tears.

"You seem," she interrupted, "to be civilized men. I had not thought to meet civilized men so far west."

Red-jacket turned back to her. "We'd not thought to see so-called civilized men ever again. Nor women. Never a woman and an old man alone like this . . ."

"We are not alone."

Red-jacket drew himself erect and placed his hand on the pommel of his saber. "Madam. You and your companion must come with us. I must insist. These woods are not safe."

"Who are you, sir?"

"Captain William Morton, ma'am, of the town of New Design, which is not only the very most westernmost outpost of humanity, but also the last refuge in exile of the Red Valley Republic, and if you have news of the world back east and how they remember us, I'd be delighted to hear it. May I ask your name? And your friend here, or is it your grandfather perhaps—who's he?"

CHAPTER 38

THE HUNT

Creedmoor crouched among weeds. Their leaves were thick and spiny and dark. They had tiny flowers, which resembled golden pen nibs. The serpent had thoroughly crushed them on its passage through, wriggling and thrashing its fat tail from side to side, perhaps just for the sheer pleasure of destruction. Not too long ago, either—the weeds still bled ink.

The weeds grew in the shadow of rocks. The beast had slithered up among them. A few of the creature's scales lay glittering among the flakes of stone chipped loose by its passage. Above the rocks stood more oaks, which the creature had slashed in passing, leaving its distinctive two-clawed mark on their trunks or tearing off branches, which Creedmoor suspected it did with its teeth. The ground rose sharply upward. Among the oaks were scattered rocks and smaller trees, pinelike, that Creedmoor couldn't name; the woods thickened and darkened.

—It seeks high ground.

There was no answer.

Creedmoor picked up one of the creature's scales. It was no larger than his thumb. It was covered with soft spines, which he carefully pressed down, wary of poison. Beneath the spines, its surface shimmered with an uncertain color—depending on how it caught the sun, it was either pearly white or a dark bruised purple—it shifted like a puddle of motor oil.

—Imagine it, old friend. Imagine what it looks like. You'll be sorry you missed this.

He waited. Nothing answered. Eventually he smiled.

—Good. Just making sure.

He leapt up onto the rocks and ran headlong into the woods.

❋　❋　❋

Destroy his weapon!—the Doctor had no idea what she was asking. Destroy it or, worse, *leave it behind,* like a Jasper City businessman forgetting his umbrella at the office—like it was nothing of importance!—the Doctor was *mad.*

If he broke the weapon, that would be the end of him. The pact would be canceled, the contract rescinded, the marriage annulled. His strength would be gone. He'd heard of it happening, to Agents caught in ambushes of the Line, caught drunk or drugged or otherwise vulnerable. The weapon could be quite easily broken, and the spirit within unhoused, sent back to its Lodge to lick its wounds, leaving the Agent only an ordinary person again, weak and frail. The obvious analogy wasn't lost on Creedmoor. No doubt if he were to explain this to the Doctor, she'd give him a knowing look and say, *Aha, you fear aging, you fear impotence, you fear loss of—* well, yes, he did, as a matter of fact. But the matter of his weapon was *also* a very real and practical problem. Without it, he'd be an old man, with no property or family or friends or land or career or prospects or pride, nothing to show for the last thirty years. . . . Without it, he wouldn't be running through dark woods, leaping from rock to rock, heedless of the branches whipping past his face, full of fierce animal joy. . . .

❋　❋　❋

He scrabbled up a sheer rock face. The creature had gone before, slithering up a crack twice the width of a man's waist, shedding scales and traces of black blood.

There was no doubt in his mind now that it knew he was chasing it. It fled. It led him on.

At the top of the rock face he stopped and looked back the way he'd come. They were high up now, him and the monster—the oaks were a shifting green sea far below. The Doctor and the old man drifted somewhere beneath them, far out of sight. The sun up in the heights was intensely bright and the sky was cloudless.

—A pleasant day. How goes it?

Still no answer. That couldn't last. Sooner or later, they'd find their way back to him—certainly if he ever returned from the western wilderness, they'd find him—and his servitude would begin again. The woman was right. He should destroy the weapon. He should hurl it from the cliff. Be broken but free.

He didn't. He couldn't. Maybe after the monster was dead; maybe then.

He turned and ran up among the rocks, on the monster's trail, which reeked of acids and oil and blood.

* * *

The slopes sharpened into a mountain, on which sunlight fell like snow. The gray rocks were made blinding white with it. The creature fled into the light. Creedmoor followed.

He'd lived half his life in the mountains—the other half, it seemed, being spent in the lowest dives of the worst cities on the flattest sunkest plains. Half a life hiding in the mountains, striking and retreating as his masters ordered, or tracking across them, scouting out paths and passes, secret routes from Station to Station—whether hunter or hunted, Creedmoor had spilled his fair share of blood on mountain snow. A rarefied kind of life, and a lonely one; sometimes he'd watched eagles soar between the white mountaintops and felt a kind of kinship with them—which was absurd, of course: there was nothing pure or elevated about him at all. Nevertheless, part of Creedmoor *belonged* among mountains. Memories crowded him; all mountains, being elevated as they were above the material world, were one, and ghosts haunted their peaks. The girl, for instance . . .

* * *

She'd been nine years old—small enough that he had to carry her through the deeper snow and over the wider crevasses, and light enough, with her well-bred delicate bones, that he'd been able to do so with ease. She'd wrapped her thin soft arms around his neck so *trustingly*—though no wonder, of course, that she held so desperately close, when one considered what was pursuing them.

Six, seven years ago—had it really been so long?

Her name had been Rose. He'd kidnapped her. And the mountains in question were far, far to the south and east, the Opals, above what had been the little trade town of Roker, and was now Baxter Station: so the mountains' pristine snows were no doubt poisoned now with sulfurous mine-tailings, their wild soaring peaks ground down to chipped ugly stubs, their shimmering clouds gone black and heavy with Engine smoke—but at the time they'd been beautiful, and new, and every footprint Creedmoor's boots stamped into the snow had been the first ever stamped by man, as he'd gone higher and higher into the whiteness and purity of it all.

But of course the mountains, though they were pristine, and clean, and white, and virgin—an unwritten page, an unblemished fair brow, and all that fine stuff—though they were silent, they were not empty. Hard on Creedmoor's heels came the Hillfolk. Or Mountainfolk, more properly, he supposed.

They were a different kind of creature from the Folk of the snowless world below. Different soil, different breeds—mountain dreams shaped them. That was Creedmoor's theory, anyway. Their manes were thick and white, peltlike, their shoulders ursine, their motions sudden, a sullen stillness that exploded like an avalanche into howling violence. By all accounts, they were man-eaters. They sure as shit had the teeth for it.

He'd have stopped and fought, and maybe won—if he had known their numbers, he would have known whether he could win for sure, but they hulked on the edge of his vision among the rocks and the snowdrifts, and maybe there were ten and maybe there were a thousand.

This was their sacred place—or maybe just their home—and he was an intruder in it, of a particularly loathsome variety. He saw their point; he *was* loathsome, and his master was worse. He preferred neither to kill them nor be killed. Better to run. Besides, there was the girl's safety to consider—that innocent fragile softness, pale skin stung a raw needy red by the winds, blond hair stiff and rimed, clinging to his Gun-arm, unmanning him. He'd not let any further harm come to her. . . .

Her name had been Rose. She was silent, almost mute, in the mountains—dumbstruck most likely by fear, though Creedmoor liked to imagine it was awe at the beauty of the mountains.

Back down in the material world of smoke and business and dirt and noise, Rose had been a chatty little thing, precocious, you might almost say spoiled. Her father was Alfred Tyrias of the Tyrias Transport Trust, the largest meat-transportation concern in that part of the world. She was an heiress, though she was too young to understand what that meant. She'd spent her life in TTT's concrete compound, living like a princess, waited on not only by a doting father but also by every dried-up craven old suit or ambitious young brownnose in her father's employ; and she was innocent enough still to think it quite normal.

And waited on also by Creedmoor, who entered the household as a tutor in writing and elocution, under the name John Cadden.

That had always been one of Creedmoor's talents: the ability to insinuate himself into the company of the good, and the decent, and the respectable. It was a rare talent among the outlaw cohorts of the Gun. It came easy to him, he liked to think, because he was himself only indifferently evil, only halfheartedly a monster.

And he was good with children. Though he, like all the Gun's Agents, was infertile, would father no children himself, he had a natural rapport with them, little half-formed creatures that they were. Rose soon adored him. He was a lax tutor, and he amused her.

Rose had put up no struggle when Creedmoor took her, in the middle of the night, and carried her out past the guards, who he'd dispatched in a bloodless manner to spare her innocent eyes, and out over the roofs and the fence and into the wild scrub and woods outside. She'd thought it was an adventure—perhaps even a dream. She'd *giggled*.

The Gun had ordered her kidnapped because of her father, of course, who had been thinking—so the intercepted correspondence said—of throwing his fortunes in with the Line. Father Alfred had been thinking in dollars and cents, shortsightedly, thinking that if the Line ran across his territory, he might lease space on the Engines, might save himself money on each cattle run, might be free to pay a stingy severance to his teams of horseback drovers and simply hand the stock over to the machines, which would run cheap and reliable— but that would only be the start of things, would only be the first intrusion of the Line on that unspoiled territory, would be the first tremor of a quake that would flatten and swallow all of father Alfred's world, and reduce him ultimately to less than nothing. . . .

Or so Creedmoor's masters had briefed him; admittedly, in all his weeks bowing and scraping and charming his way into the household's inner circle and the child's innocent affections, Creedmoor had seen no sign of any such intention on father Alfred's part, and he had come to wonder if the Guns were not running some deeper and darker scheme than they were letting on to him— offense *was* more in their nature than defense. But grand strategy wasn't Creedmoor's business.

Creedmoor took the girl from her bed at night. And he would have gotten clean away had there not been men of the Line spying on the compound from the hills with their telescopes, and had those men of the Line not wired up the woods with tripwires and alarms and bombs, and had they not had troops waiting. As it all shook out, he ended up cut off at the bridge, fled north into the mountains instead of south toward the waiting haven, and fled up and up into the snows, where the Linesmen, fat slow-moving earthbound black-lunged creatures that they were, fell behind; and then he'd have been free and clear had he not blundered across the caves the Mountainfolk called home.

"Keep them away," Rose cried into his chest. "Don't let them get me." That was when she was still strong enough to speak. He promised her he'd keep her safe, he'd always keep her safe. . . .

—You cannot keep that promise, Creedmoor.

—I can and I will.

—Do not forget what you are, Creedmoor. You are not a good man.

The Mountainfolk chased Creedmoor for days. Howling and drumming, bashing their long, long arms on the ice in outrage and loathing. Night came and went; the girl slept from time to time in his arms. He wasn't sure when she slept or when she was awake—the trembling was the same, and after the first few days, she was always silent. He broke from the shadows of the rocks and out across a vast glacial plain, a sea of ice that shone in the cold white sun so that he might have been running on air. The Mountainfolk followed behind him. The cold was so terrible as to numb all but the finest and purest feelings, of love and joy and pity and awe. Bit by bit Creedmoor stripped himself almost naked so as to wrap Rose as warmly as possible in his clothes, so that she became a formless mass of leather and linen and denim, while Creedmoor's own ugly body was exposed to the sun and the ice, and he was scoured by the cold until he looked as raw and wild and alien as the Folk pursuing him. He was kept alive only by Marmion's fires. He crossed the plain and ascended the shifting slopes of a peak that was carved square and steep like a church tower. Higher and higher . . . He was sure-footed; he'd kept his boots on, at least. And he leapt across a crevasse that was deep and black as death—and so wide that to clear it, he had to call upon all the strength Marmion had to spare, and he hung in the air over the depths for so long, it seemed he was falling or flying—and in so doing, he left the raging First Folk behind, and could continue through that elevated world in peace. The mountains were a skin of ice and air over pure thoughts. . . .

But soon enough the girl died anyway, days before he was able to make it back to the warmth of the world below. Cold, or hunger, or terror—who knew? Perhaps simply the thinness of the air, which was near-unbreathable—unlike Creedmoor, little Rose still needed to breathe. He suddenly felt her body become heavy in his arms—like the stone that sank in his gut.

But of course, it was better that way. Better that her soul vanished, sublimely, into the light of the mountains—better that than that he drag her back down with him and pass her over into the care of his masters. Probably it had not been painless, but she had at least remained *innocent*.

That was a dreadful, sickening thing to think; it reminded Creedmoor what he really was.

He scraped up snow to cover the body—he couldn't bury her in

the hard earth with his bare hands and his own strength, and
Marmion wouldn't aid him. Marmion only said,

—You failed us, Creedmoor. The girl was valuable.

Then he lay down in the snow beside her and waited to die.
Waited for Marmion to tire of him and remove its protection from
him, so that the cold would take him.

—We will not abandon you, Creedmoor.

—Let me go.

—Your life is not yours to throw away.

His limbs stiffened and went numb, but not frostbitten. His skin
wove itself into the ice so that it was agony to tear away, when finally he recovered the will. And in the end, it was the boredom that
got to him. He could lie not-dying in the snow for only so many
days and nights before his boredom grew greater than his guilt. Until he began to feel *ridiculous.*

—This is pathetic, Creedmoor.

—It is. Oh, it is.

The episode of poor Rose was just another fact about himself he
would have to get used to. Drink or drugs or women would help.

He stood, and he walked down out of the mountains, naked but
for his boots.

—Never call on me again.

—We will if we choose. And you will come to heel.

As it happened, they didn't call on him for another six years—
not, in fact, until his current mission, with the General, and the Doll
House, and poor Liv—not till this latest stage in his headlong descent into disgrace and damnation.

On the other hand, there'd been the episode in the mountains at
Devil's Spine seven years before, which had been a glorious success
from start to finish; and last time Creedmoor had been in that country, they were *still* singing ballads about his daring and cunning,
though admittedly they got his name wrong. . . .

※　※　※

In a ditch between four sharp rocks, the monster had made another
cache of corpses. Mostly bones and horn; some red and stinking
meat. Predominantly the bones were from the local deerlike

animals—but what caught Creedmoor's eye was the fairly fresh corpse of a human male, whose red jacket was torn and bloodied and had been patched a dozen times with fur but was nonetheless recognizably the uniform of an officer of the Red Valley Republic.

—Well, well. What do we make of that, then?

There was still no answer.

CHAPTER 39

LOWRY'S DUTY

Lowry wandered among the oaks. Where was he? Where was the enemy? He had no slagging idea. All he knew was shadow and sun and the hideous sound of dry leaves ceaselessly cracking and rustling, and—lately—Subaltern Collier's whining.

"Sir. Acting Conductor Lowry, sir . . ."

Lowry marched and Collier followed behind him, complaining. Collier put an emphasis on the word *Acting,* which at first Lowry had found insulting, but after a while ceased to interest him.

"Sir. We have no goal. No purpose. Sir . . ."

There wasn't anything much Lowry could say to that, so he ignored it. It was true; they were lost. They had no means of tracking the enemy. They had nowhere near enough provisions for the journey home, and even if they had, they had no idea where home was—they were going in circles.

"Sir," Collier said patiently, "we're going in circles."

Well, yes. Under the oaks, there was no way of knowing what direction they were going. The sun was only occasionally visible, and had not set for what felt like several days, and generally could not be trusted. A few sleeps ago, Subaltern Gauge had had the bright idea of hacking marks into the trees so that they could *confirm* that they were going in circles, but the marks *vanished*—and yet their bootprints in the soft dark mud did *not*. So if it was a trick, it was a stupid one—malevolence for the sake of malevolence—the oaks *wanted* Lowry to see the trick, and know their hatred for him. He'd ordered charges to be placed on the trunk of one ancient mossy oak and detonated the horrible thing, let loose a dreadful hammering of noise and weight that blasted the wood to splinters and sent the leaves scattering in a panic. That made a mark. Soon it was swallowed. They didn't have enough charges to blast a path. They didn't have enough of anything for anything.

"Sir, Subaltern Gauge has deserted."

Lowry stopped and turned to look at Collier's bearded filthy face. "Has he?" He was quite surprised.

"Yes, sir. Not sure when. He took ten men with him—they'd been lagging behind for a while and—"

Lowry shrugged, kept marching. Gauge's was neither the first desertion nor would it be the last. Lowry was no longer certain how many men were under his command. Roughly 150. In addition to the desertions, there had been suicides.

"Sir," Collier said. "I must insist we turn back. Additional forces will be coming behind us, sir, we can rejoin—"

"No," Lowry said.

"Sir—"

"We do our duty. The enemy may waver in his loyalty, but we do not. Not made that way. Don't have the parts. We can wish that we did, but we don't. We go on."

"Sir—"

"We go on."

Lowry wasn't a superstitious man or an imaginative one, but under the timelessness of the oaks, it was impossible not to entertain premonitions of one's end; and he saw himself falling in his tracks in a drift of leaves, or dead of a fever or starvation, or twisting and breaking his leg on a root so that they'd have to shoot him, or . . . The one thing all his visions had in common was that his death would be meaningless and anonymous, and he would be quickly forgotten. Therefore, it was very important that he do his duty now.

"Sir. I *insist* that we turn back."

Another possible end, of course, was that Collier might finally screw up the courage to mutiny, at which point the first Lowry

would likely hear of it would be the bayonet in the back; and then
Collier would be Lowry, interchangeable, each equally adequate or
inadequate for the task, and it would be *Collier* who'd fall exhausted into the leaves. . . .

✻　✻　✻

"Sir—"

"Go ahead, Mr. Collier, whatever it is you've got in mind, you
don't need my permission."

"Sir. There's a fire."

Lowry looked up and blinked. He took off his spectacles, rubbed
them clean, and put them back on.

They were marching along the edge of a slope. Away in whatever
direction Collier was pointing the ground fell sharply down, and
over the tops of the gently shifting oaks, it was possible to make
out, in the middle distance, a faint trail of black smoke.

"A camp, sir—a cook fire. It must be the Agent."

"Yes. Yes."

Lowry groped at his belt for his telescope before recalling that its
mechanism had broken and he'd thrown it away days ago, maybe
weeks ago. He fiddled with his spectacles again. It was a credit to
his discipline that it took him only a minute to pull himself together,
push his daydreams about death and duty to one side, and order Collier to divide what was left of the men into four groups of roughly
equal size, and to surround the camp.

✻　✻　✻

The smoke arose from a clearing in the oaks. Lowry's forces surrounded the objective with suspicious ease—either, Lowry thought,
the Agent's senses were dulled out in the wilderness, or he was lur-
ing Lowry into a trap, or possibly he was just so slagging arrogant,
he didn't care if they *did* surround him.

Ordinarily Lowry would attack at a distance, with mortars and
rockets and bombs, but of course, that was impossible without
killing the General, too. The only alternative was to rush the enemy,
bury him in waves of men. Lowry sent Collier in with the first
wave, in the hope that he'd get killed, which would save Lowry the

bother of stamping out Collier's tendencies toward mutiny. As it happened, it wasn't the Agent in the clearing at all, but Collier still got taken care of.

※ ※ ※

In the clearing were two men, standing to either side of a fire, over which they'd spitted one of the horrible misshapen deer of the forests. They'd heard the Linesmen's approach too late to run, but in plenty of time to draw their weapons. They were armed with *bows*, like something out of ancient history, and they'd have been completely comical had they not fired off two deadly quick arrows, catching Collier in the throat and Mr. Shuttle in the shoulder. The Linesmen returned fire before they could reload.

※ ※ ※

One survived.

He'd been shot in the leg and had fallen unconscious. Lowry had him bandaged, tied up, and slapped awake.

Lowry said, "Explain yourself."

The prisoner looked up in shock and confusion. He looked from Lowry's face to the faces of Lowry's men. He studied their uniforms. His eyes widened in horror.

"Linesmen."

"Yes," Lowry said.

The prisoner was a young man; tall, thin, wiry. He wore buckskin and fur. His dead companion had been an older fellow, forty or more, who wore the remains of a patched and tattered red jacket that filled Lowry with loathing and dread. Ancient and faded though it was, it was unmistakably the uniform of a soldier of the Red Valley Republic. It brought back all Lowry's horrible buried childhood memories of the fighting at Black Cap; and fuck that.

"Explain yourself," he repeated.

"I . . . Linesmen?" The young man screwed his face up into an expression of stubborn courage. "I will never tell you—"

Lowry hit him and he moaned.

"Please, sir, I don't—"

"What are you? Deserters? Refugees?"

"We fled, we fled after the—"

"After the defeat. After we drove you from the world. You ran rather than be ground under the wheels. Right. Not just you, though, is it? Not just you and the old man. Don't, don't lie to me, it's obvious—what else would you refuse to tell me? You'll tell me in the end."

"Please, we—"

"Not much fight in you. Not as much fight as I'd have expected— you were vicious bastards when I was a boy. I remember."

He glanced over at the dead man again. That uniform! Lowry shivered as he recalled nights at Black Cap Valley crawling through stinking ditches laying barbed wire, under fire from the Republic's rifles, knowing that at any moment the Republic's arrogant cavalry might sweep past, and they thought of themselves as virtuous, but they were not too virtuous to ride down children of the Line. . . .

"Are you here to meet the Agent?"

"What?"

"The Agent," Lowry said. "Creedmoor. Your General. Creedmoor's working for you?"

"Who? What? I don't—"

"Shut up. Creedmoor's working for you; either he's betrayed his masters or you've thrown in with them. And you have your General back. And you'll have his weapon, soon enough. And now you want to start it all again, and it was hard enough to put you bastards down the first time. Right? Don't lie. So where is he? Where have you taken him?"

CHAPTER 40

A MACHINE THAT WOULD GO OF ITSELF

Liv's new acquaintances introduced themselves—thus becoming, their red-jacketed leader said, not captors, but friends. Red-jacket's name was William Morton; *Captain* Morton to his men, but William—he allowed, with a yellow-toothed smile and a stiff elderly bow—to the good lady from out East.

The other two were called Blisset and Singleton, and they were brothers-in-law. Blisset's sister was Singleton's wife. Mary, her name was; Liv would meet her back at town, Captain Morton assured her. Blisset was the fair one, Singleton the dark one, unless it was the other way around, which was possible; Liv was so delighted to meet another human being that it hardly mattered what they said, and she had trouble paying attention. She had a strong urge to tell them about her research or to ask if they knew the latest Faculty gossip.

"What town, William?"

". . . a fine woman, Mary is, a pillar of the community, a very virtuous—I beg your pardon, ma'am, we don't see many strangers out here. In fact, we see none at all, ever. The town is New Design, ma'am. We have a library and high walls and productive mills and broad fields and a waterwheel on the river, all cut out of the oaks in accordance with the plans of wiser heads than mine. Two days' brisk walk northwest of here, if you and your friend are ready to travel. Are you and he alone here?"

"Yes and no. You are from the Red Valley Republic?"

"Yes, and I suppose no. The Republic is no more. We fled out here twenty years ago, after all was lost at Black Cap, before the Line could destroy the last of us. We left the world behind; we took what seemed most precious in the Republic with us. Mr. Blisset and Mr. Singleton were only boys then, and I was a younger man and didn't mind the walk, which I'm sure you know as well as anyone is quite formidable."

"Extraordinary. I know you only from history books. This is rather like meeting something from a children's story, Captain Morton. An elf, perhaps, or a troll."

"William, ma'am."

"My friend here is . . . Take a look at my friend's face, William."

Morton smiled politely and crouched down by the General's side. "He is very old," Morton said. "But I'm no young buck myself. Is he unwell?"

"Yes. Do you know who he is? Imagine his beard trimmed, imagine him twenty years younger, imagine him—"

Morton leapt to his feet. Singleton and Blisset stepped to his side, drawing their weapons, and he waved at them and said, "No. No. Down. It—" Tears ran down his cheeks. He half-started to salute, then turned to Liv and said, "Is it? Is it him?"

"So I've been told. I was beginning to have doubts."

"What happened to him?"

"The Line's noisemakers. Years ago now, I suppose. I am his Doctor."

"You brought him back to us. . . ."

"Until five minutes ago, I had no idea you existed. I did not come here of my own free will, and nor did he. We were kidnapped by an Agent of the Gun, and fled out here with an army of the Line in pursuit."

Morton kept clenching and unclenching his fists. Singleton and Blisset approached slowly and knelt by the General as if at an altar. The General's eyes wandered all around the clearing, showing no interest in anyone in it.

"The enemy," Morton said. "Even out here. After twenty years."

"What are your numbers in New Design, Captain?"

"Enough, ma'am. Enough. Singleton, Blisset!"

The two young men wordlessly lifted the General between them, each taking one arm. The General's head lolled on Blisset's shoulder and he drooled. Blisset's expression was blank.

"You are both under our protection, ma'am."

"They will come for him. Creedmoor first. Then the Line; I believe we've lost them for now, but they *will* find us. Are you sure, Captain Morton?"

"Quite sure, ma'am."

"Then lead the way."

The General whined in the back of his throat, long and high, like a mosquito, a note that rose slowly and died slowly, while Morton's smile stiffened and creaked like old canvas, and for want of anything better to do, Morton turned to the General and saluted.

Blisset and Singleton carried the General away under the oaks, and Liv and Morton went behind them.

✳   ✳   ✳

New Design—the name was a *classical* allusion, Morton explained, a phrase of one of the ancient philosophers. Liv congratulated him: *A soldier and a scholar! Rare these days.* To carve a new community in the wilderness, one must be both, Morton said; though he would allow that he did not know precisely *which* philosopher the allusion came from. Liv told him. She told him a great deal; they talked about the news, about philosophy, about New Design, about the lands to the east, about the weather. She tried not to say too much, to keep her secrets, to stay in control, but she couldn't; she was simply too exhilarated to be talking to another more-or-less ordinary human being again. Unguarded, she said almost everything that came into her head; Morton listened guilelessly and nodded, and told her the news from New Design, quite eagerly, proud of his remote little town.

Morton's little party were on a scouting mission. The beast of the forests had been coming north at nights, raiding New Design's livestock.

(Not-quite-deer and almost-turkey: that was the best of the local stock. What Morton wouldn't give for a decent mutton!)

In the last year, the beast had killed three herdsmen and a guard. In the year before that, two boys and a schoolteacher. In the year before *that* . . .

Eyewitnesses said the beast was like one of the oaks, come to life, bristling with claws in place of leaves, feeding on blood, not rain; that it was like a great serpent but also like a bear, or a man, or a machine. It must have come east from the farthest-out west, where things did not yet hold to their proper forms, and that was all Morton would say about *that* to a lady.

The mission of Morton's party—and there were other scouting parties out in the forest, to the west and east—was to track the beast's movements back to find its lair. They weren't planning to engage it; once they'd found the monster's lair, all of New Design's fighting men would come back with torches and bows and the few precious rifles.

Morton's party had stopped at the stream to refill their canteens, and in hope that the monster might have watered there itself, and that they might pick up its trail. They'd seen Liv there by the pool; they'd thought at first she was one of their own, one of the women of New Design, somehow lost. Then they'd wondered if she was some shifter or sylph or naiad, hence the bows at the ready, for which Morton apologized.

"Creedmoor is hunting your serpent-monster," Liv said.

"Maybe he'll save us the trouble, then. Maybe the monster will take care of him for us. Either way, we had best head home."

It hadn't even occurred to Liv that Creedmoor might be overmatched. She felt a sudden vindictive thrill.

※　※　※

They walked for three days. The forest remained unchanging. The oaks remained serene. They came across more of the mutilated deer, the savaged trees, but the monster's spoor was old, the corpses rotten; nevertheless, they hurried on past.

They came to New Design at noon.

It had high walls made of logs of solid oak, painted with red pitch. Before the walls, there was a wide and waterless black moat. Tree-tall wooden watchtowers overlooked the moat. On the other side of it stood a town of low log huts. Thin trails of woodsmoke rose into the sky. Turkey wandered the muddy tracks of the streets, and the deerlike animals whined and honked uneasily in their pens.

The men and women of New Design dressed in furs and buckskins, or simple worn shifts, or threadbare scraps of ancient uniforms; they dressed like border bandits, but they held themselves like honest folk.

No single house stood above the others; nothing, save the watchtowers, exceeded a single story. Nothing was ornamented. The impression was of a rigorous and severe democracy and fraternity—though later Liv would wonder if the absence of stairs was more due to a shortage of metals and nails and competent carpenters.

"New Design," Morton said. He waved an arm at it.

Morton turned to the General and stared into the man's blank eyes. "We built it in your honor, sir. That you should come to it at last in such a state . . ." And he broke down and sobbed. Singleton and Blisset stood by, pale and awkward, while the townsfolk came slowly over the moat's wooden bridge and gathered round.

Liv stuck close to Singleton and Blisset as the townfolk called out, *"Who is this? Morton, what is this?"*

Singleton gathered himself, clapped for attention, and shouted, "Hey! Hey! Stand back! Show some respect! This is the man! This is General Enver! He is! I swear it, I swear it by the fucking *Charter*! Stand back!"

✳ ✳ ✳

"Do you know what you've brought us, ma'am? Can you understand?"

Liv admitted that she could not, that she was a little confused. The Mayor cleared his throat and tried to explain. . . .

After the battle of Black Cap Valley, many of the Republic's surviving forces deserted; the true believers did not. The true believers fought on against the Line, though they knew they were doomed, and every battle after that was a rout, and soon they weren't even really fighting battles, but striking like bandits from the forests and hills; the true believers fought on because the Republic wasn't like the other petty border states and fiefdoms and kingdoms and free-towns and the like. It was not a mere organ of power—this the little town's Mayor Hobart, who was also President Hobart of the Republic, explained to Liv as she sat on the bare wooden chairs of his bare wooden office—it was the instantiation of an idea. The idea was a good idea. It gathered new lives around it. It outlasted mere mortal lives. The idea was a machine that would go of itself.

For the content of that idea Hobart referred Liv to the Charter, which she could see, if she made an appointment, and if she promised to handle the old paper carefully—they had no paper mills out here.

Like everything else in New Design, the Mayoral and Presidential office was made of oak, unvarnished; worn smooth in places by years of handling, rough and knotty everywhere else. One wall was lined with old books—works of military history and political philosophy. The other rough walls were enlivened with the red rising-sun flag of the Republic, and the bloody black flag of those who fought on after the Black Cap disaster, and a variety of battle standards. All were moth-eaten, singed, bloodied, torn and faded, and now, with the passage of decades, reduced to mere decoration.

The Mayor—and President of a Republic that was in merely geographical terms no larger than the one little town, but of far greater moral and world-historical significance, he said, far greater—was a young man. Handsome. Tall and clear eyed. Bushy black beard on a strong jaw. He wore a suit; he was the only man in town Liv had seen in a suit. It was perhaps the only such article for a hundred miles. A quite smart dining suit, though very old, of an unfashionable cut and threadbare in places. A little short in the leg. An ordinary item of clothing back in the world; out here, it was a badge of office as splendid as any king's scepter.

"I'm not a philosopher," Hobart told her. "We've got 'em out here. Philosophers, that is. Fine as any in the world, if not finer. Good men. But I'm a practical man, which is what's needed now. In fact, practicality is, as I've always understood it, a fundamental underlying principle of the Charter. But I'm not the man to explain it to you. To give you the deep thinking."

Hobart wore a gold pocket watch, not unlike the one around

Liv's neck. Like Liv's, Hobart's watch was dead, and its hands were still, though unlike her own it was silent.

"True believers!" Hobart banged the table. "My father among them, rest his bones." He gestured out the window. There was a graveyard of bare wooden poles out among the oaks on the south side of town. "The true believers fought on. General Enver fought on! Harried the Line however he could. My father was with him. At the battle of Wolf's Drift, he lost a leg and a hand. My father, that is. Came back to my mother in bloody bandages. Hobbling. Done with fighting and he was luckier than most. Brought this bloody battle standard with him."

The President held the cloth of a red flag gently in his fingers. He'd quite clearly told this story many times before. His voice boomed and was somehow both conversational and theatrical; he was a good speaker. As Liv had been led through New Design, someone had pointed out two broad oak stumps in the town's heart: Speaker's Corner and the Whipping Post. She could picture the President standing up on Speaker's Corner hollering about battle standards and blood and noble forefathers.

Something in Hobart's confident manner slipped as he fingered the threadbare cloth and for a moment he looked—ashamed? He turned back to Liv and set an expression of grave resolve.

"The General? He kept right on fighting. Deeper into the forests, hiding, striking where he could. My father dreamed of going back to him, crippled as he was. *I* dreamed of joining him, though I was only a child. But we heard the news. The victories grew smaller and smaller. The rump of the Republic's forces dwindled and dwindled. And one day, the news stopped coming and we knew the General was dead. Lost in the mountains somewhere. Dead in a lonely place with his last few men. Or so we believed, though it seems we were wrong! Quite wrong! But we believed it at the time. I don't think we were wrong to believe it even now. You can't fight forever. You can't let the fighting become everything. A man must *build* as well. But where was there a place for us in the world? Our lands run over by the Line, those bastard black Stations rising over the hills. Or falling into banditry and chaos, seduced by the Gun.

The Republic was built on certain *principles,* Mrs. Alverhuysen. I don't know if those principles are widely understood all the way back in the northeast, in, ah . . ."

"Koenigswald."

"That's right. There in the old North, the world is long since made and ordered, and perhaps you may take it for granted."

He scowled, as if to show what he thought of that. "But here we must treasure our principles. Ours are principles that flourish in peace, where men are strong and wise and free, but falter in war, and chaos, when men are frightened and corrupt. But there was no such place left in the world. So we came out here. Far out beyond even the Line's reach. To build. Those of us who kept the faith. Those of us who had read the Charter, and seen its wisdom. Children like myself, of course, I take no credit for my father's wisdom in leading us out here. My mother and me, that is. I was only a child when we came here. But I remember the dangers we faced. How we found each other; the signals by which we knew each other, back when we were in the old world, when we had to hide. My father was a Secretary of the Preliminary Society that met in secret to plan this exodus. To purchase our store of goods. To plan our way. To plan how we would live. They were soldiers, you understand; they had to find those who could build a town. A community. To find those who shared their vision. How do you lead a whole chosen people into the wilderness, *in secret*? And I remember the dangers along the way. . . . No doubt you have stories, too, Mrs. Alverhuysen."

"Yes. Not like yours. I was brought here by an Agent of the Gun. He made it seem comparatively easy.

"Mr. Hobart . . ."

"President, please, or Mayor."

"President Hobart . . ."

"*Mr.* President will do."

"You are no longer secret here. The Gun will be on you soon. I warned your Captain Morton. Mr. Creedmoor will come for us. The General is very valuable to his masters. I believe the General knows something very important to them. And somewhere behind him are the men of the Line."

"We're ready for one Agent of the Gun, Mrs. Alverhuysen. Don't worry. Do you think we've built nothing in our years here?"

"You are only men; he is something more. Mr. President—"

Hobart stood, leaning forward, knuckles on the desk, eyes flashing. "Men can do great things, madam. We've built great things. And there are those among us who think we've been hidden here too long. There are those here who'd say, build in peace, but build for strength, for *war* if you must. Those who'd say, we are the last bearers of the Charter. The last of the Republic. We were not made to dwindle in obscurity. We were made to be a beacon for the world. I am among those men, madam. And now you've brought our General back to us. What is that, if not a sign?"

Hobart sat again and smiled slyly, and drummed his fingers on the desk. "We're ready for one little lackey of the Gun. We'll deal with him. Then we'll see. Then we'll see, indeed."

"His masters no longer speak to him, Mr. President. Their voices cannot reach out here. He is no less dangerous for that—but perhaps he can be reasoned with. He is not loyal to his masters, and he does not wish to reenter their service. Perhaps we can offer him a deal, appeal to his vanity. . . ."

Hobart's face had gone so dark with fury that she was quite taken aback, and lost the train of her argument.

"We do not *make deals* with the Gun."

"Not with the Gun, but with John Creedmoor, Mr. President, who—"

"We do not make deals. That way lies corruption. If he comes here, we will kill him."

"But—"

"The matter is closed."

She studied his expression. His mind was quite clearly made up; he was seconds away from banishing her from his office. And perhaps he was right, after all.

"Very well. Where is the General? Can I see him?"

"No."

"Why not?"

"The decision has been made."

"Mr. President, I believe I was making progress with the General. More through blind luck and patience than any great cleverness on my part, admittedly, but still progress—we have a bond, Mr. President, he has come to trust me. To need me. Something living in him reaches out. This is my analysis, do you understand? I do not speak idly. I have told you: I have reason to believe that he may remember something, that he may know something, that he may have *found* something, that frightens the Gun and the Line alike. That may per-haps be a danger to them. A weapon of the First Folk, which may put an end to the spirits that drive this world mad. An end to the Great War! It is essential that we—"

"There is no end in this world to war, madam."

The President said this quite calmly. Liv was flushed, sweating. His tone surprised her. It occurred to her that she had nearly for-gotten how to talk to anyone other than Creedmoor.

"What reason do you have to believe this, madam?"

"I . . . Creedmoor told me so. But—"

"Precisely. Madam—I shall speak plainly—is it any wonder that we do not entirely trust you? Please don't take offense, madam; we are very grateful for what you've done for us. You can hardly imag-ine how grateful. You are an agent of providence, they're saying, out in the town. My citizens are saying this. Certainly you are an agent of *something*. The General is restored to his proper place, and we will take care of him. What matters now is that you help us. That you show us you are *willing* to help us, do you see? That you tell us all you know of this Agent you traveled with. Wait; collect your thoughts. Be sure you are ready to tell all. All his *filthy* secrets."

A snarl of loathing passed across the President's face. The man's smile wrestled its way back into place and he regarded her evenly; only his eyes betrayed the illusion of calm. "I want my planners and my officers and my War Secretary to hear this. Good men; don't be worried."

There was a heavy brass bell on Hobart's desk. He rang it. There was a sound of booted feet approaching in the halls outside.

CHAPTER 41

A Guest at Dinner

They found Liv a room in Captain Morton's house. Morton's first wife had died—at the end of a long and productive life, Morton assured Liv, and of no contagious cause—and he had left her room empty, building a new bedroom for his new wife.

Morton's house was larger than most in New Design. This was, Morton assured her, the result of his own hard work. It had nothing to do with the fact that he was among the first to go forward into the wilderness, or that he had been much decorated in battle.

"Though," he allowed, "Not knowin' how things are done here, ma'am, you might well think so. New Design bestows no honors, ma'am. New Design neither gives nor takes away from what its citizens build with their own honest sweat. That's the foundation of all good government."

"Is it, really? Thank you, Captain."

It was hardly what Liv would have called a bedroom. It was a little square grotto of rough logs. It was dark. Like everything in New Design, it felt rather like a storeroom in a military campsite. It contained a few sentimental treasures. On a log-hewn table, in thick dust, were a silver hairbrush and dried-up glass perfume bottle and a silver hand mirror, which contained no glass. A shelf on the opposite wall held seven yellowing chapbooks: two works of religious instruction and one discourse (illustrated with machines,

with pendulums, with beehives, with heart valves) on the power of
the principles of divided government to channel the healthy industry of . . . And four romance novels, one of which was the very one
Creedmoor carried with him. She dropped it like a snake. Guiltily
she placed it back on the shelf.

She lay down on the bed and stared at the ceiling. The bed was
made of wood and stretched hide. A few months ago, she would
have regarded it as no kind of bed at all; now the comfort of it
amazed her. She was quite unable to stay awake.

* * *

Liv dined that night with Captain Morton and his new wife. The
second Mrs. Captain Morton—her name was Sally—was much
younger than the Captain. She must have come to New Design almost as an infant—a strange life, Liv thought, and in fact, there was
something not merely foreign but *alien* about her. She was a small
brown thing who spoke softly, made very little eye contact, and
seemed to be full of private thoughts—her expression was very shy
or quietly, ineffably confident. She was heavily pregnant. Morton
beamed with pride throughout the dinner, while his wife smiled
silently and looked down at her plate, her belly, only occasionally
lifting her dark eyes to look around. . . .

Everyone who was anyone in town was there to see the Mortons'
strange, impossible visitor. Squeezed around the long wooden table
were, among others, two Justices of the town's High Court, Justice
Woodbury and Justice Rutledge, silver haired and bald respectively,
and very grave in their bearing; Dr. Bradley, lame and hunched,
short and wild haired and scarred, who beady-eyed Liv with frank
suspicion; Mr. Waite, who led the town's Smilers in their meetings,
and who was young and pretty and as earnest as befitted his position; and dour Mr. Peckham, who ran the town's farming operations, whom the others addressed variously as Overseer, Secretary,
Quartermaster, and Chief. And their wives, of course, who each
explained that they were the Secretary or Chair of some Voluntary
Society or Organizational Committee or Educational Association or
other, or more than one. . . .

Judges and doctors and meeting leaders looked exceedingly silly in furs and hides. Not, Liv supposed, that she looked any less wild. It was hard to be sure; there was no good mirror glass in all of New Design. Probably a mercy.

They ate near-deer meat and green leaves, boiled and spiced with some unfamiliar bitter herb. The deer meat tasted slightly of fish.

Morton led them in a toast to New Design, to the Republic, and to the General's return. The assembled gentlemen gave low growls of approval. The ladies smiled and dipped their heads.

"They are saying," Justice Rutledge said, "that it is a providence that has restored him to us. You are much admired as the agent of that providence, Mrs. Alverhuysen."

"Thank you, Your Honor."

"It is an excellent irony," Justice Woodbury offered, "that the General who fought for a Republic that taught us to disdain powers and providences and to, ah, to build, to build with our own hands. To build a world of man's devising. Ah, if he has been restored to us by some preternatural providence. An excellent irony." He creaked a smile and was rewarded with polite laughter, and some grave head-nodding from his colleague Rutledge.

"How is the General?" Liv asked. "Our long flight west was hard on him. Is he stronger now? Who takes care of him?"

There was an awkward silence. No one would meet Liv's eye.

Morton coughed and spoke. "Ah, the General. The stories I could tell! I recall one day when we tented on the plains of Sarf. You were there, Rutledge, weren't you? We were movin' our forces southwest from Brenham—'64, '65, it was. We were only one step ahead of the Line and . . ."

He leaned back and made wide vague scene-setting gestures.

"The plains were vast and golden; the grass was golden, too. Through our telescopes we could see them at work behind us. They built the Line as they went; we could see its smoke. The plains of Sarf throng with buffalo, as many of you know, and the Line's thund'rin advance drove those magnificent beasts quite mad with fear. The Line scattered them like a broom scatt'rin mice. Stampede was always a danger. We were only one step ahead, all the way across the plains. We'd raid at night and then withdraw. We'd played that game all over a thousand miles of Sarf. A great arc! Like a bow. Tense like a bow. You'd not think it possible, but the Line was always only one day's work from catchin' us. They had dreadful machines with them that could flatten a hill and drive the rails as easy as you or I might saw a log. I don't know that we even slowed them much. The Engine—I reckon it was Dryden Engine, but how could we be sure?—pushin' forward at the tip of that line, like poison on a speat tip. We'd dealt them a terrible defeat at Brenham, you see, Mrs. Alverhuysen, and they hungered for revenge."

Morton was a little drunk. He paused to swig.

"And yet when I brought the General his shavin' mirror that evening in his tent, he was quite calm. Quite calm. Half the camp wakin' from their first brief sleep in days of desperate flight. Half already at frantic work. We had slept in the hot afternoon and planned to continue at night. The General in his command tent, quite calm, trimmin' his mustaches with a delicate golden scissors. Civilization is an important thing, he told me. There must be room always for a certain luxury. I was a young man at the time, Mrs. Alverhuysen. Though our enemies press us hard, we must not become debased and inhuman as they are. Understand that *in his own command tent,* the General had made room for various pale urchin-trash we had picked up in Brenham. Vicious boys from that vicious rat's nest of a town, whom I regret to say we had left fatherless. Brenham, you see, had declared for the Line. What choice did we have? But there were so many survivors, who'd come out beggin' after us. The General drove off the adults; the adults had made their choice. Had chosen the Line and must suffer the consequences. But these orphan boys! And probably girls; I don't recall. The General had a soft heart. Some of our men bore a grudge against those orphans still, for their fathers' wickedness, and so the General let them stick to him. Like dogs at his heels. Skulkin' and snarlin' in the corners of the command tent. Any lesser man would have left them behind; our plight was perilous enough. But the General paid his debts. He always paid his debts. And he kept that old Hillfolk creature—Rutledge, do you recall his name? Ka-Ka-Ka-something. Ku-Ku-Ku. A wiry old monster, pale as a dead thing, shuffling around half-bent-over. Like something risen from a graveyard, painted that awful red, rattlin' bones and stones. No one else would go near him, but the General kept him close. Said he respected his wisdom. So there's the measure of the man; he was not too proud to open our stores or his own command to the worst street urchins and uncanniest Folk; yet he *was* too proud to go unshaven though the Engines themselves pursued us."

A rumble of approval went round the table.

"Kan-Kuk," Liv said. "Was the Folk man's name Kan—?"

"Something like that," Morton said. "Not important."

He leaned forward and continued.

" 'Spit it out, son, spit it out,' the General said. I was waiting, you see, while he shaved. And he could hear the men gath'rin' outside his tent. He could hear them grumblin' and pissin' and moanin'— pardon my language, ladies. He knew something was up. 'I've sorry news for you, sir,' I said. He kept his eyes fixed on the mirror, I recall, and snipped away at his whiskers. Such sharp eyes. I recall the General's old Hillfolk monster leering at me from under all that filthy hair. Like he knew what was comin' and it amused him. I recall the boys shiftin', skulkin' in the shadows. It was winter on the plains and it was dark in the evenin', you see. And 'I'm sorry, sir,' I said, 'but the men are angry. Sorry, sir, but there are rumors.' He asked me if there was a mob outside. I do believe he knew. I had to tell him that there was. Understand, madam, that we were hungry and frightened. We were trying to be better people, to be the new-model men of the glorious tomorrow, but we were hungry and frightened and tired. And there were witnesses. One of those boys we'd picked up in Bernham had been seen raidin' the food stores. We'd taken them in out of the goodness of our hearts, we'd fed them as if they were our own, and yet they were thievin'. The men were angry. Such ingratitude! Such a lack of moral fiber! Corruption spreads from within, you know. There I was stamm'rin this out to the General. He looked up from the mirror and very quietly, he said: 'Do the men demand a hanging?' " "

Sally lifted her eyes and momentarily looked pained, as if she felt that the story was taking a vulgar and inappropriate turn. Her husband was far away, staring into the fireplace as he spoke.

"He handed me back the scissors and the mirror, and as I shut them away in the leather shaving case, he walked out into the evenin'.

In nothin' but his long johns. I followed after him. There was quite a crowd out there waiting. Respectful, of course. But the General was not wrong about their mood. More than one man who'd brought rope. Don't know where they expected to find a tree out there on the plains. 'If you insist,' he said. 'If you insist, there will be a trial.'

"And there we were. There was no arguin' with him. He led us out to the edge of the camp—where we could see, against the settin' sun, the black smoke of the Line approachin', closing the miles between us. And he had the boy brought out. He struggled, but by the General's orders, he was not yet to be harmed. We chose a jury by lot. One of the men had the *Commentaries on the Law of Our Fathers* in his pack—not you, was it, Rutledge? no?—and that served us as a guide. Crime was not common in our camps, you understand. Not common at all. We sat the jury on feed sacks. We brought out torches and oil lamps for the General to read the *Commentaries* by. He was very insistent that he not serve as judge; not if he was to execute the boy's fate himself. We chose the judge by lot, too. A chaplain, I think. Could have got yourself an early start in the judgin' game, eh, Rutledge? I remember the boy's face in the light of the torches. We determined by questionin' that he was of an age to stand trial. Malnourished as he was, he might have been an infant, you see. And the sun set, and we watched the Line's smoke get closer. We watched the three black specks that rose from the Line's camp, against that red sky; we watched them come closer, closer, until we could hear the whine of the rotor blades and we knew the Vessels were on us. And still, under the General's glarin' eyes, we conducted our trial. We heard evidence. There was doubt as to whether the boy was under our jurisdiction at all, as I recall. Even as the Line approached. It was a point of principle. That was the man he was. You know, I forget now what happened to the boy. But how fiercely the General fought when the Vessels arrived! When it was time to set aside law and reason and take up a rifle—as the lead and the gas and the shatterin' noise rained down on us! Why, then . . ."

But no one was listening to Morton's story anymore. No one had been for some time. Apart from Liv, everyone assembled at the table appeared to have had heard the story many times. As Morton talked, lost in his past, his young wife had leaned over the table and asked Liv: What were the houses of the outside world like? What was it like to live in a house of stone or glass? What was it like to wear silk?

"And the Smilers?" Waite said. "Are they still doing their good works?"

"I suppose so. I've heard of them. Sirs, I passed through that world very quickly. . . ."

Waite nodded and smiled complacently. "Well, I'd like to hear more if anything comes to you. In the meantime, I'll just have faith we're doing well." Morton and Rutledge murmured approval, as if Waite had said something clever or brave.

Dr. Bradley quizzed Liv on medical science. It turned out, not to Liv's particular surprise, that he had backwards ideas about the brain. No doubt he was a good field surgeon. She tried not to embarrass him. She did not entirely succeed. He scowled behind his mustaches. The right side of his face had been badly burned, so that it was blotched and red and shiny-swollen. His eyes were very blue, very intelligent and fierce.

Captain Morton's young wife filled the dinner party's mugs— dented old metal steins, three shot glasses, a chipped china mug, the rest were of carved polished wood—with New Design's rough wormwood-tasting brew. Only for the men; the wives and Liv drank water. Dr. Bradley drank rather too much.

"Is the General in your care, now, Dr. Bradley?"

He wouldn't answer. She spoke quickly.

"May I see him, Dr. Bradley? I was making progress with him, I believe, and I believe he has vital intelligence, something in his memories frightens the Gun, and perhaps we might make use of it to defend this place. Doctor?"

Bradley barked, "He doesn't need the help of strangers."

The table went awkwardly silent for a minute; and so Captain Morton proposed another toast to the General, to his heroism and unyielding courage and apparent unkillability: *As if he's as immortal as the ideas for which he stood—no*, stands!

"Though sadly reduced in stature," Peckham said. "Like the idea, stuck out here doing nothing. Perhaps they'll both get strong again together."

Bradley nodded and mouthed, *Hear, hear*. Rutledge scowled.

The men knocked back the booze, save Waite, who, as a Smiler, was Dry.

It took another round of drinking before anyone could ask Liv the *real* question. In the end, it was Justice Rutledge who asked, "And how goes the War? Where is the Line now?"

"Kingstown. Kingstown is the westernmost Station. But they have forces as far as Kloan."

"Where is Kingstown, madam? Where is Kloan?"

Liv told them; she gestured on the table to indicate the distance she and Creedmoor had traveled.

They went silent. Waite's smile froze. Bradley emitted a barking bitter laugh. Morton's wife covered her mouth in shock.

"Ah. When we came here," Morton said, "we marched for many months. Nearly a year. From the farthest west of the settled world to the peace and fertility of the oaks, where we built New Design. . . . Now it's a quarter of that. The world shrinks."

Liv went on, "And there are forces of the Line pursuing me. They may be only days away. Gentlemen, it may be possible for us to make an alliance with John Creedmoor, who—"

"Never." Bradley banged his stein on the table. "The fight comes to us. Again. At last."

※　　※　　※

The guests departed, and Morton retired to bed. Sally tried to refuse all help with the cleaning, but Liv wouldn't hear of it. Liv took a brush and set to work.

They chatted. Liv probed gently, careful not to spook the girl—and so learned that Sally had been born on the trek, and her earliest memories were of New Design; and that her brother was a promising young guardsman and a fine shot with both bow and rifle; and that she was a schoolteacher; and that Captain Morton was very kind; and that there was a dance coming up, which would be much the same as last year's dance; and—

"Dr. Bradley seemed an angry man," Liv said.

Sally dropped her dark eyes. "I couldn't say."

"Some of you want war. Some of you want to come back to the world and fight."

"I couldn't say, ma'am."

"How strong are you?"

"I couldn't say."

"Where does Captain Morton stand?"

"I really can't say, ma'am."

"I don't wish to upset you. I understand, Sally. This must all be a terrible shock. Why, you've been here all your life. Out here alone, quiet. Raising your children in peace. What if this changes everything? I imagine it's different for some of the old men, who were used to war. For instance, Dr. Bradley and Mr. Peckham seem terribly eager to face the Line and Creedmoor both; and so does President Hobart, though he's too young to remember. Justice Rutledge thinks differently, perhaps. Where does Captain Morton stand?"

The girl shook her head and turned away. "I'm sorry, ma'am. I shouldn't speak on these things." Her voice was flat, but she nervously rubbed her pregnant belly.

"Sally—what if there were a way of ending the War? What if I told you there was a secret that would end Gun and Line and bring peace to the world?"

"I don't know, ma'am. I really shouldn't be talkin'."

CHAPTER 42

THE SERPENT

Creedmoor had left the tree line far behind, and walked on bare stone. Ahead of him, the mountain gathered into a spearlike peak, stabbing the sun. The sun was so bright that he could hardly see. The rocks baked and glittered. The beast led him on with traces of blood, scatterings of scale, and above all, the electric-oily-acidic stink of its spoor.

—So let's say I give the General over to the Knights of Labor. The union men are good in a fistfight, and they have chapters everywhere. They hate the Line, same as they hate all bosses; and they hate you, thieves and shirkers that you are. They hate me, too, after that incident in Beecher City, but maybe they'll let bygones be bygones if I give them the secret to remake the world. How about that?

No answer. It was still thrilling and a little terrifying to think such things—to be free to think such things.

—We can go hide together in No-Town, I guess, but who knows if it exists, or where, and in any case what good will hiding do?

He stopped to examine a rock on which the beast had sharpened its claws.

—I can never remember these days which Barons and Mayors and Sheriffs are secretly on our side and which are secretly on the other side or if there are any at all who are just what they say they are, still. So best not give the General to any politician, then.

There was something ragged in the edges of the thing's claw marks. It had taken Creedmoor a while to realize that it reminded him of marks made by a drill, or a circular saw—nothing animal.

—Or the Liberationists. Not much in fashion these days, too earnest, but they're decent fellows to a fault; on the other hand, would they use the weapon or just make speeches about it?

His eye caught a flicker of movement on the slopes above. A shadow moved between rocks. Had there been clouds, he'd have thought it was just a cloud shadow, but there weren't, so he leapt to his feet and ran after it.

—Or what about the Republic? Maybe that poor bastard back there was a solitary deserter, or maybe there's more of them, in which case, maybe it occurs to me I should have just joined them in the first place, when I was a young man—I could have died nobly at Black Cap or Asher!—and maybe it's not too late—maybe I'll bring them this monster's head as a peace offering!

He leapt across a crack, then leapt again, caught the edge of a rock face above him, pulled himself, and kept running. In the distance ahead, something moved again between the rocks. Motion of legs first then long tail whipping behind, a suggestion of spines. It was even bigger than he'd imagined.

—I still might just publish it in the newspapers. I still might.

※　※　※

Night fell with shocking suddenness, leaving Creedmoor stumbling in the dark. The world went red, then gray, then black. The rocks were looming shadows around him. He shook his head and rubbed at his eyes.

—Lights, please.

He squinted. Ahead of him was only blackness. No stars.

—Be like that, then.

He groped his way to a mass of rock, taller than he was, rough and still warm to the touch. He drew his weapon and crouched behind it.

Suddenly his heart thumped and he felt short of breath. His night-sight was gone. He could hardly make out his hand in front of his face, not to mention that his hand was *shaking*. It was more than thirty years since he'd last had cause to fear the dark.

The gifts of the Guns were leaving him.

He tried to recall the climb up the mountain; he'd been strong, yes, and fast—but was he still as strong as he'd been back in the world? Maybe; maybe not. He began to count the aches in his legs and his back. Perhaps that was how it worked: The voice was the first thing to fall away, then the night-sight, then—what next? There was no way of knowing.

If he were wounded, would he heal? Healing was probably the greatest of the Guns' gifts, because without it, how could one dare be so *reckless* as the Gun demanded? . . .

He reached for his knife, thinking to cut his palm, before remembering that he'd left his knife with Liv. And he couldn't find a rock sharp enough to cut himself on.

—So much for the experimental method, Doctor.

The night was silent. The monster was waiting patiently for him. It was a sporting sort of monster, Creedmoor had to give it that.

He considered running away—crawling down the slopes, maybe or maybe not breaking his neck. It wouldn't be the first time he'd turned tail like a coward, and he could always lie to the Doctor when he got back; except, of course, that the monster, sensing weakness, would surely give chase.

He pointed his weapon into the darkness and waited for the monster to come charging madly out of it. It did not.

Would his weapon fire? He examined it thoughtfully. He'd certainly never bothered to load it at any point in the thirty years he'd carried it. He didn't know how the Guns arranged for it to operate nor, until now, had he ever cared; but if the night-sight was leaving him, maybe next the weapon wouldn't fire. He stretched out his arm, winced with anxiety, and tried but failed to find the will to pull the trigger. His hand shook and sweated, and he couldn't face the thought that he might pull and learn the worst.

—Shit. *Shit.*

He sat with his head against the cooling rock for perhaps an hour, looking out into the darkness, until his fear dried up within him and blew away. He began to smile.

—Well, then. We'll see. We'll see how things are, I guess. I always said I never needed you.

※ ※ ※

He crept forward in the dark, groping with his left hand, holding his weapon outstretched with his right. Stones shifted beneath him. All he knew was that he was heading uphill. He proceeded through what felt like hours of darkness.

※ ※ ※

It became obvious that the objects that rolled and snapped under his boots with a noise like gunfire were bones, and lots of them. He didn't need to see to know that. The acid stink of the monster's spoor grew worse and worse, and behind it, there was the smell of rotting meat.

※ ※ ※

As he proceeded uphill, a sliver of yellow moon emerged from behind the peaks, like a door cracking open. Its light picked out details, made shapes out of the empty dark. He walked on a carpet of bones: mostly animal, some human, many too misshapen to say. The bones lay in a wide circle marked out by a dozen sharp toothlike rocks. And a patch of darkness that looked at first like a huge jagged rock shrugged its shoulders, swung itself round to face Creedmoor and opened two great yellow eyes like an Engine's fog lamps.

It snapped out a dark gray shape at him—something that might have been a clawed arm or a long snapping jaw—but he'd already leapt back, shouting.

—Shit—

And he stumbled as some poor dead bastard's rib cage cracked beneath him and he fell sliding in the bones. Another limb, and he was pretty sure it was a limb this time, swung through the space where his head had been. He crawled. Its thick glistening tail whipped out and scattered bones all around him and slammed into his side with the force of an exploding rocket. He went flying. He lost his hat and, more important, his gun. He landed on his feet, breathing heavily.

—Shit. Shit. I've changed my mind.

He was in terrible pain but not dead or even crippled; so his strength had not entirely left him yet. Was it enough?

He picked up a thighbone and held it like a weapon.

The creature stood fifteen feet away from him. Its huge body blocked the moon, and so its details were impossible to make out. It reared up on a long cobralike tail, thick as a tree trunk; but there was also a suggestion of several skinny shuffling legs, many-jointed like the legs of an insect or the branches of a tree, of uncertain number, which might or might not have been functional. Its eyes were huge and yellow and empty. Its shoulders were spined. Behind them opened out what looked like wings—diaphanous, ragged, the left far larger than the right. Creedmoor considered the wings irrelevant, but tried very hard to count the bastard's *claws:* he couldn't. Its scales were not precisely gray—rather, it was no color at all, as if all the misguided energy of creation had gone into its spines and claws and teeth, and nothing had been left over for mundane considerations like *what fucking color it was*—it hurt the eyes even to look at it.

The whole huge contraption whirled about its axis like a nightmare calliope, and its mouth or something not entirely unlike a mouth opened, and emitted a scream like a woman in terror, which was a sound that Creedmoor had never cared for.

It rushed forward. Creedmoor ran to meet it. He leapt and jammed the thighbone into one of its eyes—the eye shattered like glass and went dim. One of the monster's many claws slashed Creedmoor's leg open to the bone. Its mouth descended on him, but he'd already flung himself to one side, where he rolled in bones and ended up lying on his back. He scrabbled among the bones and his hand found his gun.

—Thank you. It fired.

—Thank you *thank you* shit *thank you.*

He blew two ragged holes in the monster's torso. The moon's yellow light spilled through them. The monster bled nothing at all, or possibly smoke, or possibly yellow light. It kept standing. Creedmoor fired again, and the monster's other eye went dark and its head changed shape. He pulled the trigger a fourth time, and nothing happened.

The monster surged forward, and Creedmoor slithered back, but too slowly, and it gripped his left shoulder with one clawed arm and lifted him and closed its jaws around his other shoulder and bit down. Its teeth worked like mechanical knitting needles, stripping flesh, cracking bone. Creedmoor's shoulder was full of agony, but he couldn't feel his right hand at all. He knew the gun in that hand had fired only because he heard the noise, he saw yellow moonlight pour through three more holes in the creature's body, and it dropped him, and staggered back.

He'd dropped the gun. He fumbled to pick it up with his blood-slick left hand.

He fired twice more, into the monster's central mass. One of its wings snapped off and trailed on the floor. The monster screamed again. Creedmoor shot it again. Its form began to collapse. Its internal strains revealed themselves. Some of its legs seemed to pull *left* and others *right,* and it screamed and thrashed but was helpless. He shot it twice more in its head, and it stopped screaming.

Its tail lashed out and slammed into him, harder even than the last time. It launched him into the cold night air and he spun flailing over the rocks and out of the circle of bones and he blacked out for a moment but not before he saw the monster slump twitching and maybe dying among the bones and when he next knew where he was he was sliding and bouncing down the side of a steep rocky slope.

He came to a rest on a stretch of hard cold dirt, among arrow-leafed weeds, not far from a stand of pines.

He was covered in blood and his agony had been replaced by numbness and he could not stand. Even if the gift of healing was still with him, he wasn't sure it would be enough.

—Shit.

The stars chose that moment to come out.

CHAPTER 43

A Stranger in Town

They let Liv walk the town as she pleased.

In the square next morning, she saw a young man tied to the Whipping Post and given several short sharp strokes on his back. He looked drunk or possibly simple. He made an awful, heart-breaking noise.

"A shirker, ma'am."

"I beg your pardon?"

There was no crowd of idlers watching. New Design was a busy town. Apart from the man with the whip, and his assistant, both hooded, only Mr. Peckham stood there. Peckham said, "A sad business. A shirker. Well known for it. We must all work together here. By and large, we do so gladly. This is a good place, madam. Some people even the strongest, most finely engineered republic cannot make useful without the rod. No teaching will mend them."

Two more strokes; two more yodeling screams. Then the young man was let down sobbing onto the blood-spattered earth. Mr. Peckham nodded. "A sad bit of business. A shameful necessity. Mrs. Alveruysen, would you like to see our sawmill?"

She averted her eyes from the Whipping Post. "Please, lead the way."

There were ten men at work in the sawmill. Liv stood on the dusty fragrant floor and watched them for a while. She stayed after

Peckham moved on. The men were all proud of their work. Some of them were younger than the rusty old saws they held. She wondered what New Design would do when its tools finally wore out.

＊　＊　＊

There were almost-turkeys in a pen. Docile, silent, fat. Liv watched them and they stared back. Their eyes were oddly human, and their clawed feet, scratching the dirt, seemed oddly purposeful, as if they were trying to spell out a message in an alien language. Another aberration of the rim of the world? Or were all turkeys like that? Liv had no particular familiarity with turkeys. She made a note to eat no bird-meat in New Design, and moved on.

＊　＊　＊

There was a well near the center of town. It was lined with a rough blue gray stone that Liv had not seen in the forest of oaks; they must have brought it from far away. A large pumping contraption hunched over it, its wooden wheels and gears creaking and swaying. One or two houses had tanks or cisterns; most others had water barrels. Otherwise, there was the well. She'd rarely seen a place so lacking in luxuries or conveniences or modern improvements. At least the water was clear and, to the naked eye, clean.

Liv sat by the well all morning. Around it was a haphazard arrangement of wooden water troughs, and the earth was muddy and crisscrossed with hoof tracks. All morning, the girls from the outlying pens and farms came and went with their deerlike-herds, or carrying buckets back and forth. They were wary of her. They reminded her of shy students, and the thought made her smile.

Liv made a point of smiling at them as they passed. Some smiled back.

They were not peasants, though they dressed like peasants, or worse. Morton and his wife Sally had boasted of the schooling New Design's children received. It was an admirable curriculum. In the morning, a solid grounding in the classics and the beginnings of the mathematical sciences; in the afternoons, a devout drilling in the personal virtues. Sally, who was a schoolteacher, had rattled off the various virtues, with Morton interjecting on the finer points of military virtue, and they'd both been rather patronizingly impressed when Liv explained that she knew what they were—she'd read them in the General's *Child's History*. Sally clapped her hands together.

Liv stopped a shy black-haired girl and offered to help her with her work. The girl mutely acquiesced. They hefted the buckets back and forth between the troughs. The deerlike creatures drank with long shiny black tongues.

"We do the farmwork, ma'am," the black-haired girl answered her. "The boys go to be soldiers."

"Are they very ridiculous in their uniforms?" Liv smiled and tried to make the girl laugh, in hopes of making an ally. Instead, the girl scowled and looked shocked.

"No, ma'am! They're very brave."

"Of course they are," Liv said. "Of course. I meant no offense."

The girl left soon after, in silence.

Around midday, the school bells rang. Soon the smaller children came running past, boys and girls alike in patched hide like tiny savages, scattering the hens, drinking from the well bucket with cupped hands.

A few were brave enough to ask Liv questions. What was it like in the world outside? Had she ever seen a buffalo? What was the sea like? What was snow like? What were the big cities like—did they really stink as bad as the old men said? She answered in a very serious voice; that was her usual manner with children, and after her earlier attempt at levity, she thought it best to stick to it.

Seeing that Liv was harmless, more of the children threw questions at her. Had she ever been to the theater? What were horses like?

Had she ever seen an Engine?

Had she ever been in a battle?

Had she seen the monster of the oaks?

"Enough of that! Get on!" Bradley's harsh voice scattered the children as they'd scattered the hens. "Back to your schoolwork! Leave her alone! Back to chores!"

Liv was left alone, sat on the edge of a water trough. Bradley regarded her fiercely.

He stood leaning on a heavy wooden stick. His left leg was intact, but stiff and lame, the muscles and tendons having been ruined in some past battle. He breathed very heavily through his long mustache. His hair was wild and unclean. He was short, thick. He wore a long black tailcoat. He'd worn it at dinner, too. It still retained several of its brass buttons; however, it was greasy and worn, and covered in a variety of stains, and patched in places with cloth or even fur, as if undergoing some lycanthropic transformation. He glared constantly—as far as she could tell at everyone, not just at her—and generally had the manner of a guard dog, an attack dog, a beast of powerful energies and angers going vicious in idleness.

Two young men stood with him. They could be recognized as soldiers of New Design by their posture, and by their bows and knives. Bradley had been snapping at them as he approached. Now he sent them away with a sudden gesture; they vanished promptly.

Liv smiled stiffly. It would be necessary to ingratiate herself with Bradley, she decided, if she were ever to regain her access to the General.

"Are you a doctor or a commander, Dr. Bradley?"

"Dammit, woman—both, of course."

"I take offense at your tone, Doctor."

"Don't ask damn fool questions, then. Now come along, walk with me. All right, then! I apologize. Come now. Let's talk about what you can do for us." He stamped off. Liv followed.

Bradley set a rapid pace, stabbing the crutch up and down and up and down like the pistons of a tiny snorting Engine.

"What's this place you say you found him? Some hospital?"

"The House Dolorous," Liv said. "It was a kind of hospital."

"For mad people."

"For anyone. The House was—is—presided over by a spirit of healing and protection. It was open to anyone who needed it."

"A disgrace, to put the General in with mad people. He was no coward, no shirker. It's those damn bombs. He'd still have sword in hand today, old as he is, if not for those damn bombs."

"I expect so," Liv agreed. "But he was not so lucky."

"Who brought him there?"

"I don't know."

"What does your Gun-pervert friend want with him?"

"He is not my friend, Mr. Bradley. He believes that the General knows something valuable. A weapon."

Bradley halted sharply. He stared, seemingly hard in thought. His brow—where the skin was unburned—sweated with the exertion of walking. He wiped it with his sleeve. Then he shook his head and snorted. He gestured with his stick toward the south of town, and jerked into motion again.

Liv asked, "What could the General have seen that makes the Gun want him so badly?"

"Don't know."

"Did you know the General well? Did you ever know the Folk—?"

"Great men have their eccentricities. Don't pry, woman."

"My apologies. But—"

"Don't know, don't care. It's courage that wins wars, courage and virtue—not to mention manpower and money. Real things. If in his later years, his desperation overcame him and he had foolish ideas, who are you to—?"

Bradley stopped and looked hard at her.

"Never mind. So what are you good for, then? We don't get a lot of injuries here, but we get some. A few broken legs among the hunters. There are dangerous beasts here, as you know, but they generally leave nothing to be healed. Can you deliver a child? For that matter, the deer get sick, and can you deliver a calf? Our old folk die like anyone else's, and us old folk are the only ones here who remember the old days, and the true cause and purpose of this place, and many of us have wounds. Have they discovered a cure for the cancer yet out in the world behind us?"

"I can do none of those things, Dr. Bradley. I am a scientist of the mind."

"Like in the big cities, the ones who charge a fortune to idle youths and housewives in pearls, to talk, and talk, and talk, about their empty lives and their unhappy families and all that rot and slime? We don't go mad here. We have a purpose here. We put our backs to that purpose. We cannot have the luxury of madness. So what can you do for us?"

"I have done that work. I would not dismiss it so lightly. But I came here, from Koenigswald—I came from safety and comfort, thousands of miles into the wastelands, the borderlands, into the very heart of the Great War, Dr. Bradley, and I *will* not be dismissed lightly—to study and to heal the victims of the Line's horrible mind-weapons. To heal the wrong that was done to your precious General. Do not speak to me as if—"

"But what good is that to us?"

"As if I were some—"

Liv's finger jabbed at Bradley's face; Bradley's face jutted forward on his stout neck, the veins of which stood up red.

A small crowd was watching them.

Liv swallowed her rage, collected herself, attempted a smile at the crowd. Morton's wife, Sally, stood among them—she seemed unsure whether or not to meet Liv's eyes, and shifted her hands protectively over her pregnant belly.

Bradley, clearly seeing no need on his part to keep the peace, demanded: "Do you know what makes me sick? Do you know?"

Liv listened with a thin half smile on her face.

"I was trained in a hospital in old Lannon town," Bradley said. "A big city on the south sea. We had a few headshrinkers there, wasting their time on spoiled young ladies, daughters of the shipping concerns; it was a big town. Learned my art in a big black stone hall on the hanged bodies of Lannon's criminal fraternity. Lannon's gone now, probably, or swallowed up by the Line. Don't much care. Lannon wanted to stay neutral; more fool Lannon. Soon as I'd got my sheepskin, I left town. Rode for a month. Caught up with the Republic's forces in Coulter. Never left 'em. A lifetime of sawing off torn limbs and setting broken bones and salving these beauties"—he ran his finger down the smooth burn on his face—"and I never left 'em until my own wounds were too much, and the General sent me away on a stretcher. And I begged not to be sent away. I was his best man for a while, in the sawbones business. After the mind-bombs made Doc Ullerham into a *thing*. I ran field hospitals for the whole army. Huge camp hospitals and an army under me, sawing away like little elves. Then later, after Black Cap Valley, when we were on the run, there were times when it was just me. Just me and the broken flesh. And I'll tell you what, in all that time, I never called on any fucking *Spirit* to do my work for me. Never needed to. I'd be ashamed to. It makes a mockery. . . . It makes me sick to think of some sickly vampire-thing slavering over the General's wounds. If he'd been in his right mind, in his whole mind, he'd have rather died than suffer that indignity. Have you read our Charter, madam?"

"I have not."

"Why not?"

"I was told I needed permission to touch its pages. I'm in no hurry, am I, Dr. Bradley? I can't imagine I'll be leaving here soon, after all."

"Not if I have any say in the matter. I think you know more than you're telling us. Frankly, I think you're in league with that Agent—"

"I am not in league with him, Doctor; in fact, I can think of only one man I've ever disliked more, and that man was hanged by the neck for murder and rightly so. But Creedmoor's masters are absent. He wavers in his loyalties. He *wants* to turn on them. He does not want the General to fall into their hands any more than we do. But he is too weak to do it alone. If we offer him an alliance—if we—"

"He cannot be saved. You are at best a very foolish woman. And we do not fear the Line."

"But here you are, hiding on the edge of the world—"

Bradley reached a decision. "Perhaps you'd best be a *schoolteacher,* madam. I'll not have any use for you."

He turned sharply and limped away.

She stood there in confusion. Had she really said that Creedmoor should be *saved*? Perhaps she was a very foolish woman.

※　※　※

Liv was no schoolteacher, but the children gathered to her anyway.

It was strange; she felt as though she'd been in New Design for weeks, months, years even, slowly weaving into its frayed fabric— yet in actual fact, it had been four, maybe five days? There was something drowsy in New Design's woodsmoke and the sighing of its oaks that stilled such thoughts. What did it matter how the world counted time? She was *here*. So the children came and went, and Liv had the strangest sensation that she'd seen them grow up, that she'd seen infants become boys become, the next day, young men. . . .

In fact, of course, she just couldn't keep them straight one from another. They all looked alike. So unscarred, so confident, so full of New Design's peculiar scheme of virtue, which was still so untested, so far. By the third day, they took her for granted. They still asked her questions about the outside world, but it slowly became clear that they were not so much *curious,* as they were concerned to explain to her the errors and confusions of the fallen world, and the superiority of New Design's scheme of things . . . those little soft-skinned blond children with their bland smiles and their quiet complacent manner.

Over and over—days flattening out in the quiet of the oaks and the soft drone of New Design and seeming to be weeks—the same conversations again and again. A delicate elegant machine spinning its wheels endlessly. Perhaps time really *was* different there. Perhaps the town, out on the edge of creation as it was, lifted and moved out of the world and its wars, was also lifted out of the flow of time, disengaged from its grinding gears. . . . Morton and Bradley and Woodbury and the rest of them *did* seem strangely unaged, preserved, statue-frozen. And though there was a sense of expectancy, of waiting, an excitement in everything they did, though they spoke and moved with a confident sure knowledge that they were building for the future, that one day the mission would resume, Liv thought that they did not really expect it to happen, that they did not really imagine that they would ever be reinserted rudely into the violence of time, that their precious perfect children would ever be scarred for the cause as their fathers and mothers were. War was more an idea than a reality; they contemplated it bravely, knowing it would not come.

But of course, it *would* come, and soon—but when Liv tried to warn them, they only smiled confidently and told her not to worry.

CHAPTER 44

HEEL

—Monster.

Creedmoor's eyelids were stiff and heavy as sailcloth, but he forced them open anyway. Above him were the same old stars. He'd shut his eyes so that he wouldn't be tempted to read meaning into them—dying or not dying, he was too old to go getting religion *again*.

—Monster.

He turned his head, which caused his shoulder to throb with agony. A face looked down at him. Its red eyes shone.

All around the face hung what at first looked like shadow but was, in fact, a long black mane, shifting gently in the breeze. Beneath the face were two bony knees, drawn up. It was a woman of the Folk. She perched on a jutting rock ten feet up the slope down which Creedmoor had tumbled.

—No ma'am. I *killed* the monster.

—Poor thing. Broken thing. The red men made it from their fears. Perhaps we should have turned them back when they came here, but they seemed so weak, so harmless.

—I don't know what you're talking about, ma'am.

—No.

—Are you Ku Koyrik? Your voice in my head is familiar.

—Yes. Call me no other name.

—And what can I do for you?

—What is it like to die?

—I don't recommend it. Say, ma'am, our conversation last time was interrupted, and if you don't mind, I'd like some answers before I go, so: Do you know a gentleman by the name of Kan-Kuk? Looked much like you, used to pal around with an old General.

—Of course. You could call him my husband.

—Really?

—Or my brother.

—I'm liberal-minded, ma'am, that's all right. And what was it that he promised the General, what—?

—No. I won't tell you. I don't trust you.

—Suppose I said I'd make you the same deal the General made Kan-Kuk?

—Not you.

—Or a *better* deal! You want to wipe away my masters, the enemy—well, so do I, so do I. If you wanted to wipe away all the rest of our world with them, I wouldn't blame you and I wouldn't say no; *there's* a great cause I could die for—

—Never you.

—Why not me? What's the old man got that I haven't got?

—You're broken. You belong to the broken things. I couldn't fight them for you.

Creedmoor slowly turned his head back and looked up at the stars. He considered his various pains. After a while he said:

—Are you still here?

—Yes.

—Why?

—I have nowhere else to go. Now I am going mad.

—Do you plan to kill me? If so, better hurry.

—I don't know. Perhaps I should. But then the woman will die, and the General will die, and we will have to begin again. And fail again. Our agony will be prolonged, and yours. And every time it gets harder.

—The woman? Liv? Shit. How?

—I have become less myself since we last met. It is hard for us to act here, hard to plan.

—Where is Liv? How will she die?

—Your enemies get closer. Too many to stop.

—The Linesmen?

—Yes.

—Shit.

—Your masters get closer, too.

—They do? Send them back.

There was no answer.

—Send them back. Please.

He gritted his teeth against the pain and turned his head once
more. She was gone.

※　※　※

The stars crawled and shifted. Even by the standards of the skies out
in the far West, there were an unusual number of shooting stars.
Meanwhile, Creedmoor couldn't feel any part of his body below the
neck; instead his head floated on a vague cloud of pain. Hours
passed. He wasn't dead, but nor was he healing. His head itself was
blessedly free of pain, until around dawn the word

—Creedmoor.

. . . formed in it, and his head swelled with blood and his sinuses
burned.

—Creedmoor.

—Go away.

—We have fought our way across a great silent void to find you,
Creedmoor. Nothing here echoes with our voices, and so we were
blind and lost. We suffered. We came to save you.

—Go away.

—We know what you have been thinking. The servants of the
Enemy are loyal; why are ours so ungrateful? But we forgive you
anyway. We have always loved you, Creedmoor.

—You have?

—Of course, Creedmoor. Have we not always treated you well?
Have we not—?

—You're terrified, aren't you? You're desperate. This is grotesque.
Are you about to *grovel* to me?

The sky lightened to gray, and the stars withdrew into the deep
distance. Creedmoor's left leg began to itch and ache. A shot of

agony ran up his spine, but then his master reached in and firmly pressed it back down.

—You have always been our favorite servant, Creedmoor. Do not die. Do not suffer unnecessarily. We will never leave you again.

His shoulder wrenched itself back into its socket, making his whole body spasm. His bones ground together and reknit.

—I was never anybody's favorite anything. My own mother regarded me as an embarrassing error.

—You were cunning, Creedmoor. And brave. And deadly. And proud. And fierce. And—

—You need me.

—Yes, Creedmoor. We need you. There is no one else here. The Line will take the General and his secret and we will die. Think of all we have given you.

—I wanted none of it.

—Of course you did.

His right ankle twisted back into shape, and suddenly his right leg was full of pain, and he screamed.

—Stand.

He pulled himself slowly to his feet. His legs trembled beneath him. His right arm was still limp and heavy as lead.

—There. Well done, Creedmoor.

—Fuck you.

—We promise we will not hold your insolence against you, once we have the General back. On our honor.

Creedmoor hefted his right arm with his left, and rubbed feeling back into the fingers.

—You thought foolish thoughts while we were gone. But no more. You have no choice; you never did.

—No. I suppose not.

—Go save the General, Creedmoor.

—And the woman, of course.

—If you like.

CHAPTER 45

THE DANCE

On the fourth day, Captain Morton introduced Liv to a young man—well, not *so* young, his sandy hair was receding over his sunburned scalp and he was tending to middle-aged plumpness—but well favored nonetheless, and charmingly shy and quiet. "His name's William Warren," Morton said, "the Second, after a fine father, who fought with me at the Battle of . . . but that's beside the point, now, isn't it? Our Bill the Younger's a fine fellow in his own right, and near enough the best carpenter we have. . . ." Warren stood there all the while, on Morton's doorstep, fidgeting his callused and broad-fingered hands. "Came here as a mere babe, didn't you, young Mr. Warren? There's hardly a buildin' in this town he hasn't done a hard day's work on. Anything you want to know about New Design, you ask him. I'll be busy for a spell, ma'am, with—ah, you know. Come in, come in!"

Warren shrugged, and smiled at her, and extended a hand, saying, "Perhaps you would prefer to come for a walk, madam?"

Even after a full turn around the town, hand in hand, and after a series of eager stuttering attempts at conversation on Warren's part, Liv was still unable to be sure of his intentions.

"This here," Warren said, "was built in the ninth year of New Design, as we count it, by Captain Pratt, to be a home for . . ."—

patting the logs of yet another cabin. And so on all up and down the muddy streets as the sun sank westward over the mountains, toward the wild sea beyond. Warren shone with love for every rough-hewn log of his town. He seemed to have no other topics of conversation— he quizzed Liv on the world outside, politely but without comprehension or apparent enthusiasm.

Toward the end of the afternoon, Liv decided that the real nature of Warren's intentions made no difference. Either he was assigned to spy on her, and his clumsiness was a ruse, in which case, she saw no reason to make his task easy for him; or he was, after a somewhat rustic fashion, attempting to *court* her—in which case, she was tempted, briefly, she would not deny it, but he seemed so *young*. That is, although they'd been born, it seemed, within a handful of years of each other, as best as they could reckon, Warren was so unscarred by his timeless years in New Design that Liv could not quite see him as fully a person, and it seemed cruel and somehow shameful to interfere with his blameless existence. So she squeezed his hand gently and let go of it, and told him that she was, she regretted to say, very tired, and at the mercy of a nervous headache that made further conversation impossible, and she left him standing alone in the mud, a forlorn expression on his guileless face, under the lengthening shadow of the logging mill on the west side of town.

❊　❊　❊

The next day, they held a dance, and Liv saw Warren again.

The dance was apparently a weekly affair, held on one of the fallow north fields, and attended with great solemnity and deliberate good cheer. The old danced slowly in the central ring, and the young whirled around them. The choreography was elaborate— mathematically and topologically complex, the work of clever thinkers with too much time on their hands. Morton explained that dance, like sport, like war, built strong bodies in the young, built a sense of community and respect and fair play, and that the rings symbolized . . . oh, symbolized *something;* Liv's attention wandered. She saw Warren again, but across the field, in a haze of lanterns and torches, laughing with the other men of the town, and she had to concede that he was not altogether unappealing. But then a group of boys, arm in arm, red faced and laughing, wheeled sidestepping across the field, and when she could see again, he was gone.

Perhaps he'd joined the dance. Liv had tried to step in, at Morton's gentle urging, but was unable to find her footing. The dance was unfamiliar and strenuously athletic, and she'd nearly fallen. Instead, Liv sat with Morton's young wife, Sally, who was herself unable to dance because the baby within her was acting up, and she was suddenly prone to sickness. Liv had no particular advice to give, but the young woman was in some distress, and she did her best to be kind. While holding Sally's sweating hand and murmuring, *There, there,* Liv looked for Warren, but she never saw him again.

✳ ✳ ✳

On the fifth day, they held a referendum.

New Design's men and women lined up on the long hard benches of the meeting hall. The hall's roof was a high-peaked lace of timbers, open to the sky. Around noon, a cold sleeting rain blew across the town. None of them flinched. They sat straight-backed, listening to Alderman Merrill's long ponderous speech as the rain slicked their hair black over their scalps.

Merrill's subject was property, and taxation, and points of high principle concerning both—though as far as Liv was aware, there was no property in New Design, and no taxes. Indeed, she'd seen no money at all, and had imagined New Design to be communistic, after the manner of the prophets in the ancient texts. She decided that Merrill's economics was more aspirational than empirical. He had the look of a dreamer, in a small quiet way.

When Merrill was done—to measured applause—he trudged back across the muddy floor to his place on the benches. Alderman Polk took the podium, and the townsfolk listened just as gravely to him in his turn. He wore spectacles, one glass of which was cracked, the other empty, long vanished. Nevertheless, he bore himself with dignity. Liv couldn't comprehend his subject at all.

The Aldermen of the town were also members of the Assembly

of the Republic. They spoke for both offices. The serious young man on Liv's left and the serious old man on her right both explained this to her.

Young Mr. Waite, of the Smilers, spoke briefly, extempore, on the theme of *What it says about us that we're able to have this meeting in the face of what we're all agreed would be worrying news—yes, it would—if we were the kind to give in to worry; but instead we should be very proud.* The rain darkened his fine blond hair and slicked it down over his scalp. His smile only widened as he spoke, till he put Liv in mind of a ventriloquist's dummy. He sat down amid applause, and the Secretary of Measures and Motions brought business to a start.

Issues tabled for the day: the hunting of the beast—should they continue? Or change tactics? The need for new irrigation on the south fields. Sally Morton stood and haltingly delivered a speech on the importance of infant education, which appeared to end without a point. A Mr. Dilworth's proposed adjustment to the rules of parliamentary cloture was soundly defeated, as if he had proposed a dirty thing, and Dilworth himself slunk off to angry stares.

Lastly, they discussed what was to be done with the General, what was to be done with these rumors of approaching enemies. The crowd shifted eagerly, tensely. President Hobart took the podium. The young man on Liv's left stood and clapped furiously. The old man on her right sat in wary silence.

Captain Morton sat two rows in front of Liv, sticking out in his red cavalry jacket among the gray brown of his neighbors like a peacock among hens. He did not clap. He sat very stiffly. Sally held his arm and leaned close to him.

Liv stood. There was a hush around her.

"President Hobart. The Line will find us here soon. Creedmoor will find us. You must evacuate the women and children. You have forgotten what the Line is *like,* what their weapons are like. You must make an alliance with Creedmoor, against the Line, for the sake of—"

The crowd roared with disgust, drowning her out.

Liv examined the President's face as he scanned the crowd—arms outstretched, hands clutching the podium. He smiled at his people. He waited for them to quiet down.

President Hobart's eyes met Liv's. He leaned down and whispered in his aide's ear.

"President Hobart, I propose that—"

A young man put his hand gently on her arm and said, *"Ma'am."*

※　※　※

Soon Liv was politely removed from the meeting hall. The aide escorted her across town—in apologetic silence—then left her, jogging back to the meeting briskly, his back receding in the rain, his hand on his cap.

Liv was alone—which was for the best, since she wasn't sure she could speak. She felt quite stunned. After weeks and weeks of reading the history of the Republic, daydreaming of it, conversing with its fallen General—after all that, to find it, preserved as in a museum—and to be *shut out*—it was *baffling*.

They had refused her help. They did not want her advice. She was of no importance, powerless to affect her fate. Her safety depended entirely on Hobart's wisdom, by which she was not impressed.

She wandered the town, sometimes shaking her head, sometimes smiling. She went west and quickly reached the walls, and the moat, and the guard towers. She waved to a young man high overhead, who held a rifle. He waved back. He wore a bright red officer's cap. His father's?

Beyond the moat, the oaks pressed in. A cool and inviting darkness. Liv considered fleeing into it. Abandoning the General. Creedmoor might not look for her now. Sharp mountains rose beyond the forest, purple in the west. The sun was starting to set behind them, making the snow on their peaks a shining brazen rim. The rain, still falling, thin and cold, glowed in the failing light. That morning, the impossible western sun had risen blazing from behind those mountains.

Liv took two steps closer to the bridge, and a young man stepped in front of her, blocking her path. She recognized the face—the unfortunate witch's wen on his nose. Was it Blisset or Singleton? She'd not seen them since they found her in the woods. He remembered *her*, of course. He shook his head. He would not meet her eyes.

"You are quite right, sir," she said. "It is late for a walk in the woods. I might get lost in the dark."

"Quite right, ma'am."

"You're very kind to your guests."

Liv turned back. She walked New Design's muddy streets. They were laid out in a finely planned wheel, which she had to concede was rational and elegant. It stood—Morton had explained—for some principle of order or organization that the Republic held dear.

The lights were coming on in the windows. Oil lamps or hearth fires, according to the stature of the houses. A golden haze in the evening rain. In Liv's mind, New Design was a rolling wheel broken off from a beautiful gigantic machine, some glittering clockwork of government, spinning free, diminished and alone, finally falling here, far from its parent. In a ditch. In the dirt. In a quiet distant field. Still spinning, these little lives caught in its spokes. The General had built to last.

This place was a miracle! Liv felt a sudden affection for it. It was a shabby miracle, no doubt, a tired miracle, its people falling into smallness and fixed ways—but it was the last of something splendid. Each of these people had been touched by greatness; they had seen a finer world.

As she idled through the rainy streets, Liv dreamed of saving them. A speech, perhaps? A plan, a scheme, some ingenious reversal or stratagem that might turn back the Line. Or somehow leading them farther into the West, to safety . . .

For the General's sake, they had to survive.

For the world's sake, they had to survive. If they never returned from the West, if the world never knew of them, so what? The world was a finer place while this dream persisted.

Liv passed by Dr. Bradley's house. There was a long low cabin beside it, where the hospital beds were. Captain Morton had pointed it out to her. It was every inch a soldier's camp hospital. There were three men loitering outside the canvas-curtained door, two with rifles. All with spears and swords.

Liv stood across the darkening street from them. Her hair and clothes were quite drenched now, but she'd long since ceased to care. Cold had not killed her yet. The dark-haired young man with the finest and most silver-filigreed rifle caught her eye, then snapped his head straight again and pointedly ignored her.

The General was there, of course. Held in secret and locked tightly away like a treasure the town didn't know what to do with. It made her think of those fairy tales in which a stranger brings a chest of gold, or a goose that lays golden eggs, or a wondrous machine that weaves invisible threads, or a spirit that answers every question put to it and knows every hidden secret, or what have you, into a simple village not prepared for such intrusions of the wondrous or the significant; tales in which the peasants' greed for the strange treasure would lead them to idleness, to anger, to violence, to wives poisoning husbands, to sons murdering fathers out in the empty fields; and in which, always, the headman, or mayor, or priest, would lock the treasure away, or bury it in the hills, hoping to bring peace again, and sometimes that would work, and sometimes it wouldn't.

Liv wondered if the President came to visit the General, at night, in secret, to stare at his blank ancient face. She wondered about Woodbury, about Morton, about Peckham, about Warren—who was privy to the secret?

Liv could hardly blame them for trying to hide their plans from her. She'd brought their hero to them, yes, but not for *their* sake, not for any sane reason at all. She'd brought him ruined. She'd come out of nowhere. And above all else, she had come in the company of an Agent of the Gun. She was tainted by her association with Creedmoor. She could hardly fault them for feeling that way; she sometimes felt that way herself.

Where *was* Creedmoor? Had the monster got him, or the Line? Had his masters reclaimed him? She felt very alone.

CHAPTER 46

CREEDMOOR IN THE SHADOWS

—They're gone.

—You should not have left them alone. But we will forgive you *if* you find the old man again.

Creedmoor came running, cursing, and crashing through branches that whipped his face and tore his blood-soaked clothes. He knew when he was half a mile away from the clearing where he'd left her that Liv was gone, and she'd taken the old man with her. Their scent had gone stale—and there were *strangers*.

—Not the Line. I know their smell. The red men.

—Who, Creedmoor?

—What the Folk woman called them.

—We forgive you for talking to her, Creedmoor. Nothing matters but finding the General. Run faster.

The voice in his head was on the verge of hysteria now. Beneath its calm flat tones there was an echo of shrieking. If it didn't hurt so much, he would have found it funny.

He burst out into the empty clearing.

—Gone. Creedmoor. You went trophy-hunting, you abandoned your charge.

—I left him with Liv.

—The woman has betrayed us. You should have killed her.

—Maybe.

—If we find her, you must kill her.

—We'll see.

＊ ＊ ＊

Creedmoor left the clearing behind.

—Faster. Take to the heights.

So he rose into the high crown of the nearest oak, ascending in slow forceful leaps from branch to branch, through the cold canopy of leaves, standing at last on a single narrow uppermost limb, a green sprig, wrist thin, which he willed to bear his weight. He looked out over the green world, east, back the way he'd come.

—They're coming. Faster, now. Closer.

—Yes, Creedmoor.

—We had a week or more's lead on them when we went hunting that serpent. How did they come so close?

The Linesmen weren't in sight yet, and there was no stink of them on the wind—stale sweat, grime, coal dust, fear and shame—but Creedmoor could *hear* them, the thudding of their flat feet, the wheezing of their fat throats, the rattle and dull clank of their rifles and bombs. And the treetops shivered with their passing below.

—While you were idle, Creedmoor, while you were adventuring, they gained on us.

—We'll lose them again.

—Our Enemies close in around us. The world narrows as we reach its edge. We feel a trap, Creedmoor.

—Linesmen are too stupid for traps. Without their Engines, they are stupid. Simple bad luck is our only enemy.

—Ordinarily *we* are the bringers of bad luck, Creedmoor.

＊ ＊ ＊

He caught up with the Linesmen a little after dark. They marched through the night holding buzzing electric torches, wheeling their heavy guns, heads down, wordless, implacable. He crept apelike through the branches above them and watched them go by—from a safe distance, of course. Linesmen did not, as a rule, look up; they were afraid of the sky. But still, they had *devices,* so it was safest not to go too near.

It was hard to count their numbers—the Linesmen but scattered among the oaks in groups of twos and threes. It was out of character. Generally, the Linesmen marched in columns, in accordance with their Manual of Operations.

—Discipline's gone lax out here.

—They are far from their masters, Creedmoor.

—They become more like us.

—They are a rabble. They are machines, breaking down. Do not indulge in sympathy for them.

—Don't worry. I haven't forgotten how to hate. They're moving fast. I've never seen them move so fast without their machines.

—They are loyal to their masters, Creedmoor.

—They know where they're going. How do they know where they're going?

—We do not know. A machine?

—Maybe. I guess maybe one hundred fifty of them?

—Their numbers decline. Still far too many to fight and be sure of the outcome. It depends on what devices they carry.

—Which one's the leader? I could kill their leader.

—Another would take his place. And you might die.

—Cowardice doesn't suit you.

—Go, Creedmoor. Find the General.

—I will. But not for you.

—We'll see. *Run,* Creedmoor. Stay ahead of them.

※　※　※

He ran through the treetops. The Linesmen did not look up. Within the hour, there was the unmistakable scent, not far off, of fires, and cut timber, and cattle, and fowl, and iron, and women and children. And soon he came to the end of the oaks, and looked out through a curtain of leaves across a wide waterless moat and high walls and beyond that the low log roofs of New Design, its fires banked, sleeping in the moonlight.

—A handsome little town! Better than I imagined.

—This place is a mistake, Creedmoor. These people belong in the past. Recover the General, and let us leave them to rot.

※ ※ ※

Guards in the sentry posts overlooking the moat; in the gatehouse at the edge of the bridge; standing in the streets, leaning against the log walls, holding shuttered candles . . . for a place so utterly remote in both time and space from all the violence of the world, New Design was remarkably conscious of its own security. Old habits died hard, it seemed.

Creedmoor slipped past the guards soundlessly.

—That building's the largest, yes, my friend? Oh, I've been too long in the wilderness, that shabby thing looks like a palace. I'll bet that's where their leader is. What do you say?

—We are here to take the General back; nothing more.

—Oh, but it's been too long since I was in a town, even such a town as this; I have an urge to raise hell, my friend.

—No, Creedmoor. Have you forgotten Kloan? And—

—Stop me, then.

—Be quick, Creedmoor.

※ ※ ※

A rusted and ancient bar-and-bolt caught Creedmoor's eye. It was on the door to a building not far from the center of town, small, not much bigger than a shack, built so that its rough walls formed an octagon—a church? A shrine? A prison?

He snapped the bolt between his fingers and scattered the parts in the mud.

Dust, must, old paper, stale sweat—nothing living or moving. Creedmoor was wary nevertheless as he stepped inside, eyes widening to black barrel-mouths in the windowless darkness. But it was only a kind of library. Crude shelves covered each of the eight walls, in uneven and off-parallel lines. They bore texts and ledger books and heaps of old pamphlets and newspapers.

Creedmoor ran his fingers along the dusty leather spines of works of political philosophy—military history—spiritual inquiry. Oh, how pathetic, how touching, a full shelf devoted to the Smilers' uplifting pamphlets and parables; hard to imagine who'd think that flimsy ephemera was a treasure worth spiriting away to the world's edge. There was even, brittle and moldering, a pile of copies of the *Chain-Breaker,* organ of the Liberationists. How many years was it since he'd seen those pages—those earnest humorless passionate righteous exhortations? It was almost embarrassing to look at them.

—This is meaningless, Creedmoor. Move on.

—In a moment. I'm curious. This is a strange little town.

—Do as we *command,* Creedmoor.

Most of the shelves were worthy stuff, heavy stuff, morals and politics and high affairs, but there was a shelf near the floor stacked with old romances and boys' adventure books. The paper was old, near as old as Creedmoor himself, but the stories promised on the covers—well, he might have picked them up just last year, back when he last passed through down the market streets in Keaton City.

—Things don't change much, do they? Everything gets older and more worn out, but how often do we see new ideas?

—*Creedmoor.*

—Not that I'd claim that *that* was a new idea, of course.

—No. You repeat yourself. Move on.

In the center of the room stood a lectern, bearing, as if it was a relic, a thick soft-leaved book. Creedmoor stroked his finger gently down the pages, leaving a trail of grime and sweat.

—Their Charter! That takes me back. Do you recall it?

—Creedmoor, move on.

—Of course, your kind were never thinkers, or builders. This was their sacred text. This was how they ordered relations among men. . . . What do your kind care for relations among men?

—Move on, Creedmoor.

Creedmoor stood, turning the pages, shaking his gray head.

—One hardly sees it these days, back in the world. When it does surface, it's only to be mocked. And how easily mocked it is . . . how pious its sentiments! How naïve its hopes! Oh, how worldly they thought they were being. . . . They didn't reckon with your kind, did they, my friend?

—The Line broke the Republic. The Line drove them out of the world. We would have made allies of them.

—But that, too, would have destroyed them—your touch is poison, my friend. Oh, but look here! I confess in my old age I grow sentimental myself, and I find these folk charming. Remember their recruiters, coming red-coated through town? In the open streets outside, disdaining the low dives in which I skulked! How different things might have been had I sobered up and paid my bills and gone blinking into the light to join them! I joined stupider causes, no doubt of that. But they were so . . . so *sheep*like. And I wanted to be a wolf. Somehow they sickened me. And the girls, though kind, though decent, were so plain. . . . But I, too, was young, then.

—They'd have no use for you now, Creedmoor.

—To their credit! To their credit.

—You know what you are.

—What you *made* me, my friend.

—You came to us, Creedmoor.

—Did I? I don't recall.

—They would drive you out like a rabid dog. We love you, Creedmoor. Move on or we will put the Goad to you again.

❋ ❋ ❋

A shiver of rain passed across the town. Two watchmen splashed through the mud, lanterns drawing a soft golden haze across the night. Creedmoor held still and let them pass. He turned east. He stopped and sniffed the air.

—I smell him.

—Yes, Creedmoor. The General is here.

—They've taken good care of him, bless 'em.

—He's *ours*.

—So you say . . . There, in that building; and I smell blood, and medicines . . . a hospital?

—We spend too much time in hospitals.

—We surely do. Our war is no longer young or fresh.

—Go, then, take him back.

—Not just yet. I detect the scent of our mutual friend, the Doctor, young Mrs. Alverhuysen, poor Liv—she's not too far away, over there. . . .

—Yes, Creedmoor. We know. We no longer need her.

—We owe her a visit, I think, and a warning. . . .

—Are you mad? She may raise the alarm. Go to the General.

—I think not, not just yet.

—Creedmoor, do as we command.

—No.

—Have you forgotten the Goad, Creedmoor?

—I have neither forgotten nor forgiven the Goad. But I do not fear it, not just at this very peculiar moment. You need me. There is no one else. You dare not touch me. I will act as I choose. You are only a voice in my head now. You are only a *passenger*. You are only a bad conscience, and I have long practice ignoring the voice of conscience.

—If you will not serve us, then we do not need you and we *will* destroy you.

—I know. And so I will serve you. But not just yet. The woman, first.

—One day things will be different.

—One day everything will be different. One day even you may be dead.

—Careful, Creedmoor.

. . . all this taking place in an instant, between one raindrop and the next, with the fleeting of a single black rain cloud across the moon. Moonlight fell again on Creedmoor's lined face. The rain was slackening, uncertain—a squall of wind blew cold spray past him, and that seemed nearly the last of it.

—But not today, I suppose, and not by my hand. Someday a better man than me may do it.

BOOK FIVE

The Battle of New Design

CHAPTER 47

RAISING THE ALARM

Liv sat upright in bed, her back against the cold wooden wall, her knees pulled up under the thin old bedsheet. She listened to the Mortons making love in their bedroom, a muffled anxious occasionally high-pitched noise that had kept her awake; and she watched Creedmoor climb silently in through the window. She was only briefly surprised.

He put a finger to his lips, nodded his head in the direction of the Mortons' bedroom, and smiled.

She said, "Good evening, Mr. Creedmoor."

"Hello again, Liv."

"I've been wondering where you were. What now?"

He moved away from the window and leaned against the wall. She saw that his clothes were ragged and bloody, and his hair was matted, and he looked appallingly tired. He stank of blood, oil, acids.

"Who have you killed, Creedmoor?"

"A very hideous monster, Liv. No one in town. How did you come here, by the way? Have they mistreated you?"

"How *dare* you ask me that, Creedmoor."

He shrugged.

"I spoke to their President, Creedmoor. I suggested they ally themselves with you, against the Line. I said that you could be reasoned with. They did not believe me. Was I right?"

Creedmoor shook his head and sighed. He rubbed his lined forehead with two fingers of his left hand. He gave her a strange sly sad smile, willful and resigned at once, like the smile of a storybook poisoner as it dawns on him too late that he's drunk from the wrong cup, that he's finally outwitted himself, that his time and his options are suddenly closed off, that it's too late for cunning, that at last therefore he's free. . . .

She felt sickened, suddenly close to tears. "Creedmoor—you went back to your masters. Didn't you?"

"They found me, Liv. There was no choice. There's never been any choice; we are the kind of creatures we are. In its way, it's a relief."

"You're a *coward*, Creedmoor."

"Yes. In any case, I came here to give you a warning. The Line are not more than an hour or two away. They know where this town is. They will be here before dawn. I confess the worst part of me looks forward to the scene. I do not know exactly what weapons they have with them. At least two motor guns and two light cannon. Fire, perhaps, and possibly earth-shakers, noisemakers, poison gas, screamers, barbed wire, nightmares. I thought you deserved not to die in your sleep, at least. I suggest you flee now. Or alert the town. Or you may follow me, if you choose. You know where I'm going."

He vanished out the window.

By the time Liv had dressed herself and put on her watch and her hunting knife and followed him outside, there was no sign of him.

✳   ✳   ✳

—The General now, Creedmoor.

—I disappointed her, I think. She hoped for better from me.

—Foolish of her, then. No time for self-pity, Creedmoor; go to the General.

—Yes.

✳   ✳   ✳

Liv stood in the street, listening.

Creedmoor was gone, and the town was empty, silent, touched

by a light whispering rain. It was warm, and the earth under her feet was soft.

He would have gone south, she thought, past Justice Woodbury's house, past the little octagonal book repository, across the square muddy field they used for courthouse, forum, Speaker's Corner— past all that to the long low building Dr. Bradley called a hospital, where the town held the General in secret trust. There was silence from that direction, as from all others—but then, Creedmoor had seemed in no mood for murder. Perhaps he'd steal the General away and be gone without bloodshed.

In the silence, she thought maybe she could hear the Line coming— that she could hear the muffled slap and slide of their boots in the mud—but it was surely only the rain.

The urge to follow Creedmoor was very strong, so strong that she stared almost longingly south into the night, into the rain, past Justice Woodbury's house where golden light spilled from the windows— Woodbury woke before dawn to study his law books, she'd heard— and not only because the General would need her, which was a very respectable concern, but also for perverse and willful and reckless reasons that she didn't care to examine too closely, under the circumstances. . . .

Instead, she did the responsible thing: She turned her back on them and turned decisively *north,* toward the President's house.

❈ ❈ ❈

—Something is wrong here, Creedmoor.

—*Everything* is wrong out here.

No sounds from the hospital—no screams, no moans, no raging of dying men—hardly much of a hospital at all! That, Creedmoor thought, would change when the Line caught up to this town. Soft candlelight glowed around the edges of the canvas-hung windows. Maybe even here someone feared to sleep in the dark. . . .

—I smell him. Don't you? Or whatever dim bloody thing your kind has in place of scent.

—Yes. Creedmoor, there is something wrong in this place.

—You never used to be such cowards.

—Do not be reckless, Creedmoor. There is something other than scent—there are subtle vibrations—there are points of density and absence—We *sense* things. Our kin scream at us from all over the earth and our Lodge. We must make no mistake now.

—We'll see how it goes, won't we?

There was no door, only a black hole hung with tarpaulin. Creedmoor brushed it aside and stepped in out of the rain.

The room stretched away to the left and right—turning an L-shaped right angle on the left side—and it was cluttered with beds—rusting wire-frame beds, folding camp beds, heavy oak-built constructions—and curtains—of silk, canvas, cloth, sheepskin, woven reeds—and shuttered lamps and two flickering candles—and all but one of the beds was empty.

—*There* he is. In the bed in the far corner.

—Creedmoor, there are others here—awake and armed.

—Yes. I hear them. Oh well . . .

—They know we are here. They are *listening* to us speak.

Creedmoor spun, weapon extended, to stare into the darkness behind him. In the next instant, he cried out in anger and threw his arm across his throbbing eyes, as a sudden, blinding light blazed across the room. Not firelight, not gaslight, either, but the cold white sparking neon of the Line's dreadful machines.

He blinked the pain away. Black silhouettes resolved themselves into three figures—no, *four*—watching him, at the far end of the long room, thirty, thirty-five feet away, rifles leveled at him like the accusing fingers of so many *witnesses*. Rifles and heavy handheld glaring electric lights. As if to step in for his dimming vision, Creedmoor's nostrils flared; whatever these men carried, there was no smell of the Line on them. Not that that made a difference to his sudden fury; they'd *hurt* him. They'd thought to *trap* him. . . . Creedmoor raised his own weapon, and the figure in the center of his accusers—long coated, wild haired, leaning with his left hand on a stick—his face gray and leathery and spotted with age, a smooth burn scar all down it, old, but *fierce;* Creedmoor saw the tension in the wiry fingers clutching that stick—and the old man's right hand holding up. . . . And the old man opened his scar-twisted mouth and shouted:

"Stop! Kill me and you kill us all!"

Creedmoor slowed his hand, just for a second. Just long enough to see that the shape in the man's right hand was—damn it!—another of the Line's foul little toys—and if Creedmoor did not miss his guess, if he recognized rightly the intricate little hammers and sounders and cymbals and chambers of the horrible thing, it was a *bomb*.

※　※　※

Guards stopped Liv thirty yards from the President's house. Strong arms, fur-clad, reached out from the shadows and seized her and covered her mouth.

They hid in the hills from the Line and Gun, she thought, *they fought that way for years*, of course *they know how to hide, how to strike from the shadows.*

One of them leaned in over her shoulder. His beard scraped her face and his breath was bad. He whispered: *"What's your business here?"*

She whispered, too. "The Line is here. Maybe an hour away. I came to warn the President."

"And how would you know that?"

"You must evacuate. You must evacuate at least the children. You must save the General. You must—"

"Come with us."

※　※　※

Lowry stood, hands folded behind his back, watching young Private Carr climb a tree. An ungainly procedure. Carr huffed and panted and swore. Private Carpenter and Private Dugger and Private What's-his-name hooted and cheered. *"Go on, Carr! Forward, up-ward, Carr!"*

Carr's foot slipped off the edge of a branch and he nearly fell, stopping himself only by slamming his shin down hard on the wood and clutching desperately at leaves. He screamed.

"Don't fall!" Lowry shouted. "Don't you dare slagging fall, Carr!"

"No, sir. No, sir. Thank you, sir. No, sir."

"You've got the only working telescope, Carr. Don't you dare fall."

Carr did his duty, despite his terror; he clambered up and up and dwindled into the distance, until Lowry could barely hear his voice. Eventually Carr heaved himself over a high enough branch, and lay outstretched, right arm wrapped round it, while with his left he reached slowly back to his belt and removed the precious 'scope. He extended it, one-handed, by shaking it, which made the branch quiver and leaves fall. He looked out across New Design.

The men waited expectantly. Spirits were high. The Linesmen had a proper enemy again, and a destination, and they stood straighter and their eyes were focused and they'd stopped talking treason. They scrupulously checked and rechecked their weapons' mechanisms, though the general view, as Subaltern Mill kept putting it, was that the enemy were *dead meat on the tracks,* by which he meant that he expected no significant resistance from New Design.

It had occurred to Lowry that morning that, with Collier dead and Gauge deserted, and Thernstrom dead, too, and so on and so on, he was probably the oldest man present. He was certainly the only man present who'd ever fought the Republic—and, though he'd been only a boy at Black Cap, he'd been a *clever* boy, clever enough to have survived, anyway, when thousands died, and it hadn't been lost on him that while the Republic talked a lot about virtue and honor and dignity, it fought dirty, low and vicious and cunning. . . .

Lowry grabbed the prisoner by the back of his hide shirt and yanked him to his feet. Hayworth, the boy's name was. "Stop sniveling, boy. Tell me again: How many cannon?"

❋   ❋   ❋

"Mr. President," Liv said, "the Line—"

"Yes, madam. We know."

Hobart sat behind his desk, his eyes red and his face tight and tired, wearing a patched and threadbare and ancient nightgown and cap, and over that, an old blanket. His hand ventured from the blanket to grip a wooden mug of New Design's horrible bark-and-root coffee. He'd not slept in a long time, that much was clear, but his exhausted eyes glittered with excitement.

"We know, madam. We know. Do you think we survived the Line all those years without learning a thing or two about war? Do

you think we've forgotten everything out here? Do you think we've
fallen so far from our fathers' virtue?"

"But . . ."

"*We* have scouts, and signals. . . . We know these forests. Regrettably it appears from reports that they have a prisoner." He
shook his head. "Very sad. Very sad. Tell me, madam, how do *you*
know the Line is near?"

"Creedmoor is here, sir. He told me. You must—"

"Creedmoor?"

An aide leaned in close to the President's shoulder and muttered,
"The Guns' Agent."

"Yes," Hobart snapped. "Yes, I know. Well, what's in a name?
They're animals. Less than dogs: a dog will come to its name, but
not a rat, or a snake. . . . Why dignify them with names?"

"Sir," Liv said, "he is *here*. He's passed your defenses."

"We'll see about that. He wants us to know the Line's near, does
he? He wants us to fight them for him, is that it?"

"I don't know. I don't know why he told me. He said he felt
obliged to warn me. Sir, you must evacuate the town."

"And Creedmoor says this, does he?"

"*I* say it. Mr. President, Creedmoor has gone for the General,
you may be able to stop him still—"

"We know what to do with Creedmoor."

"You've been out here too long. You've forgotten the Gun, the
Line, what they can do. Hobart, you must save what you can—"

He leaned forward and fixed his eyes on hers. "I have been waiting for this day since I took office." He spoke very matter-of-factly.
"Each of my predecessors waited for this day. I had my differences
with them, but I won't hear a word against them on this point: *No
man of New Design has not waited eagerly for the day of our return
to the world. Instead, the world has come to us. So much the better.
We've raised our young men and women to be strong for this day.
Today, madam, today we'll be *tested*. We'll show ourselves worthy
of our fathers. We'll show ourselves ready to return to the world
and take up the grand old cause again."

"You must save the General. Creedmoor—"

"Quite safe."

"Then you must evacuate him. He must be saved. Send ten men into the woods with him, flee, I'll go with them, and—"

"No. Apart from anything else, it would be bad for morale. He'll stay here to watch our victory."

"You idiot, Hobart. You shortsighted puffed-up monster. This will not be glorious. This will be just one more pointless horror in a history full of them. Will you at least evacuate the women and children? The Line's not here to fight you, to root you out, you've been *forgotten,* if you hide the women and children in the oaks, they'll be left alone, you can rebuild—"

"No. No, madam. No. There'll be no running, not this time. We've kept the spark of courage and virtue alive. We'll fight."

"You've forgotten how the world you've left behind works. Virtue won't save you—you've forgotten their *weapons.*"

"The alarm is being raised as we speak," Hobart said. "Is that right?" The aide nodded. "The alarm is being raised. Do you hear it?" And indeed, there were shouts, distant dull tones of bells, the slap of feet, the rattle and thump of drums, the screech of old bent tin-whistles, and—so close and so loud that Liv started in her chair—three rifle-shots in quick succession, then a pause, then three shots again. "No running this time. We'll wipe the stain of defeat from our splendid cause. You'll see what we can do, madam. Mr. Hulgins, will you take her and hold her somewhere where she can't interfere? We have work to do."

CHAPTER 48

THE AMPLIFIER

Creedmoor rolled up his sleeves and held out his hands, empty, palms up. He turned them over, the way a swish big-city fellow might check to clean his nails—the way old Dandy Fanshawe used to check his nails—and in fact, Creedmoor noticed that his nails were prodigiously dirty. He'd not looked at them closely for a while. For weeks, he'd not been in the company of women, save Liv, who hardly counted, and he'd not thought of such things. Creedmoor thought of the way his father's dog, that great hairy loving beast, used to come in off the fields wet with black mud and *shake,* all over the flagstones and the thatch. He had an urge to *shake.*

Instead, Creedmoor smiled and turned his hands palms-up again. "See? My hands are empty, sir. Dirty, I'll grant you, but it's been a hard road here. Would your men like to lower their rifles and we can talk as civilized men? . . ."

The riflemen's leveled weapons didn't so much as twitch. The wild old man in their center remained unsmiling, eyes fierce with hate. He shifted a little on his bad leg. It was hard for him to stand still, Creedmoor thought; he looked like he wanted to be pacing, gesturing, ranting.

The device in the old man's hand drew all eyes to it, flicking there and back fast as blinking, tugged by its hideous gravity. The little iron hammer hung poised over the striking-plate. Only the old man's thumb held back its fall, and that thumb trembled.

The old man said, "Your kind have quick hands. Unbuckle your gun-belt."

"No."

"You know what I hold in my hand?"

"My pants will fall down. This occasion deserves greater dignity than that. The meeting after all these years and miles of two honorable enemies! My name's John Creedmoor. What's yours, sir? Are you the General's new Doctor? You look a learned man."

"I *am* his Doctor, Creedmoor, and his loyal officer, and you won't take him from my care. And you are no honorable enemy— your kind are monsters, sir, vampires, *vermin*. It disgusts me that you walk our streets."

"I won't be staying long, Doctor."

"My name is Bradley. That's the name of the man who caught you, Creedmoor. That's who'll claim credit for the kill. I'll take your tail as trophy, you monster."

—This Doctor's an angry man. He lacks the good sense to keep his tongue still.

—Yes, Creedmoor, but recall the device he holds. He is dangerous.

—I daresay I could outrun its sounding and its echoes. I could be out the door before this man lets the hammer fall.

—The General is in this room, Creedmoor. Could you carry him with you so quick? You could not. And do not think of abandoning him, Creedmoor. We know how your mind works.

—You wound me, my friend. Do not injure my feelings too cruelly or I may act capriciously, out of spite. But in fact I doubt I could escape the echoes anyway. This Doctor's finger's quivering on the hammer as it is. . . .

—Yes, Creedmoor.

—I could walk away. Call his bluff. If I turn my back and walk away, he will not follow through on his threat, not if it would kill the General, not his precious General, light of the Republic, returned from the dead.

—Look at his eyes, Creedmoor. Smell his fear and his hate. He is not quite rational. He is very old. He's near death anyway. We cannot be sure what he will do. We cannot take any risks.

—Stand here, then? Frozen in mutual dread? For how long? Till the sun goes cold? Till one day the Line reaches out here and we are standing on smoky grubby streets while drab crowds surge between us? Or until the Western Sea reclaims us and we all drown, and we can stand frozen together like coral? How ridiculous. How tiresome.

—Yes, Creedmoor.

—How brave he must be, to face us like this. I see no realistic course by which he might see morning. Does he know that, do you suppose? I have forgotten how men like him think.

—You were never a man like him, Creedmoor.

The Doctor spat. His wild hair shivered as in a cold wind. "Unbuckle your gun-belt, damn you!"

"I'd rather not. You'd no longer fear me, then, and our balance would be disrupted. May I ask how you knew I was here? You were awaiting me. I did not expect that. I was very quiet."

"Do you think we fought the Line all those years without learning from them? Without *taking* from them?"

"Ah."

"I *personally* participated in the destruction of three Engines."

"Very well done!"

"We took what we could from their wreckage. We studied their secrets. There's a machine they had that listens for your kind. Sniffs for your scent. We were warned of your coming."

"Yes, yes, I know it. A black box, 'bout so high, yes, all manner of brass trumpets and breathing tubes and wire drumheads? A needle that scratches? When we talk to our weapons, our masters, their voices rise up out of a dark Lodge. Or perhaps they descend from darkness, wreathed in fire like shooting stars. Either way, there's a tearing of the fabric, a bruising of the skin of the world, a derangement in the ether—those boxes shudder at it. To within a range of about half a mile, these days, though yours is an old model, of course. There are ways of hiding from them, but I never thought to meet one here! Oh, and to think I'd begun to dream that that voice was only in my own poor head, was only the voice of my own worse nature. Thank you, Doctor, for reminding me of the way things truly are. If it's a madness, at least I am not alone. I've enjoyed talking to you, Doctor. Tell me, where were you wounded?"

"Unbuckle your gun-belt, sir. You are caught in a trap. You won't let him die. Your masters won't permit it. They have no loyalty to you, Creedmoor."

"And you? Are *you* loyal? Would you kill your General, Doctor?"

"Sacrifices must be made. If I must kill him, I will, and he'll live on in our cause."

"How zealous. How unkind. How inhumane. Think of this, Doctor. Perhaps my masters don't want the General for themselves—perhaps they only want to keep him from the Line. He holds the key to ending the Great War. Have you heard? Do you know that? Well, why would my masters want war to end? They thrive on blood and fire and the bitterness of defeat. You and I want peace because we are reasonable men, but they are neither of those things. Perhaps they'd be just as happy if he died. In which case, you have nothing with which to threaten me, and you and your men are dead, Doctor, marked for certain death. I am not threatening you; I am exploring the possibilities, to pass the time. What do you think?"

"Unbuckle your gun-belt and get on your knees."

"No."

❋ ❋ ❋

Lowry adopted a reasonable tone.

"One last time, Hayworth. Where are they keeping the General?"

The prisoner trembled and turned away. Subaltern Mill reached out to slap him, but Lowry waved him away.

"Where, Hayworth? We want to take him alive. Do you understand? We want to minimize casualties."

"I don't know. I don't know what you mean. The General's dead, he died—"

"Hayworth. We will take your town. That's just going to happen, see? We can't leave you bastards out here scheming against us. We *know* you have the General and the Agent, and we *will* take them. But if you tell us where they are, we can do this clean."

Hayworth bit his bloodied lip and said nothing.

"What do they teach these boys?" Lowry said. "What do they teach them?" He shoved Hayworth back to his knees and walked away, beckoning Mill after him.

"All right, Mill. Give the orders. Move up. We lay siege."

The Linesmen formed three columns, roughly fifty men each. Ahead of them, they wheeled their cannon and motor guns, like ants carrying leaves. They came out of the oaks and across the fields toward New Design's moat, and its walls, where Lowry now fully and calmly expected to die.

"I wanted to do this clean. I did. Have the amplifier brought to me, please, Mr. Mill."

※　※　※

Mr. Hulgins led Liv out to the yard, where he stood by her side in awkward silence.

They watched torches and candles and oil lamps light up all down the streets. The sky was slowly tending to gray, and the night stars were fading. They watched men run back and forth; first bell-ringers and drum-beaters, then a few confused and halting men woken in their nightshirts or furs or stepping out naked into the night; soon more of them, some grimly silent, others muttering with fear or shouting with glee, all of them laden with spears, bows, rifles, hoes and rakes, or buckets, or timber, or bundles that Liv could not identify. The rain softly ceased and she did not remark the moment.

Mr. Hulgins was big and guileless, slow moving, decent. Back in the real world, he might have been the owner of a butcher's shop or hardware store, most likely inherited from a sharper, harder father, or acquired by marriage to some clever woman—and he'd have been much loved by the neighborhood, and probably never have turned much of a profit, maybe lost the store to a bank, probably limped along well enough. . . . That, Liv thought, was Hulgins's natural type. He'd been badly misplaced. A man like that had no business dying for New Design.

Hulgins noticed Liv studying him. He gave what was presumably meant to be a fierce scowl, but his eyes trembled, his chin quivered. She smiled at him.

In the yard in front of them, ten soldiers of New Design performed an impromptu drill, marching left and right, twirling and locking rifles, setting bayonets, shouting and stamping out commands and code words; then they scattered, seemingly midroutine, to the town's four corners. Some saluted as they went; some held each other. Liv hoped all that noise and activity gave them confidence.

"This isn't the Line itself," Liv told poor Mr. Hulgins. "This is only a tiny distant echo of the Line. They didn't come for war. They came chasing down one man. They'll be tired. They don't have their vehicles, Creedmoor said. They don't have their flying machines. There are no Engines. They are little more than ordinary men. It's not altogether hopeless, Mr. Hulgins."

Hulgins stared out into the yard. He shook his head slowly; Liv wasn't sure what he was saying no to.

"Are you married, Mr. Hulgins?"

He continued to ignore her.

There was a noise. Liv had been hearing it for some seconds before she really noticed it—rising from beneath the hum of New Design's waking, rising quickly to force out all other, softer sounds. A noise like chalk on a blackboard; like a mosquito of unusual size whining of its horrible needs; like the ringing complained of by sufferers from injuries to the brain, to Ignvir's Lobe or Werner's Area, or by certain schizophrenics persuaded of mysterious alarms. . . . A whine, a hiss, a crackling chaos of sound, surging and then breaking, resolving into the boom of a voice, reboant, sounding from outside the town's walls and resounding from the sky: ". . . OF THE ANGELUS ENGINE. MEN AND WOMEN OF NEW DESIGN, THIS IS SUB-CONDUCTOR LOWRY OF THE ANGELUS ENGINE. I REPEAT: MEN AND WOMEN OF . . ."

Hulgins, Liv, three or four stragglers crossing the yard, a young woman just stepping outside her cabin—all looked up, as if expecting to see the voice thundering from the rain clouds; but the sky was empty and gray and still.

The voice was impossibly loud and distorted, but beneath the

howling of electricity and static were the flat dull tones of a Linesman, sounding almost bored with his message.

"CAN YOU HEAR ME? CAN YOU? YOU CAN? YOU ALL KNOW WHAT
THAT MEANS, DON'T YOU? THE LINE'S HERE." The voice stretched
and droned into incoherence. A muttering aside as loud as a
landslide—"AH, YOU KNEW IT WAS GOING TO HAPPEN ONE DAY,
DIDN'T YOU? WE REACH EVERYWHERE."

Lowry. So, Liv thought, *Lowry* was the name of the man who'd
pursued her all that way. An ugly name, an ugly voice.

She recalled standing on the Concourse at Gloriana Station, in
the shadows under the great weight of rusty iron that was the Station's roof, listening to the boom and reverb of their voice-amplifier
devices, which broadcast the Engines' commands, marked out the
hours, inflicted the awe the Engines demanded. But in Gloriana,
there had been dozens of the devices, hung in the rafters like huge
bats, so that the echoes played back and forth and the noise filled
every crevice of awareness. Lowry couldn't possibly have dragged
more than one of the devices all the way to New Design, and that in-
sufficiency was apparent. The sound was vast but not deep. The
whine was the whine of a machine pushed past its limits and close to
breaking. It slurred and howled. It *echoed*. She prayed for it to break.

"LISTEN, NEW DESIGN. I HAVE A PRISONER. I TOOK ONE OF YOUR
SCOUTS. HE SAYS HIS NAME IS HAYWORTH. LISTEN TO THIS, THEN."

There was a new voice, screaming, begging for mercy, driving
the sound up into a dreadful pitch, until it was impossible to distin-
guish the man's screams from the machine's, from the echoes still
sounding down the streets.

Silence suddenly resumed.

Hulgins stared at the sky. He held his hands trembling near his
ears as if desperate to give in to fear and cover them. Liv reached
out a hand to comfort him; changing her mind, she withdrew it and
took a step back. He didn't notice.

"HEAR THAT? HE TOLD ME YOUR STRENGTHS. HAYWORTH. WE
KNOW WHAT YOU'VE GOT. YOU KNOW YOU CAN'T FIGHT. YOU RAN
FROM US ONCE. BRING OUT THE OLD MAN AND WE'LL LEAVE YOU
ALONE. I REPEAT: BRING HIM OUT, WE'LL BE ON OUR WAY."

Liv took another slow step away from Hulgins's side.

"IN HALF AN HOUR IF HE'S NOT OUT HERE'S WHAT WE'LL DO."

There was a cough like a thunder clap. The voice resumed, but now it was hard to make out the words; the voice had started to mumble, rant and ramble and whine, drifting sometimes too close and sometimes too far from the mouthpiece of the amplifier as if Lowry swayed back and forth in neurotic discomfort.

※ ※ ※

Lowry turned his head away from the amplifier and covered the speaking-plate with his hand. He'd tried to think of some horror with which to threaten New Design, and, not being imaginative, his thoughts had naturally run straight and true back to the last time he'd faced the armies of the Republic. His mind filled with visions of Black Cap Valley—the wire, the muck, the poison flowers that thrived there, how he crawled through it, the riflemen of the Republic with their steady hands and clear merciless eyes picking off the boys on either side of him, one by one, like the children of the Line were worth less than ants. It shook his calm for a moment.

He began again.

"What we'll do is first we'll shake down your walls." He leaned in close and muttered into the speaking-plate, and it threw his voice out into the air so that it seemed the sky itself boomed with his own private thoughts. "We'll flatten your homes. We'll destroy what you've made. We'll leave only mud and muck. We'll dig you up. We'll do this because it's our duty and what the fuck else are we going to do with ourselves? You'll see. We'll send smoke and noise, the old ones, your old men, they'll remember, they'll tell you what it's like, they'll be the ones to go first, it's always the old who go first. Or the children. It's always the children who get it hardest. Choking up black dust. Bleeding from the eyes and the ears. Old men go mad. The children go old and gray, they look like they're a thousand years old when they die. I don't want to do that. I really don't, I really don't fucking care if I do or I don't. There's no pleasure in this. This is my job. But then I'll send my boys in. You'll be on your knees pleading when they cut your throats. Everything's flat and clean and so quiet after we've passed through a place, it's so easy for everyone who comes after us, but you should see what it's like for

us, at the hard edge, where you have to cut and you have to get cut.
The blasting edge. If some of you are still standing when we come
in, it's going to make it harder but it won't . . . *Fuck!*"

Sparks flew and the red-hot speaking-plate snapped off under
pressure of internal stresses and cut Lowry's cheek.

✻ ✻ ✻

There was a sudden electrical crackle, a snap, a drop in air pressure,
a silence that was full of dying echoes. The voice had gone.

In fact, Liv had hardly been able to hear a thing it said for some
time. She'd not been listening anyway. Hulgin had frozen in terror
at the first moment the voice began, and closed his eyes and begun
to mutter slogans of Smiler self-affirmation. She took that moment
to inch away slowly. As soon as it became clear that Hulgins hadn't
noticed what she was doing, she ran.

She saw Mr. Waite the Smiler by the water pump, leading a group
of boys in an affirmation of resolve and courage and pride. None of
the boys had rifles: they had spears, and bows, and knives. They
wore furs, under which their thin bodies were tense and trembling.
Waite looked like a boy himself, and Liv supposed he was, in a way:
he must have been of the generation that did not remember the old
world, that had been reared outside of time and history, and had
never, therefore, grown up. The smile on his face was ridiculously
wide and confident. Liv thought of the department store dummies
she'd seen on some of her infrequent visits to Koenigswald's big
cities, in quieter, saner times. Waite's smile had that same quality of
waxy artless salesmanship. She smiled back and nodded. She slowed
to a walk. Waite and the boys watched her as she passed. She tried to
look as though she had legitimate business, somewhere important to
be. She didn't know where she was going.

✻ ✻ ✻

When Bradley's arm tired, he lowered the bomb. He held it at his
side, fidgeting with the hammer. His face twitched and snarled.

—He feels foolish, Creedmoor. You make him look ridiculous in
front of his men. He imagined a heroic confrontation. This waiting
is farce.

—You always perceive our weaknesses, my friend.

—He is only more dangerous for it. He may act foolishly. He is keen to die grandly. His old fingers tremble.

—Do you hear that? That whine, that tremor, abusing the ether. Our pursuers are clearing the throats of their hideous machines. They are about to sing their unmusical song. Will this be the sound that kills, or are they going to speak, first?

—Every sound the Line makes kills, Creedmoor. Either the body or the spirit. Only we offer true life.

—Is that what you call it?

—Watch Bradley. If his attention falters, kill him.

Lowry's flat nasal voice settled over the town like a foul rain; it crept in through the hospital's curtained windows. "I REPEAT: BRING HIM OUT, WE'LL BE ON OUR WAY. IN HALF AN HOUR IF HE'S NOT OUT HERE'S WHAT WE'LL DO. . . ."

Bradley's riflemen went pale with dread and their weapons began to tremble; but Bradley was made of stronger stuff, and though his eyes, red rimmed, started to water, they didn't flinch from Creedmoor's hovering hand.

Creedmoor raised his voice over the din. "He's lying, Dr. Bradley. You know it. The Line leaves nothing unchanged. He won't just take his men away. He'll destroy you. It was already too late for you long before they got here. Do you know when it was too late? When they sat down and looked at their maps and drew the line of their progress, and you were in their way. There may not even be particular malice in it. You'll die here, Doctor. But something can be saved. Let me take the General away from here."

Bradley's eyes opened wide. He sneered.

"Now I know what you're thinking, Doctor: He's old, even older than you, or me, and quite mad, and what's he that's worth saving, all on his own? But hear me out, Doctor. The General has a secret. Did my friend Liv tell you that? I know what it is. I'm in on the secret. A weapon. The First Folk have a weapon. Or not so much a weapon as an idea, maybe, or a dream, or something we have no words for. They offered it to him."

Creedmoor turned to Bradley's riflemen. "You're young," he said. "Do you know that the General used to pal around with a fellow of the Folk? A caster of stones, a wise man, a something-or-other. I met his wife, believe it or not. The General made a *deal* with the Folk, I reckon. They built his Republic for him and in return—"

Bradley spat. "Shut up, monster."

"Don't like that sort of talk, eh, Doctor? Mystical bullshit, tarnishing your glorious rational virtuous origins. But listen: They promised him a *weapon*. The weapon puts an end to spirits, Dr. Bradley. A *final* end. I know you've destroyed Engines and maybe you broke Guns, but you know you only broke their housings, you know they came back, they would always come back, like the Folk themselves, like nightmares, like a disease with no cure. And so they never learned fear."

—Why are you telling him this, Creedmoor?

From behind Creedmoor's back came the sound of the General turning in bed, whimpering, muttering. Some of the riflemen glanced uneasily over at him, dividing their attention.

"See? He remembers, somewhere down in the rubble of his mind. He *found* it. He sent a letter home to his family, you see, before his last ride. Then he vanished. The Line caught him. Most likely by mistake; they throw those ugly bombs around like toys. Someone brought him down the mountain—and believe me, we'd like to know who. Somehow he ended up in an eerie little hospital back on the world's edge not *that* many weeks east of here. What if he still holds the secret? If he still deep down knows where to find that weapon? Or how to make it? What if he *found* it? He won't live long. Your town, your Republic, your world is dead. You'll never have that weapon. But what if *I* had it? We could kill the Engines. We could teach them fear. You could be revenged. Will you consider it?"

Bradley raised the bomb again, as if he intended to strike Creedmoor with it. "We don't make deals with your kind, monster. You pervert everything you touch. We saw too many nations fall to your kind. We stand on our own."

The riflemen flanking Bradley looked wary, Creedmoor noted. But of course, they were irrelevant. Creedmoor had no doubt he could outdraw their trigger-fingers, could outrun their bullets, could even take the wound if necessary.

"Suppose I fought alongside you, Doctor. If you disarm that bomb, I give you my word I'll hold back the Linesmen as long as I can. You know your people are no match for them. I can make no promise of success, but I believe I may even the odds. You yourself might survive. Do you have children here? A young second wife, maybe?"

"Mind your business, Creedmoor."

"You've played a weak hand well, Doctor. Perhaps you've saved your people. You should accept my aid with pride."

"Your word means nothing, Creedmoor. We'll make no deals."

"You used not to be so inflexible, Doctor. Back in the old days, back in the world behind us. Oh, your General and your charters and your speechifying men in medals or top hats all said, stand on your own feet; a government of laws, not Powers; have no truck with devilry . . . all that. I remember the speeches, Doctor. But even back then, you couldn't keep my kind out. Your sons and daughters dreamed of us. When your leaders were weak and afraid, they let us in. At Wolverhampton, and Tin Hill, and Syme, and a dozen other places, they called on us for aid. It's not in the history books, but it's known by those who care to know. You wouldn't be the first to bend a little."

"That was back in the old world, Creedmoor. We're a purer strain out here. Our sons and daughters are taught virtue. No deals."

"Well then fuck you, Doctor."

Creedmoor drew and fired, and the air, which had gone silent when Lowry's machine stopped howling some minutes ago, echoed again. The riflemen all drew in their breath. Bradley's body fell stiffly backwards, the long black coat opening out behind him. He let go of his walking stick, and it balanced on its steel tip for a moment then fell slowly forward. He let go of the bomb and it fell leadenly toward the earth. The hammer arced toward the striking-plate. There was a tiny screech of wire and a creak of uncoiling springs. A slow shiver and scrape of metal.

Creedmoor, already in motion, crossing the floor in fractions of a second, leaping across the beds in his path (their wooden frames sounding under his feet like drums) heard every slow sound with painful clarity. Launching himself from the last of the beds, he twisted in the air. His old bones creaked and his muscles nearly tore. He focused his *will;* the flesh could only slow him down. He hit the floor hard on his back, sliding over the hard-packed dirt. The bomb fell with a thud into his outstretched hand. He fumbled his thumb in between the striking-plate and the descending hammer. It stabbed down on the quick of his nail. It was a sharp little thing and it drew a tiny jewel of blood out of him. *Fuck,* he said; but it worked. The bomb remained silent.

—You madman, Creedmoor. You fool. What if you'd been too slow?

—Then I would be dead, or worse. You could go howling back to that dark place where your kind lodge. You could curse my name.

The three riflemen were standing around looking stupid, their rifles still trained on the place where he'd been standing the half second before. Creedmoor stood and shot them in quick succession.

He wasn't sure how to disarm the device. In the end, he simply tore off the hammer and flicked it into the corner of the room. For good measure, he prized off the striking-plate. That seemed to work. He kicked what was left of the bomb under a bed.

A terrible crash sounded outside, off in the distance, like a resounding echo of Creedmoor's own gunshots. Like now that he'd begun the killing, it was ricocheting madly out of his control: like it was all his fault once again.

CHAPTER 49

NEW DESIGN AT WAR

Dawn came. The sun rose in the west, behind thick dark clouds.. Lowry watched New Design's walls, from which no surrender party emerged, over which no white flag was flown.

Subaltern Mill stood beside him. "Time's up, sir."

"Is it?"

"I think so, sir."

"Huh." The problem was that none of Lowry's men's timepieces worked right anymore. If they hadn't been waterlogged in the rains or battered and cracked along the march, they'd stopped working for more mysterious reasons. Their hands spun meaninglessly, or hardly at all. Time out here was not yet ready to be measured. So Lowry waited, indecisively, for what felt like much longer than half an hour. He was waiting for *orders*. He was waiting for something to tick over and give him his signal. He waited, listening to the prisoner moan and pray, listening to his men mutter nervously, listening for sounds of surrender from New Design. And he was still waiting when there was a soft distant *thump* from behind the town's walls, and a line of black smoke vented into the sky, and a shell came arcing up and then down again, falling well short of Lowry's front lines, killing no one. A second shell followed instants later, and killed half a dozen.

❋ ❋ ❋

The soldiers of New Design had brought up their cannon into a beet-field near the center of town. The deerlike things that had been corralled in the pen next door had been evicted. Some of the creatures stood around looking on, nervous and whinnying and incontinent. Others fled.

Liv watched the cannon move in from down the end of the street. She peered around the wall of that odd octagonal repository of books—the lock of which was broken, and now some of the deer-things hid in its shadows and grazed its shelves.

There were two cannon. Two long metal stalks, each rising from two heavy wheels that churned the mud of the beet-field. Different models—one was much smaller than the other, and put Liv in mind of a polio-shriveled limb. Their metal gleamed in the dawn light. They'd been well looked after.

A team of men dragged them with ropes. The ground was soft, and it took ten men apiece. Captain Morton led them. When it came time to set the charges, he pushed the younger men away and kneeled down in the muck to do the work himself.

They worked quickly and confidently, they were well drilled. They had the guns in place well before Lowry's half hour was near up, even if one counted from the moment his rant began, and not from the moment the fuses fried and silence reclaimed the air. Or so Liv guessed—her own golden pocket watch was still worthless.

Morton stood looking out east across the beet-field. There was a dull glow in the distance. Not firelight; something cold and electric lit Lowry's camp.

At no particular signal Liv could see, Morton knelt again by the base of the fatter, healthier cannon. A younger man applied himself to the undercarriage of the weaker cannon and mirrored Morton's motions. Both men stood well back.

The cannons sounded.

Liv shielded her eyes from the flash. She had only a vague impression of thick black lines scored across the gunmetal sky. She went running, head down, and did not see the distant flicker where the shells struck, or the smoke rising.

Lowry's retaliation came quick. Liv heard something whistling overhead, and didn't look up. It flew with an incongruously bright and cheerful sound. She was well away down the street and through a muddy close between houses when she heard the sound of the device striking—a sound that reached her first as a dull despairing thud, as of a suicide's body falling from a bridge, and then repeated itself, again and again, harsher each time, louder and louder, gathering steam but not rhythm, until it was no longer sad and quiet, but persistent, manic, onrushing. It had no pattern; it lurched toward structure and shattered it, crashing on, and on—it had the pulse of dying muscle tissue, spasming, or the last firings of a diseased brain. Liv fell against a wall of haystacks and a fence of wet wood, and covered her ears.

The sound washed over her and was gone. Her eyes felt terribly swollen. Her nose was bleeding.

The device had struck where Morton stood. New Design's cannon were silent. Liv did not look back.

She staggered south. Men and boys ran back and forth around her, stumbling with their rifles or bows or spears. There was another cheerful whistling sound from the north, and from the west, and then the mad drone and thunder of the Line's weapons echoed distantly over the town. Neither device struck close enough to Liv for the sound to destroy her; even so the muffled echo of it was enough to make her belly lurch as if miscarrying, and she stopped to retch into a water trough. Nothing inside to expel but bad air. She slumped against the trough's side and pressed her cheek against the cold wood.

Liv watched two men go by, dragging a third, whose body was unwounded, but whose legs spasmed, and whose head twisted back and howled senselessly like a motor breaking down. She watched a fourth man, alone, stagger out from behind a barn and stumble for twenty paces before falling twitching in the dirt. She went over to him. His eyes rolled back in his head. He appeared to have bitten his tongue; blood frothed on his smiling lips. She could not bring herself to touch him. She heard men running up near and backed away out of their path. Thirty men and boys with a pawnbroker's assortment of weapons ran past, not stopping.

The sound of shooting echoed from the east, and she was glad of it; shooting was a *cleaner* death.

❀ ❀ ❀

"Enough," Lowry said. *"Enough!"*

He ran toward the nearest cannon, choking in its smoke, screaming over its noise, over the noise of his men running, shouting, loading noisemakers and poison gas. . . .

"Enough! You'll kill the General, you idiots, you *slagging* idiots, we have our duty, this is meaningless if we *don't do our duty."*

Silence fell. The men attempted to pull themselves together.

"We go in," he said. "Motor guns at the bridges, we go behind them, street by street."

But that was only one of his cannon; and the other, some two hundred feet away, on the other side of the ranks, continued to fire.

❀ ❀ ❀

As soon as Dr. Bradley was dead, and his stolen device disarmed, Creedmoor lifted the General up from his bed. The old man seemed disinclined to move of his own will—or such as was left of it—preferring to remain stiffly curled on that hard bed like it was his mother's lap. He'd been groomed quite finely, Creedmoor noticed, and dressed in a white shirt and black pleated uniform trousers that, though somewhat stained and worn at the knees, were perhaps the smartest clothes in the whole sad town. There was a red jacket, gold braided, many medaled, hanging from a rusty hook by the bed. Creedmoor wrestled it over the General's shoulders. The effect was quite striking. "You must have been something to see in your prime, sir. Ah, now, ah now, steady." The General struggled away, eyes rolling, mouth working. "You're in fine strong spirits, sir, but we must be going."

In the end, Creedmoor had to carry the General outside in both arms like he was carrying an unsatisfactory bride back out over the threshold. This quickly posed problems, for two local fellows tried to rush him with clubs and throwing-axes and it was a damn difficult trick to shoot them while shielding the General—and without dropping him, for though the earth was rain softened—and quivering now, puddles shimmering and rippling at the sound of the oncoming machines—the General was so fragile, so thin that he might break himself falling on a featherbed.

—This is going to get tiresome.

—Stop whining, Creedmoor. Flee to the west.

✳ ✳ ✳

Liv ran past the Mortons' house, and saw through the window that inside the house was no longer silent or dark. Sally Morton was awake, and working. She and three other women, two of them as young as she, one old enough to be her grandmother, stood around the dining table preparing poultices of herbs and leaves.

They glanced up for a moment as Liv came in the door, then returned to their work. There was a stiffness about them that was not calm, but something like it: *discipline*.

The old woman beckoned Liv over. "Come on then, Doctor. Make yourself useful."

Liv ignored her.

She wanted to tell them: *Run*. It was hopeless to fight the Line. But they wouldn't have listened.

Sally lifted her eyes from the table. "Doctor—"

She turned and left.

Outside it was lighter now; it was getting lighter all the time. The sounds of battle were cold and clear. She breathed deeply, and smelled smoke.

She headed south, toward the hospital and perhaps, if they were still there, Creedmoor and the General. She had no idea what she could do, but she had to do *something*.

✳ ✳ ✳

Creedmoor went loping through the town, the General cradled in his arms. The town was emptying out like an hourglass as its men went east to the fight. Two more men confronted him and, juggling his burden, he cut them down. Once one of the mind-bombs went whistling right overhead and he let the General's legs drop in the mud and shot it left-handed from the sky. The General flailed and stretched and appeared to be trying to speak.

—This old man's no light burden, not anymore. He struggles. He's full of animal spirits. His time here's done him good. This is hard work for one man.

—We are here with you, Creedmoor.

—I need help. A companion to share my burden. And do you know, I do believe I've had a crisis of conscience.

—No you have not, Creedmoor. Go west, at once.

—Or what will you do to me? We've discussed this matter, my friend. I will go on westward, but not alone.

He sniffed the air and caught her scent.

—She's on her way here, look. She knows only we can save her from the enemy.

✳ ✳ ✳

As Liv passed Woodbury's house, she heard that cheerful whistling overhead again and started running, blindly, skirts hiked up, staggering through the muddy streets, looking back over her shoulder for bombs, Linesmen, who-knew-what. She didn't see Creedmoor step out of the shadows, pulling the General behind him. She didn't see him standing in her path, grinning cheerfully, arms outstretched, until she ran right into him.

✳ ✳ ✳

She caught her breath, looked up at his face, and recoiled.

He grinned. "Still alive! My luck rubs off on you, Liv. I worried you were dead! My conscience is eased. I have a favor to ask. Your patient needs you, madam. *I* need you. I'm sure you'd rather not die here with these idiots."

Creedmoor let go of the General's arm, and the old man started to fall over. Liv rushed to hold him up. She didn't speak; she didn't meet Creedmoor's eye.

But the General would not stand, and Liv was not strong enough to carry him against his will. And it did appear that he had a *will* now. He twitched and shook. He twisted feebly but with determination. Liv pulled him up like she was yanking up a skinny weed by its roots, and he would instantly snap back down again, curling on the ground, face pressed against the earth.

—Is he *fighting* us, Creedmoor? Why won't he come?

"Is he fighting us, Liv? Why won't he come?"

She knelt down. She leaned in close. The General was silent.

"You're his doctor, Liv. Will he speak to you? Will he at least give you one of his fairy tales to puzzle over?"

"Mr. Creedmoor, why would he speak? Why would he need to? Isn't it obvious? He won't leave. None of these people will leave. This is the last of the world they built. The General won't abandon his men."

"Well, *shit*. These people are mad."

"Mad? What do you call *yourself*, Mr. Creedmoor?"

"Fair enough. Fair enough. Well, then, I think what you're saying is that to take the General out of here, we must save the town? Is that right?"

—*No*, Creedmoor. We do not care what becomes of these people. Take the General and leave them to die.

She looked closely at him, trying to figure his motives. That only made him smile.

"Yes," she said. "Yes, Creedmoor. You must save the town."

—Hear that? Doctor's orders, my friend.

—No, Creedmoor. Pick him up and carry him.

—Oh, come now. The Enemy is at hand. Don't you feel a little of the old bloodlust?

—No, Creedmoor.

—Too bad. I feel like playing hero.

"What are you going to do, Creedmoor?"

"Go to work. You should find a hiding place, Liv. Keep an eye on our charge. I'll be back for you both."

⁂ ⁂ ⁂

Lowry had what part of his forces he could still control move up to assault New Design's eastern and southeastern bridges. The first thing was to get the motor guns placed. That meant sending small five-man squads ahead, slowly covering ground while the guns were wheeled up behind. Lowry went behind the guns, crouching, running.

Behind him there were screams, and the whistle of arrows and the rattle of gunfire, and he understood that the soldiers of New Design had ambushed his forces from the rear, from the forests. There was nothing he could do about it now—because in front of him, with a great roar, the young men of New Design came charging out of the town and across the bridge. They waved their swords and their banners and cheered some nonsense that Lowry couldn't hear, because the Linesmen's motor guns immediately whirred into action.

❋ ❋ ❋

Creedmoor perched crowlike on top of the town's wall and watched the fighting.

—Senseless.

—Yes. All these people are mad, Creedmoor.

The fighting was concentrated at the east of the town. The town's soldiers fought to defend the east bridge over the moat from the massed Linesmen. But the moat was shallow, empty, more symbolic than real—a line in the sand—and should have posed no barrier to the Linesmen, who could have attacked equally well at any point, could've torn through the wall with their motor guns, could have swarmed the town from all sides if they'd chosen, like ants dismantling a corpse. But of course, they respected barriers and lines. . . .

The Linesmen fought contemptuously, joylessly. In fact, they hardly fought at all. The young men and boys of New Design—and some of the women, too—went charging over the bridge waving old swords, or their clubs or sharpened spears, and the Linesmen lazily activated their hideous grinding machine guns and reduced them to nothing. The process repeated itself. The Linesmen seemed content to let New Design's forces exhaust themselves in futile gestures.

—Why are we wasting our time, Creedmoor? These people are hopeless.

—Not all of them. Look.

There were riflemen and bowmen in the far forest attempting to pick off the Linesmen's flanks—but the Linesmen simply released their poisons, their roiling black clouds of smoke and grit and cold choking death, and the forests went silent again. The town's soldiers had more mortars and explosives still to launch, but they were twenty-year-old junk and they fizzled and misfired. On the town's side of the bridge lay the wreckage of three tripod-mounted motor guns, old models, no doubt stolen from the Line decades ago—the Linesmen had destroyed those first, long before Creedmoor started watching.

—It's a brave effort.

—That makes no difference, Creedmoor.

—It's magnificent, in its way. I never saw the point of the Republic while they were winning, but now they're dying, they're magnificent.

New Design's defenders faltered. The Linesmen pushed forward and began to penetrate their ranks, fanning out through the town.

—Shall we join in, then?

—We will not forgive you for this, Creedmoor.

— Oh, well.

Creedmoor stood, drew, shot down the black-suited black-capped operator of the nearest motor gun on the far side of the bridge. He turned and shot the operators of the second motor gun, and one of the cannon—he couldn't get a clear shot at the other cannon operator. He shot the men who came running up to take their place. He put three bullets into the overheated motor of one of the motor guns and it exploded, spraying bits of hot twisted metal. The Linesmen shouted and pointed and turned their rifles in his direction, so Creedmoor, laughing, turned away and dropped down from the wall into the town, which was now lousy with Linesmen and their ugly weapons.

※　※　※

Lowry led a force of fifteen men along the bridge and into the town. (Just fifteen men! That was what they'd been reduced to.) They cleared a path for themselves with noisemakers and poison-gas grenades, then followed implacably behind, stepping over writhing mindless bodies, doing some quick work with their bayonets.

They encountered local resistance. Several young women appeared in the windows as they walked past and let fly with bows and slings, which once again proved surprisingly effective weapons. Private Carr got an arrow right through the glass plate of his gas mask and fell down dead. Private Stack got one in his leg. The women went down to a gas grenade tossed by Subaltern Mills.

Lowry kept moving, expecting at any second that an arrow would enter his shoulder blades, or the idiot locals would get their cannon working and drop a rocket on his head, or . . .

He found himself approaching an unusually large and important-looking building, low and flat like all of New Design, but wide and sprawling. There were half a dozen guards outside it who Lowry's men shot down even before Lowry could give the order. Inside the building there was a maze of corridors, and an office containing a local in a brown suit who rose stiffly from a desk and said *"We will never surrender, Linesmen, we will fight you—"* before Subaltern Mills shot him, and no sign of the General. There was, however, a large heavily barred door, and behind that a room containing an impressive collection of machinery scavenged from the Line—rockets, amplifiers, motors, generators, drills, telegraphs, projectors, arclights, signal devices—ancient, rusty, battered, but some of it serviceable.

✳ ✳ ✳

New Design fell apart. There was no fire, not at first. The Line didn't make much use of fire. Fire raged out of control; it burned too bright. The Line favored fear, and madness, and despair, and noise, and choking gas. Creedmoor, on the other hand, was as happy in fire as a pig in shit, so he started a fire or two in the thatch or curtains of the houses. It gave the Linesmen something to worry about, and it set Creedmoor's own mind at ease. With the fire at his back, he fought through the streets. It was joyful to fight precisely because it was not his duty and Marmion forbade it, and gave him strength with an ill grace. . . .

—Kill them, Creedmoor. Quickly.

—See? I knew you'd enjoy it.

The boys of New Design watched him work. Huddled in the ruins of someone's house—burned over, then extinguished by the Line's chill black gas—a group of boys watched him go by. They'd let go of their weapons. One of their number was bleeding from his head. Creedmoor winked and tipped his hat to them as he walked past. "Good day! Tell 'em Creedmoor was here! Tell 'em, should the Republic survive into future generations, that *John Creedmoor* saved it! And make sure to note that he did it of his own free will!"

Some of them looked at him with desperate pleading hope. Some of them looked at him with hate, willing him to fail, to spare them the shame of being saved by his kind. . . .

—They will never forgive you, Creedmoor. Only we will—

—I know. I know.

He erased the Linesmen one by one. Linesmen shambled through the town in units of five or ten. Creedmoor picked away at what looked like leaders, or at whatever was easiest. Their ranks were breaking down. Their motions were becoming without purpose. The shock of Creedmoor's assault had knocked the machine off its proper functioning, and parts were spinning loose. The town was full of smoke and the black gas, so the Linesmen wore masks, which made them identical; they were things, not men. Of course, Creedmoor wouldn't have cared if they *had* had faces, except insofar as it might have made it easier to identify leaders, to identify that Lowry fellow, to pick him out from the mass. Creedmoor himself passed through the gas simply by holding his breath. When he found a clear spot, he paused and breathed in great deep joyful breaths of clean air and thought,

—This is what we were made for, my friend. Why deny it?

—More of them behind you, Creedmoor. Quick now.

※　※　※

"Who here knows signals?" Lowry looked over his thirteen men. Gas masks hid their faces, but he scanned their uniforms' insignia. One of them was a Signalman, Second Class.

"You—Signalman What's-your-name." He wiped dust off the dented casing of an obsolete model signal device. "Is this salvageable?"

The Signalman wordlessly got to work. He unscrewed the casing with the point of his knife and examined the rusting innards. His mask hid his expression. Meanwhile gunshots echoed in the streets outside, random and meaningless, fraying Lowry's last nerve.

"Well?"

The Signalman started working levers and valves, and studying fluttering needles and dials.

"Well?"

"Yes, sir. Weakly, sir. But we have the signal again. The signaling device is likely still with the woman; at least, it's here in town, sir."

"Take it," Lowry said. "You and you, carry the machine. You and you and you, guard them. Follow the signal."

He turned, drew his pistol, and strode out through the corridors, and out into the street, where he saw a man who could only have been John Creedmoor himself walking by, bloodstained and laughing and gesturing as if he was talking to himself and apparently having a wonderful time, without a fear or a care in the world, and Lowry was so suddenly so sick with *envy,* he had to lean against the doorframe a moment for support.

✳   ✳   ✳

—There, Creedmoor.

Creedmoor glanced over his shoulder and saw a short gas-masked Linesman leaning oddly in a doorframe with what seemed, insofar as one could say it of a man in a gas mask, an expression of peculiar intensity. Creedmoor shot him dead, and then he shot the Linesman who stood behind him dead, too; and then it looked like there were more of them packed into that dark corridor, each of them ready to take the others' places, a never-ending factory-line. . . .

—Too many. And men of the Republic coming. Move on.

—Yes.

He turned and ran.

✳   ✳   ✳

Liv hid at the back of a barn, surrounded by hay bales. With the hunting knife Creedmoor had left her, she tore a shirt from the back of a dead townsman and used it to bind her ears and the General's. She used the rags of it to dab ash and rose-pink bloody tears from her cheeks. She cradled the General's head and whispered, *"Calm, calm, calm."*

He was clean-shaven, for the first time in weeks. But he was also terribly thin, and terribly hot, as if fevered. There was a strength to his movements that seemed unhealthy, unsustainable. She was afraid he might be dying. She held him and whispered to him.

Slowly she became aware of a steady *tapping,* as of stone on wood, coming from overhead. She looked up.

Red eyes watched her from the dark of the rafters.

Liv said, "I *remember* you."

And from behind those red eyes, a long bone-white body unfolded itself, lengthening like a shadow, lowering itself down hand-over-hand from the rafters so that for one vertiginous moment it seemed to hang from the high beams by its knuckly feet, while its fingers rattled across the straw-covered earth, and its maned head was twisted at an impossible angle, regarding Liv with expressionless red eyes.

Then it sat by her, cross-legged, its long black mane covering its white skin and the ruby glitter of its body paint. A woman. Liv recognized her: Ku Koyrik, hound of the border.

Liv asked, "What do you want?"

There was no answer. Liv loosened the cloth round her ears; but there was still no answer. The Folk woman examined her silently.

"Did you do this?" Liv gestured at the sound of fighting all around—and now she noticed that there was shooting in the street outside the barn, terribly close. "Did you bring the Line here?"

The woman cocked her head curiously.

"Why did you let them pass? Why did you let *us* pass, for that matter?"

The red eyes continued their examination.

"What *is* the General's secret? Is there any such secret? Do you know? What do you want from him? What do you—?"

Two words floated in her mind, in a cool firm voice, not unlike her own when she was at her best:

—Quiet. Too many questions. Listen.

"What do you want—?"

—Listen. There—

There was a crack and a stray bullet from out in the street punched daylight through the wooden walls of the barn and struck the Folk woman in the back of her black mane, crushing her long skull and spattering indigo blood across the straw. She fell forward dead. Her long bones clacked and rattled and settled themselves as if cast by a fortune-teller, meaning nothing.

A brief after-shower of bullets followed, thumping pointlessly into the hay bales. Then the fighting outside moved on.

There was a smell of smoke nearby.

Liv ran crouching to the half-open doors at the far end of the barn. As she shoved the General through and out into the mud, she turned briefly back, to see that the Folk woman's blood still stained the floor, her body still lay tangled in the hay.

Outside, New Design was in flames.

Liv saw half a dozen Linesmen stagger out of a cut between barns, wreathed in black smoke, alien as Hillfolk or insects in their gas masks and eyeglasses and noise-bafflers. A crest of fire roared along the roof of the nearest barn and the whole building fell apart, sliding, burying the Linesmen in burning timbers—*good*.

And Liv saw a dozen townsmen running across the beet-field with their bayonets set, and a noise-bomb went off at their feet and they fell to their knees, clutching their heads, shivering and then going still, and Liv thought how the bombs produced that attitude of perfect *submission*.

Another dozen Linesmen turned the corner of the street. Three of them carried a large and battered machine between them. One of them looked up, pointed in Liv's direction, and shouted something that was muffled by his mask.

Liv ran, pulling the General after her. He struggled and moaned and nearly dragged her off her feet, but she found her balance and kept running. From behind her, she heard the sound of arrows, rifle fire, screaming, as the Linesmen and a pack of the town's soldiers met, to each other's surprise.

※   ※   ※

Creedmoor emerged from an alley, shot three Linesmen in their backs, and kept walking, into another alley behind a large building that in a more normal sort of town would probably be a bar or a whorehouse but here was probably some sort of solemn democratic council-house. His head was starting to ache. He was afflicted with a sickening constant smell of blood and gunpowder. Some bastard a little while ago had put an arrow in Creedmoor's shoulder, which seemed ungrateful, and though Marmion had healed the wound, it'd chosen to leave a horrible grinding ache, apparently out of spite. Creedmoor's spirits were starting to sour.

—Enough, Creedmoor.

He emerged from the building's shadow onto a wide muddy street. At the far end of it, a group of the locals were pressing back a rather smaller group of Linesmen, cavalry sabers and wooden pitchforks against bayonets.

—*Enough*, Creedmoor. This is over. What's left of the town will survive. Take the General and move on.

—I never stay to see the end of things, do I?

—They will not thank you for saving them.

—Nor should they.

—You have proved your point; you have disobeyed us. We understand and forgive you.

—Because you must.

—But now come to heel.

※　※　※

There was a granary, a tall round tower of stone, on the western side of town. Liv dragged the General behind it. He shook and pulled away from her sweat-slick grip and fell in the mud at the tower's foot.

She crouched beside him, took his hands in hers, and looked him in his wild and panicked eyes. "General. *General*. Listen to me. Do you trust me? Do you trust me or do you not?"

His eyes seemed to calm a little. His breathing slowed.

"We have to flee. There is nothing you can do for New Design now. The Line cannot have you. Creedmoor's masters cannot have you. I do not know if your secret is real or a delusion of Creedmoor's masters, but I will not let them have you in any case; you *must* stop fighting me."

His eyes went cloudy, and wandered. His shaking stopped. Maybe there was something in him that understood her, and maybe there wasn't, maybe it was just the rubble of his broken mind shifting meaninglessly; but whatever the reason, he stood calmly and let her lead him west toward the bridge.

The western side of town was quiet—the fighting was all in the east. The bridge across the western moat was unguarded, and beyond it there was a broad empty plain. Liv ran down a wide street, watched by empty windows, and was not far from the bridge when she heard footsteps behind her. The next thing she knew, Creedmoor had lifted the General into his arms and was walking alongside her.

"Thank you, Liv, for keeping him safe."

She studied Creedmoor's face. He stared at his feet and wouldn't meet her eyes; his expression was heavy and flat.

"What happened to the Linesmen, Creedmoor?"

"What's left of them won't last long. The survivors of New Design are rallying. The locals'll round up the last of the Linesmen and they can hold trials for them and make speeches and have a hanging if they like, but the old man and I will have to miss the show."

The General struggled and moaned, and Creedmoor tightened his grip. "Easy there."

"Creedmoor—"

"We've won, Liv. Three cheers. Now there's nothing left to do but bring the General home."

"Creedmoor, listen: You can defy your masters, you can—"

"Of course I can't, Liv."

He walked out across the bridge, the General twisting in his arms. He lifted his head and looked at her. His eyes were bloodshot and dark.

"Go back, Liv. Stay with the town. Consider yourself released from service, and I apologize unreservedly for ever bringing you out here. It was cruel and thoughtless."

She kept walking alongside him, and he said nothing more. After a while he put the General down and allowed Liv to lead the old man by his arm, which seemed to calm him. They left New Design behind.

CHAPTER 50

MURDER

West of the town, a river ran down out of the hills. It had once pow-ered the town's mill wheels, and now it carried their broken burned timbers away back east. Creedmoor and Liv followed it west, herd-ing the General between them. They carried him across the water where it was shallow and tacked northwest across grassland. The sun, rising at their backs, seemed frozen in its progress, as if uncer-tain, and the sky was a red that went dark and rotten as the day lengthened. Liv kept turning, thinking it was the fires of New De-sign that glowered at her back.

"Don't look back now, Liv. You've made your choice."

The General offered: "When he looked back to see if the princess was following him up the stairs of bone, he saw her only in the act of vanishing like a joke repeated too often. Transformed into stone, down in the deep warrens. Nothing from the Fairy-worlds, from the Under-worlds, from the Inner Lodges, may be looked at directly, without changing. . . ."

"See, Liv? The General knows. He's livelier, don't you think, now that sad old town's behind us? Come on, old man."

Grass gave way to stones and weeds and scrub, to a dry ashy plain. Clouds gathered and darkened but it did not rain. There was no cover anywhere. Creedmoor urged them on faster and faster, toward the always-distant hills. Creedmoor muttered, deep in thought, as if in a dream. He rubbed his head and snapped, "Faster, faster, old man."

"Creedmoor—"

"No, Liv."

"Creedmoor, listen. I know you don't want to give him to your masters—"

"Are you appealing to my conscience, Liv?"

"Of course not, Creedmoor—I'm appealing to your pride. This is your last chance to be free of them."

"That's impossible, Liv."

"Creedmoor—"

"They're listening to everything you say, Liv, and everything I think. And they tell me to kill you. Now move faster. Some of the Linesmen survived New Design. They are still pursuing us."

※ ※ ※

—Creedmoor.

—I am trying to think.

—Yes. We know exactly what you are thinking.

—I know that you know. So there we are.

—Creedmoor. Stop. Turn back. What follows us is only half a dozen Linesmen, battered and tired and confused.

—Aren't we all. And how *are* they following us, anyway?

—You can kill them easily. Turn back. Come home.

—Maybe I want to keep going west. Out onto the wild shores. Take the General and walk off with him into the sea at the end of the world. We can dissolve together. You'll never have his secret. What could you do to stop me?

—The Goad, Creedmoor.

—Not while the Line pursues us.

—This is pointless, Creedmoor. It cannot last. Sooner or later, you must make a choice. And there is only one choice you can make.

—I could snap the old man's neck. You could kill me first by means of your fucking Goad, but you would not, because then the Line would have him.

—Yes. We would take our revenge on you later, at our leisure.
Your name would be forgotten. You will not do it. You are not a
brave or a good man.

—No.

—Come home, Creedmoor. All our Agents are unruly, and we
love you for it.

❋ ❋ ❋

They kept walking. The ashy plain rose steadily into the west. Liv
dragged her feet through it. Her legs were numb and stiff. The sun
blazed behind them. They walked in silence—Creedmoor rebuffed
every attempt at conversation, and the General had fallen mute. By
midday, they were far from New Design. The sky was full of swirling
ink-blot clouds.

Six Linesmen followed behind them. They followed at a distance, not daring to come too close. The plains were broad and treeless, however, and every once in a while, the Linesmen came close
enough that even Liv could make them out—a row of black specks
on the horizon. On one such occasion, Creedmoor suddenly turned
and fired, and then there were five. Creedmoor holstered his gun
again and kept walking.

"What's the point, Creedmoor? Why are they following us?
There aren't enough of them to fight you, they must see that."

He shrugged. "No point. They have their duty." He turned an
awful cynical smile to her, and she understood, immediately and
without doubt, what she had to do.

Her palms began to sweat and her gut twisted with fear. But she
kept walking, following Creedmoor, and apparently he noticed nothing different in her stride or her expression or her scent; or at least
he kept walking, too, his back to her, his head down.

Toward the late afternoon, they began to see lights on the horizon,
behind the western hills, where storm clouds massed over the nameless sea. Not quite colored or quite colorless, the lights made Liv
think of deep willow green, and blood red; very faint, so that they
could only be seen from the corner of the eye, or for a second as one
lifted one's gaze from the earth underfoot. They towered and leapt as
if they were dancing the world into being out of the thunderclouds.

Behind them the Linesmen crept closer. Creedmoor seemed to ignore them.

Toward evening, the flatness of the plain was interrupted by dunes, mounds, of the stuff that was like ash or sand or grit; at first they were little pockmarks, knee high, but soon the surface of the plain rose and fell like a frozen sea, and the General had to be dragged up the shifting side of ash-waves taller than Creedmoor and Liv put together, and progress slowed.

And near nightfall—as they crested, with great effort, a dune of unusual height and obstructiveness, each of them holding one of the General's arms, dragging his limp legs, Creedmoor snarling and cursing as his feet slid and stumbled through the ash—Liv understood that there would likely never be any better moment, and so, in an instant, made her decision and acted.

※　※　※

She cried out, *"I cannot do this anymore!"* and she let go of the General's arm and fell to her knees. Naturally the General fell, too, limp as a rag doll, and Creedmoor nearly followed them both down. He grunted in annoyance as he tried to maintain hold of the old man while keeping his footing on the shifting ash-slope. The General chose that moment to twist in Creedmoor's arms and he staggered back, bracing his feet wide as he slid. And Liv, saying, *"Sorry, Creedmoor, sorry, I'm just so tired,"* stepped up behind him and put a hand on the small of his back as if to steady him, so that he grunted thank you, and with her other hand she drove her knife into him.

He made no sound of surprise.

She forced the knife up into the muscle of Creedmoor's back, under his ribs. It was surprisingly easy. Sighing, Creedmoor fell backwards onto the knife and his own weight forced it in to the hilt. He let the General go, and the old man slid face-forward then in a tangle of limbs down the slope of ash. Blood poured from Creedmoor's wound all down Liv's sleeve. His arm spasmed, groping for the Gun at his side, so she twisted the knife and drew it, sawing somewhat through muscle and sinew and bloody fat, across Creedmoor's side and out through his flank.

Even as she cut, the flesh seemed to close hungrily around the blade, as the power of Creedmoor's demon set about mending him. She'd known that would happen, and the sight of it horrified her perhaps less than it should have; she felt very numb. She did not intend to let it stop her.

She gripped Creedmoor by the sweaty back of his collar and set about widening the wound so that it would not heal. She was no surgeon, of course, but that didn't mean she hadn't, in the course of her medical education, practiced with cadavers; and though she'd never excelled in that sort of work, she knew how to handle a knife. She concentrated on her memories of long-past lectures and examinations and tried to forget what she was doing. Blood soaked her.

Creedmoor's arm worked its way to the Gun again and fumbled it from the holster, so she removed the knife and drove it back in under his armpit, slicing sinews, stripping the flabby meat of the underarm from the bone. The Gun fell in the ash with a soft thump and then a sudden echoing crash as it discharged pointlessly into the air, which Liv hardly noticed, because her ears were full of Creedmoor's astonished bellowing. The Gun slid heavily down the slope, making sideways slithering marks in the ash like a snake in desert sand.

Liv laughed for no reason she could clearly understand, and in a moment of inspiration recalled the delicate operation of the tendons in the back of the leg, and sliced smartly at them, twice back and forth. Then she drove the knife twice more between Creedmoor's ribs, her arm weakening, her hand shaking—and then again. Then, laughing and sobbing, she put her hands on Creedmoor's ragged bloody back and shoved him down the slope.

He lay in the creeping shadow of his own blood. He was not yet dead, and already he was healing; he pushed himself up on his elbows as if to crawl, then fell again. He still made no intelligible sound. Liv's hair had fallen soaked with sweat in her face, and when she pushed it back, she covered it with blood—which appalled her— so she took the knife and sliced away great handfuls of bloody hair—until the whole notion began to seem absurd, and she dropped the knife and laughed, and then sobbed, and then with great effort controlled herself. She could not straighten her clothes or her hair, because her hands were wet with blood, and she could not quite stop them fluttering idly at her side; but close enough, close enough.

Beneath her, Creedmoor was healing rapidly, but she no longer had the will to hurt him further. The moment had passed. She could not and would not do it again. Her heart pounded and her legs were unsteady. She went sliding down the slope to retrieve the General.

❋ ❋ ❋

The General lay tangled in the wet ash. His shirt was torn and soaked with blood. There was a neat tiny bullet wound in his side. His breathing was labored, and there was a little blood in his eyes.

"... *How?*" she said. Then she remembered how the Gun had fired as it fell, and she'd thought nothing of it at the time.

Now the weapon lay a little way away, and it was still.

Creedmoor moaned, wrestled his torn and broken arm back into its socket, and sighed with deep satisfaction. He held up his hand as if testing the fingers; they spasmed. He tried to sit up but failed and coughed blood.

"I'm sorry, Liv," he said. "But what did you think would happen? What did you think my master would do? If we cannot have the General, no one will."

"He is not dead yet, Mr. Creedmoor. The bullet passed through. He may live."

Creedmoor rolled his head to see the body. "He won't." He looked away again, up at the sky. "I'm sorry." Creedmoor attempted to sit up again. It seemed to Liv that something important in the muscles of his back or belly had been damaged and not yet mended, because he only twisted and fell and swallowed ash.

Liv sat by the General's side. She brushed his forehead and made it bloody.

Creedmoor spat the ash out; he said, "The murder was well done, Liv."

"Thank you, Mr. Creedmoor."

"You're not finished yet, though."

"I have lost the taste for it. I cannot and will not do it again. I refuse. Are you not in the most tremendous pain, Mr. Creedmoor?"

"I'm used to it." He laughed and gurgled blood. "Oh, Liv, that's a lie, of course; my master takes the pain from me. I am a terrible coward."

"I know."

The General stared up into the clouded sky. His breathing came loud and painful. He seemed to be trying to form words.

Creedmoor spoke again. "What was your plan, Liv, if I may ask?"

"I thought I would kill you, Creedmoor, and take the General away from you. Perhaps we might find survivors in New Design, who would help us back east into the world. We could bring his secret back, if he ever had one, and . . . I think I began to have heroic notions."

"I know how that is, Liv, I know how that is."

"If we couldn't go back, I thought we might walk together into the west, into the sea, and be unmade together. No one would have him; not you, not the Line."

"A good plan. Better. Simple, decisive, wise. Suicide is often the best course of action. If I tell you how much I sympathize with you, you will not believe me. And now no one *will* have the General's secret, because he is dead."

"Not yet."

"Soon. What will you do now?"

"I am not brave enough to go into the sea alone, Mr. Creedmoor. What will you do?"

"I don't know. I'm healing, which means my masters have not yet decided to dispose of me, despite this debacle. Maybe they've gone to their Lodge to debate what tortures to visit upon me."

He grunted as he twisted his left leg back into place, and held a hand to the ragged tendons at the back of the knee. Pain, despair, relief mingled on his face.

"More likely they'll forgive me. The Great War goes on. With Fanshawe gone, and Abban, there aren't many of us old dogs left. I'll go home, I guess. Back to work. *I* had heroic notions that I might break free, but I guess that's all over now."

From over the edge of the dune, there was the sound of stomping, sliding footsteps; shouting; grumbling; the rattle of packs and cans and weapons.

"Or perhaps not," Creedmoor said. "Perhaps not."

The footsteps came closer. The voices of Linesmen carried on the empty night air.

"My Gun, Liv," Creedmoor said, trying to stand, and failing. "Hand me my Gun, please, Liv."

But Liv was already off, and running, over the dunes.

※　※　※

Liv fell to her belly—standing, running, would only expose her to the Linesmen's rifles. She crouched and slithered and crawled through the ash, through the hollows between the dunes. She put some distance between herself and Creedmoor and the General. Lying on her belly, she lifted her head a few nervous inches over the crest of a dune and looked back.

She saw them coming.

Five men. That was instantly clear, though all Liv could see were tiny silhouettes against the spoiled dawn. Short, heavy, heads down, not running but gracelessly stamping forward. A row of distant chimneys squatting the skyline. They went up and over the top of an ash-dune and were gone from view. When they reappeared, they'd grown larger, and she could see the black of their uniforms, the hard jut of their weapons. Two of them carried some kind of heavy box between them; as they came closer, they threw it away and started jogging.

When they were close enough that she could see the gas masks that elongated their jaws into inhuman forms, she slipped down out of sight and slid away. The ash whispered beneath her shifting body and she froze, inched forward again, froze again. She crept away with nightmare slowness. She heard gunfire.

※　※　※

Creedmoor crawled on his belly through shifting ash, to where his Gun lay, some way upslope and hard to get to. He kept sliding back down. Behind him he heard the wheezing and panting of the Linesmen as they negotiated their own shifting nightmarish obstacle course of ash.

—The General is not yet dead, Creedmoor.

—He will be soon.

—But not yet. *Fight,* Creedmoor.

His veins flooded with fire. He lunged, closed his hand around his weapon, and rolled over on his back. He shot twice and killed two Linesmen, but his wounds slowed him and he could not get off a third short before the last three Linesmen got their rifles up. Their mechanisms rattled and coughed and Creedmoor screamed as a bullet hit his hip; then he screamed again as Marmion said,

—No.

. . . and began to force his bones roughly back together.

Then the Linesmen were on him. They stamped on him and kicked him and tore the Gun from his hand and kicked it away.

—You deserve this, Creedmoor.

—Yes.

Liv heard Creedmoor screaming, cursing, roaring obscenities, laughing and taunting, as if he'd never been happier in his whole hateful life. . . .

Why didn't she run? She wasn't sure. She told herself it was safest to stay still and silent. She told herself that perhaps she might still somehow save the General. The truth was she found herself oddly reluctant to leave Creedmoor.

She hoped they killed him.

She didn't want him to have to die alone.

What if they heard her? The sound of her own breathing roared in her ears. The tick of her pocket watch echoed. . . .

And in fact, now that she listened to it as if for the first time—now that it seemed so loud as to drown out Creedmoor's roars and screams—Liv sensed a horrible familiarity in its off-kilter ticktock, its rattle and rush. She *knew* that sound, that rhythm. She held it to her ear and heard in brittle miniature the Song of the Line, the Song the Engines beat out over the continent. She held it in her hand and stared at its blank gold-plated face. It was too heavy. She knew with utter certainty that if she could unscrew its gilt backing, she'd see some oily black iron parasite lurking in its bright clockwork. No wonder they'd never lost her. How long had they been spying on her? Had they gone through her luggage when the Engine carried her west?

She swore and dropped the device. She shoved it down into the ash, grinding it with the heel of her palm. She covered it over and crept slowly away.

❋　❋　❋

The last three Linesmen stood all around Creedmoor, kicking and spitting and shoving him down in the ash and watching him heal and wounding him again; and Creedmoor spat back and called them every filthy name he could think of in every language he knew; and they could probably have stayed like that forever, but eventually the Linesmen got tired.

Night had fallen. There was no moon, and only a miserly allotment of stars. What little light there was came from the glow of the thunder in the west. The Linesmen fanned out and searched in the ashy gloom for Creedmoor's weapon.

"There."

"Where?"

"I see it. Mr. Mills, sir?"

"I see it. Looks so harmless, doesn't it?"

"Don't know, sir. How do we get rid of it?"

"Explosives should do the job. What do we have left?"

They bent low, planted some of their devices in the ash, then jogged to a safe distance.

—No. Fight, Creedmoor, stand up, fight them.

"Watch this, Agent. Carpenter, hold his head up. Watch his teeth."

Creedmoor laughed and spat, "Carpenter? Fuck you, Carpenter. I'll—"

There was an immense thumping noise, like a body falling from a great height; and the ash exploded, blasting outward in a red-and-black peacock crest of fire and ash and a cloud of nightmarish black smoke that stank of gunpowder and blood. The air was full of a terrible pressure, and the stars seemed to shudder and withdraw. Then there was a long deep silence. Creedmoor gasped and sagged as the full pain of his injuries hit him, and the fight went out of him.

—Marmion?

No answer.

A fragment of red-hot twisted trigger mechanism had flown out of the explosion and hit the one called Mills square in his head, killing him; Creedmoor's master's final act in the world as it fell back screaming into its Lodge.

The two remaining Linesmen didn't seem sure what to do next. Carpenter let go of Creedmoor's head and stepped over him. The two Linesmen stood side by side in confusion.

※　※　※

Liv heard the *thud* of the explosion, and moments later she choked on the stink of powder and blood, and she felt the agonizing pressure; and she understood at once that Creedmoor's master was gone. It was too late, but the thing was finally gone. Its vessel was broken and it had gone screaming back or up or down or who-knew-where into what Creedmoor had called its Lodge.

She waited a little while, thinking. Then she crept back.

Creedmoor lay still on one slope of ash, his hands bound behind him. The General lay on another. Both of them lay in their own blood, and both looked dead.

Two of the five Linesmen survived. They were busy with some task, bent over and with their backs to her.

After a while, she realized that they were attempting to bury their dead. They dug with their bayonets and their bare hands in the ash. It wasn't working. The ash poured back into every hole they dug.

She'd heard that the Linesmen did not bury their dead—that they fed them to their Engines. Apparently that was propaganda—she wondered if it was the Linesmen's, or their enemies'.

She felt a spasm of sympathy for them. It passed. As she watched, they came to seem like insects, working from cold unconscious instinct; like engine parts grinding away; like there was no feeling or kindness in what they were doing, or even duty, but only habit.

Creedmoor rolled his bloodied head to one side and saw her crouching in the dark. He smiled grotesquely. She looked away from him.

One of the dead Linesmen's rifles lay discarded in the ash. Liv crept closer and picked it up. Its mechanism was very complicated, and she wasn't sure how to fire it, or how to operate it without making noise; and she couldn't bear to use the bayonet; so instead she held the thing like a club and crept closer again, and struck the nearest Linesman on the back of his neck.

Pain ran up her arm. The Linesman fell like a sack of coal, into his own poorly dug grave. The other one turned very slowly, and she swung again and hit him in the face, bloodily breaking his jaw and his teeth—and possibly his neck, because he fell and did not get up.

She wondered if either of them had been—what was the name of the man on the loudspeaker? *Lowry*. She decided she preferred not to know.

She dropped the rifle and staggered limply over to where Creedmoor lay grinning.

❋ ❋ ❋

Creedmoor's face was bruised and bleeding; pale and *old*. His bound hands were swollen and red. His nose was broken, Liv observed, and his cheek torn. He seemed smaller, frailer.

"Well done, Liv. I thought you said *never again*, but I know as well as anyone that it only gets easier each time. I suggest you put a stop to the killing now, before you develop the habit of it, and cut me loose."

"Why should I, Creedmoor?"

"My master is gone."

"I know. Will it return?"

"Not to me. At least I don't think so. It doesn't often happen that our masters are broken and we survive. The Linesman did what I could not, bless 'em, they—"

"You're bleeding badly, Creedmoor."

"Not as bad as it looks. Much of it was healed. Untie me and bandage my wounds."

"I should leave you to die, Creedmoor."

"My master is *gone*, Liv."

"That excuses nothing."

She left him and walked over to the General. He didn't say another word.

※ ※ ※

The General, like Creedmoor, lay on his back. His arms were splayed. Blood formed a strange shapeless shadow around him. At first Liv thought he was dead—but then, as she approached, he took a single heaving ragged breath. Blood spattered on his lips, on the beard and mustaches that the doctors of New Design had so neatly groomed. After that, his breathing was shallow, rapid, but constant.

Liv touched the wound gently. The flesh around it was stiff, blackening, as if poisoned. The General was muttering beneath his breath. His face was terribly pale. She held his hand and it was cold. He stared up fixedly at the dark sky, the few harsh phosphor stars. Liv held his hand helplessly and waited for him to die. His eyes were fierce but unfocused in time.

His voice slowly rose into audible registers, quavering, sounding as if from a great distance. His hand tightened in hers as if he knew she was there, as if at last he desperately wanted her to be there.

". . . again," he said. "Once again. Dying once again under the stars, alone. A cause that is always failing and faltering. Another lost battle, and another."

Liv felt an urge to reach for a pen and notepaper. Instead she clutched at his hand—no longer cold, now tense and feverishly hot—and leaned in close.

"And every time, I promise myself again to the cause, to the stars, to the future. And I come back down the mountain colder and less human. I hardly know my daughter, my wife. Everything changes on these nights. Oh, it's hard to go on. . . ."

He spoke as if he was repeating himself, mouthing the lines of some speech—as if he were finally forcing out words he'd been holding mutely inside for years.

Creedmoor came crawling closer. Liv raised a hand, and he held his distance.

"Death and rebirth. I thought this time might finally be the last. I went up the mountain. . . ."

CHAPTER 51

The General Speaks

~ 1878 ~

The General went up the mountain in the early days of spring, when the snows receded. Birch and pine breathed cool life into the foothills. There were vibrant purple pine-flowers underfoot. The white topknots of fat shy quail whistled through the underbrush. A clear and cold quality of sunlight. He took the time to comment on those matters to Master Jodrell, who was taking dictation on a sheet of paper flattened over the rusty lid of their ammunition case. The General sat stiff-backed on his shooting stick; Jodrell crouched at his side.

"Don't write that down, Jodrell. Don't write that down."

The boy paid the flowers, the pines, no mind; that troubled the General. A man should have a sense of nature and of beauty. One might so easily become less than a man, in those desperate last days of the Republic. Striking from the shadows, hiding in the alleys, the remnants of a great cause might become monsters. And on the mountain's barren peak, and in the troubled darkness beneath, it would be easy to forget. . . .

It took an hour for the General to finish dictating his letter. He addressed it to his daughter, and to his granddaughter, whom he'd never met. It was impossible for him to write to his wife—the General was not brave enough for that—but he hoped one letter would do for them all. He promised them: This is the last time. This is *truly* the last time. The end is in sight. In the halls of Kan-Kuk's people . . .

Kan-Kuk himself stood among the trees, some twenty feet away, still and tall and thin as the pines, gnarled and bone white as birch. Watching with disapproval. Silent as a stone. The secret was for the General alone; the General was their confidential agent in the matter. The General shivered under the gaze of those dawn-red eyes, and changed his mind. "That's enough, Master Jodrell. Pack it away and come along. No need to write to them, eh, when we'll see them all soon enough?"

But the next morning, as they passed up into colder hills, over bare stony ground, as Kan-Kuk strode on ahead, the General called for the boy Jodrell again and sent him away down the mountain, carrying the letter, and certain other papers, and money enough for a new life.

"And Jodrell. Tell my wife . . . tell her that if we come back, we bring hope. Tell her if we do not come back, there is no hope. The world will devour itself as it always has. Tell her to take our people from the world. Go west. She will understand."

Maybe Kan-Kuk noticed Jodrell's absence; maybe he didn't. The General was not sure that Kan-Kuk distinguished among the men. In any event, Kan-Kuk never said anything.

It occurred to the General later, as they navigated a difficult creek bed, that he should have sent some message of more *personal* affection. But it had not crossed his mind at the time, and he could spare no more men.

❋   ❋   ❋

There were twenty-four of them—not including Kan-Kuk. A small party. Deerfield and Darke had been trappers before they'd come into the service of the Republic. There was banditry in Mason's past. Now that the last remnants of the Republic were reduced to hiding in the hills, men of that sort had come into their own.

The General had sent the remainder of his forces on to Broad Kills, there to make camp, to await his return, and should he not return, to prepare for exodus. These twenty-four had split off at Dunhayne, gone south, traveling by night, hiding by day, through lands under the shadow of the Line. They'd passed for long miles through hills looking down on the tracks, and watched the Engines of Dryden and Gloriana and Arkley pass each other, again and again, with terrible regularity, cutting across the plains with contemptuous, monstrous ease. . . . They'd gone up into hills where brave men had once panned for gold, for dreams; hills that were now hacked up, ground down, burned over by the greedy mining machines of the Line. They'd gone without their uniforms, in simple buckskins and furs, and the patrol of Linesmen that caught them creeping across the blasted black plain in the shadow of Dryden Station took them for ordinary bandits and got overconfident. The General lost only two men: Boone and Caldwell. They were pursued for a while by a larger force, but they evaded it, went to ground in the hills, moved again only when they were sure their pursuers had lost interest. They passed southeast out of the lands of the Line without further incident.

They forded the freezing Shayle.

They lasted out the winter in Huntsville, where the mayor was friendly to what was left of the cause—though of course, they never told him Kan-Kuk's secret, and the General never gave his own real name or rank, but claimed to be only a former Captain, and before that a tailor, now looking to retire in peace.

Linesmen came poking around the town like hungry black wolves, and the mayor and all his people lied to their faces: *There ain't no strangers here.* Eventually the Linesmen went away. A kind and brave show of solidarity. In the privacy of his attic room, the General grew misty eyed and sentimental regarding the virtues of ordinary folk.

Kan-Kuk absented himself from their company, his alien kind not being welcome in town. Maybe he went and burrowed himself into the earth for winter; maybe he went stalking the cliffs in the snow and wind. The General didn't know. As the weeks went by, the General began to wonder if Kan-Kuk had ever existed, had ever come to him like a ghost out of the dark hills and rumbled: *You are chosen.* To wonder if he'd never gone as in a dream following Kan-Kuk away from the dead and the wreckage of the battlefield and into the hills above Asher, which the men said were haunted, and down into the warrens, and into the beautiful and ancient cities *beneath* the warrens, where white faces and long thin bodies like veins of marble surrounded him, and probed him, and drank him in with their unearthly blood-warm eyes, and tapped stonily at him as if to see if he were *hollow*, and whispered secrets to him in the harsh and grating voices of fairy-tale ogres. He'd begun, in fact, to settle into the rhythms of Huntsville's life, to forget the burden of his destiny, to think of himself as a man among ordinary men again. . . .

But Kan-Kuk called for him again in the spring. He woke at midnight to hear the echo of Kan-Kuk drumming on a river-rock, out beyond Huntsville's edge. He gathered up his men. The sharp-shooter Sam Hart, who'd lost an eye in the fighting at Onakha, stayed behind with a local woman, and the General swallowed his sorrow and pride and envy and gave them both his blessing.

❋   ❋   ❋

— Come away, General.

—Is it time?

—It is.

—Do you remember when you first came to me?

—It was only moments ago, General.

—Forty years for me. More than that. A lifetime. Long enough for a civilization to come and go.

—I remember.

—I lay on the field of battle after Asher. Wounded in the shoulder by a lucky shot and bleeding badly. Under the stars, in gorse and briars, by the bridge. Our first defeat. It might have been the end of us. The death of the Republic, before it was born. I told myself it would not be. It would not. I called on all my will and . . . And then you came to me. At first I thought I was mad.

—You *are* mad, in your way. That's why we chose you.

—Beneath your warrens there was a city. I have not forgotten. And we made a deal.

—Yes. I gave you what strength I had. I helped you make the world over.

—You did.

—I warned you it would not be enough.

—Forty damn good years, though. Or near forty.

—Now it's time, General. You owe us your services. We have waited long enough.

— Too long. I know.

—Come home.

—Why me?

—You know why.

—You'll give me the weapon?

—Not a weapon.

—What then?

—You'll see.

✳ ✳ ✳

They went up out of Huntsville, and through ancient woods, just a few miles west of the ruins of what had once been Founding, the first colony in the West. They went up into the foothills north of Founding, looking for a particular sullen hunchbacked mountain by the name of Self's Mount.

✳ ✳ ✳

—There. And beneath it.

—I am an old man.

—You promised. We gave you forty years.

—I honor my promises. But I am an old man, and frightened.

✳ ✳ ✳

They went up, and up. They spent a day hunting around the foot of a cliff face of golden brown stone. It caught the sun; its crags and outcrops, its caves and eagle nests cast stark shadows, made its surface as ornate as a cathedral. It was square as a big-city bank. Birds came and went overhead like congregants, like clerks. It was the last homely thing in the mountain. They scrambled up a lunar waste of scree; they delved through the ocean-floor shadows of a crevasse that cut up into the mountains at steep unnatural angles. Kan-Kuk went ahead of them, always, on fierce striding legs, turning his head full of sun-red eyes to glare back at them, urging them on. They stumbled across a wolf pack, hungry and maddened by the long winter, and lost young Martin Hulme. If that was the most fear-some guardian they faced, they agreed, they'd be lucky; and they burned Hulme's body. Kan-Kuk said

—We are near. Do you hear it?

—No. But I don't doubt it, old friend, I don't doubt it at all.

—You will be tested.

—No doubt. No doubt.

❋ ❋ ❋

"Sir. We ain't alone up here, sir."

The General followed Deerfield up onto the scarp in the windless lee of which they'd made a brief camp. At Deerfield's gesture, the General crouched among the mossy rocks. Deerfield pointed down over the valley. Black ants crawled over the scree below. . . . "The telescope, please, Mr. Deerfield."

"Yes, sir. Sir, I count twenty-two of 'em."

"Yes, Mr. Deerfield. Ah. Aha. Twenty-two men of the Line. No vehicles. No Vessels overhead."

"I reckon we can take 'em, sir. I been watchin'. They're lookin' for someone. I reckon they followed us up from Huntsville, sir. But they don't know where we are yet. If we strike first, we can take 'em before they can bring out their bombs or their gas or all that."

Deerfield's instincts were generally sound—but he was a hunter, a trapper, he saw no further than the immediate kill. He did not un-derstand the stakes, or the weight of responsibility on the General's old shoulders. They could not take risks now. . . .

The General collapsed the telescope. It made a pleasing firm sound. His mind was made up. "No, Mr. Deerfield. This is a mo-ment for circumspection. Discretion is the better part, as they say. We'll avoid them. They don't know why we're here. No one knows but us. This is nothing but damned bad luck. They think us ordi-nary bandits, or ragtag remnants of the Republic. They'll forget us soon enough."

❋ ❋ ❋

But they kept coming. Up into the cold and the dark, among pines as sharp and hostile as bayonet blades, scrambling over frost. The

Linesmen had caught their trail—that much was clear—and they were closing steadily. Shots were exchanged by long-rifle, more for show than for any serious purpose; they pointlessly wounded the trees, or were swallowed by the dark. The Linesmen were distant but coming closer. They *glowed*. . . . The General's men labored under thick furs. The Linesmen fought off the cold with electrical heaters, the filaments of which burned an angry buzzing red. That was all that the General could see of them—like fireflies in the dark, in the pines. As they got closer and closer, there was a hum, a hiss, barely audible.

And at last the General came to the end of the pines. A level hollow of bare flat stones stretched out before him; no cover. Kan-Kuk waited there. With silent resignation—indifference?—Kan-Kuk fell in alongside the General's little band. They ran for their lives headlong over the bare stones. Over the sound of their own ragged breath, the clatter of their own boots, they heard the whistle of the bombs. . . . Then that terrible *noise* began, and the General fell into pieces.

CHAPTER 52

LIV CHOOSES

The General's voice had begun to fade. Every word now took more breath out of him than he had to spare. Liv leaned in so close, her ear was almost to the General's mouth; her head was nearly lying on his heaving chest.

"*. . . falling into pieces. Bleeding away. Dying again. Waiting to be reborn again into struggle again and again, when the stars turn and morning comes. Every time . . .*" His lips moved weakly, effortfully, but only a thin murmur of breath escaped, only a sigh, only silence.

※　※　※

"Hah. Ah. If that was all it took to open his mouth, we should have shot him weeks ago."

"Shut up, Creedmoor. *Shut up.* Oh, I swear I'll kill you if you say another word."

※　※　※

Liv waited a long time for tears to come, but they would not. There was a dry ashy bitterness in her eyes and her mouth. She thought she might never cry again.

Eventually she stood. She scraped up ash in her hands and threw it over him. Two handfuls to cover his face; three, four to cover his chest. Ash settled in his slackly open mouth. It dulled his deep green eyes and the polished medals on his red jacket.

She should have closed his eyes and his mouth.

She looked west, into the thunderclouds over the Western Sea, and she looked back east. There was no sign of dawn yet.

"Not a weapon," she said. "A cure."

"Liv. Liv, untie me."

Liv ignored him. She covered her mouth, sick at herself, and began scavenging the Linesmen's bodies for provisions.

"Liv—where are you going?"

"Back to New Design, Mr. Creedmoor, to look for survivors."

"The survivors won't welcome you back, Liv. You brought the Line on them; you brought *me* on them. You let their General die. They'll give you a trial and a hanging."

"That may be true." Two of the Linesmen had carried packs. One had been torn by Creedmoor's—by Marmion's—bullets. She hefted the other and found that she could carry it.

"I'm sorry."

"Perhaps I'll go back east, then. Over the Worlds' Ends and back home. I shall stop for my friend Maggfrid. I think we're entitled to go home—no one could fault us for it."

She cut off a Linesman's belt and examined the pouches. A small knife, wirecutters, some white powder, something heavy and wheel-toothed that when struck made a small blue flame.

Creedmoor tried to sit up. He gasped and fell painfully back. Liv turned to watch him.

"If I untied you, could you walk?"

He looked at her for a long moment. Then he nodded.

"Not well. You hurt me badly, Liv. The healing began but didn't finish. Not before . . ."

She studied his expression until he closed his eyes. Then she turned away.

Each of the Linesmen had a steel water bottle. She unscrewed them one by one and found that they were all empty.

"Self's Mount," Creedmoor said.

"Yes."

"Self's Mount. The old man said it. He mumbled and he was

cryptic, but I heard that distinctly. He was going to Self's Mount when they caught him."

"I heard him, too, Creedmoor. Do your masters know that?"

"No."

"Are you sure?"

"If they knew they would have sent me there, not here."

"Then no one in the world knows that but us."

"That may be true, Liv."

"Except the Folk themselves, I suppose. What is this thing, Creedmoor—this weapon?"

"I don't know. Honestly. I'd tell you if I did."

Two of the Linesmen had heavy metal implements that, when a copper plate was depressed, emitted a dull red light and some warmth. Not enough to cook with; enough maybe to prevent freezing on cold nights. Liv took one.

"You deserve to die here, Creedmoor."

"I do."

"The General spoke of a cure. Where is this place—Self's Mount?"

"Far away. The foot of the World's Ends, in old country, within the lands of the Line."

"You know where it is, then. But one could also find it on a map, I expect."

"I expect you could."

The Linesmen had better knives than hers. She took one.

"In Line territory, Liv. The Line has held that land for two hundred years or more." He turned on his side and spat blood. "In the shadow of Dryden, right in its fucking shadow."

"But they don't know it's there," she said. "One assumes."

"But they dig everywhere. Nothing can be buried so deeply they won't dig it up in the end. It's only a matter of time. They'll find it and take it and be unstoppable, Liv—"

"I doubt I would make it back alone, Creedmoor."

"Back to New Design? Maybe."

"Back to the world."

He nodded. "Likely not."

"So." She sat near him. Not too near him.

"So," he said. His wrists were bloody where he'd struggled against the rags that bound them.

She trailed the point of the Linesman's knife in the ash. His eyes fixed on it. He tore them away and said, "We must find it. We must find it before the Line does."

"We, Creedmoor?"

"You'd never make it alone, Liv, you said so yourself. There's months of wilderness between—"

"Then you'd bring it to your masters, instead."

"No. No. Not them. They're gone, Liv. I'm free. We can keep it for ourselves. We can turn it on Gun and Line alike. End the war. Think of the fame, Liv, think of the *glory*."

"I don't care for the glory, Creedmoor. And I don't care to be involved in this . . . madness. Look what it's done to you."

"I have friends—even now. I know people. I can find us allies. I can take the old man's weapon and *use* it. If we don't, Liv—the Line will grow, Liv, it will conquer, it will *eat*, it will conquer Gun in the end, and once it's swallowed the West, it will swallow the East, too, and your Academy and your home. There's no stopping it. It—"

"Maybe, maybe not. Nothing you say can be trusted."

"No. But it's true."

"Your hands are tied too tight. You may lose the use of them."

Real fear in his eyes, real desperation.

"Even if you don't, it will be some time before you can walk unaided. You wouldn't make it back alone either."

"That's true, too." He nodded vigorously. "I know that. I do."

"I don't trust you, but I do think you understand self-preservation."

"You can't just go home again, Liv. You know you can't."

"Be quiet, Creedmoor. I'm thinking."

※   ※   ※

Liv climbed to the top of the dune and looked back east. In the night, she could see nothing but more dunes; the horizon was close and constricting.

She said, "Are you watching me?"

"I can't see you, Liv, not from down here—you'd have to untie me—"

"I wasn't talking to you, Creedmoor. Don't speak. You'll open your wounds."

She looked west. In the distance, the mad clouds roiled, glowing, forming and unforming. She recalled the General's words: *beneath their warrens there were beautiful and ancient cities.*

"Ku Koyrik. You let us pass. Why? Did you mean for this to happen? Did you mean for the General's secret to come to me? Is this accident or design? What should I do?"

There was no answer.

She knelt, somewhat self-consciously. She stretched out and pressed her ear against the earth, feeling suddenly the great rightness and sanity of that action—but though she remained there for some minutes, she heard only her pulse pounding in her head. There was no message for her.

If she'd had a coin, she might have tossed it, but she didn't, so the choice had to be hers.

❊　❊　❊

She made her decision and acted at once. She slid down-slope to the ash where Creedmoor lay, and knelt to saw through the oily rags that tied his hands.

He was silent for a long moment. Then he sighed and said, "Thank you, Liv."

He sat up, stretched his stiff swollen fingers, and winced.

"Hurt less when they were bound. I ask you, does that make any damn sense?"

"Be still, Creedmoor. Let me look at your leg."

"Ah, Doctor. Doctor. You're a very wise woman."

"Never forget it, Creedmoor."

ONE: ENGINE SONG

~ SIX MONTHS LATER ~

The Engines go thundering back and forth across the continent, on scar tissue of tracks raised over the plains, in hideous scarp-sided canyons cut and blasted through the hills. They drive through tunnels and their Song echoes in the darkness, drums beneath the earth, comes crashing out the tunnel mouth into the light in a booming, belling note. New tracks go down, opening new routes. Humboldt to Gloriana, over the wetlands; Antrim to Dryden, obliterating the hills and the villages there; Firth to Coffey. The mesh closes tighter. Lines converge. The tracks are like fences: no one dares cross them. Children come out from towns by the new tracks and stare in awe at those lines stretching into the distance, into the future that waits downline for them. On clear nights, the Engines' Song beats and drones out over the prairies. Everyone hears it. Everyone, everywhere, knows what's coming, unstoppable, implacable. . . .

But there's a new sound in the Song. Something off. A beat that stumbles. A tiny, brittle wrong note. Nothing any human ear can pin down—not in the brief moment of the Engine's presence, as it comes howling out of the East and receding into the West—but something that's always there. An impossible impurity. The Linesmen shift uneasily at their posts. They have sleepless nights—they look grayer even than usual. Their hands shake. Construction falters on the new towers of Harrow Cross and Archway. Wiring goes astray and papers are misfiled. Beatings are ordered but morale does not improve.

The Engines sing to each other: *Lowry has failed. Lowry has failed. Months go by and no return. Lowry has failed. The trail is lost. What will come out of the West? What will come?* The sick note is fear, is not-knowing when their end may come. The continent shudders with it.

TWO: JEN OF THE FLOATING WORLD

The Floating World overlooks Jasper City from up on the bluffs. By day it's invisible among the trees. In the night they hang paper lanterns on the branches, and gaslight glows from behind the crimson silk curtains in the girls' rooms, and the Floating World hangs over businesslike buttoned-up Jasper like a lurid dream.

Strangers come and go by cover of darkness. The girls of the Floating World are famous far and wide, but not all the strangers are there for the girls, and there's more than one kind of business goes on in the Floating World. Everyone in Jasper knows that, and knows to keep their mouths shut: too much curiosity about those strangers can be fatal. . . .

Knoll comes in after midnight, slamming the door open and letting in the cold, slamming it shut again and rattling the lanterns and making the girls jump and scatter. The patrons look at their feet, sidle out of the room. Knoll's furs stink. He's big as a bear, and filthy. Hanks of matted black hair sway from his belt. Hillfolk beards. He collects them. He serves the Gun these days—as the monstrous sledgehammer-sized rifle slung over his back, riding him like a dumb animal, plainly shows—but his masters don't begrudge him this recreation, so long as he does what's needed when they Call.

Jenny, scarlet-haired Jenny, smiling Jenny, Jen to those who know her well, madam and proprietor of the Floating World, greets him over by the fire. She claps her hands and her girls scatter, leaving Knoll and Jen alone. He looms over her like a storybook ogre. He shifts uneasily in his tree-stump boots. He belongs in a *cave*, Jen thinks. Jen laughs, and he bows to kiss her gloved hand, and she keeps laughing as Knoll remains stiffly stooped. Under her scarlet skirts, on her thigh, there's a Gun silver and sharp as a needle. Jen of the Floating World thinks,

—Knoll.

—Ma'am.

—You look different.

—Never seen you before, ma'am. They don't let me in places like this.

—I should think not. But I didn't mean you. I meant your weapon. Or what rides it. It used to belong to a friend of mine.

—Yeah? Dead now. Mine now.

—You're a crude one. A lot of the young ones are crude. These are crude times. I hear you're a tracker.

—Yes.

—There's work for you. The Lodge is close, here. Look into the fire, Knoll. Listen. They speak to us in the flames.

Knoll kneels by the fire, and the flames leap. There's a bloody blackness at their pulsing core. A voice sounds from a great distance, both familiar and deeply, perversely strange.

—Knoll.

—Master?

—This is not *your* master. You may call me *Marmion*. I blaze bodiless now in our Lodge. Creedmoor bore me into your world, most recently.

—Who's Creedmoor?

—He is *not* dead, Knoll. We would feel it. Thirty years he served us, sometimes well though never faithfully. We would feel it. He is not dead, and yet the months go by and he has not returned.

Jen thinks,

—He should've come here, Knoll. I was the contact. He should have come here *if* he was coming back to us.

—Who's Creedmoor? Never heard of him.

—He has not come back to us. He has *betrayed* us. That woman has led him astray.

Knoll furrows his brow:

—Master?

The one that called itself Marmion said:

—We need a tracker, Knoll. We need a simple man.

—That's me.

—I will come with you. I am *angry*, Knoll.

Three: Rebirth

Mr. Waite, leader of the Smilers of what used to be New Design, and is now *New* New Design, finds his faith in a sunny disposition and a positive attitude sorely tested these days. He was never suited to leadership, but the town's handful of survivors turned to *him* in those dreadful cold months after the Battle, first to keep their spirits high with singsongs and improving homilies, and then, when no better candidate emerged, to be their President. *No, no,* he said, *we must keep the secular and sacred functions of government separate;* and it was pointed out to him that the people of the Republic now numbered 233, and were long past caring for matters of principle; and in the end, how could he say no?

After the winter, they numbered an even two hundred. Leadership in such times is a terrible burden.

He married Sally Morton so that her unborn child might have a father. It came out wrong—marked *in utero* by the Linesmen's bombs. It came out thin, and gray, and silent, and cringing, and habituated to fear. Another child is on its way, and Waite is cautiously hopeful.

Waite's face is no longer smooth or boyish. Leadership has hardened him. He looks a lot like the old General, now, thin and severe. He smiles only for good reason.

New New Design is built in a river valley, a few miles east of the ruins of the old town. The survivors wintered there in the caves. Now Waite goes walking, once a week, in the ruins. It's part of his new routine.

He tells his people that he goes walking in the ruins so that he can absorb the wisdom of their dead comrades, and also so that he can scavenge for useful tools. In fact, he goes there mostly to be alone.

He stops among the razed barns on the west side to remember how rich New Design was—how finely engineered a society it was—what a remarkable and generous achievement! And then he thinks that he has no notion of how he might go about building such a thing, and he sits with his head on his hands on a heap of charred timbers.

New New Design is rebuilding again. It's spring. New houses cut from fresh logs are going up. The children, who number ninety-eight, are being schooled. A schoolhouse was the first thing they built. It's Waite's job to rebuild the world. No wonder he needs to be alone sometimes.

He watches birds settle in the rafters.

On the scorched floor, trapped beneath the timbers, is the skeleton of a Linesman, wrapped in a slick gray coat that does not rot and wearing a singed gas mask.

Waite unstraps the gas mask and kicks it with all his strength. Which is not inconsiderable—he used to be a fine athlete. The mask sails, flapping its straps over the ruins of poor dead Mr. Digby's barn, and lands with a splash in a water-logged bomb-crater.

There's an answering *crack* from the earth under Waite's feet, and he jumps and puts his hand to his gun.

The crack repeats. It sounds like a stone being broken with hammers, by roots. It repeats again. It sounds like a man cracking his knuckles, over and over. It sounds like barking; like laughter. The earth shudders and quakes.

Waite feels warm and cold at once. He starts to laugh.

He stops laughing when a white arm shoots up out of the roiling earth of the floor of what used to be Mr. Digby's barn.

The arm is terribly long and thin, like a bone-white sapling. It *stretches*. What follows, lifting itself up and shaking off earth and laughing, is the maned form of a female of the First Folk, rising from death.

She looks Waite's way with brilliant ruby-red eyes, and he slowly moves his hand *away* from his gun.

She looks all around her, head cocked, listening. She seems troubled. She climbs up the timbers of Digby's barn and looks west.

She tumbles loosely back to earth, and opens her fist; it's full of stones. She scatters them. She pokes among them. She seems unhappy with their answer.

What she's doing, Waite thinks, is very nearly like *shaking her head*. Or *drumming her fingers nervously*. In her troubled uncertainty, she suddenly seems remarkably human. Her gestures are nearly human gestures. She might even be beautiful.

She looks Waite's way again. With a crackling of joints and a shifting of her mane, she shrugs her bony shoulders as if to say, *What can you do?* and she smiles.

Waite turns and runs from the ruins, and he never goes back. When Sally asks why, he tells her it's time for a fresh beginning.

Her second child, born in summer, is healthy.

FOUR: GOOD-BYE

And when the letter finally arrived at the Academy of Koenigswald, it bore the stamps of a dozen postal services. Between the House Dolorous and the Academy, it had crossed the continent with the uncertain dithering flight of a butterfly. It was addressed to one Dr. Grundtvig, who had retired several years ago, and so it gathered dust in a pigeonhole that no one checked anymore, until one of the porters noticed it, opened it, called for silence, and read the highlights to his colleagues: *It is with a heavy heart that we inform you that Dr. Alverhuysen was taken from us . . . the responsibility is ours . . . no ransom demand so far . . . an Agent of those Powers that bedevil our land . . . we must now presume her dead . . .*

In one of those coincidences that are so impressive and terrifying to the weak-minded, but are in fact inevitable in the nature of things, it was a mere two days later that the enormous mental defective Maggfrid showed up at the Academy's August Hall—banging on the great doors in the dead of a rainy night, bellowing to be let in—and confirmed the sad news. He was unable or unwilling to explain how he'd accomplished his return across the world, beyond the words *I fought*. There was something wild and savage in his bearing. He resumed his janitorial duties, but now a certain glamour attached to him, and the students sought his conversation.

The Faculty commissioned a commemorative painting. At the insistence of Agatha, Liv's dear friend from the Faculty of Mathematics, it pictured Liv in a white dress carrying a book down the Academy's summer lawns. They hung it in a shadowy spot at the back of the Hoffman Library, where overworked students liked to take afternoon naps.

There was a small quiet farewell service. Dr. Ekstein gave a speech, praising *that noble spirit of scholarship that knows no frontiers, that fears no peril!* Maggfrid sat with solemn dignity. Agatha, mildly sedated, muttered *good-bye, good-bye, my dear* over and over; and those colleagues who were inclined to say *well what did she expect going out there* or *I told her so* were at least able to hold their tongues until after the service, when sherry was served and decorum somewhat loosened.